The Gospel According to Lilith

I0683212

BOOK ONE

TRANSMORGRIFICATION

An Original Novel
By
Lonnie Hicks

Chapter 1

Among the heavenly spires, upon the highest balcony, Lord watched Lucifer conduct the Worship of the Universe Services for all the heavenly hosts.

"This cannot be." he thought to himself. He felt a slow-moving anger build within him.

"How could this happen, yet escape my eye?" he said to his minister who appeared beside him. "How can all of you sit at my table and not know? Someone knew, someone must have guessed, and, yet, none who sat with me—none counseled me in this the most evil betrayal of all betrayals."

He cried out in anguish and faces looked up from all over the realm knowing that Lord was angry and justice was to be meted out to one or many. They tensed, waiting, knowing that anyone of them could fall dead and no one would know the offense or the difference.

"See him," Lord said still looking down at Lucifer whose beauty was undeniable. "I made him my most beautiful angel. I raised him on high. I made Lilith the most beautiful woman in the entire universe and this is how they repay me—with treachery?"

"He bewitches her and she becomes pregnant with his child?"

"This is all done in my very bed in the night?" He turned to the minister. "So you say she is with child and that child is his?" Lord said suddenly.

"Yes," my Lord, "it is so."

"You say she confesses such?"

"She did my Lord."

"Bring her to me. I would hear her. Bring her to me. I need to see her, hear her response, see if she will offer me false regrets or perhaps a plea of how she was deceived, or bewitched."

The minister stirred to leave, heart pounding, unsure if his part was beginning to be perceived by Lord—who would guess in time that he, the minister must have known of the liaison, but did not convey that truth to Lord. As he traversed from the throne room, he feared he might be struck down before he reached the door.

Down each step from Lord's throne, was a step into his own hell for surely the wife would betray him to Lord, if pressed, to save her own soul. He was lost in the end.

"All this," he thought, "would have consequences far beyond a simple tryst and that this would ignite, among all in heaven, far reverberations. There would be here," he thought, "fatal sin, inexpugnable, wide-ranging and irremediable; and possibly war."

The minister survived the last step emerging out into Angel Air where the hosts were completing Worship Services.

In the pulpit, Lucifer was mesmerizing. He was magnificent. There was no denying that. His arms were outstretched in flowing robes as he told the angels to rise up in praise of Lord. They all took their wings and made them rise above their heads and move slowly up and down in a rhythm with his words, "Lord is good. Lord is great. Lord is on high." The minister Raphael could see how Lilith could be bewitched by him-everyone was. His heart went out to her.

He swept by angels and Cherubs, certain that his mission would not end to the good.

He found Lilith in her apartments red-eyed from crying, eyes which grew wide at his entrance, guessing, he guessed, why he had come. She crossed her arms around her stomach instinctively, he guessed, as a protective move. She was clearly pregnant.

He said "Lord demands your presence."

She nodded. "I understand." she said.

She roused herself robotically and prepared to leave. Even sad and crying, Raphael marveled--she was a beautiful woman. She was the most beautiful woman in the Universe. How could any not love her?

Chapter 2

Lilith's trek to Lord's spire was seen by thousands who looked upon her and looked away, fearing to look at her—least that act be noticed by those who could then report she had been looked upon favorably—and then, make this known to Lord, where interpretations could be made that, in looking at her, their loyalty could be questioned.

Lilith moved slowly thinking it was true; she owed much to Lord. He had given her beauty above all others, had elevated her above all others and made her his wife, making her immortal and almost his equal.

She knew his wrath would be severe. It would mean her reduction from her elevation—an elevation many had previously thought undeserved from the first instance. He would punish Lucifer as well. And she wondered about the child. What of the child?

Lord, at Lucifer's installation as Minister of the Universal Service, praised him mightily.

"I am, today, appointing Lucifer, whom I have favored to be Leader of Worship in the entire Universe. I have granted him the gifts, of beauty and grace. I have given him the power to inspire and the greatest gift of all—immortality."

"I have placed him on this high ground because he has found favor with me. He will lead you in the Celestial Rites, in the Universal Sacraments and, mind you, these are no mere routines. Without this infusement of my Spirit in the service all becomes dull ritual and does not cleanse the soul; and uncleansed, we see the contamination of the Spirit and some will fall--fail to make the Holy stance and become shadows whose dull lights, bring the dark, and bring to many, even angels among us, to the fall. Lucifer, I now name you 'Morning Light'."

"Here me now, Cherubim, elevate your dreams and aspirations to levels which, by my hand, you Lucifer, now possess. I give you him to imitate. Follow his example such that you might rise as well to the highest highs."

Lilith was hesitant because she remembered that Lord had broken the rule of Strict Equality in taking one among them, no two, Lucifer and her—raised them up for others to admire—but, in doing so, made them a target for envy.

She spoke out loud to herself rehearsing what she would say to Lord.

"My Lord, am I to convey in this my gratitude or my remorse, because in being high, I have only earned my own isolation; I sought to cling to the only other who understood my plight, Lucifer. We were attracted to one another, enveloped in praise of you, but drawing, also, remonstrances from others. We were two children caught between shinning much for parents' sake only to earn the envy of all the siblings."

"You are wise, Lord," she thought to herself. "Surely you understand, indeed foresaw, this circumstance. Surely, Lord you knew we, your creations, would be attracted to one another in our mutual need. So, Lord how can it be that in this, I or we, must have all the sin; can you not share in this as well--because in creating us, these events progressed and were inevitable? Can you relieve and, perhaps even eschew, the sufferings which surely your wrath might bring?"

"Bring to your heart forgiveness in this Lord," she said out loud, "for surely that way lay the peace." Her step was livelier now buoyed by this new ready defense. She drew closer to Lord's chamber. Her new thoughts, to her, seemed to make her prospects more bearable and her heart gained strength feeling there might now commence a reconciliation, not a condemnation; a negotiation, not blame; an opportunity there for redemption—hers and Lucifer's. Things might be mended back to whole again-if she could make Lord
understand.

She neared the chamber door, still thinking, "How could I not love him; it was fate set in motion by Lord himself."

She entered and Lord surveyed her deliberately with Raphael at his side. Lord's mood to Lilith was one of anger mixed with agitation.

He did not speak but stood merely looking at her. Then, slowly he drew his clothing aside and sat upon his throne. Raphael took his place beside him.

Finally, he spoke not looking at her. His light was so great Lilith could barely look at him.

"All my love was gathered in you, Lilith. I took you out from among the Cherubim and pronounced you to be on high, scarcely a whiff from my own status. I loved you with the deepest fire within me. No soul gave more, Lilith, than was given you. No heart pounded greater than this heart pounded for you."

Lord paused. The tension was almost unbearable. All of heaven seemed to hold its breath. "And now, word comes to me that this was not truly reciprocated by you. While accepting my gifts you secretly stomped upon them, besmirched them, indeed transported them to another, giving to him what I had given to you; twisting all that is precious, tainting it to something clandestine, dark and betrayal-ridden, pursued in the night as I lay sleeping!"

Lord paused.

"Tortured, I in these moments, bled for you Lilith, from these wounds inflicted. First my thoughts were to find fault within myself. I did an inventory of where my own shortcomings might lie. I wondered what I had done to facilitate this happenstance."

"I cannot Lord…" Lilith began but he stopped her with a raised hand.

"No, I will have my say, I need to have this pain, to make fully visible to you my wounded entrails; to make them visible for all to discern."

"Oath betrayed," he continued, "if that were not enough, there is to this even darker news. What can be the shade darker than darkest night? What is worse than this?" Lord stood; his hands clasped together, a great sadness in his eyes, as he wept. He cried a wailing cry.

"A child, Lilith?" he asked? "Here adds a three-fold foment, a new offense which is dagger sharp in my heart. A child is spawned of this dreadful match-a child. A child, whose heart, whose lungs, whose very existence conjures in me forever, images of the coupling, the sexual seed. The very face of betrayal is now alive, inside you, coming into the world. A deeper cut is made on the wound; a new affront is made visible here. I see inside you the fatal scar which will not heal. I am clubbed to my knees."

Lord stood mute for a long moment.

"A child, Lilith, no doubt conceived in the love meant for me--a child whose very existence will be testimony to my cuckold!"

"Tell me of it," Lord said suddenly his eyes continuing to tear, "tell me though I might die from the hearing. Tell me that I might understand not only the act but, as well, the circumstance. Tell me that I might feel and see what was in those fair nights destined to be me with you, in our bed, destined to be my child, not his. Tell me straight away, I have the need to know even if every word will be a rapier to my soul."

Lilith hesitated.

"Tell me!" he commanded."

"Lord…" she began.

"I must know." Lord said slowly,

While she paced before him, Lilith began sputtering and said, "Lord he was too beautiful and I sought most times to avoid his eyes because to look at him was to take me too close to feelings I sought to throw over-board. I am sure he was the same. I had to go to Service, and like the others, I looked upon him, and to do so Lord was to fall. My eyes would, once fixed upon him, could not look away. I was transported. I floated. Even while seated, he drew me with his spirit and his words. He was your emissary Lord, and I, like the others, were filled with his praise of you, his words were spoken so beautifully. The combination was over-powering." She paused.

"Go on." Lord said.

"One day I walked at Sermon's end, meaning to return to my apartments, but suddenly he was there, by my side. I looked at him startled, looking back to the pulpit to see if he was still there, but, no, he was there beside me. I froze at his booming voice, that sublime presence."

"He said to me beautiful words, Lord. He said I want to touch you in your violets and blues and indigos, and, I know I should not. I long to be with you he said."

"I have had no other thought," he said, "I have watched you sleep, Lord at your side; I could not resist coming each night to be near and hear your heart beat."

"Was that you? I asked him, Lord."

He said, "Yes."

Lilith was quiet for a moment and bowed her head as she remembered that conversation. "I thought it was a dream, but I knew it was his face. It had been him. And I, too, could feel him upon me those nights. I could feel his caress down my spine, all the while laying there in bed with you Lord, yet he came to me again and again and lay with me irrespective."

"I asked him if was him in the dream and he said, 'It was me'."

Later I said to him, "Lucifer, do you not know that I have this baby within? Are you aware?"

He said, "I had guessed and I am of the view we both should go to Lord and say we are in love and have the subterfuge to an end."

"I cannot," I told him. "It would crash down all the heavens. No, we must take the time to think it through, as to the best way to surface the news; for we must fully understand the moment of all this and what can be the foreseeable consequence."

"I do see," Lucifer said. "I'll agree to a wait but no more than two days. I'll not have fear guide us in this; we have little to apologize for except love moved us to bad judgment."

"Indeed," Lilith said, "bad judgment-is all it is, and it happened in a dream."

"But events transpired to overcome that plan." Lilith said. "Lord, you found out it seems before the two days expired." She paused. "I now stand ready to confront what I have done and make what amends I can."

Lord looked at her and finally spoke, "Do you love him?"

Lilith did not speak.

"I said do you love him?"

Lilith said, as she looked into Lord's eyes and saw the pain therein, "Yes I do, Lord. I am helpless not to, he has my heart, my soul and try as I may to resist, I cannot expel him; now the child makes that doubly difficult. In this Lord, my will is powerless," she paused. "I am lost."

"So you are lost, you say? But Lilith," Lord said leaning toward her, "I have given you and he the will to resist. Yet you say to me that my gift to you does not exist? Surely you know that your helpless claim cannot subsist in a loss of will? You have been given that from me forever. Give me another explanation for that one does not ring true. I am your Lord, responsible for your very being. No one knows better than I, your tendencies and capabilities."

"There is more to this, I suspect," Lord said smoldering "than that which you have thus far given me."

He leaned close to her face again. Lilith blanched, fearing Lord's explosive temperament.

"What more, Sire, can I cite? I am honest with me as I can. He seems to me not resistible and him, me. What is this "more" of which you speak?"

Lord spoke slowly, each word measured. "I am of the suspicion that you have not run to him, but rather, away from me. I am of the suspicion that you enjoy the pleasures of pride as much as that of love; but the final end is that you and he covet not only Love's Sweets but perhaps more; an entire kingdom, which has now a potential heir within your loins."

Lord paused and then continued, "Star-crossed lovers merit reprieve but none, I say to you, will be forthcoming for rebels and revolutionaries. Here before me plain to see is not only the seed of suspicion but the seed of a new dynasty, one which clearly, is designed to replace me."

Lilith, dumb-founded, could not speak.

"Leave me now, I will ponder these thoughts in my private, and see where they lead. I need now to think of larger things."

Chapter 3

Lilith went to Lucifer and he gave his thoughts.

"That did not go well, I see. He gained details and the details changed his whole view. We are no longer star-crossed lovers but pretenders to his throne. Lord will now eschew thoughts of forgiveness and treat us as rebels. You and I, and the baby, are the greatest possible threat, and, he will act swiftly as he must, because to linger would be, in his mind, disastrous."

"We must act. We must gather the Cherubim whom we can trust and plan for what surely will be an attack. You and the child must be given over to a safe place for the goal in all of this, from Lord's view, will be to take the child from you."

"Take the child?" Lilith asked, "What do you mean?"

Lucifer looked at her sadly. "I mean that he will likely not want to see the child survive."

Lilith touched her stomach aghast. "You mean kill the child?"

"I fear," Lucifer said simply, "or least we must be aware that he, or one of his minions, might attempt to do so. So your sequestration is critical in this. You must not be taken at all costs."

"Now," Lucifer said "let's go off to the garden spot and speak with those who might cast their lot with us, who understand the gravity of what we have before us."

Lucifer and Lilith moved under cover of veil and scarf after having sent word to key Cherubim leaders that they should meet on a matter of critical urgency.

In a flice, Lucifer stood before the small group of fifteen, "As many of you know Lilith and I have a situation. We fell in love, we were unable to turn our heads from one another, and that love, I am reporting here, was consummated and Lilith is with child."

There was a hush and then an audible gasp from the group, "With child?"

"My!"

"Lord will be furious, does he know?"

"He knows," Lucifer said. "Lilith told him hours ago and he has taken a different view. He does not view this as an affair of the heart. He believes that it is a part of a plot, a plot to over-thrown him and that it is his kingdom we want—to supplant him and place ourselves on the throne with our child as heir. Lilith is persuaded that he will not relent in this view. This presents, Lucifer said, "ultimate danger not only to us, but as well, to all of you."

"To us?" one in the group cried, "Why us?"

"I have not told Lilith this until now, but I have gotten word that he now regards all of you, and any those associated with us, as suspect and his plan is to smite one and all and your families as well."

Lucifer paused as his words sank it. "I am sorry to have brought this onto your shoulders. But, I don't know what to do. My first thought is to sequester Lilith and the child to safety somewhere, but beyond that, I also hear that Lord is ordering his closest guards to arms and plans to demand that all the Cherubim proclaim their loyalties to him, or to Lilith and me. He is not allowing any middle ground or time to ponder. Those that hesitate at the question will be killed."

Another in the back of the group spoke. "It's true, my wife has been summoned. I did not know what it was about."

"And mine too," another said.

"My son," said another.

There was the slow track of recognition as they all realized that some among them had been targeted and family members had already been summoned.

Lucifer said, "I am not asking you to make decisions now, but time is running in my view. We must summon those of you who plan to join us, combine all our powers and take up arms to protect ourselves. Lilith and I have the powers of Heaven with us, and, if necessary, we can defend ourselves against Lord's hosts and defend others as well."

That said, the night-shade came and all departed agreeing to meet in the early morning and report what responses there might be or rumors.

Lucifer and Lilith lay that night to contemplate how future events might transpire and what fate might fetch for their unborn child.

Lilith said in that quiet time, "I am for you in this, but I fear for the child."

Lucifer responded, "I will not back-step one wit for, if this is what we must do to preserve the child, then, so be it. If we must take up arms and provide the defense, so be it. If war it must be, then war it shall be, because there is no higher cause than that of defending those you love."

Lilith offered, "But are we right in this Lucifer, will the end be peace or destruction, and, if the latter, who then the winner? What if it is only a desolated world our baby seed will inherit?"

"I am not sure of what lies beyond these words we utter in the dead of night," Lucifer said, "the future is often shaded. But, if I take this single candle, if it will be all I have-the only beacon against this night- then, this small illumine will have to suffice."

Chapter 4

Before morning the reassembled group went to the garden to count the ones who would take up arms with Lilith and Lucifer, and, to retake from Lord their missing family members. Word had spread that hundreds were gone, taken by Lord who had chosen the women and the young, apparently thinking that they would more easily reveal intelligence as to who the plotters were.

There was anger in this Cherubim group at this—many had brought their thunder sticks, fire bolts and spears clambering in the meeting to storm Lord's castle and take back their kin; to declare that a new kingdom be proclaimed where Lord would be taken down, forced to reform and recognize the rights of Cherubim.

Lucifer stood before them and stated that a plan such as that "would only decimate our meager ranks. Rather," he said, "no, we have not the strength for a frontal assault. We must wait to gather strength and add numbers to our ranks and choose a spot and way of our own choosing for the assault. Gather now our brethren in this; come to, by morn, the high spot near the pulpit such that we can speak again and plan."

With that, and murmuring, the group dispersed and Lucifer looked at Lilith saying "You know what this means—he'll know we are gathering, he probably has already been told by someone from this very group; and headlong now we all rush to warring; all creation bates it's breath as to what will be this outcome."

"I agree," Lilith said simply.

The presence of arms in the ranks that next day underwent inspection by Lucifer who had to gauge what strength lay among his battalions. He had a battalion of higher angels and a battalion of arch-angels, Cherubim, Ranklings, Soarlings and others who stood before Lucifer and Lilith, eyes open, some bulging, all showing fear—the fear of the unknown, of rebellion, death and mayhem, of going up against Lord.

"None know," Lucifer said, "and I can not tell you the outcome, other than we must fight and get our families back."

Gathered then as one, they mustered to the planning of the initial battle scene which was to attack the arsenals, where the sun-bursts lay, deadly weapons, which could spew deadly radiation across whole galaxies. Several of these could take the battle to Lords' forces but only Lilith and Lucifer and Lord could trigger these weapons so great a force was needed to set them off.

Lucifer said, "We must first take them from Lord's arsenal because deprived of that explosive force might force Lord to early negotiate and spare us all a fiery death."

Lord gained word of Lucifer and Lilith's plan confirming his worse suspicions and this sealed the antagonism and hardened his heart. He told his ranks, "All the rebels must be killed." The word went out among Lord's battalions that all the rebels must be killed, and the cataclysm exponentiated.

"I will show all who rebel against the kingdom, the ingrates who conspire, that vengeance is mine and that my righteous wrath is great." He spoke to his assembled hosts charging them with battle plans, the first of which was to protect and guard the sun-bursts sequestered in the arsenal.

And, so it was, too, that Lucifer's hosts—banners waving--rode, in war's fever, pushing back both fear and common sense, supplanting them with glory dreams and ideologies- promising promises. The red robes of Lucifer's sermon garb became the flags of the battalions, some others yellow stripes; some merged these to give the assemblage color and inspiration.

They marched to music made by members of the heavenly choir; they were singing inspirational songs offering encouragement and said, "Think of your families and your children."

Lord's wards, two-thirds to Lucifer's one third, felt confident of their numerical superiority. Raphael said "At best, this "war" will be over in a day."

Their mood was uplifted since Lord rode with them at the head in full view of all the hosts. Lord had his chariot and stomping steeds that mounted the arsenal hill standing there snorting magnificently. Lord fingered their reins.

He spoke aside to his general who said "Their
numbers are puny most Lord; we shall no have difficulty
in running them through. We only await your word in this
and we will down upon them and they will run Lord, they
will not resist. Tell us now when to bolt and we will all be
home by tomorrow."

Lord peered down among them seeking Lucifer,
finding him sitting a winged horse seemingly calm. The
general said from his own look "he seems confident Lord-
-almost complacent."

"Let's then," Lord said, "offer him, in this, some
discouragement."

With that and a wave of his hand the general sent the
signal down the ranks to drive a wedge with the chariots
to break through the middle line of Lucifer's infantry,
which, the General thought, would fold rather than hold,
and once split, the general would take advantage of his
superior numbers, would take down Lucifer's divided
troops in small groups.

The down-hill race had begun with Lord's charioteers
plunging into Lucifer's ranks in the middle and,
immediately, the center of Lucifer's infantry line broke
retreating allowing Lord's charioteers to enter at the
center. But five ranks in, to Lord's astonishment, Lucifer
swept down with his own charioteers on the flanks and
had Lord's charioteers surrounded on all three sides; a
trap Lucifer devised, had been sprung. Every horse was
speared and wounded, went down, as chariots, charioteers
and horses from Lord's ranks floundered on the ground.

The chariot men—not used infantry combat—were
no match for Lucifer's infantry forces now reinforced
with even more infantrymen. Meanwhile, Lucifer
dispatched more infantry from the rear to prevent Lord's
charioteers from being reinforced while Lord looked on as
his finest fought bravely but finally succumbed.

The shrieking of men, horses baying, lives ebbing,
banners down, some limply waving, painted the scene
where heaven's hosts took the look of a red hell, of red
blood flowing.

There were some who stumbled blinded by lance or
spear, by blood from head wounds; some wandered,
mumbling incoherently. All in the gathering dusk faded
from view underneath the gloaming.

Later, Lord sat in his Council of State; his ministers were glum and sour. Lord said, "This Lucifer has the faculties given him by me. I shall not again underestimate his use of these. Make me now a single plan to prevent the sun-bursts from falling into his hands. We meet here again in an hour to see what you have contrived and, mind you gentlemen, failure this time is not an option. If we visit defeat again, I will spell for each and every one a consequence which will not be liked."

The next day Lord's Angel Hosts assembled at the launching point and Lord surveyed their ranks and spoke, "I have given you the high assignment to protect our people down below as they seek to secure the sun-burst beams. Your job is to swoop low, drop your maiming hooks and swoop up again to cause mayhem in their ranks and then release the Swooping Prey back down among them as human bombs." Lord raised his hand and said, "Fail me not. Fail me not."

The Angel Hosts flew high, each carrying a Prey, a tiny demon cherub, who would swoop down aiming toward the eyes of the enemy, thereby blinding them. As thousands of Angels lofted, surveying the field, seeking Lucifer's hosts and spotting them, made Lord to know they were in place, awaiting his word to attack.

Meanwhile, Lucifer muttered to himself that "This is not a good development." This was a surprise because Lucifer had no aerial counterpart to challenge the Angel squads of Lord. He murmured to his general, "Do we have anything to counter this, we are exposed to attack from above and must need, therefore, to hunker down and take the blows?"

The general was glum and only said, "We have nothing, Lucifer, and must pray the damage is minimal."

Lucifer's forces arrayed themselves on the ground and moved to close positions, one to the other, each spreading his shield or wing to cover one another against the diving demons, who sought to split the seam between the covering wings and shields and find the eye of its holder.

The battle started. Immediately there were screams as the demons smashed irises and blood spurted from the unlucky targets; Lucifer, despondent, saw his ranks waver and his hosts break and run, fleeing. He knew he would likely face the wrath Lord would muster for he was, indeed, a vengeful Lord.

But from the air came a trumpet sound and looking up Lucifer could see Lilith at the head of new hosts who came rushing in on a tremendous cloud, around her thousands of her personal hosts and Cheribums, who she had been busy in recruitment. This sight for Lucifer was a welcome one. Lilith flying above was the picture of a fierce woman warrior crashing down upon Lord's angel hosts and cherub demons—her angels counter-attacking, spewing cloud-gasses which enveloped the Prey, blinded them. Eyes aflame from the cloud-gas, the demons shrieked and sank to the ground there crushed by shield, sword and lance.

Other hosts fell from the sky as Lilith's hosts shot cloud-darts which, just head-size, enveloped shoulders and face, and then the scream, as the demon hosts clasped both hands to face, cried for Lord, and began the deadly plummet to surface ground where, amid gathering shields, Lucifer's hosts again swarmed over them.

Once grounded, the fate of Lord's flying demons was sealed. Demon Prey were up-tossed from the mayhem; severed Angel limbs and angel parts lay aground; de-feathered wings and screams, bloody hearts lay strewn all upon the battlefield, signaling a rout.

Silence then; deafening, as both groups paused to intake the final scene where Lilith floating just above the ground, her hosts all around, saw shock on the faces of Lord's hosts, dismayed at the outcome before them.

But Lucifer looked to his recruits; thousands were blind meandering, crying out, and asking for comforting. The battle was won but at great cost.

The battle was won to Lilith's credit but, it also entailed many losses to Lucifer's minions. No new battle could be waged soon by them. Lucifer took his place beside Lilith surveying Lord's form on the far hill. He stood still and then turned away. Lucifer knew there would be another battle line drawn and that one would have a different outcome.

He and Lilith embraced as the hosts cheered. She took his face into her hands, planting a kiss. Lucifer said "I understand this is one battle and many more will have to be before we can declare victory. But know in all of this I stand with you for all eternity, for we have been given the gift of immortality, and shall live together for best or ill, for all time. I pledge here now my hearth and kin to stand with you now and to the very end."

Lucifer cried softly holding her, feeling that seed within her, and said, "All my effort and purpose is growing inside you and my equal pledge is to love and honor you. We have this mold cast, have set ourselves upon this path; have by this primordial scene fixed our future. We cannot go back, or mollify what destiny has planned for us. If this then is the primordial fork, then let it be that we shall play out our part, not retreat or soft wield our deep felt commitments and sentiments."

The hosts rose in one voice "Hosanna, Hosanna," they all voiced as one.

"We now bury our dead," Lucifer said, "and pray them on to peace and prepare ourselves for the next onslaught."

Lord, too, made vows of his future intent. "It was she," he said to his lieutenant, "turned the battle with her treachery, it was she who came to manifest how far she has gone into treasonous treason; it was she who wielded the spear which pierced my heart on that battlefield; it was she who rallied my enemies, turned my Angels against me and clambered down to destroy the loyal angels."

"I shall mark this day the beginning of time when fatal sin came to this kingdom. I shall this day mark the forked road--one fork leading to my kingdom—the other to sin and treachery. Here a new history begins and I shall judge all by these new standards. In this new era, all is will and no will, chose or eschew, chose which road beckons you. Mercy shall not visit those who diverge from the righteous path; rather, blood shall be their destiny and I shall visit upon them a terrible judgment and cast them into fiery hells where they shall burn forever."

Here, Lord. issued the first decree, for in the kingdom, previously, there had never been treason and hence no need for decrees. But, here now, was a new era beginning and all knew Lord's new terrible wrath now commenced and new decrees would be placed upon them. Loyalty and obedience to the word was now the primary order.

That night in his Throne Room, Lord sat his head awry—in his mind recasting the day's events, reliving the horrible sights he had seen from his hill-top perch; mindful, so mindful, that he must prevail next time or lose all he possessed.

"But how best to defeat them," he mused aloud as he thrust himself up from the throne and began to pace, "to accomplish that task? Am I to don the warrior-cloak while still grieving grievous loss? How can my mind clear if my heart chokes off in my chest? What is my prize of gold or kingdom if my soul dies quietly in the infirmary pierced asunder?"

"Even now I have her face before me: Lilith," he said, "how could you abandon me? How could you not love me for all I am is in you? I gave you immortality so that I could always be with you. I feasted in my heart of hearts each moment near you. Betrayal is crime true, but the greater loss is not to be able to be near you; the former is mere effrontery, the latter is murder most supreme— mine."

"This is murder which does not allow death, the death without the dying, an eternal damnation, a carving out of my being— from all existence—until I stand here now a hollow hulk, speaking, breathing, talking, commanding, but my essence has been exorcised. And that, as all can surmise, is true murder done without the dying." Pausing, Lord said, "These two shall, in due time, clamor down to the gates of hell begging to be let in, once my wrath is upon them."

At light Lord woke amassing his resolve, conjuring the plan for the day's assault knowing his scheme, if executed well, would crush the rebellion and rebels; all would be thrown down the Pit of Wells to fiery hell, to their final end. He would start again with new, loyal, hosts, with a new ethos and would again grant kindness without regard or thought to its consequence. He had made Lilith and Lucifer powerful, close to himself in their majesty, and now he faced them combined against him. He would not make that mistake again.

He spoke to his assembled hosts, "We, today, will cast off yesterday and face this new sunrise and, I say to you, I guarantee that this day all, unto the last one of them, shall fall; that the last unto the last of them shall

19

drop their treacherous shields, flee, or be destroyed; that one and all of them shall break before my judgment, be captured and thrown down the Pit; that each and every one of them shall recompense the heavenly balance sheet."

A roar went up among them and Lord sensed a refreshment of their faith and resolve. "Now mark these times," he said "newly minted, for all creation is now re-born, a new time not so innocent, is upon us, one which has been marked by this stain—a stain which must be expunged, a debt to be paid."

Another roar echoed and each rank made its bow pledging to Lord a victory for one and all.

The field where the battle was to begin was on a softly rolling plain with seven rising hills, where each detachment could rise to the fight, but, before hand, each battalion was hidden from each other behind a hill's crest. It made surprise easier for both sides but more difficult to see how the battle progressed since, in this scene, there were many skirmishes but no one single, large, battle scene. It was terrain made for tactics and maneuvers, not massed pitched battles.

Lucifer surveyed it all, Lilith as his side. She said, "This is not the ground I would have chosen because my aerials cannot hit the mass, but must swoop down upon fragmented groupings, thus, losing the element of efficiency. This day will then be long and nothing can be counted as done until all the small battles have been counted, and even then re-massing will be difficult meaning we shall not know for a time who or what has won."

"My fear," Lilith said, "is that we might win most skirmishes and still will not have won the battle. They outnumber us two to one and we cannot lose more hosts than they or we are done."

And a gargantuan battle it was. A thousand, thousand, hosts descended among the seven hills and many ranks were, therefore, invisible and commanders could not coordinate as they would wish since there was no line of sight view of the battlefield.

Lord rode the between the hills and the valleys offering encouragement. Lucifer and Lilith flew above relaying commands from ravine to valley.

There arose a first volley from Lords' hosts upon the central hill as their hosts sought to mount the top of a hill held by Lilith's forces. These were met with an aerial bombardment from Lilith's hosts and a push toward the top, as well, from Lucifer's infantrymen. Backing down, Lord's ranks shrank, pushed back into the valley below with Lucifer's minions in hot pursuit. But Lucifer miscalculated in allowing that pursuit because he could see Lord had planned to have his infantry descend into the valley with hosts he deployed from behind yet another hill. These combined to surround Lucifer's forces. Lucifer's hosts pursuing were now the pursued. There were cries of anguish as the plan hatched and Lucifer saw the loss of an entire battalion, now being decimated rank after rank, outnumbered three to one and they soon fell beneath Lord's forces of purple and green.

Lucifer said to Lilith as they watched; "We see our dream die here at arms and we are helpless. We must choose between hope and clear futility; do we fight on or spare lives and take what fate awaits us before Lord's Throne?"

Lilith spoke quietly, "Not as yet. I'll have my aerials launch another drop to see if mayhem can cause the scatter and help us yet re-coop what our eyes reveal below as sure disaster."

Lilith's forces flew high, their cloud-gasses shooting out, enveloping, but, this was of small consequence since Lord's forces and those of Lucifer were in such close proximity—the cloud-gas had to be sparsely used—least Lucifer's infantrymen be felled along with those Lord had fielded. A drag of time later it became clear that none and nothing would appear to save this battle or to save this day.

Lucifer raised his hand to halt the proceedings, telling all his hosts to cease in resisting and he took Lilith by the hand to begin a slow march through the ranks aimed toward Lord's position on the high hill;

each face in the angel hosts looked up to gain sight of what they all understood was the march of surrender, the final battle act, the end of the rebellion.

Slow march and longest time, Lucifer and Lilith then stood before Lord, his mount stomping ground, his eyes piercing down—his judgment ready, his wrath unsheathed, his words coming clear, addressing one and all.

"These two," he began, "were given my greatest fruits, all the gifts I had to give, all the love I possessed and yet, they saw fit to betray me, in my own bed, in my own house and still yet harbor the spawn-seed of that awful union."

"You shall be," he said to Lilith and Lucifer," seated before me and I shall pass judgment upon you befitting the crimes of which you are guilty."

Chapter 5

It was before the assembled hosts that Lord summoned the two to hear sentence passed against them and for them to receive from the parchment read, their fates and transmogrifications.

All hush came upon the group as each stood at Lord's command whereupon he began to read from his rolled up scroll. "I have given each of you the gift of immortality, and mark while this I cannot revoke—this gift is irrevocable--but note, beauty is one gift which is redeemable and I, herewith," he said, raising he sword high so that all could see lowered it over Lucifer's head spoke, "revoke from you the beauty I gave and give you the appearance of the animal of the field with cloven hooves. I place upon you the face of the goat and horns to mark your treachery." Sudden, it was that Lucifer had cloven hooves, and horns on his head, that his whole body was crimson red. A gasp went up from all the hosts.

Lord continued, "You shall have the pitch-fork tail, signal of the forked tongue used to deceive and all shall know you by these presentments and you shall be so named for all eternity, and more, all your hosts and Cheribums shall be as gargoyles—hideous—and they shall cleave with you in this punishment."

Lucifer stood now the image of a redden goat; ugly now, with his beauty gone, evaporated.

Lucifer spoke, his mouth was smaller now, but, he still had his eloquence, "You, Lord, have pronounced, and I have received, your judgment and punishments for a crime that has no precedence. I accept your pronouncements but ask Lord that you contemplate that when love given and received is put down viciously, without a shimmer of forgiveness or understanding, when this simple relationship is judged wanting and deemed a threat to kingdoms, what then is the true meaning there? How balanced is this judgment against Lord's own values and sentiments?" How can Love be a crime? Especially since we, Lilith and I, were by your own creation, fated to be attracted one to the other? Should not you Lord forgive and understand that you might have had a hand in the whole scheme?"

Visibly angered, Lord leaned down from his throne-perch and fully-faced Lucifer's new countenance and said "Your sentence is pronounced and you shall be cast down the Pit. You ask if your punishment is just. I answer you that to escape these deeds with your life intact is, in fact, mercy, more mercy that the angels you led received, which now all around us, lay dead. They have not life or limbs whist you walk about full-bodied, uglier true, but full-limbed. Nay, you have mercy."

He turned then to Lilith and spoke close to her face, his tone softening.

"I gave you my all; nothing retained, and allowed all to flow away from my heart to you. I did not anticipate that my reward would be menstrual blood in my own bed and another's embrace round you and conception too, in that very same space. How could you?"

Lord's lament was monstrously sad so great its depth.

"How could you." he said again?"

He paused, "I," he said raising his sword again, "strip from you my beauty gift and make of you a snake to crawl upon your belly henceforth."

And Lilith was, in the instant, a serpent upon the floor.

Lord peered down, gazing upon her lowly form.

"I raise by this kingdom's highest heights this further judgment upon you. So, as the seed you carry is evil sent, I smite it from your belly and thereby prevent its birth in this world and, too, make it such you will forever in your womb be barren."

The hosts gasped as Lilith, even as serpent on the ground had a small bump, which in Lord's pronouncement was gone and dispensed of. Her cry, even with serpent lips was audible in the midst of the hush now over the assembled hosts.

Lord thrust his sword even higher and said "I condemn you and your hosts to the Pit where you will be thrust down its fiery depths. I hereby condemn you, Lucifer and you Lilith, to spend your hideous immortalities on Earth."

Chapter 6

The Earth in that time newly forming was a place of exploding volcanoes, fierce lava flows and it was formless and lifeless. Meteorites and asteroids rained down daily in terrifying numbers, creating huge sulphur and methane gas clouds.

Lord's pronouncement had been carried out instantly and Lucifer and Lilith found themselves on a fiery crag where the heat was unbearable; where their bodies burned with red hot heat, with white fire and a blue blaze but, being immortal there was no relief for their torment. In that instant Lucifer said "we must get away from this Hell and find some place for shelter."

As he spoke, he heard Lord's voice was booming, "And I banish all the hosts who cleaved to them to Hell as well."

All around Lilith and Lucifer could see angels now made into demons descend to be with them exiled by Lord. Thousands arrived, each a gargoyle, no longer the beautiful angels they once were, all cowered and astonished to be in such a place but happy to see Lilith and Lucifer. Many took heart that at least all would be together in the place.

Under fire with brimstone hurtling from the sky Lilith was able to with a great effort take herself from the serpents form temporarily said, "I am able to resume my old form for only brief moments so let me speak while I can." She looked out over the many thousands there-- many injured, most frightened--and offered them hope for the future.

"We are in this Hell; true, but some of our strength still remains. Lucifer and I can change our forms, but only for small intervals, so I appear before you in woman form in order to speak with you and to let you know we shall not lose heart despite this circumstance. Place your faith in our resources, even as I know many of you now suffer, sharing a fate which comes from having given us your support. Know you well that we shall survive this and rise again and deny the fate decreed us from Lord. We shall go down this crag and found a new dynasty below. Lord has banned us but he was not able to take from us all our powers. Lucifer and I have many powers left we shall build anew here. Join us."

Lucifer said, "Bear the pain as you will; I see below cooler valleys and we must gather ourselves and clamor down to the valley floor where we can begin to structure a new life."

It was a horrific descent where hot lava and steam burned many horribly step by step. There were cries and pleas of mercy to Lord even as they moved slowly down, passing burning boulders, fiery heaps, steam gardens and pyres. Lucifer could hear cries in his ears-some of the hosts asking for mercy, asking Lord to forgive, but these cries were not heard by Lord. There was only silence from above and in a crevice made of molten sulfur they all sat, to rest before the final descent to the valley below where Lucifer had promised accommodations would be more bearable. Lilith looked at the faces and whispered to Lucifer, "It is clear that, naturally, some among us regret this turn of events and will likely seek redemption from Lord's decree and that will likely be rejected, thus, then, dear one, they will likely turn on us as the progenitors of their now unbearable torment. We, too, shall see," Lilith said, "rebelling rebels and revolutionaries in short order. For that we must have a plan and not be caught by surprise and, thus, suffer more in this horrid place—from a wedding of the specters of Hell and the specters of Politics."

"I agree," Lucifer said, "this is foreseeable."

They arrived at the valley floor to survey the landscape for shelter points and Lucifer pointed across the crevasse to a high cliff which appeared to have caves embedded midway above the valley floor. "There," he said, "we can find a cooler spot away from this murderous inferno and sit to speak of our plight and our sojourn here."

They all agreed and began the trek up the cliff wall to the cave Lucifer had identified, sore and injured many of them, dispirited were some of them, resentful were others. Lucifer could see the frustration and confusion mix that inhabited them and knew that some of this would spill out and contaminate the new life he and Lilith were planning to build. His thought was to confront the riffs before they became disastrous and thereby cripple the whole enterprise.

That night in counsel, in the cave where they had gathered, he spoke of these issues and more.

"I know some feel our fate here is hell itself and that Lilith and I led, therefore, must take blame for urging you to rebel and now this, 'unbearable eternity.' I see this view. I understand. I understand that some would want to make a plea to Lord to take you back, to forgive and, thereby, relieve this suffering; ask forgiveness for the blasphemy. If that is the wish of some of you I would hear you on this. Stand and let yourselves be seen; how many are of this view? I, myself will help, in this, to see if Lord will recant and punish Lilith and I, but relent among you innocents and take you back. Let me see by standing up, how many are of this view?"

The pause of thought ran threw all of them as they sought to see and feel where their own inclinations lay, and, at some long pause-point, several hundred of the thousands there stood up.

"I see some have declared." Lilith said. "Here, then, is the plan. Choose among you delegates and then prepare to present to Lord your best case. We will then communicate on high and see if Lord will repent. It is a course to try; it is a cause of worth. Let us sleep this night and tomorrow make the attempt to communicate to Lord your desires and see what transpires."

All nodded to Lilith's plan and began to make arrangements for sleep. As they busied themselves arranging the space Lucifer spoke to them soothingly, "We will on the morrow make a permanent shelter from raining rocks, create a space inside this cave where we can all live normal lives, sheltered. We must plan in our exile to make a new city in this Earth."

The next day the delegation for Lord's review assembled in front of all the hosts and called Lord's name.

"Oh, Lord," the delegation leader said, "we are here, some of us, beseeching you, asking your forgiveness—to take us back, take us away from this dreadful place, to return to your kingdom, give us your salvation."

There was a silent pause and no response came and the group hesitated and started to disperse when that familiar voice, that booming thunder-box of Lord's occurred.

"I hear you; I understand your words and your anguish, and your pleas for redemption at my hand. This makes my mind tend toward salvation for the truly repentant. Here this, I make no promises here, but I will hear from all who want to come to sit with me and make individual personal pleas. Ready yourselves all who would come and I will transport the lot all at once."

The group of several hundred looked at one another understanding Lord would hear them out and in a flash all hundred were gone, taken from where they stood, by Lord for counsel with him.

Astonished, the remaining hosts looked at one another and finally turned their gaze to Lucifer and Lilith who stood stock still mindful that a pardon from Lord for even a few might create an avalanche of those who would, too, ask for forgiveness, thereby abandoning Lucifer and Lilith to a lonelier still, haggard exile.

But Lord's voice instantly returned and was again back in the room; his pronouncement clear.

"I have smited your delegation each and every one."

There was a hush of disbelief spreading among them and a murmuring twinged with fear and loathing.

"How could you Lord?"

"Know this," Lord was saying, "my decree is one of suffering. You have all sinned against me and have, thereby, earned your punishments. There shall be no reprieves. You shall suffer from my command for all eternity. Let this be for you clarity; sin and punishment are not to be severed, but are welded together irretrievably."

There was stunned silence in the room at this.

Lilith spoke, "Lord I can see, especially in the case with me that such a betrayal, from your view, falling in love could warrant the hell you have bequeathed for Lucifer and I, but I am not able to see where such a harsh meting of punishments has been earned by those who merely followed their consciousness. I am of the view that mercy is not a sign of weakness but of strength yet, you by this, show no inclination for forgiveness and, thereby, in my eye reduce your presentation from on high down to lower motivations and pettiness."

All were stunned at Lilith's statement. There was no immediate response from Lord. But soon the cumulative effect of Lord's silence and Lilith's statement ignited among them a cumulative dread awaiting Lord's response to Lilith's speech.

It came.

"By the kingdom which is mine to rule, that the creature I created would affront me so and repay my gift with insolence, blasphemy, and such rejection pains me. Such salt on such wounds do not heal. Such deeds cannot be expunged. These are such dire acts, from which there can be no retraction. As deeds are done, so, too, are they punished, and, you all shall have to suffer yours; and from me know, there will be no, I say again, no reprieve."

"You ask, Lilith, that I make an exception for you and honor your love for Lucifer and stay the hand of punishment. Understand, in this, despite my love for you, I have not allowed in this an exception for myself, even though in my heart, I might sorely wish to…"

"This is done." Lord said with finality.

An awful silence fell. There was no sound or response. Everyone there knew matter had ended.

Lord's disembodied voice was now gone silent.

They all stood mute.

Lilith spoke and said "This is our new home."

Chapter 7

So, it was that the rein of Lucifer and Lilith began on Earth and they, with their fallen angels, began the work of making hospitable their environs. There was no reshaping the Earth to make of it a paradise—Lord had quietly rebuffed their efforts to do this, allowing only minor changes to the terrain, forcing the group to hard labor for the simplest gains.

Water was had from geyser steam and from these the group could bathe. Small algae plants grew even in the lava beds and from them soups and broths were made. Evolutionarily the time passing was eons on Earth and Lucifer, Lilith and the hosts saw the Earth slowly begin to support life, evolving from simpler life forms to higher ones. This was a welcome development for it made life much easier because the food supply became more plentiful for the many hosts.

Lucifer and Lilith saw their small colony prosper but it did not grow. Lord had made all of the hosts barren as well, therefore, for none could there be children, only immortality.

Lucifer was especially grieved and grew morose from lacking a sense of being able to see his own progeny take a place on Earth.

"It is our home now," he said to Lilith, "it seems fitting our kind should have a place on this new Earth. Why can't we conceive a methodology to have it so," Lucifer mused.

"It is so," Lilith agreed, "there must be some way to give this place a future which includes our progeny. We could," Lilith said, "suddenly seek out an animal here and alter it in our own image and have it progress to be, not us, but something akin to us. Could we not have a mortal being be our progeny?"

Lucifer mused again saying, "We would be as Lord himself. I remember that Lord once said that he took mortal beings and transcended some to high being.

Perhaps, we too, could learn that trick and thereby make on Earth a legacy."

They both sat with eureka eyes and thought to see what animal would be most suitable for that experiment.

But, word of their nascent intent reached some of the hosts and one among them assigned himself as leader and approached Lilith and Lucifer with a singular plea.

"We understand you have the desire to make an animal here fertile to produce a being in your own image and would have of this an heir. We find this alarming and full distressful since many here are more qualified, and, too, have demonstrated loyalty. Yet that loyalty would, in this plan, be eschewed in a project, sire we think frankly smacks less of practicality than of vanity and dare I say pride. Did not Lord himself regret his own creation of you and Lilith? That deed if done, if I may say, would seek to rise above strict equality and ends in mortal mischief. That is the lesson there, I think, for us to consider. What manner of being, is this would be birthed, what powers would this being possess?"

Lilith spoke, "My womb was made barren. My seed was taken from me in a violent rage and I was publicly humiliated, made bereft, and more, shamed. I admit it is my desire to see progeny, as is true with Lucifer, we both do. It is nature to seek this, to desire this."

"But Lord has machinated to prevent conception in me and I must, therefore, seek other remedies. Now eons on this planet life has become abundant, we, Lucifer and I, seek some creature, some small cherub looking similar in our image. Our plea that you, Cherubim, will understand and not take offense, for surely that is not the intent with which we proceed. Indeed, it is clear this is our home now and we think, it proper, to explore the possibility of life in our image which we think can't help but rebound to the benefit of all--our new seed and Cherubim."

Gathered in the great cave place, the Cherubim paused to consider this and finally Lucifer spoke. "You all had taken from you your former beauty as was mine wrenched from me. We were made to appear to be gargoyles and demon-like. That is crushing blow enough. But in this, our survival, we have endured. Speaking for me, I naturally seek to recapture to myself and for all of us, what had been lost. We can re-build here not only in

31

our image but, in doing so, may discover that which can give you all a new look, one more pleasing than the countenances you all now endure. In this we all might see new benefit and a new stage in our evolution here."

With that the Cherubim calmed seeing that something of this could benefit them, and relive the misery the mirror brought each day when they dared look in it.

So it was that Lilith and Lucifer sought among the creatures extent on Earth one suitable for the experiment. They began the survey of the two legged ones but found at first only those which crouched low and scurried along on all fours. Lilith inspected a baby child secured from its mother who looked on, not afraid, more curious, because Lilith had made herself appear similar to the mother and her species which had gathered at the edge of a glen.

"Now mother," Lilith communicated, "I mean your baby no harm I simply need to see how your baby ambles and moves about."

But, it was plain that Lilith was pleased to cradle a child, motivated by that baby seed memory Lord had forestalled.

She was now in full pursuit of it, and this child had rekindled that fire anew. A sigh came from her. Her eyes closed as she held the baby close.

Lucifer retired to his own pursuits as Lilith started her plan to teach the mother how to teach the child to walk, up-right, to teach the mother how to improve her species' lot. Lilith fully intended to conjugate a new beginning on Earth through the mother and the baby.

In days and years to follow she traced for the Earth animals each step which might, at end, present a new race closer to hers and Lucifer's. She labored on skeletal development and brain growth such that these might increase the intelligence; she taught them all, assembled in their small group, how to use certain tools for improvements in the housing, and in their diets. Most concentrated, she sought to teach them to speak, to communicate above primitive sounds and body gestures.

One day she called Lucifer and the rest to see what her labors had wrought. Once assembled, the small creature lined up awaiting Lilith's signal; and, at that point, on her signal, the child, now a young female adult, began a fully erect walk. She initiated her trek with an exaggerated gait and her lips curled to what looked like a smile similar to Lilith's own.

A mother's pride glowed in Lilith's face and all applauded the work done. Lucifer stepped to give Lilith's charge a warm hug and to Lilith he then exchanged a tearful smile for this was truly a tiny miracle and the first one on this new Earth.

And then, the young creature was heard to utter what all there was sure a "thank you" sound which astonished the assembled but was clearly heard. Lilith's pride was now without end because she had not tutored her charge for that sound and clearly saw, while the child was imitating sounds heard, it also meant that the creature was capable of potentially communicating and inventing words and meanings on its own.

But, time was not a friend to this enterprise, because one day Lilith arrived to find the mother awash in tears the girl cradled in her arms; expired. Lilith had no end to her grief. On the day she taught the mother's group to swaddle the girl in clean linens, how to put beside her small mementos, how to bury her, the latter customs being unknown to them.

By the graveside, (the young girl had no name) Lilith stood, herself in white linen, spoke her sorrow over the death; her grieving tones carried high into the earthen sky. "I have in this bound myself and our kind to you, Earth's kind. Our sorrows and our destinies are now fully intertwined, and yet, this is not the end point but only a pause in the march we make toward kin-hood and the species-knit which I think will make both our futures more secure. With this, the first step, we'll see more clearly the second and the third and beyond, until we reach that success I believe, is yet to come to its final stages--the blending of our exiled set and Earth's woman and man."

By fading light, this first child was laid to rest and, the hands clasped across her grave, sealed a pact set between Lilith's kind and the creatures of Earth's forests.

But, not known to any of them was Lord's high observation of these proceedings and brooding in his throne room. He observed the transpiring events below.

Musing out loud he spoke his inner thoughts, "I will not continence this evasion attempt to circumvent my decree. There will be no progeny for you Lilith, no progeny for you Lucifer by natural means or these artificial ones you may conceive. There will be no creature proxy, no orphan adoptions for you. I will smite all progenitors natural or otherwise as I have smitted this one."

Lucifer and Lilith had no knowledge of the real causes of the child's death and proceeded anew to find other children and means to bring to Earth a species in their form. For eons on they had some beginnings of success only to find that by accident or unknown means failure, death or deformity overtook all those efforts until one day Lilith sat with Lucifer and spoke.

Lilith breathed, "I cannot bear this dark disease which seems to blunt all our efforts here and, despite mighty efforts extended, all has come to accident, failure and grief. What is at play here?"

Lucifer eyes narrowed from recognitions his mind then perceived and spoke, "Yes, there seems a pattern here, cleverly disguised, but such common outcomes, can only mean one thing--Lord has intervened here to frustrate our efforts--for surely he has been aware yet we have received no communication, no warning, no threats. That can only mean he has seen all and directly set things askew placing his hand in all of this to murder our attempts at progeny."

"I fear your theory makes most sense," Lilith said, "it would explain our experience. I had forgotten that must of what transpires here must perforce come to the awareness of Lord and, given his penchants for adherence to his pronouncements; it comes clear that he would act to forestall our efforts. But, what now to do?"

Lucifer, in conspiratorial tones, took Lilith aside and said. "We must make our effort opaque such that Lord cannot observe. There is a way this could be done as I have discovered. It can be done with an admixture of gases I have concocted here."

"What is that?" Lilith inquired.

Lucifer said, "Sulphur gas provides, I have discovered, shields us from Lords' eyes if we place a sulfur fire at the mouth of the cave, Lord will not be able to discern what transpires within. I have tested this. We can this next time hide what we do such that Lord will not be able to observe.

So Lilith's next pupils were tutored deep in a special cave. Lucifer erected by its mouth a special fire of sulfurs he gained from volcano cores. The sulfurous gasses, foul though they were, made observation by Lord and his cohorts, impossible.

New activity thus began in these deepest depths and went on for, in Earth time, eons till one day Lilith emerged from a lesson given to say, "Lucifer I think we are ready."

Lucifer came alone to the cave's mouth to accompany Lilith to a cave branch deepest most into a chamber Lilith had decorated in bright colors to observe a young man who appeared to Lucifer to be near twenty and was, in appearance, most beautiful.

Lucifer looked on in wonderment saying, "Truly astonishing this—you have created a creature most beautiful, and in our likeness. I am Lilith, most proud and curious."

Lilith said, "Of this we must converse, but not here in these depths; let's retire closer to the surface and perceive the plan as to where we go from here."

They sat in a secluded cave alcove and whispering, Lilith spoke said "I live in fear that Lord will surmise from our sheer activity that something is amiss and send someone to investigate and thereby smite our latest effort and give us again only dust as spawn. I fear that tonight, tomorrow on the next day yet another funeral and nothing here to celebrate except another defeat. What shall we do to protect the child?"

Lucifer spoke slowly and said, "You should immediately create a female counterpart and have them mate and make them fertile as stars in the sky and have them then disperse quickly as they can to the far corners of this Earth. Install in them wanderlust such that Lord will not easily find them for the kill. Make them live, too, in caves where they will not be easy to discover. We must make it difficult for Lord to exterminate the fruit of our labors."

Lilith went back again into the cave to initiate Lucifer's suggestions which she found most wise and perceptive. Lucifer gathered together the elders in a group to teach them the arts of sulphur concealments to ward away prying eyes from the goings on in the cave. Lilith moved to her second task—the creation of a young girl for the match to the young man already born.

She too, once completed, was beautiful and in her, Lilith was most pleased. The two stood before Lilith and Lucifer as separate entities. Both had been given only preliminary awareness of who they were and both were as yet unnamed.

Lilith spoke, "I am Lilith and I am your mother. This is Lucifer and he is your father. We have given you life upon this Earth for a grand purpose. Yours is to found a race, to give birth to nations, to go out and multiply and populate among all the animals in this place. We have given you consciousness of yourself, in this new form of life, and we have placed you here as first exemplars."

The two stood in bewilderment not really comprehending but Lilith spoke soothingly, "Do not be of concern that you don't yet understand, because I will impart to you the knowledge you will need to succeed in this wildernesses. Lucifer and I will impart to you the fertility you will need to succeed to spread your seed across the plains, the mountains, the valleys and the seas. Hear me and your name young male shall be Narob and you young princess shall be called Sarah, such that by this you shall remember us both and your origins."

"Come," she said, "gather between us, because even in this touch, much can be imparted. We shall teach you of the mysteries of life, of love, of sex and your mission here; we shall teach you not mechanistically but organically; your need will be to learn, to continuously adapt, for the road you will travel will be harsh, and strewn with many dangers."

"You shall learn to survive if we, your progenitors, happen to be gone one day and thereby igniting your need to survive on your own. I have planned for you curricula, the tools you'll need to acquire before you begin your journey."

Their tutelage began first in the survival skills. Lilith led.

"You are in a frontier world, and therefore, must learn to use the tools at hand and not be inclined to harness yourself to rigid rules and stern practices. Your way must be the way of adaptability for that will ensure our survival. You must marry outside your small group for this ensures variety and variety is a foundation of adaptability. Be liberal in your assessment of others because, if you accumulate enemies, you'll not be surprised to find yourself surrounded by enemies. Always forgive, for in forgiveness is the possibility of new beginnings; avoid long running feuds and separations. Be learned in the arts because the arts open the closed doors of the mind and this practice is life-saving. Be not complacent and yield always to curiosity-yours and that of your off spring. Wander about your world because there is danger in concentration—you'll be more easily be discovered and, thereby dispatched, if massed. Remember you are not enemy-less in this place; there are forces afoot which would rather see you fail to prosper."

Respect things of the body, and you Sarah, are to make from your womb a new race and a new beginning to populate this New Earth. It is not a bad thing to lay with the young man; it is the means to your survival and the pleasures which accompany it. We have given you the ability to be fertile most months such that you may proceed toward that goal with joy."

Lucifer said, "Learn of the trees in the field, the animals, large and small because from them you can gain medicines for your healing and the secrets of agriculture. Carry your burdens lightly and highlight the joys your new lands will bring. Look to your spouses and children because you are weaklings in the wilderness and many animals have greater strength than you possess, and you must, therefore, live by your wits and the ties of family, loyalty and intelligence born of that curiosity and wanderlust Lilith mentioned. Remember that the prize goes to those who know best the needs of others both animal and plant. This is the map, which will guide all to success, defined as all living together on this green and blue world understanding its underpinnings and requisites."

It was these instructions that Lilith and Lucifer gave that infused the budding two as they left from their instruction lessons. They began to speak to one another seeking greater understanding of who they were.

"I am puzzled most," Sarah pronounced, when he and Nabob were alone, "as to who is my mother most--she who lives in the cave and is the hairy one--or she who soars the skies? What and who is my true progenitor. I must ask this question in my next lesson with Lilith."

Lilith when asked simply stated, "You, my dears, are hybrid born of, mortal flesh yet raised higher than mortal flesh commiserate with the higher purpose you have in this place. Hybrid, not animal fully, but descended from same, yet more than these origins because you have received additional gifts from Lucifer and I. Your race is mixed with ours in founding a new dynasty. What awaits, we cannot yet see, but it is yours to explore that future which is surely yours and we beseech you to not avoid but take that future to embrace."

With this instruction kit the two left the cave where Lucifer and Lilith lived and moved out upon the Earth's landscape to found their own settlement.

Chapter 8

It was then that the waters of the Earth were plentiful covering most places. The two learned to live near the creatures of the sea and planted their feet most often on land close to the sea. This allowed them to explore more quickly using the shorelines to navigate by.

Narob, still innocent, lay on the sand by the sea with young Sarah, and asked. "I wonder how just we two can be expected to populate this huge place. What births are there to be and how many must we conceive to have an opportunity to complete such an awesome mission? I for one stand mystified."

"Our mother," young Sarah conceded, "told me in lesson class that within already grows that seed even as she prepares another young male from the cave nursery to match with what grows in me. These two we shall engender, as more are produced from mother's nursery, such that enough numbers are reached to produce the number needed to guide them across these lands and abound to prosperity."

Narob was not appeased and he said so. "I am not agreed with this procedure. My love wishes to plant my own seed in your womb. I have not wished this nor have I been consulted. You and I are not relatives and, therefore it seems to me, able to conceive and produce our own offspring; and, I this day, propose we try."

Sarah, was taken aback by this, abruptly it seemed, thrust upon her by Narob, who was further saying, "I will prepare a place this night in the far cave there and see what we can do to further this. I have this need to feel you in my arms and yield and reciprocate this love I need to give and receive."

His hand moved to her breasts as they lay in the sand. She felt her nipples swell to anticipate each stroke and maneuver. Encouraged, young Narob murmured in her ear, "I was born as well as you to accomplish this, to consummate our love in this way. I want to see your belly swell with our mutual seed. By this way, it seems to me, a more natural means for you and I to be together here, rather than by inseminations artificial."

Sarah's eyes agreed in Narob's estimation and he placed his hand on her heart; there on the sand, and his mouth on her mouth, his genitals on hers without penetration and sought to meld there on a sandy rise, by the sea, in the warm sun, but consummation eluded them.

"Tonight," he said, "we will further experiment, and we, like our parents, can mold our own future through our bodies which alone can sate our mutual need."

Lilith and Lucifer watched their creation from afar; parents keeping a watchful eye of protection over the two. Lilith said "I think we should not interfere; what about you?"

"I agree." said Lucifer. "We have set in place forces which cannot and ought not be held under strict control. No stronger force than love, our history exemplifies this, and we ought not deny this to our own children. Our role is to keep them safe from their enemies and teach them from afar and protect them; have them learn the habits of safety, and, for now, we see instinctively, they seek the shelter of the cave for security."

That night Narob ignited the sulfur fire at the mouth of a small beach-side cave as Lucifer had taught him to and prepared a place where he and Sarah, would lay; his heart pounding, anticipation in his body, driving it to distraction both loving and frenzied. Sarah lit candles unsure of what, and how to be in sexual embrace, assuming Narob would have the capacity to meld her body with his. Narob did not know the mechanics of it, for obviously he had never been with Sarah, who in a linen dress was transparent lit before the fire.

It was the first sexual embrace for each of them, young Narob thought, and he worried that it should have proper moment and significance. He also wanted that Sarah would take comfort from it and that the two would, this night, to produce a child.

She sat her legs crossed and fixed his gaze and then lay back to encourage him to place himself beside her— she was impatient for his embrace, remembering his earlier touch beach-side, and how her nipples had responded. The breathing between the two, she thought, was a first step, but, it was between the two that touch, the first touch was the explosive part. His hand, lingered and floated down to her aching center and she felt for the first time his member enter that entry-way and reacted so strongly to his finger-tip that the aching shook her body explosively again and again. It was, too, his mouth on hers, his hand inside her moving slowly. It was a fire lit inside and the fire lit beside them that combined to bewitch both and what happened next was ordained. She felt his hardness grow and sought it out to replace his finger there, because she wanted more of him to penetrate, more of him for her own lips down there to embrace, to explode against.

She moved to roll over atop him to take him into her hand and place him within as he laid back his own body-quakes rocking him. She rocked him, moved him side to side, thrusting her body over his body and withdrawing it as fire embers exploded from popping wood soared to the cave ceiling-a fireworks for their mutual consummations, which exhausted, the two who lay side by side now quivering, dumb-founded from the experience.

Lilith and Lucifer from an unseen view looked on. Lilith smiled, "Perhaps I over-did the sexual sense. But no matter, we see they will populate, and in doing so, take, too, the pleasure of it."

Sarah's belly did not grow that night and the two of them wondered what had gone wrong. Sarah asked Lilith about it the next day and Lilith told her than in human form a baby would take a longer time; but that, nonetheless, the two of them should prepare for the baby's birth and to learn how to navigate the new environs the planet presented to them. Sarah resolved patience.

Such was their time there—an idyllic life, with abundant food, fuels and prospects. They retired at night and lit the fire and talked of the wonders of their world. In the day time there were cautious keeping to the forests and glens, only occasionally exposing themselves on the white-sand beach. Sarah said one night before the fire in the cave, "I wonder if the child within will have traits of you and I, or of our parents mixed. Or, if they will have our cave parent's traits first, ours second, and Lucifer's and Lilith's third. I wonder what the look will be and the temperament."

Narob stared into the fire and agreed. "Surely it is speculative to wonder in what these origins will eventuate."

Came her time, Sarah called Narob to sit with her by the fire because she had felt all the signs that Lilith had told her to look for. Her face was red in the fire's glow from both fright and anticipation. Narob took a linen cloth and boiled it in water as Lucifer had told him and placed it, once cool enough, beneath Sarah who spread her legs to accommodate the impending birth. Narob looked to see if she had crowned, meaning the baby's head was visible at the opening, while she started the deep breathing she had been told by Lilith to exaggerate. Secretly unknown to them, Lucifer and Lilith stood by watching, declining by prior agreement to intervene, and understanding the need for the two to gain confidence in their ability to manage birth.

Narob gave a push and he could see the head move forward until there was a forehead and then a nose and then a face. His heart pounded within him. Narob laid back and followed the rule book Lilith had given her, to breath, push, relax, breath, push relax. There was in this a ritual she thought, because she was breathing new life onto this exile planet, she was uniting its flora and animals with those of her other parents and thereby, simultaneously giving birth to yet another branch different from either of these.

The baby was still struggling toward the light.

Lucifer and Lilith looked on teary-eyed.

"I think this progeny," Lucifer said, "shall not possess our immortality but will be more resilient in its toughness and survivability in its native branch. These two strains combined shall prosper," Lucifer offered, "the better on this planet."

When the birth was reaching it apex and the little feet were released from the womb origin, both couples looked on in awe. "My, he is so beautiful," Lilith cried and Lucifer beamed with pride while Narob delivered the child to Sarah's arms, thereby, put into place the first creation Lilith and Lucifer had made in this place.

The boy was named, Abram and was strong and sturdy-limbed. He grew apace. Before long new children were in seed. Sarah gave birth to seven children in turn who mated with those Lilith created similarly as she had done with Narob and Sarah. These began families on their own and their children grew and multiplied into many strong beings. Lucifer and Lilith had them all assemble one day undercover of night in the mammoth cave which could accommodate them all.

"Standing before all of you," he said. "we meet because in a short time our numbers will be too huge to be sheltered from view, in any other venue. Now you are all assembled, Lilith and I need to one last time plant the vision of how you all shall proceed to migrate to other places where your futures lay."

He surveyed his and Lilith's handiwork and said, "We have here given birth to a new nation of women and men, who are now at the embarkment's edge, and will be scattering up and outward across the topography, up and out of the darkness into the bright sun-shine less afraid, more proud."

"Your mother and I came here many eons ago. Much has not been said, much is even now unknown to you and here I will, this night, give you heedance to our story and let this be a guide to you in your future endeavors to play out this destiny your mother and I have bequeathed thee."

Lilith stepped forth. "Your father and I were once high in a far off kingdom and fell in love. That love was deemed unconscionable and illicit by the king of that kingdom and he let it be known that it was true, that we should not have lain together, and, more, we produced a child. Lord of that kingdom, often forgiving, could not forgive that part; Lord of that kingdom could not forget the transgression that involved a child and a possible heir and there followed a terrible conflagration, terrible killing and war."

Lucifer spoke, "Many died on the battle field, many hearts burst as war pierced and impaled the most vulnerable among us and we, losers in this, Lilith and I, and our adherents, were exiled to this place at a time when Earth was a hell of searing heat and volcanoes. We burned in that conflagration, too, for many eons, still dogged by Lord who looked down, after tearing the child from

Lilith's womb, preventing her, too, from ever giving birth henceforth--this even after tearing from us our child, our beauty and grace. He made of us a further mockery by giving us ugly countenances, stooped gaits, and myself, the hooves of a goat and a tail of spikes."

"But we," Lilith spoke, "did not relent and designed up a plan to recreate in this place a likeness of our former selves and we set to accomplish this after eons of meandering and suffering. New life had taken hold here and we hit upon the idea that a new race, too, could here be conceived, given birth to and be disseminated. First, and here me close, the former Lord got wind of this and murdered the first of these. We took then to the caves and devised a plan to remain concealed until our numbers grew large enough to brave the daylight, to make the trek to disperse from a few to the many."

"We are now at that gauge point where we feel we can risk a bold trek in the daylight. You are it. You are that step. Understand your origins, from that your destiny and understand that we are with you and will appear at desperate hours to assist, because you are those we love, those who live not only your destines but ours, as well."

The throng bowed to the two, among them Narob and Sarah now older who took their place at the head of the throng in the march up and out of the cave.

Chapter 9

How then, did this trek transpire and, once out in the open, did it remain concealed? It did not.

Lord, in his throne room, pondered this human development. He observed these earthly hybrids marching; and made his calculations. He first set upon them catastrophes and thereby exacted still more punishments upon on the progeny of Lilith and Lucifer. He made upon them fires of the forest, tornadoes, and fierce hurricanes; he set upon them drought and climate change; he allowed diseases free rein among them. He made lightening strikes at their homes and marauding beasts to enter their camps and tear at their limbs. But always they would retreat to their caves, light their fires at the caves mouth, and disappear from his view. They lit fires within the caves to keep beasts at bay and survived.

In the caves they wrote upon the walls, learned incantations, invented arts to amuse themselves while in that dark, venturing out while he, Lord, was pre-occupied somewhere else. with other outbreaks of human-beast hybrids expanding into new territories. They were, Lord noted, resilient; they had been taught well; they rebuilt after the killing winds, they replanted after killing drought, and they progressed in curing diseases set upon them, and they grew smart, and smarter still until Lord realized that he was loosing the race to put them to an end. Their numbers continued to grow despite Lord's best efforts to quash them.

Chapter 10

But despite Lord's failed efforts to blunt their growth, the Lilim breed, as they were called, did not, therefore, have a smooth path. In the eon After the Cave Dwelling, (ACD), some of the Lilim's newly born, as they grew to maturity started to resemble more and more the curse Lord had put on Lilith and Lucifer. Some of the male breed grew increasingly short and stocky with huge lobes at the forehead after several generations. They became aggressive against their brethren Lilim. The females slunk low and learned the arts of winding dance and the solicitudes of the sexual arts. These traits combined to split these creatures of Lord's curse from those whose temperaments seemed to have taken most from the new land.

Lucifer said, "We have in this land, now clearly, two breeds; one breed where Lord's curse remains herewith to haunt us and these now manifest themselves in some of our people in ugly war-like traits. The peace is already broken between these and the Lilim. Mounting skirmishes come to me on report. These 'Regrets,' as they were called, are instigators of the mayhem and the Lilim seek only peace."

Lilith said, "We must step to make the mark since failure to act in this could cause us to forfeit all gains we have made in this place thus far. I have consigned myself to think on this and concoct a plan whereby peace is made without the risk of a permanent split between the two breeds. A delicate remedy is needed--one skillful and sure. I have heard the Regrets have maimed and killed many among the Lilim who flee in terror from them--their visages so horrible to see."

Lucifer added, "And more, as the Lilim see these horrid looking beings, they are, reminded that they resemble us more in our cursed state than the Lilim who now appear, by contrast, more advanced, indeed, overarching even us. There is a dangerous appearance in things."

Even as they spoke, a representative of the northern Regrets appeared and asked for an audience. Lucifer and Lilith took on the appearance of the Lilim and beckoned him to step forth.

The representative of the northern Regrets appearance was fearsome indeed; exaggerated by war paints and tattoos, clearly designed Lucifer thought, to place the Lilim in terrible fright.

The Regent said, "I thank you Lilith and Lucifer both for allowing me to come before you to balance off what I am sure has been an unbalanced case made against us, so let me please make my plea as to…"

Lilith cut him off, "You come here unannounced, to tell a story? What I am most concerned with is the stories of the blood you have shed. In most reports, you did this unprovoked and brutally, showing no mercy upon your weaker opponents, the Lilim. What I seek before sly justifications are regrets from you Regrets and apologies. If not I shall by the native powers I possess strike one and all of you wherever you are on this Earth!"

Lucifer, feeling the mood was moving too fast toward hostile, softened his words and said, "Your name, sir?"

The representative said "I am called Ra, leader of the First Council, gatherer of the Cave Mavens and Lord of the Arms." He paused making a bow.

Lucifer could barely contain his anger instigated by the realization that the Regrets had built a society of their own with armaments and politics without this having been approved or discovered by him and Lilith.

"Am I to understand that you have created armed battalions and used them in combat with your fellows, killed maimed and murdered them?"

"Give me," Ra said, "a moment to make my case Lord, I beg you."

Lucifer slowly sat back, by this indicating he was prepared to listen. Lilith did likewise while clearly un-reconciled to all she had heard thus far.

Ra began, "In children born to our women, we began to notice they looked different and as they grew older they were different. Some few, at first, took on the appearance of the ancient curse, of which we had heard-gargoyle-like;

some were born clearly to the appearance of the Lilim. Initially these ugly ones were smothered in their beds, tossed aside, thrown down wells or destroyed on pyres of fire."

But our women revolted, seeking to protect their children, deformed though they might appear. They said, "They are our progeny sure as the Lilim and should not, because they lack beauty or grace, be murdered in their nurseries."

Ra paused and then continued, "So secretly we began small colonies of these first Regrets and hid them in the old caves nurturing them, bringing them food. This was more that 20 Glicks ago. But their numbers grew and their births to our women more frequent. Ultimately more of them began to be born to our women than Lilim. We had thrust upon us the realization that it was a dominant genetic stain marking a rift between us in our development and that of the Lilim."

Ra looked at Lilith and said, "Highness, it came to pass that the Lilim discovered our caves and in the stealth of night came and murdered the entirety of one cave colony, and aghast, we found the Lilim had taken some of the young ones and roasted them on fire chanting "Lord's Curse is Here Fulfilled—Long Live the Lilim"

It was for us an infanticide, a monumental tragedy, especially when we learned that this was done in hundreds of caves across our land. Unable to contain the anger, I and our leaders sought peace and restitution from the Lilim who averred that the deed was done by renegades from among their number and did not represent the sentiment, desire or intent of the majority of the Lilim."

Ra continued, "But it seems," he said, "these words were not true; we learned the Lilim council knew of these abominations, indeed, had provided direction to them, aiding the renegade crew in locating where our nurseries were located. The Lilim council provided these renegades with provisions for the long marches it took to reach our outermost hiding places."

"I could not," Ra said, "hold back our own hotheads against these developments, especially when at one point a burned chard of a baby child was tossed at the council's very door. They gasped at this horrific sight and rushed to the armories and secretly by night set out upon the Lilim which they slaughtered in their beds as they came upon them, burned their children in restitution in huge bon-fires they lit in market squares and villages. This, Lilith highness, has been raging now for two Glicks and we of the council cannot aver or forestall it. It grows by extension and leaps boundaries each day like the forest fire from village to village."

"I have come to you for assistance." With that Ra fell silent awaiting a response from the two.

Lilith spoke, "If what you say, Ra is true; it is deeply disturbing and must be rectified because to allow it to progress, beyond this, is to bring down all we have worked to build here. Thank you for your recitation. Lucifer and I will think on this and reconvene this conversation in the morning.

"We shall, too, send our envoys to ascertain the facts you aver."

Lucifer and Lilith sat in consultation that evening.

Lucifer reflected, "Such cruel irony here, we are faced with Lord's curse now eons later on this planet and we, too, face rebellion where the risk is to splinter the unity we worked so hard to engender. All this could be splintered in a flice, if we take the wrong decision and appear to favor either side." Lilith responded, "To think that the off-spring I worked so assiduously to create could be tainted such even at this distance from Lord's curse. He has demonstrated here the capacity for eternal punishment and, thereby, crashes down upon us true eternal retribution. We must, in this place bring this curse to its end and place upon this planet a new hybrid breed not subject to Lord's curses. I shall go among these warring factions to mend their ways. No, Lucifer I know what you will say, but I set in motion the sequella and I will fix this once and for all."

It was decided that Lilith would decide the fate of the Regrets and the Lilim. She trekked to the hinterland where she called the combatants to a wide meadow. They all took the look of fear, knowing well Lilith's ability to incinerate them all, everyone of them—even those not there—where they stood or lay. Their minds were most concentrated as she sadly spoke, "I am the womb which gave birth to you and that womb now bleeds. The carnage here is the carnage of my seed. This bleeding weakens me, brings upon me a feeling to faint and horror at what you have done."

"This carnage will cease. As a body memory I shall, henceforth, have all women bleed each month as a reminder of this since, against my womb you all have perpetuated a terrible crime against me; this will be a reminder, that in this, you have offended me mightily."

"All shall lay down their arms. There shall be a truce and truth made wide spread among you. There shall be reconciliation councils created and each shall have an opportunity to tell their story, tell the story of their loss, and tell the story of their grieving. Mind you, if this is not done with dispatch, I will come back and make to pay each who disobeys. I will, too, have the atrocity caves cleansed by teams from both combatants such that the mend will be as joint as the war was severing."

"These are my decrees and I shall leave behind my emissaries to see that this is done. And woe," she said leaning in toward the group, "to any who would defy me in this, woe to each and everyone, who would make of himself or herself, an exception and believe that my absence means I have no longer a care, simply because I take leave. My promise to you all is that is not the case. I will have restoration, that failing, terrible retribution."

***

Lilith spoke with Lucifer upon her return. He asked "Tell; what transpired?"

Lilith gave him her account but spoke more slowly after completing her report and said, "These measures I have taken are a temporary balm, which will only temporarily salve the wound; but the deeper issue remains in place; we have here in these hybrid races, a bifurcation where one side has the nature of war and the other carves peace, where one carries the taint of prejudice and the other the taints of deadly victim-hood and from this a thirst for blood, too. How shall we purify these hybrid genes because clear to me is that this kind of conflagration will occur again and again among them?"

"Your thought in this?" Lucifer asked.

"I fear I shall have to remake, again, this breed of Lilim and see if the fault can be corrected and make of this yet another race. It is a starting over plan, I know but," Lilith said wistfully, "I know not what else to do."

"I shall unhappily undertake this new mission," Lilith said "however, I remain steadfast and renewed in my vision and in my courage."

"I am agreed." Lucifer said.

They lay together that night with special intent because the events of the day had been shattering. It was as if the intensity of their love-making that night could re-cement their resolve, and their powers to effect the healing needed.

Lilith, skilled in the love-making arts promised with her eyes special ardor for Lucifer's receipt even as she sensed he had his doubts as to her mission.

Chapter 11

Lilith took to her task of molding from earth materials for a new hybrid, one which would avoid the curse of the Regrets. She moved among them and said, "I will take a child from each group make the attempt to expunge from that child Lord's curse and re-grant to the child the capacity to partake of beauty again, yet avoiding the war-like traits the curse involved in each.

The small Regret group parted as Lilith moved to see the small child they had prepared for her.

One among them said. "The mother and the father were killed in the cave raids and she is orphaned with no kin or relatives. She is our choice for you."

Lilith parted the small netting protecting the child and at once her heart was drawn to the tiny form, eyes of jet-black and smile which immediately was warming to Lilith. She took the baby in her arms and raised it high and said, "I will take this child and make from it the possibility of a new beginning for the Regret nation, to strike from its genes Lord's curse still raining down among us. Grant me your hopes and dreams that I might succeed in this."

She then took the child and laid it before the Lilim encampment at their high council which had prepared for her as well, a Lilim child. She looked at their child offering and received it with this lament to the Lilim council, "I am sorely disappointed upon seeing the carnage you visited upon Regret children, whose sole violation was they had from you a different visage. This visage was afflicted upon Lucifer and I long ago by Lord. I am angry with you over this in that in elevating beauty above all you have utilized this prejudice to kill the gargoyle beings and to lay them low. I am disappointed in you. I will, as I did with the Regrets, mark each woman with the monthly menses to remind one and all that only harmless blood should be spilt in my realm. You have in you this fatality where life is easily snuffed out by you on the most specious of pretenses. Part fault is this is my own and I am bringing these two children together to make of it a correction. So, hear me Lilim, make of this a fork in the road and stay with the one which is signed peace."

Lilith took both children home for Lucifer's inspection. He, too, was taken with the children, and said, "I see something beatific in both. These are promising choices. Perhaps we have here a smattering of our old home on high to work with."

Lilith took each child testing each for genes, temperament and grace to see if she could isolate the fault. She was shaken by the experience of seeing what each breed had done to the other. It was clear that each breed was capable of awful deeds. It was as if what they had done was a rebuke from Lord, a vindication of his sentence upon them.

Lilith spoke as she gazed upon the two children. "Is this necessity? Lord's ultimate sentencing such that Lucifer's and my progeny shall carry our taint within forever; shall cruel punishment be visited upon these children for the sins of the fathers and mothers for all time? I, my precious ones, have the prospect of righting this over-punishment for the sins of the few, sins, I say; is love so bad it requires timeless degradation, and more, is this to be visited also upon the little ones? I am not in accord with this eternal damnation sentence." Lilith said finally.

She worked to install in each breed a propensity to forgive and make amends before the violent turn would be used. She understood the need for war at times but installed in each a sense that it be implemented only as a last resort. These things she taught the children as well in their curricula.

"Children," she told them, "the first obligation is seek the peace for they that do so shall be blessed." Harness all your energies and, if war you must undertake, even with the first shot, begin to plan the peace, plan from the very start to minimize war's length and impact, for investment in war can grow. If it lingers long, it can warp your societies' growth making your societies too wedded to a need for constant warfare to meet the distorted needs wars brings. All of this is neglectful of peaceful needs. No mother has a dream to see the child she birthed crushed, burned, maimed, or dead. If the multitudes are busy making war machines the price will be high in mothers' tears."

Lilith began her project brimming with hopes that she could correct the defects Lord had sought to inculcate in her and her progeny. It was, at once, difficult to exorcise the genes because Lord had embedded them, resulting in the gargoyle traits, but, as well, because in her attempts at correction, bizarre unanticipated traits occurred.

In one pairing, the two adults she created, were sycophantic to such degree so as to have none of the traits Lilith knew they would need to survive the wilderness. These two had little of the toughness in their capacities for initiative and aggressiveness--traits needed on the frontier to hunt the beasts of the Earth for food and clothing. But, it was not to be, these two waxed passive and were unable to do more than repeatedly ask Lilith for instruction as to what they should do and when to do it.

Disheartened, Lilith determined to abandon these first two, she with Lucifer, aligned them lovingly in burial plots she first used for the Lilim. These defects had lead to their deaths from bodily diseases.

Lucifer spoke with her consolingly after a visit with the Lilim and the Regrets. "It must be with them a delicate balance it seems. I am sad to report that, in my monitoring of the peace between the Regrets and Lilim, events are making clear that reconciliation is less and less apparent or even possible. The two seem to have ingrained an additional curse from that of Lord. This new curse carries with it an inability in each to tolerate the other. More crime and mayhem is slowly building such that it will, I foresee, go again full bloom and we shall see the return of the atrocities you so arduously sought to stem in your visit there."

Lilith was, in this news, overcome with a upsurge of both anger and regret. How could this so bravely begun have come to this unhappy consequence?

"When, Lucifer said, "shall we be free to rid ourselves of Lord's bitter seed which stymies us even now as we seek to consecrate a new beginning on this planet? I fear his reach is long and unrelenting."

Lilith said, "And unremitting. I pray some day to break his hold."

Lucifer said in a sadder tone, "Your work with the new hybrid is of great moment now because there is more I have to tell of my view that the attempt to get the two races to live together will come to naught because of this inbred fault we have identified. One or the other must go if there is to be a chance for either to survive in anything resembling a livable peace. I say clear, I am reaching to a remedy, to exterminate the Regrettable ones and thereby clear the decks for the two you are seeking to create and this may therefore, make beauty and its subjective traits less of a pretext for renewing war among the remaining ones."

Lilith looked at him, wide-eyed. "Do you say all to be smitten down, and done away? Do you say that all those by their affliction of being beauty-less shall therefore go down to death and destruction? Do my ears hear clear on this?"

"It is sad to bear this decision, but I am convinced here we have to choose between this; genocide or peace," Lucifer said slowly.

Lilith took her head in her hands, "Sad this day more than any I have ever known. But, I too understand if you need to do this, do what you must. But I cannot bear to join you. My heart is now pressed to replace these innocents who we now must bury."

The very next day Lucifer came out among the Regretables and told them of their decision. Consternation, mayhem, weeping, horrible fear, rage, and lamentable laments greeted his words and all said as one, "Say Lord, we shall not have to bear this burden unto our own deaths when we have no crime with us except in being ugly to others. Say not this is our crime for it is not what issues from our character but only from the accident of our births. Say not you will do this unto us because all eternity shall from this point note that the Justice-bell rung awry and mis-gonged commemorating the tale of this."

Later their leader came forward to embrace Lucifer privately and said to him. "We have talked among our selves and decided, that in your name, we will summon the courage to submit to this. Tell Lilith for us that we understand her heart must be torn as ours are at this circumstance."

"Take us, if you must, for peace is a higher goal and some must ready the sacrifice if it is to have its chance to flourish."

Lucifer had them all gather in their thousands from all over Earth. They stood silent before him their heads bowed in prayer; some with children at their sides, women with children in their bellies, many eyes wet with remorse and tears, great gargoyles tears, heaving chests and humped backs they all stood ready to receive death from Lucifer, their father's hand.

"We are," their representative said, "able to die, but insist, that this be abiding with our consent and our honor intact. To die as warriors is our destiny we understand that, but seek only the way to accomplish this with honor your highness."

Lucifer allowed them time to make their laments and to adjust to the inevitability and, after a time, the gargoyle leader stepped forth, his sword in hand and delivered the first blows to his wife and child and then to his own torso.

There were others in his entourage who followed suit until there was left only the mass of Gargoylim who waited for Lucifer's final blow.

Slowly, deliberatively, Lucifer raised his mighty sword and circling it over them and in wave after wave their regiments disappeared until there was only one mother and child. Lucifer closed his eyes and ere they opened, Lilith suddenly appeared and cried, "My heart is severed, too." She raised her sword and with her own blow dispatched the mother and child, uttering, in the still of that morning, "With love in my heart, it's I who pass this on to you in this exile world."

The horrible task completed, Lilith and Lucifer took leave from the field which from that day was referred to in legend as the "Field of the Regretables." All over Earth from that time their sacrifice down the eons has been emblazoned upon glyphs and statuary from the Mayans to the Tibetans, from the Goths, to statuary in the mighty churches of the East and West and on the walls of the tombs of Egypt.

Their story was told and retold down the eons. The memory of them and their deaths and deeds noted in dim memory were etched from that day's events.

Chapter 12

Lilith returned to her new hybrid task with a sad vigor now impressed with the gravity its results could portend. There were three ingredients needed; a presentable appearance, a balancing of penchants between creation and destruction enough to ensure survival, and the capacity for creative invention and adaptability.

She brought her new creations before Lucifer for his inspection. He would test the couples Lilith created to see if they could balance between them the rigors of coupling. Beyond this test, he would send them out amongst the Lilim, to see if they could blend, mesh and integrate undetected. But again and again some fault appeared. This couple fought terribly. Lucifer found the husband dead from knife wounds and he sought the woman's eyes inquiring "What have you done here? What is the meaning and justification here for homicide?"

She looked at Lucifer and said, "He sought to make of me a slave. I am no man's slave and I silenced him and his predations. It was just."

Lucifer could only send her back to Lilith with his judgment, "Needs more work, homicidal."

Another man in his twenties, his paces just begun, challenged Lucifer to a duel making the claim that Lucifer was an old man, and that he, the young man, had seen Lucifer in his real demeanor, that of a goat. "I say to you Sire, that your time has expired in this and now alive I see you are not matched for youth's vigor. I challenge you, Sir."

Yet, another two creations lay slovenly together never leaving their room in never-ending sexual embraces and showed no interest in others. One woman polished a stone to a mirror and spent all her time studying her face in it. Two more hatched a plot against Lilith to replace her and Lucifer and found a new dynasty.

One night, Lucifer and Lilith sat discussing the difficulties all this presented. Lilith said "I am weary most and cannot crack this conundrum to create that ideal blend and match we seek. Instead, for mite and minute differences, we get large variations, something I cannot fathom how to control. This being-creation activity may be beyond our capacity and fraught with permutations and perturbations more that we reckoned or could anticipate."

Lucifer could not help but assent understanding that in myriad attempts success still eluded them. "I have only one other string," Lilith said "to unwind and that is rather than create couples, two by two; perhaps a better approach is to create an entire race and have them then be fully realized and to be instantly the counter-balance to the Lilim which now exist. The gain from this approach is a détente and while each individual may be flawed, the sum of capabilities in the group might be larger than individual ones combined."

Lucifer surmised Lilith's vision, while possible could, if incorrect, result in instant war rather than détente; "But still," he said, "it is worth a try."

Lukim was to be their collective name and Lilith had given them faces fair and intelligences superior, she discovered, superior to that of the Lilim. It was not her intent but, it was clear from the first years, that this new breed was a cut above the Lilim who in a fashion displayed an eagerness to learn from the new strangers among them and took from them ideas on irrigation, and sanitation, hunting and agriculture which the Lukim seemed to generate naturally.

The two groups cross-fertilized, but in the fifth Glick, new trouble loomed where Lukim men were being favored by Lilim women and Lilim men were left without brides to marry or women to father their children. Their farms and enterprises began to suffer

from lack of labor while Lukim farms teemed with children fathered by Lukim men and Lilim women. In time the brideless Lilim men grew more impoverished lacking supports children bring to farm labor. Prosperity grew among the Lukim and resentment more and more became the male Lilim's lot. It was clear a riotous clash between the two groups was imminent.

The young Lilim men took to the hills where they armed themselves and began to raid Lukim farms stealing off with food and "liberating" Lilim women whom they took to their mountain-side caves for a rough life of debauchery and aimlessness. The Lilim women protested and some escaped and returned to their Lukim homes thus enraging the Lilim men all the more.

There was in this a scab forming on the social wound -all this created by Lucifer and Lilith's attempt to correct the misalignment brought on by Lord's punishments. At last Lucifer and Lilith had to survey the situation, admitting that this last attempt teetered on failure and that they had to decide what to do.

They went down among the Lukim and gathered further the Lilim nation and sought to broker between a peace and understanding before actual war ensued. "

It is, 'the Spike of Inequality.'" Lilim rebels opined. "You, Lucifer, gave to Lukim men more gifts than those afforded us and we, the Lilim, have been left behind to take table scraps from those clearly favored by the two of you."

A murmur of assent went up among the Lilim men and agreement seemed near unanimous among them. Lucifer looked at Lilith to see if she had a plan to influence this rising, and dangerous sentiment which once loosed would not be easy to put back level again. The Lukim people were in this, models of restraint and did not counterword the claims of the Lilim men; rather they looked to Lucifer for guidance as to what turn and maneuver to make to the Lilim claims.

Lucifer, mounted high so that both camps could see and hear him proclaimed, "It is true that Lukim have come to this world with more skills than many Lilim possess, partly owing to the potentialities Lukim possessed at the time of their creation. Strict equalities here on this planet are not possible; even as we see that this principle has been our bedrock, it does not seem possible in this land as it was on high .Whatever gifts each may have at the beginning mark will soon differentiate each from the other over time. I cannot make a guarantee to each Lilim soul that no Lukim one will supersede and garner more skills than any Lilim may possess. Indeed, this is beyond both mine and Lilith's capacities. You must, therefore, relinquish this expectation of us and of your selves. Lilim you undervalue your own treasures and count them as naught against those Lukim possess. Lukim you overrate your own gifts and under-value those Lilim possesses. We know because Lilith and I created you and our assessment is accurate."

"Take down these words, I say, and come to understand that a mix these aspects is what will be required to survive here and to keep the peace. Lukim share your lights with the Lilim without arrogance. Lilim make clear to the Lukim those peaceful aspects they have not apprehended, which has allowed you to survive on this planet for so many Glicks. The secrets you both possess cannot be exchanged in an atmosphere of aggressive, hostility and hatreds."

"Now there may be some among you some who cannot learn these new tricks, Luke looked at them all intently and lowered his voice, "or scoff at the vision I laid before you. There are some who may not, in fact, be able to modify their behavior and thought process to meld Lukim and Lilim. Some may not comprehend practically my words and thrust or agree."

"You shall become known to me and I shall identify you as unsuitable for progress here, and a hinderment to the peace that we have decreed must prevail on this planet. If you are not able to modify and reorient then you shall make to us your own case for eradication."

Lucifer's words echoed on the landscape with a heavy gravity for all understood--his ultimate intent having been recently demonstrated in eradication of the Gargoylim and their disappearance into that void for which both Lucifer and Lilith had the capacity to inflict.

On that day promises were made for change and alternative slants presented—promises from both sides made that the strictures Lilith and Lucifer would be adhered to. But, dear reader, it was alas, not true. In a short time these fervent promises evaporated. As each side came into close contact they once again began to disagree on the simplest routines and tasks.

The Lukim made each task a speedy test and wanted nothing more that to complete it and move on to another one. The Lilim wanted to tarry with each part and savor its aspects in detail, and did not like rushing along forgetting in the process the point of the project.

"Each aspect," Lucifer thought, "had its merits but conflict over these aspects soon again threatened the social fabric causing still more out-pouring of mutual resentments between Lukim and Lilim."

Lilith foresaw this eventuality and told Lucifer of a new plan she had considered. "It was," she said, "a fact that societies could best be cemented with family ties and marriages." Her notion was to decree that intermarriages take place among the royal families of the Lukim and Lilim where daughters and their dowries would be offered as exchanges to make war less likely; where one's daughter could be held hostage if aggression ensued from her father's encampment. There was to be also princes who had to go to live in Lukim or Lilim courts so as to provide additional insurance against unjust attacks, since to do so from an aggressive king would deprive that king potentially of his own heir who could easily be put to death while residing in the opposite's court.

She once again gathered Lukim and Lilim and made an announcement. "By these presentments all the young at 13 shall be betrothed outside their kingdom and families to an opposite Lukim or Lilim kingdom or with families which are geographically contingent. This shall hold for high and low, royal and commoner, citizen and non-citizen for the benefit of all Earth's denizens."

"So as it is stated here, so shall it be done." Lilith said to them, "I tell you to go and make these arrangements and come back to me in two Glicks to demonstrate that my will has been done and implemented."

The word of Lilith's decree spread high and low and there ensued much discussion as to its workability and practicalities. Some said, "Lilith, herself, would not agree to these new strange arrangements, yet she imposes them upon us," the women complained.

The men, especially the Lilim, protested that a dowry was in fact, a marriage tax and only augmented their poverty-a new expense they could ill afford. This, in turn, only augmented their subservience to the more prosperous Lukim they said.

The debate between the Lukim and Lilim continued for two Glicks when Lilith returned to see what progress had been made. She arrived promptly at the fore-stated time and proceeded to her evaluation of how well the bulk of them had followed her stricture. She visited households, talked to stalwarts and doubters alike; she surveyed the young princes and princesses asking how fared the arrangements that had been made for them. Two Sikes later she summoned all of them to make known to them her assessments.

"I have," she began, "made my survey and am satisfied that most you have begun to obey and in that I am pleased and make known to you my esteem for your having done so. Some however, have only responded with subterfuge and evasions, thin and translucent. For these, I have ordered they be brought forth to set the example I would make.

From a group of men and women some among whom were young princes and princesses; Lilith selected the first two for judgment. "You Kamim and you Argent did willfully disobey both me and your parents and sought to cling to your stated love for one another. In doing so you refused to make the journey to your appointed betrothal villages. This resulted in bad faith charges between your encampments poisoning relations between your two villages, relations which now await mending and repair. What have you to say to us."

Kamim, a young girl of 13, her eyes red with tears, asked, "Oh, Lilith, Mother of us all, please, we thought you of all would understand since it was your love for father Lucifer which drove your defiance of Lord and set in motion the events which brought us all here. I pray you'll understand love has no boundaries and against it many, if not most of us, are weak and defenseless and cannot predict or control where love's arrow lands."

Lilith stooped to peer into the young girls eyes and began, "I cannot gainsay love's attractions, nor deny its powerful magnet which can clamp two together helplessly. I'll not deny my own history in this and that love, which began so long ago on high, is still strong with Lucifer and me. But love, by itself, does not justify all things; love alone does not excuse behavior that can cause the fall of an entire village. Nay, as a princesses you should understand, even if your years are young, the responsibilities therefrom and, as your station is elevated above others, so too, will be the punishments succeeding your transgressions."

"In this it was clearly made known to you your duties. Rather than obey, you squandered your responsibilities for love, which you are too young to know, for a love which may not even persist beyond a single Glick. No, the risk you took endangered many and I here now pronounce you shall pass, with your partner in this, from being to non-existence."

With those words the two simply disappeared occasioning a gasp from the assembled host. Next, were two men who had refused to pay the bride-price claiming excess poverty, which in full defiance had made a spectacle for all to see, flaunting their disregard of Lilith's edict.

Lilith's jaw was clearly set and all could see that this judgment would not go well for the two men. "In your own defense, place before me words which might make my hand relent," Lilith said. "Make my wrath remain sheathed from its penchant to make quick work of thee."

One man, clearly afraid stood forth, and made a plea, shaking as he did so. "Lilith, my Queen, spare us for lack of resources. We heard the stricture on the one hand to multiply but cannot pay the price required to marry, all this through no fault of our own; indeed, it is iron circumstance which has governed us in this."

Lilith contemplated his words for a long moment finally said, "I have not the mirror to see inside minds and intents. I have to take my decisions from behaviors made and those which manifest obedience or defiance. You have made a case to me where defiance is not denied; all you have offered me is reasons. Reasons for individuals may be as many as grains of sand at the edge of the sea, but my demand is for compliance and strict behavior. I can make no exception here."

The men were dispatched and only a small heap of white residue remained from Lilith's handiwork. So it was among the several hundred who lined up before her in that judgment day, so it was that Lukim and Lilim came to know Lilith's quiet, quick and severe punishments. It was they who all learned that arguments were only in second degree to compliance.

Lilith later spoke to Lucifer. "I fear that the longer I am here the more like Lord I become and more the more these earth hybrids stir in me feelings I do not know I possessed. These times are strange."

"Yes," Lucifer agreed I fine myself changing as well."

But despite Lilith' demonstration of her demand for obedience subsequent revisits by her made clear that all was not going as well as she had hoped.

She said to Lucifer. "I see here it matters not what creation we set aground; friction and murder bubble up and dark deeds ensue which require constant correction. What are we to do to preserve what has been created here?"

Lucifer said, "It appears that contentiousness continually manifests itself in whatever creature we place aground here. We have the Lukim taking advantage of the Lilim who are too passive for their own good. I confess that our choice is between the Lukim and the Lilim and, alas, it is clear the advantage built-into the Lilim is that their passivity disallows war, destruction and mayhem even if the price there-from, is stagnation, lack of initiative and only small dollops of imagination. I say, reluctantly, that we are stymied and our last act should be to eliminate the Lukim as yet another failed experiment, and allow the Lilim to progress along at their admittedly slow pace but one which is peaceful. What say you to this proposition?"

"I agree," Lilith said, reluctantly. "My heart is cracking from these disappointments. My hand cannot take on this assignment Lucifer. Could you not take the lead in this and do what must be done?"

Lucifer agreed that it was appropriate for him to devise a solution in dispatching the Lukim. He resolved that rather than a public means a disease should over take the Lukim and have it appear that his hands were clean and he, Lucifer, had done nothing to motivate the disease's inception and devastation.

He loosed a terrible botulism upon the Lukim, a flesh-eating malady which made is progression visible to all. The Lukim were terrified, after a time, realizing that they were the only ones afflicted. They retreated to their former haunts in the caves leaving the Lilim on the surface alone.

Delegation after delegation came to Lucifer. They pleaded, "Our ranks are devastated and we have fewer and fewer to plant the seed, therefore, there are no crops or stores in our granaries, we die from starvation as much as the dreadful disease. Give us supports."

Lucifer, his heart asunder from his secret knowledge, pretended to give aid but never gave enough to ameliorate much of the disease or the hunger which afflicted them. In their diseased state they were grateful to receive whatever was given to them unmindful that the pittance they received did not even last the journey back to their villages. When asked if succor was had from Lucifer, they replied, "Nothing was given us; they had nothing," they said, "to give."

The rolling death of the Lukim ended after five Glicks. Lucifer and Lilith agreed that it would take further time to conjugate a true remedy, since both agreed that still a variety was needed to add to the traits present among the Lilim. But none was at hand.

Chapter 13

Lord had observed these activities of Lucifer and Lilith satisfied that their progress had been stayed and began to concoct his own plan, whereby, the weakling Lilim could be over taken, by a new species that, he, Lord, would create. This new Earth race would have the traits of rapid births, and intelligences which would allow them to quickly disperse and follow, if necessary, the Lilim to their cave retreats. Lords new race would make of the Earth a garden of farms watered with irrigations and the domestication of some of the useful wild beasts and, thereby, become the dominant race on the planet.

At some point, he thought, there might be the pitched battle between the two races and the dispatching of the Lilim would occur such that Lord's people would alone in full possession of the planet.

Lord weighed his plan in his mind thinking he would name the male of the new race Adam and the female Lilith after Lilith, whom he still loved.

The new two would love their Lord, having had rebellion distilled from them. They would be as well the instrument whereby his new race would displace those rebels Lilith and Lucifer sought to mint.

His hand went to work where he decided to make them similar to those created by Lilith and Lucifer had made on Earth because that would mean they could mix and mingle undetected once there and could provide to Lord intelligence of things transpiring among them.

He fashioned both from the dust of the Earth, because these materials gave them the look and origin he thought they would need. He named the man Adam and the woman Lilith so as to confuse things among the rebels if his two were discovered.

His thought to make them adherents such that they would never rebel against his will; they were to be beings that loved their God and he eliminated from them any free will of their own; a momentous decision since it was this trait that the original two, Lilith and Lucifer, had been used to betray him. There to be here no replication of that event, because in Lord's estimation, the sequella had been inestimable and had resulted in a most deadly consequence for him and the Kingdom.

No, these two were to be constructed minus that trait. He work went quickly, and completed, he had them before him for his inspection. Bringing them to consciousness slowly, Lord made them that first day to understand their mission and to test the results of his handiwork.

He said to them, "I am Lord, your Master, and I have created you. I lay claim to your absolute loyalty and devotion, because you are my children and have come to exist for my purposes, not your own. My expectations are brief and clear, you shall hold no other Lord before me; mete out to me according to my strictures a full measure of your devotion. In turn I shall protect the life I have given you and make of you a success in your life on Earth."

His drew breath at the sight of the woman. She was the exact Lilith from on high, his erstwhile wife, except in this earth Lilith's demeanor there was none of the deceptive traits he had despised so and certainly not the rebellion. Both Adam and Lilith were beautiful in their faces and their bodies clean and well scented. He did not make either immortal since that too, in his estimation, had caused mischief.

"I am preparing a place for you which is to be your home on planet," Earth he said to them "look and gaze upon what it looks like now."

With a wave of his hand Lord showed the two Earth vistas below and right away Lilith asked, "Who were the people there who looked to be similar to ourselves?"

"These are the evil ones," Lord said "I forbid you to mix with them except as I direct. They have been tainted with the sin of pride and have been exiled there where they continue to wage war against me, where they still, continue to mutiny against me and embrace perniciousness, sin and perdition. You shall have no truck with them, and you are, upon my word, to strictly avoid intercourse with them."

Lilith and Adam looked at each other and, in their innocence, were curious, if not fascinated, by the beings Lord had shown them. Lord noted this silently, saying only "Prepare yourselves for the descent."

67

Chapter 14

Lord's Adam and Lilith came down to a grassy field, in the new world and immediately heard Lord state, "Prepare a place for your shelter with the materials I have gathered for you. Learn to sustain yourselves against the beasts in the land and above all hold no thing, person or object above me, your God."

The two looked at each other and Lilith said "We must gather mud and twigs and fashion from them a home as Lord has said."

The two first made a lean-to for the first nights repose and lay side by side seeking to understand their own creation. "Why are we here?" Adam queried, knowing well Lilith, herself, did not know, but anxious, nonetheless to discuss and regurgitate what Lord had said.

"Well," Adam began, "I am sure Lord has for us the mission of leading pure lives and making this place one where his glory is to be made and maintained. He was clear to state that we must not integrate our seed with the others he has shown us, and we are to make him in this world, by our activity, proud of us."

The two busied themselves with constructing a home for themselves and finding food for themselves. Lord told them of the animals he had created and showed them the domesticated ones. "Goats," he had said, "you will tend these for the cheese and milk. You shall build a house where your animals shall dwell below and you shall sleep above. Three times a day you will pause to pray and contemplate and you will avoid all those things I have said to you are sin."

"There shall be no idle pleasuring; your seed is precious and shall not be spilt on the ground. Intercourse is my holy writ and is for creation purposes alone. There shall not be nakedness in my temples and you shall cover your head in my holy places. You attend to your Lord's purposes each seventh day such that you might address me in your dreams and prayers."

Adam and Lilith proceeded to obey Lord's demands and sought to make that place the vision they had been given. A small home was built and animals gave them the meat, cheese, and milk they needed to survive those first few days and months. The toil of it they did without complaint or resistance. Lord observed from on high now content that his new minions were good creations, and, in them, he was well pleased.

But this was not transpiring without being observed by Lucifer and Lilith, exiles, who wondered what Lord's intent was in creating the two. "She looks exactly like me Lilith said, or exactly as I used to be."

"Yes, Lucifer said, "it appears Lord still has you in his heart and he looks now to replace you with this human one."

Lilith did not respond. She understood well that Lord had by this action make clear his continuing involvement with her, Lilith. She sought to divert the conversation.

"I wonder if Lord has deemed them exiles too, but I can see they are not treated as such and such devotion I see, they kneel and pray to Lord thrice each day. It is clear to me that he has placed here his own improved loyalist species, one to compete with those we have created, such to make of this a population race; his minions versus those we have in place. Lord is clever here, his thought is that the settlers will have the planet in the end and we and our creations will, if Lord has correctly surmised, be pushed back and away into the barren hills and eventually be decimated, or killed. Lord has his plan for us and it does not bode well."

The two made pact to observe a while, noting that these two new arrivals should be observed for a time.

Adam and the new Lilith had no independent sense or will of their own, as was Lord's wish, and, therefore, also lacked initiative of their own volition. Lord came to them one day and asked why they had not planted the crops with the seed he had given them.

Adam responded, "Lord we await your instructions in this."

After a time the Lord came again and asked, "Have you not planted yet?" and Adam replied "We had morning-prayer and knew not how to construct a plow and awaited your instructions in this."

Lord grew restive, and said "You must use your inventiveness; else you will not survive here. I gave you life to grow and thrive here not to stagnate awaiting my instruction."

***

But the two did not show initiative, rather, made plaintive pleas for Lord to be patient with them. It was clear that Lord was growing more and more impatient with his two creations and for a time he neglected them not responding to their entreaties, and endless questionings. Adam's Lilith wanted to know which plants were safe to eat, which animals were clean, what rituals Lord desired at prayer time, what sex was permissible. Adam wanted to know how to memorize prayers, which prayers were pleasing to Lord and which were not.

Stumped, Lord sat in his throne room assessing the qualities he'd created in the two and whether they would survive day to day without his daily assistance. He devised a thought to have them mix their seed and produce a child, who could assist with the labors and begin the process to populate the Earth against the creations sinful Lucifer and Lilith had set in place. The child must evolve, he thought, higher creativities.

He spoke to Lilith's name-sake, "You shall lay with the man and conceive a child, the first of many I shall require of you. Your mission is to spread my word and my children across this land such that all might know what I, Lord, require of them. Prepare thy womb for the receipt of this and I will tell you how to make yourself clean for this first child in this place."

Lord's Lilith went to Adam and told him of Lord's requirements and how he had told her the preparations she had to complete before the sex.

"Come" she said "I will show you."

She led him inside their lean-to and said, "I first make a fire in the ground, in the floor and set within this dug out space firewood, sticks and incense, and sweet twigs, found in the forest. These will form a smoky cloud and I will then straddle it, whist these smokes and fumes rise up into my clothing- they cleanse my body scent in the way of Lord. Lord has given me water to wash with and ointments to use such that when we lay together tonight I shall have been purified and worthy of the conception."

Adam watched as she prepared herself following Lord's instructions—first squatting down above the ground fire—her face starting right away to show the perspiration that the hot fire created. It did not look to Adam, comfortable, but he murmured to her "Lord's will be done."

It was that she had also secretly prepared an admixture of plants she had discovered which she sipped, saying to Adam, "I have drunk of this and it puts me to, I think a greater state of readiness, for you and for tonight when we come together." Adam took the bowl with the yellow brew and sipped it absent-mindedly, and after a time, noticed that indeed his brain shifted to a state of excitation and euphoria. He looked at Lilith noticing her eyes were narrowing in what, he guessed, was a state of bliss.

"How came you by this plant, does Lord know of this discovery, what will he think?" Adam asked.

Lilith smiled a half smile because she knew that Lord would not likely approve an elixir he, Lord, had not personally approved. She finished her fire-cleansing and drew close to Adam allowing him to embrace her as dusk descended; as both knew that the night would bring new life to Lilith's womb and their lives in that place would be forever altered. Elevated in their mood by the plant narcotic, they settled together to learn the steps of intercourse, neither of which, of course, had done before.

Adam was beguiled by the fire scents now in Lilith's skin and by the oils glistening from her. He slowly drew her outer garment away from her body seeking to see all of her, his excitement growing as he was able to see first her breasts, then her stomach, and finally her center space. In wonderment he first gave the touch to her breasts in tentative exploration, but then with more intense probing. He reacted to her responding to his sensual activity and it excited him, especially at his center.

He took his finger and probed her center seeking entry there to understand of how this sexual activity was to proceed, anxious then, just a little, to avoid in Lilith's eyes any hint of disappointment.

Lilith hummed sensual moans at Adam's touch, these first accentuated by the plants effects, and decided there was nothing more exciting in this new existence than this—Adam's touch. He probed to her inner-ness and she responded pushing his finger tip deeper within her. He was at her breasts now suckling and her nipples swelled, intense in response to his swirling tongue, darting over them. He put his face on her stomach and below.

Fire there, he made her warm with his breath and she responded by grabbing his hair forcing upon him encouragement because she was then determined to sate that urgency between her legs now lifted high above her head to make herself more accessible, more available to him. Her cries in the night were those first heard in the smoky dark, in their new place, in their new home on planet Earth.

Adam then took his member in hand to replace where his finger-tip had sought to trace and seated it home at Lilith's center possessed now with an all consuming urge to join with her, to merge. Lilith arched now, so she could ungulate and makes a wide space for Adam to consecrate what both thought was to be conception and a child soon to be in the new place.

Both lay trembling in the fire's glow, both amazed at the experience and Lilith asked, "I wonder if the baby will be here by morning." Neither understood the dynamics of pregnancy. Simple-minded, they thought the baby would arrive in minutes or hours...

The next day both awoke and Lilith asked "Can you see any thing there, is there a baby or sign of one?"

Adam told her to lie back and he placed aside her garment and bent his head to have a look to see if there was anything visible. "I do not see anything, no baby can I see. Perhaps it will be on the morrow."

"I wonder," Lilith said, "if we did it correctly? We might have to try again. What do you think?"

"Perhaps, we should ask Lord in our prayer today what we need to do."

"Let us sit the prayer mat and ask Lord how to proceed."

They knelt in supplication and Adam prayed, "Lord we lay together last night and followed the ritual as you instructed. Lilith lit the fire of purification; we prepared the ground, we added scents and Lilith squatted down drawing up into her all these cleansing agents and followed on Lord then the intercourse. I probed her center seeking the baby-making way. This morning we looked to inspect but found no baby and wonder what we are doing in this that is amiss."

Lord's response was not favorable and terrifying. Lord said, "I have given you instructions in sex and you have taken of it to make it a drunken unclean thing tainted by narcotics taken from the forest. I have given this to you for procreations sake and you have diluted it with idle pleasures and brought shame to my strictures. You have defied my will and placed yours up against what I have decreed. What say you to this? What shall in this be your punishment?"

Lilith, clearly taken aback, said, "Lord, surely we meant no defiance in this, we earnestly sought to implement your will, your decree, please don't punish us for we are novices in this."

Adam stepped forth and said, "Lord, if anyone, the fault lies with I who took too much delight in Lilith's body; it bewitched me and drew me down to faulty judgment. I alone merit punishment. Take thy anger out on me because I am the only one deserving of your wrath."

Lord paused before his next comment, finally decreeing, "So, that pleasure shall not be the outcome of holy creation, I here decree that pleasure shall be balanced off in Lilith with painful childbirth. That seems a just adjustment, a balancing between the violation and the punishment. For you Adam, for your role, I decree that you shall toil in the fields and I shall remove from you all the seeds I have given you. Your lot shall be hard work in the fields and you shall have to brave the beasts in the fields for survival and the meat you eat. You'll not have an easy life of agriculture and husbandry. The animals of the field and indeed, some of my plants shall poison you and you'll not know which among the flora and fauna is friend or foe. You'll carry this burden, you and your progeny henceforth, and know your Lord's word is meant strict and cannot be compromised, evaded or diluted."

Now, it was that Lilith's and Adam's lot on Earth was hardened as Lord had decreed. They were sickened by plants not knowing which were safe and which were deleterious to their health. Animals friendly to them before were not after Lord's decrees. From the bugs in flight that had not hitherto landed to bite, to the lions on the veldt, to even ants beneath their feet, there was a changed attitude and new dangers from each of these and all.

It was the new world of Lord's punishments such that Lilith and Adam themselves became hardened, too, and sought to shield their activities from Lord's view least new violations be espied and bring with it new punishments. They learned to speak a disguised tongue to shade their meanings from Lord's ears and now over several years there was no talk of conception or child-bearing. Lord seemed to have lost heart in them and they, too, welcomed a distancing between themselves and Lord who less and less frequently addressed or visited them.

"I am so lonely," Lilith said, "we are orphaned here by our creator who sees us now in disappointment and regret, and yet we have no path to re-coop his trust and mend this rift and regain our former life. We have been set adrift assaulted by fauna and flora alike."

Adam marked from this point his decent into depression and hopelessness blaming him self for Lord's disappointment and for the retribution that Lilith now shared while she was, in this, blameless.

"I have the sorrow, my love, in this knowing I have, and I alone, have brought this calamity upon us, this disaster, transforming what was for us an idyllic life to one now of ceaseless war against creatures, and the nature of this planet. We will not survive nor produce any children after us unless we break this cycle and find a new path. My plan, I have thought upon, is this..." He halted himself mid-sentence, and motioned to Lilith to follow him to a near-by cave they'd discovered hence, where they surmised Lord had difficulty in hearing what they said one to the other.

Once there Adam began," I think we must shatter this imbroglio and need new inputs, hence my view is that I shall trek beyond this clime to make contact with the Others Lord warned us against."

"No," Lilith, interrupted, "that would only bring new retribution if Lord found out, and our plight as a result, would only worsen. You cannot do this for surely next time Lord's wrath will escalate beyond punishment to our very extinction. No, cautious moves we must make here, least we adopt solutions which worsen our lot; and besides Lord's animosity toward the Others seems so great, there is no telling what he would do. No, best we endure and wait to see then if time can temper his anger and his rejections."

"But love," Adam, said, "there is this other piece; if we are not to be the first and last of our kind, we must know--for our own sakes—we must learn the trick of reproduction. The Others know this thing. We must learn it from them. I mean we must have a child, no many children. If we learn how to produce a brood, Lord will soften once he beholds them and we will, by this, also be reprieved."

At this Lilith, began to waver, her desire was strong to have a child and Adam's enterprise to learn from the Others carried with it the possibility that the two of them could learn to conceive; and that had attraction for her.

Then go," Lilith said, "be swift through the mountain pass where I have seen the smoke of their campfires and you should be back, if you succeed, in no more than three nights and four days."

Chapter 15

Adam set out with meager provisions on the mountain trail, leading up to the pass over-mounting the top to the valley of the Others which lay down the other side. He had no clue as to whether communications would ensue, or, if they would consider him an enemy as Lord did them. But the risk was necessary, he thought, to take for his and Lilith's sake. He left purposeful bent to have the full exploration of it and whatever lay on the other side of the mountain pass.

He climbed high and higher along the pass seeing better, as he rose, the surrounding country side. Of all that greenery he thought looking down in the valley, none would guess that his and Lilith's lot was not assured--to the contrary--at risk. In defying Lord in this trek he took all to risk and knew not then what retribution Lilith and he might then suffer.

He was at the peak and began to descend when darkness fell and he decided to rest until the morning so as to be fresh upon approaching the Others' village. The break of light awakened him and he gathered his provisions and put his foot on the downward path keen to see—anticipating--what kind of reception might await him. How much he wondered he might blend, or would he be immediately seen as alien and not of their kin. The picture Lord had shown flashed by fleetingly so it was unclear to Adam w how much of a resemblance in detail existed between him, Lilith, and them.

He planted his feet upon the outer rim of the village perimeter and noticed a man in a field forging a furrow with a wooden implement. He looked up at Adam's passing but did not take further notice. Adam was both astonished and relieved to see that the Others, by this man's representation, were indistinguishable from Lilith and him.

He cautiously walked toward what seemed the market square where he felt he would best blend and not be noticed; where he hoped to gain the intelligence he sought. He was surprised to see the abundance of foods available in the village stalls and the vendors hawking their wares. He pulled his scarf across his face so to avoid

too close scrutiny and meandered from stall to stall noting
fresh vegetables, tomatoes and squash and other fruits
unknown to him. There were brightly colored garments
and raiments dyed with dyes in stall after stall. He paused
to inspect a water wheel at the edge of a well where he
stopped to sit to observe what he could see surreptitiously.
The women there were numerous and walked freely in the
throng and some, Adam noticed, had little ones trailing
along, children he guessed, who were smaller in height.

"Grapes, fine grapes, sir," a voice said, "very
reasonable." Adam looked up to see an older woman, her
hand extended, and a basket of grapes on her shoulder.
"Grapes sir?" she repeated and Adam shook his head
amazed that he had no trouble at all understanding her.
How can that be he wondered?

Meanwhile, Lilith and Lucifer aware of Adam's
sojourn had instructed their minions to do him no harm
and to take no notice of him at all. Their plan was to
identify what was Adam's mission and later, to present
themselves directly to him in the village in pleasant form
to interrogate him themselves.

The opportunity came when Adam sat at the edge of
the market under the shade tree when Lucifer, in the form
of a shepherd, approached him with Lilith at his side.

"Hello stranger," Lucifer said, "we welcome you here
in our village and offer you our every hospitality and
inquire if we may, as to your origin."

Lilith said, "You have the look of a journey on you
and must have the desire to refresh. Let us not worry him
at this point Lucifer, instead offer him a chance to bath
and cleanse at our house," Lilith said. "What say you
stranger, would you avail yourself of this offer, tendered
to you with only kindness and generosity?"

Adam accepted the proposal and walked with the two
of them to their house not far from the village square. He
was given towels and scents to bath with and, upon
completion, was invited to lounge with his hosts as their
guest.

Adam marveled at the structure much grander than
the mud structure he was used to. Clearly these two were
people of means. "How shall you be called?" Lilith said.
"What name do you use?"

"I am called Adam," Adam said, "and how are you called."

"I am Lilith." Lilith said.

Lucifer said "You may call me Lucifer."

"I am from the other side of the mountain," Adam said "My wife is there and she too is called Lilith. I have traveled here on a mission seeking information of which I have need which is precious to me to achieve in the shortest possible space of time."

How may we assist? What kind of information is it you seek?" Lilith said.

Adam said, "I and my wife seek to conceive a child but are not able to despite trying for several years. We have sought remedies we know are available but none have worked. We fight against poisonous plants and have had to build defenses against the beasts in the field. I am here to learn how to combat these things and have our family become a reality."

Lucifer and Lilith looked one to the other realizing that Adam had no clue as to their identity nor indeed, the history which lay behind his creation, nor, obviously, did he know whom he was addressing. He had no memory beyond the date of his own creation. Lord had obviously told him very little.

"Sit," Lilith said "there is much to impart to you, of us and of your own origins. There is no time to tell all the tale but right now I will give you a brief outline of us and our time here and what is surely your Lord's intent for you. Take this cup of tea and recline. Let us waste little time for of that we have very little."

Meanwhile, Adam's Lilith on the far side of mountain heard Lord addressing her inquiring, "Where is Adam." I cannot see or sense him? Has he dropped himself out of sight into a well; has he descended deep into the cave where, unseen, he labors. Why would he leave you here alone to toil the field and dig roots?"

Quavering, Lilith responded slowly, looking around as if looking for Adam, "I would concur", she said, "with your guess that he is deep in the cave's recesses busying himself with this or that. I am sure he will be here at prayer time as usual."

Lord's response was not forthcoming and Lilith was soon aware that he was gone.

Meanwhile, Adam was being told the story of his creation by Lilith and Lucifer. He was amazed—overwhelmed with its import. They spoke to him of their knowledge of many things, of life, death and birth, of things in the field; how to grow their own food and domesticate animals to provide foodstuffs for lean times.

After several days he took leave in the early morning eager to share with Lilith what he had learned.

He struck out straight away back over the mountain to tell her warding off in his mind the terror growing there because he knew now the scope of their predicament, the very reasons he and his Lilith had come to exist and, furthermore, what peril this new information meant to him, to her, to life and limb.

He scurried mountain-ward determined to make Lilith's side by night and to lay out for her this new information and danger.

He came to the mud house, silent now, with night fall and placed his foot on the mat looking up to identify the sleeping bed which he and his Lilith shared. He could see her dim form sleeping there and reached her side to awaken her with his news.

But she would not awake. Lilith was still as death, which Adam did not know, but became alarmed as his attempts to awaken her failed. Slowly he began to see that she like animals in the field and lay dead before him.

Instantly he guessed that this was Lord's retribution for his adventure, a retribution terrible indeed and one extracted at Lilith's expense.

He shook his fist at the ceiling, "Lord thou are a cruel, Lord. Why have you taken her when it was I who transgressed? Why have you sucked away the capacity for forgiveness within your own being? We are but creatures on this planet, creatures of your creation, why torture us?"

Lord spoke for Adam plain to hear, "I am your Lord and in this and many things you have transgressed and I now see that in your creation I have erred grievously. There are some beings who wax worthy of me and some who do not. I shall, perforce, wipe this slate clean and start anew."

Adam bent to his knee and then stood wandering from the mud house to prepare a place for Lilith's body as he had been taught by the Others in his time there. It was a linen wrap and with oils and scents. He prepared an ossuary of rocks and stone inside a cliff's face on the mountain he had topped, days before.

Beside, her resting place he paused to pray his final prayer for Lilith.

"I came to life, to this life, with you and toiled. I have come to grief with you and I cry by your side. I came to many joys with you and laughed. Now, I too, share your death, unearned, in my view, undeserved, yet I will endure; sure only of the loneliness I now feel and will feel in times future. My Lilith, my heart lies with you inside this tomb to brighten the dark gloom which is my sad grieving shroud."

With his hand at the lever he moved the stone to roll it closed with his precious Lilith sleeping within.

Chapter 16

With days passing, then months and a year Adam's depression grew to such degree he made the mark to address Lord directly. He prepared a place, apprehensively, since it was unknown to him what would be Lord's reaction.

"Lord," he said beginning his soliloquy, "I am a wretched creature here, here in this wilderness, I am bereft of companionship, toil my only solace and yet remain childless. My loneliness is such I have laid with beasts in the field so deep my desperation. Lord I desire companionship of the woman kind. Where is future in this decree you have placed upon me, where will this tact take us, where will be its end if I am denied woman and progeny? I trust you will understand and take consideration of a need for a new wife for me. It seems both logical and needful since the Others grow larger and larger in their numbers and clearly one time soon they shall rocket down the mountain and over-run even my abode here and I shall, however, long lived will be pushed aside by their them who will populate this clime and submerge, my children, if I have any." Lord was silent.

"I need, Lord, to know that this has reached your ear and that you will at least consider a portion of this plan for its logicality if not its merciful bent."

After a pause of time Lord spoke, "I cede that less than needed to be was given by me of your settlement in the wilderness and, further, I cede that I am too, a prisoner more than I should be, of my history with the Others and their minions. You, my Adam, maybe, speak the truth, and are the unwilling casualty of those factors. I must then reconsider and come to clarity concerning my mission for you."

There was again a pause. Lord then spoke again.

"I will think on these things and come back to you with a fresh plan, anew. Meanwhile, it is my wish that you prepare a place for a transformation I have in mind. You shall make a mud tower five cubits high and one cubit wide. I will have there my fully realized plan for you and shall grant your wish for a wife and companionship. But tamp down your expectations for a rapid change since you shall not only have to prepare for this but I have in mind for you and her an alternate abode."

With that said Lord fell silent.

Adam stood down from his prayer platform and clutched his heart at the prospect of a new help-mate— one to share his life there in this lonely Garden of Eden. He remembered Lord's word and began the gathering of bottom sediments, mostly fine grains, for his cubit mound. Lord had said "It must be of the finest grain, red in hue and free of debris for the creature I shall make of it must be free of contaminations, taints and sin. You will cleanse this," Adam remembered Lord's words, "and I will make for you a woman of purity."

Lord sat in his lonely hour to contemplate his next creation resolved not to make a similar mistake in his fashioning of woman kind, not to replicate another Lilith, a Lilith on high who sought to mount rather than be mounted.

But all models of such which passed his mind veered always to aspects he still adored in Lilith, in her beauty, in her smile, in her very irresistibleness. These were not mere minor aspects; they were inherently fixed to him of what woman was. How could he create a new woman who lacked these traits? And more, there was the heavy load of Lilith's sexual nature and capacities. He drew upon all these things and his feelings still present for her in remembering. She was, he ruefully thought, his finest creation above all others. She had been given the gift of creating life, previously only reserved to him; she had been given sexual prowess surpassing even his own, beauty and immortality and other capacities he now pushed aside in his mind.

Lord would not have another like her on Earth. Already, the Lilith he had expelled from Heaven along with her lover, Lucifer had magnified their power to create creatures that would soon be numerous enough to overtake all of that planet's resources and make of their exile a near paradise thereby nullifying his decree that they should suffer for their betrayal of him. No, they had taken Lord's gifts of knowledge and immortality, and with these gifts learned to fashion weapons, now used to defy him. He hoped not to replicate, in this new person, that mistake. This he thought, would take some devisement.

Chapter 17

Meanwhile, Adam awaited Lord's return but this did not occur soon and mighty was his growing impatience. One night he lay at rest and footfalls outside came below in his manger house.

"Fear not," a voice said, "we are come as friends." Adam peered over the out-jutting to look below to see in the dim three people one of whom, from the voice, he guessed was Lucifer.

"May we come in?"

Adam peered, blinkingly, and said, "Yes. I will come down." He descended and joined two; one was now visibly Lucifer and the other Lilith. The third remained outside in the dark background.

"We are here, Adam, to apprise you of an action we took some time ago and now see it was wrong not to let you apprehend it and its meanings." In the dark came forth the form Adam now clearly could see. It was his dead Lilith now fully alive but strangely quiescent.

"How," he said, "can this be? How can this be? My heart, my heart." he said to this resurrected Lilith.

He moved, first slowly and in disbelief and then he let out a joyous grasp as he pulled Lilith to him saying, "So many nights and dawning's I have longed for you here in my hold. So many times my very soul was wrenched from me laying in the dust of the earth barren and not to grow I thought or ever come alive again."

He pulled back to look at her. "Is it really you? Are you my Lilith?"

"I am your Lilith, Adam," she said "I am come again, but for only a short time; Lucifer and Lilith, the Mother of many, came to my stone grave and revived me. I am here for one night only and then I must return to my resting place."

"You mean," Adam said, "you will become dead again?"

"Yes." said Lilith. "Lord's power is great and he will take her again once more. We are powerless to prevent that. What I have done is to take her spirit into my self and part of her will to bring her back. She will be returned to rest before the dawn. These are the few hours you have."

It was a shocking turn for Adam to absorb. Even as they spoke he raised his regard to the sky wondering aloud, "Even as we speak we may be being observed. We should retire to the cave in the cliff face where it is possible to speak more undetected."

In the cave's bosom they spoke of trends and news since they last met and Adam's joy was mixed because he would have his Lilith back for on a few hours.

"But, come Lilith," Lucifer said, "lets us leave them to their own precious few hours."

We must go," Lilith said, "Lord will be missing her."

Lucifer said to Lilith as they departed. "In bringing the girl back you lost a bit of your immortality. It was a kind act but a foolish act. You are becoming more and more like them."

"I know," Lilith said.

Then they were gone, leaving Adam to matriculate through the circumstance which he was now confronted. Surely, Lord would return and carry out his plan for a new creature woman for him and yet his heart was still with his Lilith. At dawn after they had lain together he reached for her and she cried as his hand could not touch her. She had become spirit. "You can not touch me now" she said. "I must return to rest, and moments later she was gone.

Days later Lord spoke to Adam, asking "Where then is the mound completed I have asked you to build?" I see only a partial attempt yet the time has passed for it to have been done thrice I think. What has happened here? Why has this not been done?"

"I have," Adam began, "been sore pressed by the plantings, Lord, and, alone, my work load has seen doubling. I am new at all of this." he said. "I must learn my chores and those Lilith had been accomplishing," he murmured.

Lord's silence was long. At last he said "I will return in five days hence, let us commence the ritual of the new woman for you."

Adam bowed indicating his assent and grasped his hands to his mouth wondering "What resolve can make of this predicament a positive outcome, for surely now it careens toward disaster and a downward trend."

84

Adam took to molding the mound as Lord had insisted and thinking deep on his preferences, when with sudden flash Lucifer's Lilith was there by herself at his side. "Come let us quickly to the cave where we can be unobserved. I have a plan to suggest for your consideration and comment."

Adam wondered at this solo visit and what could be Lucifer's Lilith intent?

They both retired to a deep cave branch to continue the conversation. Lilith began, "What would you say to the proposition that you come, over the mountain into our protection and leave behind Lord's strictures and rejections of you. You would have our shield against his wrath, you see; we have the ability to protect ourselves and would also shield you. In this you could find a new mate and have children of your own. We would prepare a place for you and your future progeny. Why spend more lonely days here?"

Adam's instinct was to agree and move quickly. And it was under stealth of night he went with Lilith over the mountain pass and in a new home, special built for him by Lucifer and Lilith.

Adam, at the door of his new abode thanked Lilith and Lucifer and said. "Many things have happened here so quickly. There is much to talk about in the coming days."

He bade them a good night with those words. He was troubled, but willing to through in his lot with Lilith and Lucifer.

Chapter 18

Lord on the other side of the mountain returned at the announced time and did not find Adam in his place. "Adam," he called. "Adam where art thou? I see you have dis-encamped and gone. What manner of insolence is this Adam?" he roared. "I shall have the bottom of this and know what is afoot here."

Lord could easily surmise the circumstances; Adam had left to join the others on the other side of the mountain. He soon hovered above the small village and announced to them "I, Lord, have been sinned against, again and again. People of the exile, know that Lucifer and Lilith have stolen from me, my creation whose name is Adam. I will have him back or I will burn this city in fires of hottest hell. You will suffer that all your children will die in this my retribution. Or, you can deliver to me Adam, and I will consider what mercy and punishment will be due. Give me out him I seek—or know that Lucifer and his whore, Lilith will have brought down upon you more calamity obedience would bring."

A crowd gathered in the market square to see Lord's apparition in the sky there. Lilith, Lucifer and Adam his peered up to see the blinding cloud surrounding Lord.

Lilith and Lucifer moved quickly to the balcony to speak directly to Lord. Lilith's face was of the sternest cast, her steps purposeful. "I am here Lord." Lilith said. "And I say to you that we exiles ask you to rethink this plan, not come upon us with fearsome threats against the many here, the many that have not harmed you. It is Lucifer and I you seek. It is against us you have the grievance. Take what retribution as you may, take vengeance if you must, but, please reconsider this. Adam is now social mixed with humans here; he is no more a creature solely of your creation. He has now his own will, his own desires. You should rejoice in this."

Lord's response was booming. "Rejoice you say; I should gather all thy transgressions and make of them a dance of joy? Am I to contemplate that you, Lilith, can dismiss all manner of betrayals and deaths in the name of love—a selfish love-one which, even if true, costs too much, and in this Earthly form and manifestation, continues, continues," he boomed, even louder, "to produce this unholy alchemy where your precious love causes blood to run red in the streets. At what price this liaison for you and yours, for Adam, an innocent and young Lilith, an innocent, for the obsession of two? What is to be the judgment in this--equal and fair? Shall more die this day for your obsessive love which by your own word you are helpless against, such that many are swept to their death because of it? Tell me, how many have to die for this love?"

Lilith turned from the balcony with Lord's voice outside, still heard. "Here me people of the outcasts, by dusk, if I am not in receipt of the one I seek, the fires of night will light this city and none will be spared. The tides of dusk are my deadline, and as sure as the sun's dip will occur and night begins, I shall give fire loose upon you."

With that said, he was gone.

Came the darkening sky, the three sat as inhabitants of the village came to speak with Lucifer and Lilith while Adam looked on.

The village elder spoke to Lucifer and Lilith later saying "We are in the fear that the conflagration Lord threatens will destroy us and all we have built in this place. We want to know, even as we prepare to arms, that this effort is warranted. What say you of the merit of his threats? Can he destroy us as he attests? Tell us that we might reassure all the others who need to know as darkness descends upon us."

Lilith spoke to the representative and said, "We have in this planet's time spent eons in preparation for this affliction which we, eons ago, anticipated would come; and now it has. We are ready for it. We have prepared a shield over all, to protect us, and you.

"Lord's power is great, this is true; we cannot give positive assurance that all will be insulated from all harm, but we are sure we are well defended. Our council and our experience is that Lord's pronouncement is without negotiation. He will try to do what he has said he intends, if we fall one whit short of his demands."

"Then why," the representative said, "not give them the one and preserve the peace and avoid destruction here, and why take this risk?"

Lucifer spoke, "Lord's demand encompasses more than his desire that we repent. Rather it is Lord's wish that we fulfill his decree and suffer here. It is less focused on Adam but on the defiance we represent in ameliorating that sentence, nay thriving, when what he meant for us another thing. We have sought to avoid a struggle with him over this; but if not this place, it will be another in train. We prefer to battle here since it is our best fortified position. Our calculation is that of all spots on this Earth this is the best spot to make a defense, which is the reasoning behind why we settled here."

Mollified, the representative left to prepare for the on-slaught all there were sure would come at darkness' peak and sure it came, announced first by Lord's voice, which past the midnight hour spoke from a high cloud illumined in the midst of a crystal night.

They all looked up to hear him speak slowly. "I have given warning to all of you of my desire to have the man Adam returned to me as my rightful creation, he whom I have chosen to populate this place. You have, I see, chosen to defy me that reasonable request. By all the thunder within me I shall this night loose upon you my righteous wrath and visit upon you punishments attuned to the caliber of your defiance."

With a thrust of his arm a terrifying bolt streaked out, electrically charged, headed straight for the abode of Lucifer and Lilith. Adam stood wide-eyed watching. A counter bolt rose up immediately from Lucifer and Lilith's arms extended combining their bolt of fire which met and squashed Lord's bolt mid-air. With a thunder clap of riotous sound the two brimstone missiles each cancelled the other out, to be followed in rapid succession by another bolt and then another, the bolts dueling in the night sky over the village. Remnants from their clash rained down on houses with roofs of straw which ignited to mix with flames from other houses from the fallout of the thunder bolts. Shouts of horror and then villagers formed a rehearsed brigade to quell the flames with water, gaining confidence in their ability to maintain control over these fiery events even as the battle waged on above them.

Lucifer took a moment in the heat of it saying to young Adam, "Take my hand you have some smaller power to also throw fire into the sky. Take my hand, point your arm and capture fire in your mind and release it."

He showed Adam once again with an arm thrust and Adam responded with small bursts of his own. He grew acclimated to the technique of it. They were able to make larger bursts until all three combined were of an equal if not surpassing those rained down by Lord. It was this that turned the tide in that first skirmish and roused Lord to unsheathe more bolts plucking them from his terrible quiver; still more of terror and destruction from the sky.

He swept his arm across the dark and sent down demon beasts small in stature but who could enter the abode of all setting flame to the inside of homes, cold-cobalt blue flames of death. Thousands of these demon beasts spread out flattened on the night sky and as a mass started their descent. Some landed in homes to rent their horrific destructions.

Quickly, Lilith rose on the night sky, her power directly confronting that of Lord. From below Lucifer and Adam joined once again in the fray combining to cast a flesh-killing spell upon the demon-beasts. Aghast, Lord could only watch, occupied as he was with missiles from below propelled by Lucifer and Adam coming toward him hovering in the now blazing white sky.

And it was then that battalions of the demon-things had their fire boomerang back upon them by the combined fire from below. They fled seeking to avoid the fire of their own making, and their sizzling bodies were consumed in the ensuing flames. All in an instant was heard their terrible screams as they met a fate intended for others. Lilith and Adam maintained their steady rain of fireballs causing each and every demon-beast to explode mid-air and plunge downward to their fiery graves.

The vision of Lord, once burning bright in the night sky, dimmed, flickered and ultimately quenched itself leaving a black hole where Lord once stood. Down below a great cheer erupted while villagers below looked up to the three standing on the balcony. "Hosanna, Hosanna," was their cry and the three rose, put their hands together forming a temple, offering to the crowd their prayer of thanksgiving.

Lilith spoke, "Make no mistake this is but one skirmish in a longer running punishment which Lord will continue to seek to rain down on us. But tonight we can take some small solace here—that we have prepared and now achieved some confidence in our ability to defend ourselves. Make no mistake, Lord will not relent, he will cast down his thunder again... This is our lot here, on exile Earth. Next time will surely be a flood, blight, disease or fire again. We cannot but brace, be prepared as we can, and hold steel and iron in our own defense."

Adam spoke, "I am, it is true, Lord's creature here for only a pittance's time compared to how long all of you have endured this place. But know my gratitude to you; your stout defense is without measure. My appreciation runs deep and will not be forgotten"

Chapter 19

Lord was still with all the hard sentiments congealed in him from the battle, where he had seen Lucifer and Lilith; once again, combine against him, this time adding the nascent capabilities of Adam to their continued defiance of him.

Lord spoke aloud, "I have, in this, sought righteousness and have made the attempt to balance the karma of the universe—for every action an equal counter-balancing reaction. Even as I lay claim to Justice and it requirements, all that happens, it seems, is an ugly counter-balancing that grapples with my will wrestling to stalemates unresolved and unrelieved."

"I am now captured in this conundrum and seized of its dynamics rendering me to appear powerless against my own creations who defy me without risk; ruining my authority in the eyes my own adherents. I will think on this catastrophe and seek its righting for, without an adjustment in this, all the universe will veer surely off into chaos, from which there is no return."

While Lord contemplated a re-righting of the Universe, Adam settled down to life in the village.

Adam lay on his bed of straw that night, mourning his loss, unable to digest it and its meanings, when Lord appeared to him at his bedside. Startled, Adam looked up trembling.

"Be still Adam, I have not come to do harm to you but explain what I have in store for you. I have prepared a new place for you and will make a new wife for you, in a special place I have prepared in another land far from here. There, you can find bliss with your new wife and I will give you all the things you'll need to survive. I know you have had concerns in those things and I am prepared to strike out a new enterprise in this place and want to know if this is something which might please you. Think on this. In several days and I will return for your answer."

Adam awoke the next morning the night apparition in his mind and deep with his thoughts. The next day he contemplated all of the options, choices, and twists and the turns in his saga in this place. At days end he made his mind clear as to what he would do and further to tell Lucifer and Lilith of his decision.

He told them, "Lord's apparition came to me last night and offered to have me back and make anew a relation between me and a new wife. I am inclined to accept this and to make reconciliation. No more, needs here to die because of me.

I know that you two have made me as one with you and my debt to you is great. This enterprise, this time around, with Lord will succeed or fail; I cannot know at this juncture and can only guess; but try I must, because there is here much that smacks to me of my destiny and I, therefore, should play out this thread."

Lilith and Lucifer listened quietly and embraced Adam jointly, Lilith whispering to him that "You are perceptive, I agree. It seems your destiny is to gather round your Lord's plan and see what comes of it. Understand, we are always a refuge should you need it and we are here in case. But, go with our blessings and understanding."

With that, Adam took leave and took the mountain pass to his mud abode awaiting Lord's next appearance. It came swiftly with Lord appearing telling Adam to prepare for the journey to his new home. "Lord," Adam said as he made preparations to leave, "I have this heavy beating in my soul. I beseech thee Lord, in your great powers, to heal her Lord, heal my Lilith and bring her back; to give her beauty back; and allow her to come back to me to share this new place you have prepared for me."

Lord said, "I understand Adam, what it is to have the woman you love wrenched from you. It is not in my power to undo the deed once done, but what I can do is make your loss bearable. Come kneel before me for the application of my remedy."

With that he pressed upon Adam's brow a single finger saying, "With this, I erase each trace, mote and memory of your Lilith from you and release you from that emotional prison which currently envelopes you and all your sentiments. I free you to love another."

Adam was beset with a groggy feel and ultimately could not remember anything except Lord taking his finger away. Lilith was lost to him, erased from his memory. His heart was freed. Newly compliant he went to work on preparations to travel to the place Lord had provided; a changed Adam.

Chapter 20

The place was the Garden of Eden, a garden of rushing waters, abundant fruit trees, shade and the blessing of being a place of peace. Adam entered from the South wall into an oasis, where outside the garden was desert and devoid of people. It was here that Lord told Adam he would settle with a new wife, Eve. It was to be also where Lord would take Adam's soul to reinvent it to match it with that of his new wife Eve.

He induced another deep slumber in Adam which caused him to sleep whereupon Lord sought to correct in Adam what Lord felt was wayward tendencies. He gave Adam a resistance to the wiles of Lilith's ilk; he was convinced that Adam had a weakness there. But he made the pair attractive to one another but only moderately.

He sought as well to plant within the new Adam more of a free will, having learned that a Tabular Rosa creation with a slavish attitude lost the ability to freely choose Lord's way. Free will was a risk, Lord understood, but one he was willing to take, again, even though free will had given Lilith and Lucifer the means to disobey him. That free will, Lord had learned from Lucifer and Lilith's example on Earth, also created the initiative necessary for survival in the wilderness of Earth. It was a matter of how much free will was a balance between rebellion and sycophancy.

Lord had pondered long on Eve's temperament, her freewill, her tendencies in sex, and on her capacity for defiance. He concluded that sexual aggressiveness was to be eschewed in her, and, while free will was to be her endowment as well, it was not to be in the portions Lilith had possessed.

Eve was to be a being oriented toward hearth and family rather than adventure, traits a wife needs in the circumstances on Earth. He made her a creature of beauty such that the pair would mate. He made them both from the red clay of the earth and matched their temperament and tendencies to follow the ways of heaven in their new paradise.

The two awoke and Lord said to them, "I am Lord, your God, and I have made you in my image and have made for you here a garden such that you might live your days on Earth in peace and keep the ways of your God in this place. You shall populate this planet in my name, you shall be fruitful and you shall multiply and carry forth my name and my commandments here.

Adam looked blankly, stammering "Yes Lord."

Eve said "Yes you are Lord."

"Eve," Lord said, "does this man please you?"

Eve looked at Adam very closely inspecting him. "Yes Lord he does," she said at last."

"Adam, Lord said, "Does the woman, Eve, please you?"

"Yes she does." Adam said.

"Now come Lord said I will show you the garden." He took them through the garden and told them what strictures they must observe.

"You may eat of any fruit in the garden and I have placed here an abundance so as to make your life here one of ease. You shall not want for sustenance. But of all the trees in the garden I forbid you to eat of two trees—the Tree of Life and the Tree of the Knowledge of Good and Evil. Of these trees you may not eat. This restriction is mine and cannot be superseded by your thought or desire nor should you allow any thought of yours to intercede your will for mine."

"You shall not have concourse with any of the humans outside the garden--these are the fallen ones, the ones who have displeased me and have fallen into sin. Do not have any concourse with them."

These were Lord's tests made known to Adam and Eve for their own protection. Knowledge of good and evil would speed too fast, in Lord's estimation their development, since while they were created as adults they were in fact as babes at the breast. He would bring them slow to consciousness and not have them rush their passage to full blown awareness. And he certainly did not what them to associate with any of Lilith and Lucifer's kin outside the garden walls. The Tree of Life he did not speak of but it had the power to grant immortality.

As such Lord left them to began their exploration of their new home the two talked for the first time.

"Eve is my name. Is that what Lord said?" Eve queried.

"Yes," said Adam, "my name is Adam and I have some sense of precedent that I have been alive before, but it was not in this place. It is in me, a memory of another life, but faint, and not present to mind. I cannot re-conjure it, try as I may."

Eve took his arm and he wrapped his arm around hers and the two walked through a shaded glen and sat beside a gurgling brook.

"Such a beautiful place," Eve exclaimed. "Such beautiful animals live here." She stopped to fondle a beautiful bird which twittered offering its plumes for caressing. Neither was clothed at all and neither noticed the others' nakedness.

"Who or what is the name of our creator?" Eve asked, as they sat under a Banyan tree, "Who is he and why has he gifted us so?"

Adam took her face into his hands, and offered "I am not sure, but he is powerful and clearly our benefactor, such that we must count ourselves extremely fortunate to be here."

Later under the starry night, they could hear wild beasts outside Eden and both clung together feeling more secure that way. Lord was wise, they thought, in creating for them a haven to protect them from the dangers outside.

In clinging together that night, both felt more secure in holding one another. Adam felt his pulse beginning to respond, upon looking at Eve's body moon-lit in the night; he moved from behind her to touch her breasts, and then turned her head to kiss her open mouth. Eve responded to his kiss returning it awkwardly.

There was something pure in these innocents, totally lacking in experience, which allowed for a full intensity to envelope them, meaning that all that transpired then was without defense, pretense, or expectations.

Adam sought Eve's center as they faced one another lying side by side. Eve welcomed and received him willingly as God's non-human creatures in Eden heard the sounds of the first human mating in paradise. Many watched.

Eve made a gasp as Adam's size surprised her and she sought to accommodate him. He felt her depth and warmth all enveloping, carrying him to the brink and then awash like the ebbing tide, he came back again into her only to feel the rush of new crashing waves come over him as his body ebbed and flowed matching that of Eve's torso which arched up to him and then made the trough and then the crest and then the trough again, to deepen him within her, deeper in out and then again; bottomless.

Lord surveyed the scene satisfied that what he had wrought this time was good and would sustain.

*****

Lilith, too, could see the events in Eden and surveyed the new Eve from a distant observation post, and said to Lucifer, "She is beautiful. Adam should find in her many satisfactions. Lord, it is clear has crushed in Adam all memory of his Lilith and given him this Eve in substitution."

Indeed the latter seemed true because Adam took Eve to his deep soul-source and seemed happy and content with her.

Chapter 21

Lucifer looked upon this Eve with lust. That evening he confessed to Lilith his deepest thought on Eve. "I have in my glimpse of this Eve recognized all that I have endured in this place—in this bitter exile. I miss more than Lord's punishment that my beauty was taken from me. Nothing would please me more that having that restored. It is a loss I have yet reconciled even after eons here."

Lilith turned on elbow to face him, "Such is my identical thought. I find my self looking with frank lust on this new Adam but I hesitate for him to see me serpentine."

"I wonder," Lucifer said, "if this is a new temptation for us is yet another of Lord's traps wherein we would, if tempted, be given new more hideous outcomes and in this be secreted away, our freedom to be entirely lost."

"That is not entirely", Lilith said "without possibility. Lord is clever and cunning."

The next day they spoke of this again, with Lucifer saying "I'll not regain my beauty here naturally, but my mind wanders to Eve's impregnation to see if a child of that union could dilute, if not restore, my beauty through the child; creating, too, a new hybrid progeny."

"It is not impossible to contemplate," Lilith said. And the two devised a plan to steal into the Eden garden where Lucifer would lay with Eve and procreate a new line for Lilith and Lucifer on Earth.

It was just after dark when Eve lay resting that Lucifer came to lay with her after causing Adam to fall into a deep sleep. He awakened her after having made himself to appear to be Adam himself. Eve eagerly welcomed his hands upon her. The two made consummation with Eve murmuring "I love you Adam."

Adam awoke later to find her sated and returned to sleep unaware of Lucifer's transgressions. Lilith's quick question upon Lucifer's return was if he had emptied his seed full into her womb and Lucifer said he did as much. But Eve was a different being and Lucifer, was not sure how all would proceed. He resolved to continue his night time visits with her to be sure.

Eve in this began to change in subtle ways from Lucifer's coupling with her, urging Adam in their love-making to higher and riskier techniques; her satiation points escalated pressing Adam to more exertions and more exotic sexual experiments.

Adam drew, away from her at one point saying softly, "What is in you such that less and less of what I do satisfies you?"

Eve said, "I am only taken with this thing and I expect I will work my way through it and it will pass. It is the newness which attracts me."

But unknown to Lord and Eve alike, Adam had had a dream where Lucifer appeared to him. Adam was delighted to see Lucifer appear and remembered him vaguely from his mountain passages. After greetings and hospitalities in the dream Adam told Lucifer of his dilemmas with Eve. Lucifer said "You say despite your ever expanding offerings nothing now satisfies her need for more?"

Looking away, Lucifer asked, "How long have you been aware of this?"

"Some time now," Adam said.

Lucifer knew the origins of Eve's sexual initiatives. But he did not reveal this to Adam, even in a dream. Adam had been his erstwhile friend, and Lucifer later told Lilith, "I could not reveal to him the truth even in the dream."

"It is I think," as Eve had said, "her proclivity in this will only have a limited span of time. She will come round back to a lower level of need. I think I am in this correct. But we shall see."

Lilith, upon hearing Lucifer's decision not be honest with Adam decided to visit Eve in a dream and offer her advice. This she did and said to Eve, "Contemplate, your husband's needs for sure but do not make the mistake in this of abandoning your own, because if you do neglect your own needs you will lack the means for your own growth and you will see resentment grow within you."

Eve took Lilith's advice to heart and redoubled her efforts to maintain balance between her desires and Adam's needs. But despite these good consultations, Eve's new awareness, brought to her not only new heightened needs, but ones which pressed to know more

of her new life and its restrictions. She found herself
wondering what of the Trees and what of the
consequences if the fruit of that tree entered her mouth,
was taken into her body. What would be the consequence?
Would there result a heightened awareness resulting or,
perhaps, more balancing in that regard? What if the eating
the fruit would be to plant in Adam a new appreciation for
her new sexual proclivities, something to bring him to her
now elevated level?

"Could this tree," she said aloud while sitting
underneath it, "have magic enough to transport Adam and
I to a higher mental realm as well? Perhaps, too, equal to
Lord himself? "Perhaps," she thought, "its forbiddances
were the answer. Perhaps, it very forbiddances was
because the fruit gave power equal to those of Lord
himself?"

She burned to know the answer to these questions
because these questions were coming to her in her sleep.
She spoke of it to Adam. "I am dreaming dreams where a
man comes and lays with me. At first I thought it was you
coming to me to sate me, but in flashes you changed in the
vision to another man, one who looked like a goat-man, a
demon. This it is very disturbing me because this man is
asking me if I know of the tree and what its powers may
be. What is your thought on this?"

Adam asked, "A face that is not me, but is the true
me, in the dream? How often does he come to you?"

Eve said, "Several times he has come in the week.
Especially upon departing the face is red and glowing and
has horns jutting and the eyes have golden glow
alternating with the color rouge. He is frightful looking
but I am not sure if it is I, who is making this vision in the
dream, or if it is part of the dream itself."

"And what transpires again?" Adam asked.

"He, I mean you," Eve said, "is very amorous and is
not soon sated. Often, it seems for many hours he, I mean
you, is with me. It is not unpleasant, were it not for the
vision."

Adam rose up, his eyes narrowing. He said, "I find
this vision familiar with something embedded in my
memory. Your description makes me think I know this
man. But, more, Eve, I too, have had a vision in my
sleeping, but mine is of a woman who comes to me in the

dark night, and gives me sexual offerings and satisfactions. I thought at first it was you, altered in the dream, but you. But of late, I have migrated to the view that she is not you but another. And Eve, she took feels familiar to me, especially when she speaks."

Eve asked, "What manner of sexual advances does she do upon you? I would know more in this."

"Well," Adam said, "her desires are so many I have to recollect the ones which she craves most intensely. She demands that I lay back and she is upon me where she seems to delight in holding me deep inside her as she rocks me to her satiation point; I am pinned down and am only in receipt mode. Then she has the need to take me in her hands for soothing inspections and I let her."

Eve sighed, "Such dreams are these! I am nearly convinced the questions they evince can be resolved in the mystery of the tree. Let's have a test of that theory and eat of that tree. What is your thought Adam on this?"

Adam was silent, blank and did not respond for a time. "Lord has said that we were not to eat of those trees. We should not do the very act you suggest. His wrath, I am sure, would be terrible and swift in coming."

"That I agree," Eve said, "is most true. Lord was clear and explicit about that tree. Yet, my mind thinks that surely Lord would not allow us these thoughts if there were not something to these visions, dreams and their contents. Is this, for us, a test from him, and a puzzle he expects us to solve?"

"Perhaps," Adam said. "perhaps a puzzle?"

The two slept.

***

But the day that followed, from sunrise to sunset, both thought of little else except what the dreams meant and how they related to the shimmering trees in the center of the garden.

Adam said to Eve at their retirement, "We shall, each of us, make the effort to concentrate in the dreams to remember more detail, if we each should dream again, and straight away compare our notes in the morning light."

Eve agreed and they allowed their eyes to close for the night. Meanwhile, Lilith and Lucifer heard their plan and the prior discussion and sought to devise what should be their own reactions. They decided each to dream-cycle with each that night.

"I think," Lilith said, "I should come to Eve in her dreaming and make explicit that the key to the dream lies in the eating of the fruit of the tree. For, I too, cannot anticipate why Lord has made of it a mighty test. Perhaps it does hold some secrets that I, too, am now pressed to know what those secrets might be."

***

But Adam and Eve had devised their own plan, even as Lilith spoke. Under cover of night they crept from their sleeping place to stop below the trees now gleaming in the moonlight, their fruits sparkle-flecked alluring. Both plucked a low-lying leafy fruit from the 'Tree of the Knowledge of Good and Evil.'

Eve turned it in her hand and held it to her mouth pausing. Her lips pursed for the first bite and she remarked to Adam, "Its aroma is wonderful; it is a delight, but now to the taste to see if I gain some understanding from eating of it."

She bit the apple, her mouth opening wide-and she swallowed silently offering Adam a bite of his own. He took the sphere, now missing its crown from Eve's semi-circle bite, and took his turn, munching slowly. "Its taste," he said, "is true ambrosia and I am pleased with it."

He said to Eve "Do you feel anything, have you a sense of transport or new clarities? Is there in this single bite any clue to the puzzlement?"

"I have none," Adam reported, "I have noticed nothing here at all."

The two gazed at each other and Eve suggested, "Perhaps another bite?" She took the fruit from Adam's hand biting another bite and handed it back to Adam for his second one. Both ate and then waited for a time, at last, concluding that perhaps too much had been made of the eating of the apple.

There was in their dreams that night visits from their two respective sprites, Lucifer and Lilith who offered, each in turn, encouragement for what they had already

102

done, each said in their vision, that if knowledge was the outcome then this was something good.

"However, after these visitations from the two, both Adam and Eve started to receive yet other visions in their dreams, horrible visions, ugly creatures who hissed menacingly saying to each "You are inferior beings on this Earth and like the Lilim your place is undeserved. As sure and day follows night you shall perish here and not survive. We Gargoylim are the only rightful heirs to this wilderness."

Lucifer and Lilith also became aware of the Gargoylim vision and undertook to identify its source, making the resolution that the return of the Gargoylim was a most serious event. If they were alive and spawning all on earth could be threatened.

Meanwhile, in the morning's hazy light, Eve awakened and looked upon Adam and saw his face alternate between his normal visage and one similar to that of the Gargoylim she had seen in her dreams. More to the point, she was seeing, him in his nakedness. To her shocked eyes his member was alternating between his normal look and that of a serpent.

"Adam," she exclaimed, "I am seeing strange things, your member plays tricks on me, now in this moment it is ok but in the next moment a serpent. Do my eyes here prove faulty? Tell me this is not transpiring."

Adam looked down for his own inspection and he, too, saw what Eve had reported. His member was in one moment normal, and the next serpentine. "And you," he said, "you, I am seeing something with you. Your center to me is, in the moment as it should be, but in the next, I see it has grown teeth which bulge gave it a hideous over-bite."

Eve looked to see what Adam had seen and she, too, saw the apparition there alternating.

"The tree," Adam said. "We ate of the tree and this is our punishment."

"Oh!" cried Eve, horrified. "Lord will surely notice and swift will be his retaliations. Quick, we must cover ourselves, and hope his eyes will not see."

They took up their normal routines and later that day, they heard Lord's voice calling, "Adam, Eve what hast thou done?"

Adam and Eve both instinctively touched the fig leaves they had used to cover their nakedness.

"What are you in hiding from me? What I see is clear. Who has made you aware of your nakedness such that you need to conceal it from me? The only source for this knowledge is from the tree. You have eaten from the tree of 'Knowledge of Good and Evil'. This is plain to me. Confess that I would know that my suspicions are true. Tell me if this is so."

Adam, much afraid, spoke, "It is true Lord we did eat, thinking it was a test, a puzzlement you had set for us to solve on our own. We both, too, had dreams urging us to this conclusion. We are but new here Lord, forgive us this trespass. We are not tutored."

"I do not doubt," Lord said, "that you had urgings from the two evil ones who likely invaded your dreams with the express intent to encourage you to these transgressions." There was a pause.

"All I had planned for you is now changed. I will have to think on this. Carry with you now the warning I give. I am not pleased in this. I made for you a garden paradise and you ate of The tree which was forbidden, and more, you have trafficked with the evil ones. You have now placed upon you the stamp, their evil stamp. All is tainted here, you are my creations and now you have rewarded me with a monstrous sin. I will think on this."

Adam and Eve watched as the vision of Lord shimmered and disappeared.

In terror mode, both sat talking in the dark night, a full moon rising, unable to fathom what would transpire next, afraid for their lives, when suddenly with a thunderous sound, Lord came and spoke. "Adam, Eve, come before me now in this dark night, I have a pronouncement to make in retribution of the trespass you have confessed to; I have a dark heart to heal, even as I hammer down the arm of righteousness upon you, even as I grieve for you whom I have loved, and made a place for you. Hear me in this my judgment!"

Adam and Eve in the now ever cooling night, shivered knowing Eden was no longer inviting to them; Lord's very breath seemed icy as he spoke. The two huddled together for the warmth.

Lord spoke and said "I pronounce upon you, Eve, forever the pain of childbirth and all of your progeny for having first eaten of that which I had said was forbidden. Adam, I make of you and Eve an exile, for you to toil and dig in the earth, to break your back to make a living outside this place. This Eden is now closed to you; you shall be ejected from here and must make your way out among the hordes, many of whom are disciples of the evil ones. You shall toil in that wilderness forever for your sins. My hope for you is that you will remember and choose me your Lord over the followers of the Goat and the Serpent one, over Lucifer and Lilith the evil ones. Teach your compatriots of this, my regime for them, make them know of the choice before them and bring them to my fold as compensation for your sins here. This is my charge to you."

"This day in paradise," Lord continued, "is now forever known as the day of your original sin which you shall carry forward with you forever—unto eternity. And Eve, I say special to you my heart's greatest pain was in my recognition that in your womb the evil one has placed yet another spawn liken to the one he had done many Glicks ago. In this sacred place I cannot bear yet another humiliation by that one and now you are his vessel to yet another sacrilege, another affront to my face."

"For both of you then, this is my decree; you shall be exiled from this place to go out among the Lilim progeny of the Goat-man and you are to make amends in that sinful sea and, thereby, hopefully to make me proud of you, proud enough to redeem my faith in you."

Chapter 22

Adam and Eve were ejected from the paradise garden and set upon the path, out amongst the Lilim peoples.

Lucifer and Lilith met them on the road appearing to them offering shelter, food and succor. But Lord immediately set down upon them thunderbolts and shouting "Gather not with these two, make your own way in the world, I command thee!"

Lucifer reciprocated shouting back, "You have made these orphans in this wilderness and I shall see to their survival. If you are wishing upon them suffering unto death, strike them down dead now; otherwise leave me to be about their rescue. They are now your ambassadors. Let this then proceed to be about what you yourself have acknowledged is your wish for them."

Lord shouted back, "This raw attempt at usurpation shall not go unpunished." Lord was silent and then after emitting a blinding flash of light, caused them to shield their eyes. He was then gone.

Soon after this encounter, Eve took to her sick bed having already begun to feel the pains that child-bearing was to bring to her.

"Now," said Lucifer to Lilith the night after settling the two in a temporary house, "we are embarked here upon a new hybrid species; these two from Lord, and the Lilim, now both to intermix all around on planet Earth."

"Lilith," Lucifer said pensively, "let us call the child Cain."

Chapter 23

Eve had five children in rapid succession, the first Cain and a second male, Abel; then twin girls and another male Seth. Eve named the two females Ariel and Sara.

Lucifer determined that Cain, the eldest, was to be introduced when he came of age to the Lilim community, and further there was to be a marriage between him and a Lilim princess to make there an immediate blood pack between those of the garden and those of Lilim. Many of the Lilim lived in the caves for parts of the year and each year their numbers dwindled. Many welcomed Adam and Eve as a new hybrid who came to mate with them. But some among them questioned the wisdom of admitting what some regarded as Lord's Trojan horses into the community.

A leader among them spoke to Lilith and Lucifer, "We have this hesitation, Sires, because these are creatures of Lord. Even though exiles they might be, as with us, but, that not withstanding, they are not of the same stock as we, and, who can predict their tendencies in terms of the ingredients Lord might have planted within them and their genes. We are remembering the Gargoylim and the sad ending to their existence; and that of the Lukim, and understandably, we seek here not to replicate those sad stories."

"What assurances have we," the Lilim representative said, "that this episode will not have a similar ending and we, Lilim, again might be victims of yet another failed species? And more Sires, in this elevation and the marriage planned are we not creating a new hierarchy and compounding the inequality we all agree is destructive?"

Lilith let the assenting cries die down before she spoke and insisted, "We have," Lilith began, "sought a balancing between what gifts Lilim have to give and those necessary to survive here, nay to thrive here. Alas, it is also true, that in our attempts in the past, we have had our grievous errors and challenges. True, in making those attempts, we experienced more failures than we care to remember. You, Lilim, are my chosen ones, but alas your numbers do not grow, and therefore, there has been insufficient progress in producing food enough for everyone, at pace rapid enough, to sustain the community. We must, as I have decreed eons past, mix our blood with that of other species and produce the genetic variety to assure the mix of skills needed. We must have more that one arrow in our quiver to avoid deadly stagnation. No fault lies here. It is a matter of biology, genetics, and careful planning."

In seeking that variety," Lilith continued, "we must be relentless. Here with Lord's spawn we have another opportunity to see that goals' fruition. Bear with us, obey in this, and you shall see augmentation in the survivability of us all."

The Lilim, in majority, assented although some still made their disagreement known signaling their belief that this experiment was doomed to rank failure, if not a sad repeat, of previous experiments.

***

The marriage arrangements for Cain, son of Lucifer and Eve, and his princess were made and the day set for the ceremony where Cain, as eldest, would marry the Lilim princess Elena, "a true beauty," Lilith said of her "she is strong of limb and fearless."

As the day drew near Lucifer took the young Cain aside and gave him, fatherly instructions such that he, Cain, might know what lay in his destiny.

Lucifer said, "We have short time and I have much to convey. Know that I am very proud of you, my son. I have seen you come of age clear-eyed and start to gather the parts of wisdom you shall need to bring together two people, teaching them the skills of harmony. Know this is the plan for you and, further, the skills you must garner to yourself. First you must look to agriculture; irrigation and trade for these are the vehicles which will allow our exile kingdom to accumulate the treasure and leisure necessary to progress. You must lead a contingency from among a number adherents I shall create for thee to settle beside the great rivers of this Earth, the Nile, the Tigris, Euphrates, and the Yangtze of the Far East. With this plan you will make a new garden on this Earth which shall be ours. Cain nodded his understanding of his father's plan and he, in fact he said was one who took readily to tilling the Earth and animal husbandry.

But Cain suddenly took on a moody stare and caused Lucifer to inquire. "I see you have a trouble, tell me what it is. Do not hesitate, let your sentiment fly. I am your father and in these things I offer comfort."

Cain stammered and blurted out, "Father I cannot in good conscious, complete this marriage because I love another."

Lucifer gazed him a steady gaze but said nothing.

"I cannot deny, though I have tried," Cain said "to deny this is so. But the very fiber of my being tells me this is true."

Thoughtfully, Lucifer looked at the young man now only 13 years and said, "Wait here a moment, Cain. I would have is this Lilith's counsel." Moments later he returned with Lilith who sat the scene quietly as Lucifer resumed his interrogatories with Cain.

"Now repeat for me your sentiment such that Lilith here might hear as well."

Cain retold his story for Lilith's sake and she paused asking quietly, "Who is the fair one who has captured your heart? Tell us that we might know. The princess we have chosen for you is beautiful beyond compare, who can surpass the beauty she possesses? She, I am told, is most enamored of the image of you we sent her. This marriage seems destiny. What say you Cain, come confess to us your heart's secret."

"She is," Cain began, "Ariel."

There was a clear shock at this revelation. Lucifer, gap-jawed, blurted "Do you mean Ariel, your sister?" Your sister is the one in your heart?"

He looked at Lilith whose face, too, registered shock. Lilith looked back at Lucifer and said, "I had no knowledge of this, no awareness whatsoever." Looking at Cain she said "Whatever love may be between you and Ariel Cain cannot be. She is your sister. Has this love between you two been reciprocated by her, is she aware of this and, I must ask, has this love between you two been consummated? Have you two lain together?"

It was a deadly silence befell as Cain did not immediately respond and he fell mute; thereafter, not speaking at all. He was clear to see he was traumatized by his own revelation because he had not expected the two to take such exception. Cain was not schooled in the ways of incest and saw no harm in his sentiments for his sister.

Lilith said, "This must be wearying for you, Cain, let us suspend this discussion for the time being and take it up on the morrow. We have time to measure this and produce some resolution which will provide a path toward solution."

Cain departed, leaving the two to discuss in detail the conundrum he'd presented them. "I wonder, most," Lucifer said, "what the answers are to your questions, Lilith. There are tremendous unknowns in this. I suggest we have Ariel in and see what her conceptions are in this."

"I agree." Lilith said more of a wisp in her voice than usual.

Ariel was a true angelic vision in her appearance, having been named so by Eve at Lilith's suggestion, a name which brought to Lilith's mind the angel allies she had recruited on high in the kingdom, angels who had turned the second battle there from sure defeat to victory even though temporary.

Ariel's entrance was with a grace which was evident. Even at 12, and she was full upon her womanhood. Lilith could see Cain's enchantment with her, any young man would be proud to have her as wife and mother of his children.

"Yes, Sires," Ariel said politely, "Cain came to me after leaving here, and I am of the opinion," trembling as she spoke, "this matter is causing tumult and consternation."

"Tell us Ariel, what of the relationship you have with Cain, when was it initiated and what is the nature of its character, its consummations." Lilith spoke the last word enunciating each syllable of the word.

"Consummations?" Ariel replied. "I assure you both there has been no consummation, no sexual intercourse between he and I. Did he aver as such? I am sure he did not and would not. Cain is an honorable boy and he would not say it was so, when it was not. No, this has not occurred, nor broached nor even temptation's lure has arisen here because all there's been from my side is an

110

occasional glance and flirting look, but, nothing above this."

"Has Cain," Lucifer leaned down to her to increase his scrutiny mentioned to you?"

Lilith touched his arm signaling him to stay that question saying," That is all we have in the way of questions for you now Ariel, thank you so much for your straightforward answers to our query."

Ariel turned to leave and behind her Lucifer said, "And please, Ariel if you will, do not discuss this with Cain until we meet with him again and gain more detail in his perspective on this."

Ariel, turned, her small face shining. Lilith could see she had spoken honestly.

"I will do as you ask Sires," she said and retired.

Lucifer stood to stretch to his full height, and said, "I took your meaning in staying my last question..."

"Yes," Lilith said, "we'll not want to allot to Ariel the unnecessary burden of believing that any of her actions were factors in forestalling the wedding. Clearly she is not wrapped up in this romance as Cain is. He, apparently, is engaging in a love affair that lives mostly in his head."

Cain retuned after being summoned looking now more chastened than before, sensing that his love for Ariel has complications more than he understood.

But still, when Lilith asked him the extent to which he was willing to relinquish his feelings for Ariel, for his duty as a prince, he faltered. Lilith asked him straightway, "Cain can you forego this love you profess for Ariel, and have it give way to your duty as prince of this house? Will you and I know this is asking much, leave this love aside, no matter how strongly felt, and move forward in this life and in this marriage to the princess?"

"I can only state, at this time, I have only moments ago become aware that such a love is not to be. My mind reaches out to me offering reasons that I should relent, but, my heart sweeps away that offering and cannot at this moment, thrust the dagger into it, into my own side. In this I am asking my sore heart to do this thing which is to my heart suicide."

Lilith spoke, "We understand the weightiness of what we ask. Think on it now, ponder it more this day and night, and we shall speak again tomorrow."

Cain withdrew, as Lucifer and Lilith watched him depart, Lucifer whispered to her, "This parenting has windy roads and steel traps which rips away huge chunks in my very soul."

None of this was revealed to Abel and the others, whilst Lucifer and Lilith continued their talks with Cain, who seemed to be relenting, Lucifer and Lilith guessed, after possibly speaking with Ariel who likely clarified her feelings to Cain, indicating to him they were not as intense as his. This was known because Ariel came back to report to Lilith that this had transpired. "He has relented," she said and confided in me that he will do as you wish."

"Thank you Ariel," Lilith said. "I guess we shall have our wedding."

Plans for the wedding proceeded among them but Lord became aware of the wedding and made his own plan.

He encountered Cain in the fields and told Cain that he, not Lucifer, was his true father. "I created Adam and Eve, your true parents and you must make to me, as your true father, a proper sacrifice and acknowledge my paternity."

"You are my true father?" Cain said much confused. "What is true here?"

Cain, fell into a much depressed state, as he listened to Lord, tell of his origin and original circumstance.

"Your mother, Eve, lay with Lucifer and thereby damned herself and you, and her progeny, to curses I have placed upon them for all eternity."

"But what can I do?" Cain said plaintively. "I have only in this the fault of being born."

"But you," Lord said, "can make to me a sacrifice to indicate your loyalty and perhaps, therewith, alleviate these circumstances which bind your kind and theirs on this planet; and more, I could agree to plea your case for marrying Ariel with them directly."

At this Cain's interest grew and he agreed to make a sacrifice to Lord to gain his support.

But unknown to Cain, Lord had made a similar proposition to Abel, who was also smitten with Ariel. Lord instructed Abel to make an offering at the rock altar and Lord told them he, would judge whose offering gained his favor and his support of marriage to Ariel.

Separately, Cain prepared his sacrifice to be a bale of fresh hay bound with the finest hemp from the grain fields and took to the altar and placed it there for Lord to acknowledge. But Lord did not appear. Cain afraid that his absence might be noticed placed the gift, and after a wait returned to his quarters.

Abel, too, had decided to cooperate with Lord's proposition understanding that as second son his options were limited and, that Lord as a powerful ally was not something to be eschewed. He choose a sacrifice of fresh lamb's blood as he had learned to do from Lilim scribes who told him that his life as second son was to be that of a headsman whose wealth was measured in the number of sheep, goats and herds he owned.

It was in this, that the initial split between the descendants of Abel and those of Cain occurred, a separation between headmen of the desert, wanders, keepers of the simple life, and those of Cain whose descents, under instruction from Lucifer, were pressed to build huge cities supported by the plentiful agricultural bounties that settlement by rivers can bring.

The gifts from the two brothers were measured by Lord. He looked upon Abel's gift favorably since the life of the simple shepherd was the one Lord favored. The gift of Cain was rejected by Lord as associated with the goals given him by Lucifer and Lilith.

He said to Abel "Your progeny shall go forth in my name and live the simple life of piety as I have commanded and you shall not to fall to the influences of the evil ones who will congregate in the teeming cities and fall sway to false worship and paganisms."

Cain's gift was thus rebuked.

Crestfallen, and feeling the sting of it, Cain added to this his recent realization that Ariel had no feeling for him. He wandered to the moonlit altar where Lord had made of him a mockery. He meant to understand why Lord had rejected him. He had rage in him that grew thinking that Lord, Lucifer, Lilith, Ariel and yes, Abel were likely engaged in a plot to destroy him. Against the three, Lord, Lucifer and Lilith, he felt powerless to act. However, Abel, his brother, Cain could challenge and exact his revenge.

But even as these thoughts enveloped him, he heard a voice and turned to see none other than Abel, who by happenstance, had also come to the alter. He had no doubt, Cain thought, to savor his victory with Lord at his expense.

"I have come here," Abel said quietly, "on chance that I might see you here. Lord came to me an hour ago and told me that he has asked you, as well, to make a sacrifice and that Lord, had chosen mine. This was first I was aware of this."

Cain rose in a mighty rage, shouting, "You lie in this, you all have lied in this!" With a mighty blow he brought down a heavy rock against Abel's skull and it made a sickening thud sound, where in the dull moonlight, Cain could see blood come from the fissure and Abel's blood spill out on the ground mixing with the lamb's blood already there.

The scene transfixed him for a time and panicked.

He made haste to hide the deed, to bury Abel, and to leave the scene before he or Abel would be missed.

But Lord, on the next day, appeared to Cain still in his bed and said, "Where is thy brother Cain? What hast thou done?" Lord repeated to Cain his demand. "Where is thy brother Cain, what hast thou done."

Cain responded sharply, "Why doest thou ask me Lord, am I my brother's keeper?"

So it was that Cain severed his ties with Lord and Lord with him.

***

Cain hurried to Lucifer and Lilith in the next several clicks, to make them aware that he would fully cooperate in their plan for him to marry and that he would prepare himself for the wedding as they had asked of him. He would, he averred, take his Lilim princess and build the cities as Lucifer had asked.

Lucifer and Lilith replied to Cain, puzzled at his change in attitude, but grateful for it and said "Thank you, Cain. I know this was not an easy thing for you to do."

But Lilith became suspicious when Abel turned missing. Lucifer and Lilith called Cain to their side to ask him if he had any knowledge of his brother's disappearance.

"What can you say of this, give light to what you know or may have heard? We have looked in every cranny, but Abel is missing."

Cain did not immediately reply saying only that he had heard a rumor that Lord had come to Abel in the night and asked of him to switch his loyalty and return to Lord's fold. "Other than this, I have heard nothing."

"Perhaps this is so. He is second son and that position can be a frustrating one," Lucifer said. He and Lilith looked at each other; sure that Lord's intervention was possible and resolved that if it was so Lord would likely hatch a plot against the wedding as well. They dismissed Cain telling him to prepare for the wedding and vowing to make themselves more vigilant in the event Lord made an attempt to disrupt the proceedings.

The next day all huddled to make plans for the wedding.

Elena, the chosen princess, was preparing for her wedding at age thirteen. She held an etched picture of Cain, upon a polished metal plate sent to her by Lilith her future mother-in-law. Elena spoke of her impending marriage with her mother, Lorna, who could trace her Lilim origins back generations.

"What of the marriage night that I need to know mother," Elena inquired on the eve of her wedding. Lorna, a beautiful woman in her own right smiled.

"Well I was hoping you would ask me that, dear." Lorna said. "But first we must review the importance of the event and I need not tell you that this is not an ordinary coupling. You have been chosen by Lucifer and Lilith above all of the other girls for this honor and I want to impress upon how important it is that not only the wedding go well, but the marriage, as well.

"Here, listen closely," she said. "Be vigilant that you please your new husband and he pleases you and neither of you should shrink from the hard work that is marriage.

Look at Lucifer and Lilith—never has a couple suffered more, yet have retained Love's spark, over eons. See their example and take heart."

Elena said, "Mother I will be mindful of your words," Elena said "and will make you and father proud of me as I carry this burden, but, know I am still a girl and have a heart to feel and love to give. Tell me the things I will encounter as woman and what shall I, in that regard, press to sincerest regard. What of making babies and births, what of sex and male anatomy? How will I know what pleases him?"

Lorna sat back in her chair for what she knew would be lengthy conversation. She gathered her breath, sighed and began, "The male anatomy," she began, "is deceptive at first encounter, you look at it and it seems flaccid with small sacks hanging directly below and you wonder which is which and why are they there. I cannot say; I was expected on my wedding night to attend to their servicing and I decided, not to dwell there as this was not my lot, at least at that moment, and concluded my husband, your father, had the equipment and this was to be, therefore, his problem."

"Flaccid?" Elena inquired.

"Why yes," Lorna continued, "at first glimpse its architecture resembles that of a fig leaf with two figs affixed but it is not that in arousal, and we certainly hope that comes easily for your sake; then note that aroused by the sight of you it can magnify its girth and length by three or four fold, until at the business end you encounter a massive shaft which he then proposes to plug into your private parts. The shock of it, I can tell you, is not lost upon you each time this occurs. There is not preparation nor memory of this it seems, at least to me, because each time, I and my private parts, register shock, pleasurable shock mind you on entry but shock nonetheless. But, I suppose, I am too frank with you one so young in years. Keep in mind it is different with everyone but I have given you the broad outline."

"And babies?" Elena promoted.

"Ah babies," Lorna said wearily, "there is no description from sheer memory I can give but think of the sexual act I just described as the going in and child birth as the coming out, but not pleasurable, but painful. But the mind's eye causes, me at least, to quickly remonstrate and forget the pain of it and in months, strangely, my body cries out to have another child and I am dragged along in this and find myself producing yet another child such as you my dear. I am content this is enough for you to absorb now. This is not the only opportunity we will have to converse on this. We are close nearby your future husband's lands. We shall have many, many visits."

Chapter 24

Meanwhile, two days before the wedding, Lord sent to Lilith by private courier, a secret message in which he identified Abel as murdered at the hand of Cain and invited Lilith to inspect the grave where Cain had sequestered him. Suspecting a trick, Lilith told Lucifer of it and he suggested, "You go alone and have your inspection, and I will have my word with Cain upon your return. No word of this, if true, should reach the ears of others and thereby put the ruin to our wedding plan. No, you go this night so as not to be seen and cleanse the area and bury properly, if necessary, Abel's remains."

Lilith, donned drab garb, left that night quick to the place Lord's note had said was Abel's burial place. She had with her Eve, because she thought Eve had a right to this knowledge. If true, Lilith would need someone to assist with the burial, if necessary. Beside, Lilith thought, Eve had a right to grieve.

The two stepped close to the altar rock expecting to see Lord's apparition there; but none appeared and, in the inky night, the dull red glow of blood was clear on the altar. Eve said weakly "There is blood here, there is blood there; the blood of my son lay splattered here?"

"Perhaps, perhaps not," Lilith said tentatively. "This must be, in part at least, the lamb's offering Abel made. Let us track to the spot Lord has said Abel lays."

In a short ascent from the rock along a narrow mountain trail they came upon a stone covering a small cave where Lord had said marked Abel's remains. Lilith took the stone aside easily and it was clear, even in the dull moonlit that a form lay on a stone slab. Eve peered down onto the face she knew was that of Abel.

So sad this grieving scene; there Lilith and Eve joined in mutual grieving, both locked and interlocked for the first time with the realization that the fratricide was true, and accomplished. Cain was the guilty one.

"What turn can this portend," Lilith whispered to Eve "how can this vaunted wedding, signal a high new beginning also can be seen underneath to have been initiated with a rank murder? How auspicious can this be such that the launching of this new species carries with the rancid smell of a foul deed?"

"I perceive your harsh judgment in this," Eve said, "but remind you that the murderer, as you suggest, is delivered of my loin, was suckled at my breast, and was pain of my pain from his delivery to his growth and now, new pain is this for me to endure. However, much the killer he may be, every mother knows despite these suspicions, or even realities, he is my son still; he remains the fact of my mothering existence."

Lilith softly touched Eve's sleeve. "I meant no disrespect. I am sorry to have interjected into your grief, forgive me. Of course, Eve, we all understand, foul deed, true or not, a mother's love must be constant for that is how we are built."

The two closed the rock and slowly walked down the mountain both wedded now in the memory of that which could never be revealed; that which must be silenced and concealed even from Adam and Lucifer—locked behind the rock's face—inside the mountain.

Chapter 25

The wedding retinue was resplendent at the bride's home; Elena was radiant in a beaded dress of satin sheen, glowing with pearls sewn in at her breast line and bust. Lilith had given her to wear a special Tiara of rare mixed jewels, plucked from deep in the Earth—these Lilith had secured in their early volcanic years on the planet. On Elena, they gained an extra gleaming.

At her side, her father, a tall man purposefully fit the vision of the father of a wedding princess; and her mother, whom Lilith had not met beforehand, was a beauty herself. She was a handsome woman, who had, from the looks of things, made an altogether handsome wedding for her daughter and her future son-in-law.

The assembled hosts in their thousands stood mute, all aware of the momentousness of this coupling--Lilim bride and the bride-groom from the garden. Eve took Cain's arm and the procession was begun with a canopy of flowers hovering above as Eve and Cain began the march, as a hymn last heard in the kingdom on high-one which Lucifer had used in his services. The hymnal strains produced were exceedly lovely to hear on Earth, as Eve and Cain made their approach. Lucifer stood ready to make Cain and Elena wed.

Eve and Cain paused and turned to face those seated near and to face those thousands assembled there.

Elena and her father began to move toward them, her flowered corsage at her wrist, her father beaming proud. Elena had a beautiful smile, and there was true love in her eyes, Lucifer thought. Thanks to the young, he mused quietly to himself, "they always, without instruction, choose love as their first preoccupation, and, thereby save the world again and again."

The four were now planted face to face—Elena unbearably beautiful—her bell-like voice was clear as she picked up a wedding bouquet and spoke her wedding vows softly to Cain.

"There are twelve rose buds in this bouquet I give to you," she said.

"This one is my mind for it has learned that our two minds melding will provide light for our way."

"This one is my Heart for there can be no courage without it—Faith its underpinning."

"This one signifies my Body which here now unfolds only for you and under your touch it will bloom-buffeted by Innocence Betrothed which smothers the Cynical Twinge."

"This fourth bud is where our Future resides, curled up fetal-style, because indeed our marriage is just beginning."

"Home is this bulb making our mutual effort flower."

"This one is my shy steel devotion which will not waver or fail you, us or myself."

"Here is my wish for children who will reflect what we seek to grow here. They are the earthly angels humans are allowed," Elena said, tears welling up in her eyes.

"My Spirit and my Soul are these rose spheres which inhabit our aura.

"This last Silver One, which is my Love, opens its flower petal wings signifying how you took my breath away with your mere reflection."

"Under your touch, I, for the first time in my life, will bloom from the smell of rose-bud bouquets and new beginnings of Tomorrow's and Tomorrow's, of Futures, and the making of beautiful Yesterday memories we will have shared."

"These, in the end, are not mine to give, but, merely pass them on to you and us in the way that Nature intends—that we make of them our bond, sealed with our vows, making them strong enough to last all the years. From these are made true Weddings and true Beginnings."

Cain took his turn, "I am here mindful, so mindful, of how imperfect I am. My hands are not beautiful; my heart came here today lit solely by the prospect of being your groom. My needs are many I am grateful that you have the strength not only to love me, this I feel, but the kindness to heal.

Elena, if there is magic in the air on this Earth, it has come among us in these brief months since I have met you. You have enveloped me, opened my eyes to how fortunate I am to have the prospect to spend my life with you. I have the prospect anew to become a better person because my heart had the sense to love and marry you."

"Therefore, I step forth, the fortunate one, and, as your vows make clear, the one who has a lot to learn from you, where despite your youth you display wisdoms far in excess of your years. I plant my soul in your soil today, invite it's fertilization with your tender ministering, hopeful that, I too, may bloom way beyond what I would have been capable of, alone."

"I will take you, if you will take me; I give to you my solemn vow to be faithful with you and you, alone, as my wife."

Lilith, Eve and many, many others felt the tears run, all knew the import of that wedding.

Chapter 26

Cain was true to his promises with both Elena and to Lucifer. He did proceed, with Lucifer's help, to build cities as Lucifer had requested. Lucifer gave him ten thousand fully grown Canaanites to help in the effort hoping to gain the mixture of genes he and Elena represented to spread quickly across the planet. This miracle was much admired as these ten thousand massed standing before Cain as they prepared to set out on their journey to explore and claim the Earth. The families stood by as well for the farewell.

"We have made you," Lucifer said to the ten thousand, "to go forth and populate this Earth as your ancestors from us have done. You shall seek no war with Lilim or others; rather you shall seek out the great rivers of this world and build cities, centers of learning and advancements as you have been instructed. Your mission is central to our survival here, to the Lilim, to myself and Lilith and we wish you the sturdiness and pluck to persist, despite, any hardship. We are sure you will endure where others have failed; you will succeed to rise up great towers and new civilizations where none now exist."

After some years some of the Lilim dissidents, with the creation of the ten thousand, were mollified because these new Canaanites, in some locales, produced abundant crops. The Canaanites instructed the Lilim in how to triple their crop yields. But some Lilim resisted citing that the Canaanites were overrunning their towns and villages even in the short time they had been on Earth and putting the Lilim population in a bad light.

But, on balance, most Lilim were pleased because Lilith eliminated the custom of bride price in many villages, and in those, young men were better able to afford marriages.

Thus, the start of the main 'Diaspora,' as Lucifer called it, while not perfect, seemed auspicious.

Lilith encouraged them sending messages such as, "Scatter, and by our vow, do not fail."

###

Ariel had attended Cain's wedding and its beauty affected her. The thought that she was not in Cain's affections, that she had been supplanted by Elena changed Ariel. She had a feeling being left behind; Nno longer the object of attention she once was. All talk after the wedding was of Cain and Elena. Both left at the head of an army of ten thousand settlers and almost daily there were reports of what adventures they encountered in their treks. Cain had become a hero and she felt forgotten.

Her disquietude grew from a nagging vein to full blown jealousy then anger, much of which was directed at Eve, Lucifer, and Lilith, whom she came to see, had curtailed any relationship she might have had with Cain in favor of this state marriage. She withdrew within after Cain's wedding into herself. Eve, noticing, sought Ariel out in the days after the wedding to see what her trouble was.

"Tell me love, I notice you have been despondent and I notice you have become more withdrawn in conversation and your affect lacks the sparkle it once displayed. What can you tell me of what is distracting you from your normal self?" asked Eve.

Ariel said, "I am well, mother, it is that recent days have been taxing upon me, the busyness of it; Cain marrying, of course. I am in this losing a brother, one who has been near all my years, and now he is charged to be gone, and I and you .too, have no knowledge of, if or when, we shall see him again."

Eve allowed as how that was much to bear in one so young and was content to let the matter lie without an attempt to further pry. But it was not easy with Ariel; the loss of Cain started within her a progression of negative feelings that became an obsession within her.

She was by the altar stone one day, where she went often to think, and Lord appeared to her and said. "Ariel, I am the father of your father and have created you through him. I am Lord God."

Ariel had heard of Lord but this was the first time she had ever heard him speak or had seen his shimmering vision.

"Oh, Lord," she cried, "I am in full fright of you. I have not thought to ever see your very vision. What concourse do you have with me? Is it my father or my mother you seek?"

"No Ariel, it is you I seek and I have done so because I have chosen you for a special mission which very important, one where I am asking you to found a nation in my name."

"I don't understand," Ariel said.

"Ariel," Lord said, "I will impregnate your mother again and she shall bear a male child who is to become your husband. You and he shall live 900 years and in that time I shall add to your numbers with immense fertility and new beings, I myself shall create, and send you out to populate this land."

Ariel was strong affected by this appearance of Lord and did not speak of it to any one. But sure to Lord's prediction days after, Eve announced that she was, to her surprise, pregnant again.

"It is much to wonder about," Lucifer said, "but I am so pleased to have another child in this house."

Ariel understood the deep meaning of Eve's pregnancy but still chose not to speak of it wondering if she had merely imagined the encounter with Lord. But, true to the prophesy, Eve not only gave birth but did so to a young man who appeared fully-grown to be two years older than Ariel, herself.

Eve had awaken one night in her ninth month expecting a delivery in twelve more days hence and found standing beside her bed a beautiful young man. "Who are you?" she said frightened. "What are you doing here?"

"Do not be afraid, Eve," he said "I am your unborn child set in your womb by Lord for he is the true father. He wants you to know your impregnation was not by Adam but by him. I am that progeny whose destiny on this on this Earth has been assigned; I am to marry Ariel and found a new nation in Lord's name. His wish is for Seth, to join this effort as well."

"Found a new nation, I and you?"

"Yes," he said.

Eve was still thunderstruck by this revelation and did not know what of it to make. The young man started to fade saying he would reappear when the time was right.

Leaving, he said, "I shall be the one to appear when Ariel is to marry. Lord has commanded that you make preparations for the event which shall be in only a short time. Look for me to present myself for her hand and you are to seek me out in the Northern tier by the Red Sea, for that is where my family lives."

Eve went to Adam and told her story, her belly now flat and void. "What shall I say to everyone when they inquire?" she asked Adam.

"Well we can say, of course, the baby was lost, but you say this young man appeared and announced he is to be Ariel's groom? How strange is this to contemplate," Adam said. "We shall look for this young man, where you were told he resides. If you see him again, could you recognize him?"

"Yes" Eve said, "he was brilliant against the darkness; his vision is burned into my eyes permanently."

All the hosts, Lucifer and Lilith were told that the baby was lost and they offered their laments at the news. Ariel pressed Eve for more details, suspecting there was more to the tale.

"Tell me mother, did you get a visitation from Lord?" "I did." said Eve

"You," Eve said, "you received a visitation from Lord as well? Was he a young man just your age?"

"No," Ariel said, it was Lord himself, "but he did tell me of a young man I was destined to marry, and thereby," Lord said, "I would found a nation. He said it this was to be."

Astonished, Eve said to Ariel, "I think I was shown your new bride-groom in a vision from Lord. He was standing there beside me and bright and clear as a new moon."

Ariel, moved quickly to her side.

"Saw him?" she repeated, "Tell, me, mother what he looked like, what was his vision, what features did my bride-groom have?"

Eve sat back to collect that memory and began to describe to Eve what she had seen and the conversation she had had with the young man who appeared in her tent. "He was tall and fair skinned with shiny black hair and eyes dark as charcoals in the fire, a beautiful boy to be sure."

"What did he say?" Ariel pressed for more details.

"Well," said Eve, "he said that Lord had made a plan, that he was of a family just north and he told me where to travel and when to fetch him there. He seemed to think that a marriage between him and you was urgent in Lord's estimation. I told your father and he is to travel hence to meet the boy and his family and, if necessary, make arrangements for you to be wed."

As Eve said the words she seemed herself to be astonished by them as she uttered them.

Ariel was thrilled. "I am to be wed? Soon? How wonderful!" she exclaimed "Then Lord's words were true!"

Lord's plan in this was plain to see. He would launch a new nation concurrent with the Canaanite Diaspora. These two would have a contest for the new Earth rather than he, Lord, forfeit, it to the Lilim.

Eve, Adam, or Ariel could know or suspect the deeper plan there-that it was no accident that the wedding of Ariel and her groom happened in the same year that the Canaanites took to the face of the land following Lilith and Lucifer's requirements for dispersement. No matter Lilith thought. Let's have the wedding first.

Ariel's wedding was a cause for excitement. And it was a thing of wonderment for all who attended. Lucifer and Lilith expressed surprise that the young man's parents had agreed so readily to the wedding plan and, too, Ariel pressed upon them her desire to wed as soon as possible.

With the hasty arrangements made, Lilith and Lucifer deferred to Adam and Eve the decisions around details. This pleased Ariel and she was delighted to have found her prince. Lucifer was especially happy at the prospect of her wedding and married life with her new groom— whose name they found out was Abram.

Chapter 27

Came the wedding day the wedding parties from both camps assembled in the field below where Abel's remains were ensconced in the ossuary in the cliff above. Eve and Lilith took their places in the wedding march bathed in this irony, remembering that moonlit night and that discovery.

Abram's family included a younger brother, slight of build, and a sister younger still. His father had more than three hundred animals and had fathered many children, more than twenty-five of them. The family had many head of sheep and goats and pastured them from summer meadows to the nearby mountain highlands following the migrations of the game they used to supplement their diets in winter.

Adam was satisfied that Ariel would not want for shelter or food.

Adam stood before the couple at the wedding and said, "I am come to this land by the hand of Lord and once I resided in a garden of running brooks and abundant fruit. But that origin gained a cloud of misunderstanding over it and Eve and I were forced from that life to begin anew outside that Eden. We were met among the Lilim with the kindness of Lilith and Lucifer and we have made a home here in this place."

"Today, my Ariel stands for marriage with Abram to start a new line. Our hearts reach out to them and press to them our good wishes and fond hopes."

"Ariel," he said turning to her, "I have built an arch of flowers for you and your bridge-groom to stand under, marking that garden you are descended from, and place upon your lips wine that you might sip for comfort and enjoyment, for these you will need in the cold nights this dry land brings. You will marry here today with my blessings and my sturdy love with is always available to you in any and all circumstances."

He turned to Abram and spoke again, "You have come to us from the Northern place where the plains about the mountain range and my Ariel has found in you high and honorable traits abounding. Take these and simmer them with those she has, too, in abundance and make of this your marriage—the treasure it is meant to be. Know that your bride comes to you with love such has been her nurturing. Take this gift, do not squander it and accrete to it that which you have to give. In these things I pronounce, this day that you are now by my assent, man and wife."

A roar come up from those assembled. They gathered round to congratulate the couple who received their best wishes. The couple were lit by the glowing pride of parents and friends.

Lord looked upon the scene undetected and was satisfied that with Abram and Ariel he would give birth to the counterweight against Lucifer and Lilith's activities.

That night as Ariel prepared for Abram, Lord appeared to her and said, "You have done well today and this night you will lay with you new groom. As I have said, yours is a singular destiny. On this Earth, in my name, you shall mother a nation. You have my heart in this and I wish you well. I shall visit again soon to further discuss these things."

Chapter 28

Ariel and Abram took leave of Adam and Eve's house and transplanted themselves north to Abram's family home which was a large encampment near an oasis. Ariel was curious to see how plainly his people dressed especially the women who eyed her curiously as she arrived with Abram and his family. All were in white linen. Abram's people seemed calm and serene in welcoming her.

She was shown her quarters and Abram sat with her after for a simple meal of lamb and rice. "Our people," Abram said during dinner, "value a simple life, one which does not have the patina of striving; we value a life attuned to the tending of the herds and the seasons. This is Lord's way."

This was not like the routines she was acquainted with where all activity centered on the village and the market square. Abram's people were nomadic and tied more to the needs of their wards, their goats, and their sheep. Their tents could be easy dropped and packed upon a donkey's back and moved in a convoy to the next waterhole or watering spot. She could see that in this desert land all centered on time and distance to the next water source.

Abram and she lay together after dinner and Abram talked to her of his memory of his origin. "It is strange," he said, "Lord came to me and told me of my mission, which it seems is the same for you that we are to found something new in Lord's name."

"I am proud," he said turning to Ariel, "that he chose you for me and my promise is that I shall not let him down and make with my heart a wedding bed with you."

He was, Ariel thought, so kind and so beautiful that it was easy for her to cleanse herself, as he did, and to make preparation for the wedding bed. She lay awaiting him to finish his lavation, her own oils wafting around her making her slightly dizzy.

It was not that Ariel had knowledge of the sexual act, but she was not the least afraid and felt comfortable with Abram's guidance. He was to be sure, a novice too, who lay beside her his hesitant touch gliding first from finger-tip to finger-tip and then to her shoulders bared, allowing his full palm to spread over one shoulder and then the other. His flattened hand took her breast full-scoped allowing her body to feel a streaming sensation from his hand strokes which ultimately reached her center where the sensation igniting a full explosion within her. He noticed this and did more there where she could feel his member touch against her side, extending, pointing there and she felt it thicken and grow.

Not sure of what was transpiring she reached to touch where she felt it lie and he gave a sign of relief as she explored tentatively what was offered there.

It was not a memory of what happened next because that occurs in the brain; rather what happened between them was a body quake followed by tremendous lurching. She felt her body meld with his as they both moved beyond the mental to a stupendous spiritual and sexual release leaving both astonished later lying side by side under those desert stars on that first wedding night. The union was made.

Chapter 29

This first initiation into marriage brought a pregnancy in Ariel--a development which pleased her very much. She and Abram were very excited about it. Lord came to the both of them to instruct them in his wishes for the child and them.

For two days Lord was with them and imparted to them these enunciations.

"You shall know that I am Lord and thee shall have no other Lord before me; you shall cleave to my commands and live a chaste life as I instruct you in what foods you may eat, what animals are clean and unclean, what utensils you may use in preparation of meals, what plants you are to avoid and which are poisonous."

"You shall not make graven images or idols or pray to them, as these are not of your Lord's favor and to do so will be regarded as blasphemous. You, in all things, in heaven and earth, shall have no other Lord's or God's before me because I am a jealous god and will not brook disobedience."

"I will rain down iniquity upon those who betray me for that is fresh in my history."

"For those that love me my mercy is and shall be endless."

"You shall not utter or reveal my name nor hold my name in vain, nor speak it in unclean circumstance or among yourselves in conversation or secret thought."

"You shall make one day of every seven for my worship where you shall remind yourselves of these commandments and your duties to obey the word I have given you."

"You shall avoid the sins of the cities, the towns and villages for within them multiple temptations abound and there live the fallen."

"You shall not kill."

"You shall not steal."

"You shall not bear false witness against thy neighbor."

"You shall not commit adultery, or covet thy neighbor's wife, thy neighbor's goods or his wealth or his house or his animals."

"You shall honor thy earthly father and mother."

"You shall prepare an altar of unhewn stone in my name and make upon it burnt offerings of sheep and oxen. In approaching my altar and places of worship thou shall cover thy head against nakedness which offends me in my places of prayer."

"These are my words, Lord said, "these are my commandments and I place upon you the task of seeing they are observed among you and your progeny."

Abram and Ariel took these words to heart and taught them to their children and their children's children, saying "Lord had given these laws and placed them upon those he has chosen to do his work on Earth.

Lord, as well, gave to Ariel and Abram, ten thousand newly created women and men. He gave them herds, animals, and implements and pressed upon them that their life was to be without sin. Their life was to be one of piety. They, as children of God, were not to be tempted by the Lilim, or Lucifer or Lilith or the Canaanites who dwelled in the cities and towns because theirs was an impure life.

Lord's apparition came before them as they as gathered for dispersal and said "You are the children of Lord," Lord said, "your lot is not to be an easy one but one more rewarding. I will, in due time, take from this Earth these city sinners and apply to them their just due. Do not crave the wealthy life or the life of grubby tradesman; retain your hold upon the land since that it the way of independence. Heed my Law that I have given you remembering your Lord is with you."

With that thousands and their animals, began their dispersement to the North, South, East and West. Lord was sure they would give competition to Lilith and Lucifer's minions of a similar number.

These ten thousand were the twelve tribes of Israel.

Chapter 30

Lucifer and Lilith looked on this spectacle of thousands of Lord's adherents moving out across the Earth's terrain.

Lucifer spoke, "See how he equips them to most effectively form a sea of pastoralists who will surround us in our cities and cut off our supply lines in the conflict that will surely come. We shall have trade routes, but these will have to cross lands they occupy. It is wise for us to dominate the seas and rivers least we be strangled in our quest to prosper and grow. And we must be sure to keep the land and sea shipping lanes open."

Lilith said, "Yes, let us make a map of their traversings such that our strategic choices will be most meaningful in countermanding Lord's strangulation plan. My, he is clever. But, ere, and I speak most clearly here, we must, as well, plan for the inevitable clash of war coming for as these populations expand at a similar rate the result will be a bottle neck at some place and arms will come to the fore. There will be clashes on land or sea or both."

In days, thereafter, Lilith made a pact with the Canaanites to match their ten thousand number to those Lord brought to the field and to have them to settle in areas close to Lord's minions. They were told to build walls around the great cities close to the supply routes and to prepare for war.

Chapter 31

All of this took place in the nine generations after Adam. The Lilim and the Canaanites sought to quickly build while Lord's minions took the nomadic life. Both sides viewed the other warily and their paths criss-crossed frequently. None of this went smoothly for Lord's disciples.

There were nine generations after Adam in which Lord saw Abram, Ariel and Seth move to minister to the thousands he had created for them and their progeny. Those generations included the generations of Enos, Cainan, Mahalalell, Jared, Enoch, Methuselah, Lamech, and that of Noah.

But it was that over these generations there was unrest among the descendants of Ariel and Abram. They chafed under the severe requirements Lord placed upon them. It was clear that many were defecting from the faith to take to the cities listening to Lucifer's entreaties to abandon the hard life of the desert. The tens of thousands had become over two million in nine generation's time, scattered from Ur to Egypt and to Sidon in the east. It became clear from the first that city dwellers and the nomadic peoples of Abram, Seth and Ariel were destined to clash. It was clear that Lucifer's cites were great temptations.

In the very first generation of Enos, the human creatures Lord placed upon the Earth after Abram and Ariel began to name themselves "Lord," and "King," and made idols of gold and silver which had been strictly forbidden by Lord. More, they took Lord's name in vain making of its utterance a swear word and an unclean thing. And most disappointing to Lord, even as they engaged in sexual activities, they called out his name. Disheartened Lord watched becoming more and more restive.

He called Enos of the second generation to him to discover the origin of these trends.

"Lord," Enos said, "they cry out to me that Adam, himself, has used thy name in vain and they see no harm of it. More, they proclaim that you, Lord yourself, have said that we are all made in your image and therefore, partake too, of the divine spark within. They see no harm in making it known that their piety comes from you, from your words and from your example."

Lord, was not persuaded by this rationale and told Enos that his word had been written clear. There was to be Lord said "no circumventions and clever evasions."

Enos said, "By the example of my father, Seth, I shall, convey these words."

Enos told the people of Lord's wishes as they gathered in his town by the well. He told them that Lord was unhappy with them; that he wanted them to repent and re-new their faith, that they should abandon the worship of idols, things of wealth and the sinful life.

At first the people complied but this soon lagged with the passage of time, until there was a full relapse and many returned to their blasphemous ways.

Kenan was the son of Enos. He viewed his father's obedient ways with Lord to be outmoded. He was openly defiant of Lord's way, building a handsome house for himself as a tradesman. He held the pastoral life in contempt favoring the more lucrative trades of the city. He built himself a small business working metal and doing blacksmith contracts for arms and swords.

He was hammering at his anvil when Lord appeared and inquired of him, "Why have you rejected my wishes and flaunt my desires for thee? Have thou not piety enough or fear enough to heed the warnings I have sent by your father. Why Kenan? Do you have in you the genetic stain of Cain from three generations ago; has that seed infected you and made of you a rebel? Have you not heard that I have promised to destroy all of mankind in this world if my words are not heeded? Tell me what your mind in this is? Do my words have impact upon you?"

Kenan stood by, fashioning his plate of metal. Having been there when his father, Enos, spoke with Lord in the past, Kenan was not afraid of Lord, although many would have been afraid. He had not fear.

"Lord," he said, "I have heard, your words, but I see that our enemies amass all around us huge fortunes in trade with which they use to buy arms, to some day utilize in attacking us. I have built me here a home of metal against that day, which I can see will surely come. Such as it is, I have built a fortress to protect my family and keep them from harm and, I make available to our people, arms with which to defend themselves against that future clash sure to come. To me Lord, this seems prudent and is not meant to exhibit any disrespect for you or your strictures."

"Your words, Kenan," Lord said, "come smoothly and carry a persuasive air, but in your presentation, you have clearly made a substitution of your judgment over mine. This is a rendering of you my creature, placing yourself on the same plane as I--nay, above. Am I to turn from this, allowing your example to persist among human kind?"

But Kenan would not relent and said to Lord, "I am not able to see Lord kindness in the threat to destroy the world in a flood, as I have heard, drowning our women, and indeed, the children."

Lord took his leave of Kenan that day and continued to remind all of his displeasure with many of them. As the Diluvium Day approached, he saw that Kenan had constructed a metal bell in his workshop. Lord spoke to him, "What Kenan is this machine you work upon? Have I knowledge of its purpose?"

Kenan spoke tersely, "Lord, this is a diving bell which will hold my family and I and enough oxygen in it to survive the flood you have prophesized. It was the only devisement I could conceive which might allow me to protect them."

Lord looked on, his anger rising; but he paused and spoke deliberately. "I see you mean to defy me is this and other things continuously?"

"Not defy Lord, but I am taking some initiatives to protect the things I love."

Kenan did proceed to build his diving bell and came the flood he did sink beneath the waters inside the diving bell to await the end of the flood. All in side could hear the thrashing of the waters that day and felt secure. Lord looked upon this and gave Kenan and his kin bladder infections such that he and his kin, in the diving bell beneath the waves, drowned in their own urine.

**

137

Mahalalell and Jared, in the two generations before the flood, did please Lord although the trends Lord saw continued among the descendents of Adam. He decided in the Enoch generation to lose upon them a plague such that they might know his displeasure and the seriousness of their violations. He sought out Enoch to apprize him of this and to rescue him from the plague by bringing him on high to be with him, Lord.

He spoke to Enoch and said, "Enoch, I have a bitter disappointment in human kind and plan for their demise. I look upon you as one of most pious, though even you I see are sometimes seduced by the sinful life and the temptations of the devil demons. What say you to this?"

Enoch said, "It is true, Lord. I am not above reproach for relapses happen to me more often than they should. Demons like Azazel, the goat-man, appear to me and make such reasoned words which, in that moment, make sense to me, and I forget where my bearings lay. I am pressed, Lord, to stay the course when all about me others are abandoning the course you have set and laid for them."

At the mention of Azazel, Lord grew angry. "Azazel," Lord said, "was once one of my high Council members and he and his fellow angels did fall among the humans on Earth, did marry among their women, taught my people warfare and weapons, taught the women mirrors, and cosmetics, made men to be animals of violence, sloventry, and vileness. He passed to my people, astronomy, astrology and mathematics, prematurely, telling mankind by virtue of these knowledges they had become as Gods themselves."

"Yes, Lord," Enoch said, "it is true. The fallen angels you righteously threw down from heaven for offenses now wreck havoc among us. They have raped our women and the spawn of that union with our Earth women, these Nephilim, grow larger in number everyday and pollute our ways. The demon Goat-man, Azazel, has with him now thousands of these Nephilim and as well, thousands of the fallen angels you cast down to Mount Hermon. They have emerged from that place to teach men how to make knives, and shields for wars. They have engaged and practiced witchcraft, Lord. They have made a course for

138

men and women to follow—a path of wickedness. I am unable, Lord, despite my attempts, to put an end to this blaspheming. Even now Azazel's leader, Samyaza, boasts that Lord is weak in influence among his own people."

It was also that Samyaza's and Azazel's activities on Earth did cause a rift between Lilith and Lucifer. Lilith was outraged because these fallen angels had the visage of the Gargoylim which for Lilith evoked terrible memories of their despoliation of the Lilim. More, in their hideous appetites, they had the habit of grappling the Lilim, who were a mild people under Lilith's protection, and eating them over roasting fires as the Gargoylim had done.

She said to Lucifer, "These fallen ones are the Gargoyles returned, war-like and hideous, they have, like their former brothers, taken to cannibalism and eat my people; and more of this I will have no truck. I will strike them down. They have sought to hide their ugly faces by intermarrying with Earthly maids, but that has only produced a hybrid race of Gargoylim of prettier face. This must be stopped!"

"But Lilith," Lucifer said, "why would we intervene if Lord's own acts here decimate the ranks of his own adherents, not just Lilim? Lord now speaks of genocide and wiping out all of his unfaithful kind and starting over again after plague and flood. Why intervene here, which by God's acts and those of his unfaithful, are careening them all straight toward self-destruction?"

Lilith said, "We cannot be sure that Lord will follow through on this or merely be content with threats, and besides," Lilith said, "there will sure be survivors among the humans and Nephilim as well, not to mention Azazel's lot. They are hardy demons and may likely emerge alive even if weakened. No, we must make it certain that each and every one of them is dead and done to protect the Lilim. That is my design. I will gather forces to confront their numbers. It will not be easy. It is stated they number in the six hundred thousands."

Lucifer lost his patience. "This is folly, Lilith, even if amassment is successful, six hundred thousand of our brethren, and your Lilim will be placed at risk and for an enterprise which has no guarantee of success and one which will surely see our forces emerge less strong for it and most certainly weakened. Lord could easily, if he gets notice of our plan, hold his hand on the flood and see us weakened from battle within. Nay, I cannot consent to this plan."

"Consent, Lilith said coldly. "I am not meaning here to request consent--yours or that of any other. I mean to set my course and make this so"

Lucifer, now very angry, shouted, "Lilith, do not defy me in this. Do not do this!"

Lilith turned upon Lucifer and said coldly. "Are you my master?"

Lilith gathered her Lilim, but, many among them were afraid. Nagreb, their leader, said to Lilith in conference, "We have suffered here, a terrible toll. The fallen ones, giants they are, many fifteen feet tall, raid our towns and villages, rape our women and steal our food. The fallen ones made us give tribute to them in crops and animals from our herds.

They threatened that if anyone spoke of this they would return and burn our villages to the ground. They made babies with our women and had them come and live among us such that we could not reject them as our own children, and such was the mix we could not tell their spawn from ours until it was too late. We now have Nephilim among us but none can tell which is which except by the memory of the old ones."

Lilith was much surprised by the rapidity with which all of this had transpired. "How," she said, "did happen so quickly?"

"They use magic and witchcraft, your Highness, so as to have the children mature quickly and before we could adjust, hundreds, nay thousands were fully grown, confronting us."

Lilith said, "All of this reinforces the need for all the tribes to gather to arms for surely the hour-glass runs toward empty. I will have them at the drilling field in two Ticks time. I will give them instruction in the plan to make the assault upon the Nephilim stronghold where they have made a coalition with Azazel at Mount Hermon.

Tell them to cast aside fear because only by cleaving together victory shall be ours."

In the interval between the two Ticks, Lilith went to the Canaanite leaders, descendents of Cain, and made with them a conference. "I have come to enlist your arms to join with mine to rid this land of the Azazel scourge, and with my Lilim, make sure my prophecy that victory will be ours. You Canaanites have force of arms and I have a confidence that you will acquit yourselves well on the battlefield."

The Canaanites had a group of council leaders, twelve in number. One of them rose to speak for all. "We have suffered under the fallen ones, and have seen our people and our lands despoiled. Thus, we have great empathy for the mission upon which you are embarked. We have had our women secreted away never to return. But Lilith, Highness, we have retreated to the mountain caves and made our defenses there such that the demon hordes and the Nephilim have not be able to penetrate. Most have settled for a stalemate and have left the majority of us in peace. We are now adequately protected."

"Besides, Lilith, as you are full well aware, Lucifer has not acquiesced in this maneuver by us; in fact, he has warned us clearly not to become involved in this Azazel venture of yours. Makem, another Canaanite leader, spoke slowly, "he warned us not to join you in this least we risk his unforgiving anger."

"Am I to understand that he warned you not to cooperate with me in any way?" Lilith inquired.

"He did." Makem said.

Lilith peered into each face in the room to see both fear and anticipation of her words. In some she saw the hope that she would be able to convince the fearful ones to join her in her quest. In others she saw defiance.

"I," she began, "was exiled here by Lord many eons ago and sought with Lucifer to take this place from the hell it was meant to be by Lord, and make of it a paradise fit for living. You, the Lilim, and others are the product of our effort in this. I had in all these Glicks but one aim—to secure on this Earth an enduring peace. I have in times past had to make terrible judgments but always the aim I sought was in that measure, to make a place for the peaceful, and, yes, the meek to lay their heads down at night and not have to wonder if their children would taken away and eaten, not to have to wonder if their very lives hung at the whim of powerful ones far and near. My goal is and continues to be to support those who chafe under the decrees of tyrants and those who countenance enslaving others for specious grandiose dreams. Our people have the capacity for peaceful functioning, and distaste for a stratified slave existence. Eschewing this life," she said "brings to us true independence. My statement, then and now, is: free will is not free if it is has no meaning to the individual."

"We should not allow the pretensions of class, hierarchy, wealth and hierarchy suck from us our life blood. You Canaanites and rebels must surely in your heart of hearts think this is as I do."

Despite their fear, the Canaanites were stirred by Lilith's words and agreed to join her in the offense at Mount Hermon.

Lucifer soon got word of that development and convened his lieutenants. He said to them "What am I to make of this defiance? Am I am to thrust my love for her down and raise my sword against she who is, she who has been all these eons—my love, my only love? Has she, in motivating this, said as much to me? Has she spoken by her deeds—that those leather bonds of intimacy—have snapped in her eyes? Thereby, I am flung away from her and all we have shared?" How much in this is rank betrayal, how much is misguided affinity for her Lilim? How much oft this is rebel seed which she and I shared that long ago against Lord has come home to roost here? Will all rebels' fate be to teach rebellion to their own progeny and future generations? And what in this dizzy mix shall be my proper response? How can I, in the extreme choice, raise my sword against her and strike her full in the heart and kill the thing I loved most—for dead principle, for form and power's maintenance?"

No requiem, Lucifer thought, is sadder than requiems for family; no beast of retribution uglier than the beasts born of the same blood that turn upon one another."

Azazel came and spoke to Lucifer, "Lord, there is in this survival at stake. Lilith, pardon my own observation in this, was more loyal to the Lilim than to you Sire. And surely she gave little support to you in your attempt to rise up the Lukim, who now lie abandoned in the caves. It is only my view sire. Where goes loyalty which is only one sided?"

Lucifer took his hand to his forehead. "We have been long on this planet and I keep getting this splitting pain in the head. Too long here, I fear means we are more and more subject to the foibles of the humans and others here. My mind fogs, more and more. My origins dim. Perhaps, this is Lord's ultimate revenge."

"My aim in this becomes clear. Lilith and I no longer share the same vision for this place. After sifting through all the conjugations there is one disgorged at the other end—she must not love me enough to cause her to pause or to allay her course. By these acts has her sword's thrust pierced my heart, and she has given to it, a further cruel twist."

"Gather the arms—we prepare for the struggle against her."

Chapter 32

Lilith's plan was tri-fold. Her offensive was to be against the human hybrids, the Nephilim who in intermixing with humans made it difficult to identify and dispatch them. Therefore, she could not know who was foe and who was enemy. In the battle to come, Nephilim could suddenly appear in human form as Azazel's reinforcements. This could cause confusion in her ranks and her stalwarts would not know they were enemy until those human-looking stalwarts turned to Gargoyle minions arrayed against them.

In the time before the battle, Lilith had her minions to spread among the Nephilim to gather intelligence as to what sign identified the Nephilim. They found there was, indeed one; the pentagram. Her order was to have each and every one with the pentagram marking dispatched on the day before the battle so as to deny Mount Hermon reinforcements and Trojan horses.

A second part of the plan was to gather the eggs from Nephilim women thereby eliminating new births among them. Finally, she had thousands of her own personal demons come to the Nephilim men in the night and take from them their raw seed such that they, too, would lose their capacity for reproduction.

All this was done days before the battle.

**

On the day of the battle itself, Lilith stood surveying her assembled hordes. She saw the sons of Cain on the plains before her and inspected them for their readiness. They had indeed learned warfare techniques from the Nephilim more so than Lilith had realized.

"Show me your shinning blades!" Lilith importuned them.

They in their hundreds of thousands shouted, "Cahch!" which was the Canaanite war-cry.

"Show me your flaming sticks!" Lilith shouted and there arouse thousands of flaming sticks which Azazel had shown the Nephilim how to produce, which the

Canaanites had adopted and had used to defend themselves.

"Make ready your flags," she said, "stiffen your resolve because this day we march to the Mount of Hermon. Lilim and Canaanites shall together shoulder to shoulder, avenge the wrongs done us here; take back our women and children wronged, and take back our grain stores filched, such that we might survive lean seasons where we have no crops or food."

"For these," Lilith said, "we fight!" The assembled army began its march toward Mt. Hermon.

Now, it was that at the head of the marching column Lilith recognized Armel a great, great granddaughter of Ariel who sat up her saddle and made her salute as Lilith approached.

"It is good to see you, Armel, descendent of Ariel, I knew your great, great grandmother!"

"I am here," Armel said, "in support of this and her memory. I heard in my childhood many stories she told of you."

"Fate is ours," Lilith said in acknowledgement.

Chapter 33

The fallen angel band on Mount Hermon had made a fortress 500 cubits high. They had a secret water supply and had stores of food against a protracted siege. Lilith knew, too, that they, from their great height above the plain below, would have the advantage that height brings for the downward flight of their arrows and missiles which would gather deadly velocity once loosed from on high. She knew, as well, that Lucifer had sent Lukim into the fortress to support the Nephilim ensconced there. Their numbers were unknown.

The fortress had come to symbolize for Lilith all that she despised in the Azazel trend. This is where Lord, in tossing these fallen angels down to Earth, set loose consequences which, in train, threatened all peoples living there. It was not just the war and mayhem they brought to Earth. These fallen angels, with their superior powers, created the death and destruction and spread its techniques among the humans. It was their thirst for conquest and their teaching Earth people the habits of war which had the greatest impact. The teaching of arms to one group demanded greater and greater arms as group after group was drawn into an arms race. Each side was in a struggle to build larger fortresses and more deadly arms. The fallen ones introduced the need for labor to build these forts, monuments and cities prompting one neighbor to enslave another neighbor to get them built.

It brought, too, cause for the accumulation of wealth solely for the purpose of arms- making and, ultimately, subjugation and more vile, slavery. All this she saw happening in the cities Lucifer and the Nephilim built where striation ran amok with Pharaohs, Kings, servants, slaves, and concubines. All this Lilith was full in rebellion against even as Azazel, then the Nephilim, became Lucifer's converts. Many humans too fully embraced city-building, self-regarding monuments, cruel human sacrifices, and degradations without number. Atop these structures, many millions were martyred in numbers that often exceeded those lost in a full out war. It was, she thought, the scourge of the priesthood and kings and the end of strict equality that threatened to destroy what she had sought to build from wilderness Earth.

Lilith could see that these developments would destroy everything already begun.

Lucifer had, too, reinforced this development. He, in her mind, had changed to become a warlord selling arms to both sides in the many conflicts, enjoying this new role of scourge-bringer to the minions of Lord. He was willing to sacrifice all in this in his battle with Lord. Lilith was not willing to do that.

This, then, was an assault upon not just the mountain fortress but her decision to break with Lucifer and Lord. The direction both had come to embrace ended in a ceaseless war. A crossroad here was clear. There was no going back. The Lilim gave her a scared name, Asherah which could not be uttered ever out loud.

She ordered the first ranks of her battalions to advance and to draw upon themselves the first bursts of fire from the mountain top. They were then to retreat and await her next order. The purpose of this was to test the positions of the arrow-throwers, to identify how many and where they were located on the mountain. She was ready.

Chapter 34

At the base of the mountain, on the plain, Lilith advanced, at first with only twelve columns of men and women so as to allow the Azazel's forces to underestimate the true strength of the forces arrayed against them. Lilith had them advance at a very slow pace to draw fire from above.

The Canaanites shouted their war cry, "Cathch!" Cathch!" with each forward step. The Lilim swayed from side to side as they advanced, their formations were square and this done by thousands made them a moving target for the arrows.

Atop the mountain, Samyaza, Azazel, and their ten chiefs in council surveyed the plain below having received word of the impending attack. They were making their last minute plans after surveying the strength and formations of the army assembled below them.

Samyaza, their leader, peered down with Azazel at his side and the ten chiefs of council and heard a General state: "We have counted 200,000 angels and humans with 100,000 in reserve," General Rajob said. He was a burly Gargoyle who once held the rank of Arch Angel who was cast down with Samyaza's early group. "We can dispatch these with little harm to our selves Lord," he said.

Azazel, said, addressing Samyaza, "Sire, I am told there is a schism between Lucifer and Lilith in this and she initiates this confrontation without his support. I would surmise she has only these fighters and probably only a few more in reserve. We command the heights and she will find our fire and arrows will rain down and blot out the very sky. Their force will wither and become immobilized under our assault. We then can flank them with our reserves as they lie flat in defense. Then we deal them the coup de grace—perhaps even take Lilith as our prisoner."

"We shall," Samyaza agreed, "deploy them-post haste."

Lilith sat her white steed giving survey to the scene, her heart repelled by the ugly faces she could see of Samyaza and Azazel who perched high above her on the mountain rim.

She spoke to her forces, "We are embarked here on a great battle where history on this planet is to be made. You all, all of you, have at stake here, the future we envision or we succumb to one the Nephilim envision. Shall that future be one of war, evil, cannibalism, fear, damnable treachery, or shall we create here a place where the peaceful may live without fear, without endless war, retributions, feuds, and exacted vengence after exacted vengeance. We stand against the former; we fight for the latter. We give our lives for this."

"Lilim," Lilith said, "let me say, and future generations may record, that evil was in this place atop Mount Hermon and we rooted it out; ground it down into the dust of the Earth such that our children and their children's children may be safe."

She raised her sword and shouted, "Fail me not! Fail me not!"

Even as she spoke, the sky filled with flying demons from the mountain top swooped down among her troops frightful terrors, their demon eyes bulging large, their fearful claws in gripping mode grasping at Lilith's front line troops to make of them an example. They snatched at Lilim heads with bloody claws and grappled them from Lilim torsos and flew the heads high only then to toss the bloody heads back into the faces of those below. Shrieks were heard everywhere.

Immediate terror was the effect but Lilith shouted to the front ranks to "Hold steady!" she said. "They have shot their best arrows, we have endured the worst, hold steady; use your shields to protect the man next to you. Pick the arrows out and toss them back!"

She committed then her sally force of angel flyers and their canisters of gas she last used on high. They flew straight to the crest of the mountain into the innermost ranks of Azazel and Samyaya who had not expected an aerial assault. Lilith had identified their bunker atop the mountain and ordered her angels to gas the bunkers inserting gas between the observation slits. Samyaya and Azazel were horrified at the diving squads which planted their deadly gas full-square in the bunkers where the high council itself had gathered to observe what all had before hand thought was to be a sure rout.

They fled as thousands of the winged ones dropped amongst them, gas bombs. Azazel and Samyaya's group made a number an attempts to leave the bunkers at the back end, only to be greeted there by still more angels from the air whose deadly cargo landed among them laying flat. All heads turned to watch because it became clear that the true objective of the battle was not the troops massed below but the small leadership group above. It was clear that, if Samyaza and Azazel and their compatriots were killed, the others on Mount Hermon would surrender, or turn and run.

So swift was the gas delivered that, stunned, all sought in the obscured scene to see who among the leadership had survived behind the gas clouds. It was clear after minutes passed, that all who had stood there moments ago had been dispatched or disappeared. There was from that high perch no direction given to the troops below and the Mt. Hermon contingencies simply stood motionless and leaderless.

It was a stunning contemplation since this battle had been initiated and won is less than one Earth hour.

On the plain below, thousands of the confused Samyaza forces surrendered easily, confused and disorientated. Lilith surveyed them in their surrounded group. Most were afraid, although some were still defiant. There were in their tens of thousands. Her commanders told her that it was possible that some Nephilim had escaped through an underground back passage and Lilith instructed they should be pursued. "I will take the mountain," she said, "and see what is left of the demon leadership."

Chapter 35

Now at the summit, Lilith assured herself that the demon leadership was done or gone and, ordered that the inner caves of the mountain be searched for food, water and hiding combatants.

She took all the Nephilim hybrids from the battle field and ordered that each and every one to be executed, and further, their family seed be made dead in the female wombs and that the seed of the men be sterilized. She then ordered that the same be done with the Lukim soldiers who had joined them.

As she spoke, she received word that an inner sanctum of the fallen ones had been discovered and that she should come to see the terrible deeds which had transpired there.

There was in the mountain center a large crater which had been hollowed out by a past volcanic eruption forming a natural amphitheater. But centermost in this theater, which was 250 cubits high and 150 cubits wide, was a mountain of bones fully 150 high and 75 across--the cannibalistic remains of Lilim eaten, tortured and tossed aside there.

The Lilim wailed, stuck down by grief and their cries echoed through the surrounding mountains.

**

Lord was completing his talk with Enoch when word came of the defeat of the Samyaza and Azazel, the fallen angels at Hermon.

The courier said, "Lord, her Angel hordes directly descended upon the demon command council and dispatched them all in a group with their gas bombs. It was a fierce, brief battle because when Nephilim hordes saw their leader's dead, they surrendered or fled. Many now, I understand, are being tracked down by Lilim forces; apparently Lilith means to have each and every one, demon and Nephilim destroyed."

Lord said, "These angel-demons of Lilith are fearsome indeed. But, Enoch," he said turning to Enoch again, "I'll not at this news, veer from my prime concern which is the conduct of my people and the faithful."

"I have seen," Lord said "that you are a pious man, yet even you have been tempted by the Devil-Lucifer and his kind. My heart grieves at what is happening among my creations there in the Earth space. All is chaos and grinding sin, whist the forces of Lucifer and Lilith run amuck unregulated. No matter, I shall exact a remedy to make the people aware of my displeasures in all of this, but for now hear me. "You, Enoch, I shall raise on high and I shall punish the unfaithful below with a plague. Then we shall see if there is a reformation among them."

And there was on Earth, at this time, these momentous occurrences: Lilith sought to establish the hegemony of the Lilim in a peaceful place while protecting them from periodic assaults from Lucifer. Lucifer now joined with remnants of the Nephilim bands and scattered Gargoyle groups, who had managed escape from the Mount Hermon battle to regroup. They fled seeking to disperse quickly across the land before Lilith forces could hunt them down for their dispatch.

Lucifer maintained his grand goal of dispersing his minions along Earth's great rivers teaching his city builders secrets of war, witchcraft, astronomy, astrology and metal working. He promised many that if they gave him his due, they could learn in time the secrets of *immortality*, as well. The quest for immortality among men became Lucifer's most salient selling point among them.

Lord, as he promised, loosed among his adherents a fearsome plague. There the flesh of the skin was made to pus from head to toe in blisters, putting the victim in agony. To walk or sit caused huge globs of skin to drop from face or eyelids or other parts of the body, pulled down by gravity or the slightest movement. Enoch watched his former friends die horribly and the suffering was so great he went to Lord who had raised him on high and asked for leniency.

Enoch said, "Lord you have brought me to this high place to sit along side you in a place of honor. For this I am grateful. You are a merciful Lord, and I am acutely aware that when I was on Earth, I was not a perfect one, nor were my friends and those who allowed themselves to be tempted toward the unclean, who abandoned their birthright which is obedience to the ways you have designated. But, I pray you, Lord, to understand these are imperfect beings and they are buffeted in that wilderness by hardships and the temptations of Lucifer and his kind press upon them. Spare them further suffering in this, grant them mercy, alleviate the suffering the plague visits upon them. Allow them surcease."

Lord said, "Enoch, I am resolved in this; spare the rod, spoil the child, and we would only come again to this same point in the future. I would have double grief as against this singular one. I mean to have an end to endless redemptions and my people below must understand this. I am, in this, without further patience."

A pale moon came upon them in Enoch's hometown; there was then seen a green gas settling at each door and one could hear from within, screams as the gas took hold in the lungs of those within. In this Lord was unrelenting until each and every soul in Enoch's old city lay down dead or dying.

Lord, received a prayer, offered to him from a nearby town which called up to him from an prayer altar pleading, "Please, Lord, spare us more suffering from this terrible plague, we are not yet struck but see its beginnings here as well. Please, Lord, relent. We have all pledged to change our ways and to go out among the people and seek their redemption in your name. Please spare our town."

Lord spoke to them and said, "I have given you, my Earthly creations, my best intents, but you as a race, have violated all of them. I have given you my blessings and ask only that you keep the covenants and, lo, I see that these are disrespected and set aside in your judgments, demonstrating by this, that you know best what my plain words mean."

"I fear that you all have defects born of my own creation and I look to find just one righteous man among you to stay my terrible hand which will rise again and again and slay each among you until there is not a single soul left."

A man stepped up to say, "Lord, Enoch was right, the Devil, Lucifer, set among us the demon Azazel who had worked his witchcraft among us and against our will. He made of us his accomplices. Give us, Lord, your understanding in this. Slay, at least the Nephilim first, such that we have a chance to cleanse ourselves of sin induced by them. This will allow us to return to your flock."

"No." Lord said. "Know this, I am not pleased with you my creations and mean to send a great flood to destroy all of the Earth, so great is my displeasure."

***

Lilith sought the Nephilim, aiming to rid the earth of them. But, the Nephilim were resourceful and went back to the old traditions. They hid themselves in caves from both Lilith and Lord's forces and devised new ways to disguise their young so as to be indistinguishable from the ordinary humans. No one could know if their compatriots were Lilim, Canaanites, or even fallen angel survivors in disguise. Their pentagram marking was not used and they took to secret meetings and to the life of fugitives.

Lilith took a generation in the hunt, but at last she realized that the many intermixings of Nephilim, demons, humans, Lilim, and Lukim was an impossible trend to retract. The act was complete and irreversible.

Chapter 36

The next generations after these events, were the ancestors of Lamech, who was the father of Noah. Lamech was a descendent of Cain who had rebellion in him promoting him to violations of many of Lord's structures. He was the first of Eden's descendents to marry two wives in blatant disregard of, and respect for, the community and Lord's word itself. Lamech spoke openly and favorably of trade, of living in the cities and abandoning the pastoral life for one which would enable the gathering of wealth and a life of ease. He hinted that there was merit in amassing slaves and spoke of the benefits of hierarchy, priesthood, Lords, and Kings.

These were in direct contraction to Lord's decrees which embraced a life which was the opposite of these. Lord called Lamech to explain his ways.

"I do not comprehend why your faith is not strong enough to resist these temptations and nay you preach openly and flaunt my word. What manner of punishment do you imagine, if you were I, would you think this deserves?"

Lamech was unrepentant. "You, yourself, Sire, have said that we on Earth have been given free will, and if so, why punish us if we prove to be precocious students of yours and seek to meld your wisdom with that of others and make of our life here on Earth more bearable? I cannot, in my feeble mind, see where there is a divergence from the base of your teachings. For are we not here to worship you and the make of this life one compatible with the holy ways? And if so, whatever makes that more possible seems to me advisable."

"You have said," Lamech continued "that we are simple shepherds of our herds, that we are the fishermen of the sea and that the city-builders are the sinners and by our very lives surround the sinners ultimately cutting them off as the sea does the land. But I have seen Lord that these city-dwellers have many ideas such that even we, of Lord's way, can learn from and make progress all the more come faster to us and make the hard scrabble life of the desert more bearable."

To Lamech, Lord did not make a reply sensing that his work on planet Earth had gone awry and could not be corrected except with drastic measures.

Lord decided to make his plan for the world known to Noah, Lamech's son. He called Noah before him and said, "I have in my will to destroy the world in a flood of devastating proportion. Noah, tell the people that this will be so and can only be waylaid if, you Noah, can find among them, for my inspection a single other righteous man."

"Lord," Noah said, frightened, "I believe this deed need not be done. But I shall immediately be about this work and bring to you such an individual."

But Noah, as he searched, found that Lord's word had been abandoned, that even as Azazel's minions had been killed, many of the Nephilim had survived to maintain the corruption of the people, teaching them how to make more and more deadly weapons from metal and more alluring cosmetics for the women from antimony, and deadly black magic was introduced among the people. There was, too, sexual transgressions. The spawn of Azazel, from these unions took up sodomy, conducted orgies and debaucheries and other sexual deviances. Noah came back to Lord with his lament. "Lord, I have failed in this mission. I can find no one who meets your requirements."

Lord warned many of the coming flood but there was little heed among the people to correct their sins. The degradations of Azazel had taken root among them even as Azazel himself had been dispatched by Lilith at the battle of Mount Hermon.

Many chided Lord for his promise of a flood and said amongst themselves, "It was not Lord who raised the power against Azazel; it was Lilith who did the deed. Lord, it seems, cares not a wit for what happens here on this Earth. He does not protect us from the degradations of the evil ones."

But prophets did go among them and made the plea to them to mend their ways because retribution sure was to be among them from Lord's wrath.

Lilith knew that Lord would not relent on the promise of a deluge and went among the Lilim and the Canaanites who were much concerned that their support of Lilith at

Mount Hermon would result in Lord singling them out for sure destruction. Lilith addressed their representatives and said, "I have recourse and remedies against this flood to protect you all from the tall waters Lord has promised to come. Gather your animals, your tents, and utensils .I have prepared a place for you at Sela in the high ground. There, I have made the water to flow from irrigation. There you will be safe from the deluge."

The Canaanites and the Lilim were first wary because Sela had become a Nephilim stronghold where they had retreated to after their defeat at Hermon.

Lilith said, "Fear not, we can regain this place and make there to grow a garden. The Nephilim can be defeated there."

Sometimes called Petra, this mountain place had deep meaning because both Azazel's fallen angels had once lived there, as well as Nephilim. It was also the place where Adam and Eve first settled, once out of Eden. Lilith's proposal to make of it a new space for her, Lilim and Canaanites was greeted with wariness.

Lilith said that they should fear not. Petra was to be their refuge from Lord's storm and rains; it was, too, in Lilith's proclamation, that she and Lilim were to inaugurate a new regime on Earth's ground separate from those of Lucifer, Lord and the Nephilim.

"Do not be afraid!" she urged of them.

The group spoke again to Lilith as they prepared to leave for the new home, and said, "We are determined to follow you to the new land, this mountain, upon which our survival rests. In you we place our trust. But know that in doing this, that among us, there are some Nephilim that still exist. We cannot ferret them out, since they have taken from themselves all marks we used to use for this purpose. We may well be, on this transport, accompanied by Nephilim in disguise, latent in their true loyalties and purpose."

Lilith said, "Let us not lift this burden now, even if it may be true. We have weightier-weights to carry as we seek to fix our new home high above the flood.

It was that the caravan of over nine hundred thousand set out East to Sela underneath then gathering clouds and sounds of unrest in the heavens. Their column stretched miles and miles long; it was days before the last set out

157

after the first set foot on the path. Lilith guarded the rear while the Canaanites took the flanks. The Lilim spoke to those in passing towns seeking provisions and water for the horde. Many of the people from these small towns choose to join, fearing Lord's wrath would soon be upon them for their succor of Lilith's hordes.

This proved all too true. Scarcely had the group traveled the first leg of the trip, Lord's apparition appeared before them. The apparition demanded of Lilim's advance group, the circumstances of their march. They told him of the impending flood and their need for shelter.

"Thus, you march as such to avoid my dictum?" Lord demanded. "Know that your Lord will not continence this attempt by Lilith to circumvent what I have decreed." At that moment, many in the Lilim group turned to run in terror from the apparition only to see Lilith come from the rear to confront Lord's apparition speaking in a great shout.

"These are my people and are under my protection. I seek a peaceful passage to our new home far from here."

It was the first time Lord had seen Lilith. She instantly grabbed his heart anew at the mere sight of her. His voice betrayed the emotions within which still resided there. "Lilith, you have first now, after all these eons, come before me, before my visage and you have not changed in mine eyes, in my regard of you. Have you designed to take these people under your protection and seek safe passage for them and intend to shield them against the deluge which even now gathers above us?"

"I do," said Lilith. "It is my plan. These are my people for I have given life to them long ago and I have sheltered them from Samyaza and from Azazel and even now from the flood which you have decreed for the descendents of Adam."

"I see," Lord said. "Your instincts still are attracted toward protecting the meek and mild and in this there is much to admire. What of Lucifer and your divergence from him in this. Is that still in place or has there been, as I have been told, a major schism and fracture?"

Lilith pondered Lord's word for a moment then stepped forward toward His apparition. "I cannot speak of that in this roadside vestibule. Let me say to you straight away, Lucifer has his concerns and I have mine. Now I must go to Sela before these rains you have prophesized wash us from our path."

She wheeled away from the apparition of Lord and showed her back to him. She looked at the faces of those trailing many miles afar. When she turned again to gauge Lord's reaction, his apparition had vanished. She raised her right arm so that all might see and lifted her voice so all could hear, "On, hurry, do not tarry, we must make the mountain by nightfall."

But in short time, the rains had begun in such sheetfulls that many in the caravan were blinded and their frightened animals bolted and left the column and had to be retrieved before progress could begin again.

Lilith moved up and down the trudging line, urging them on in the muddy sand, now turning thick and resistant to any steady progress. "We must," she said "be on the swift. It will be deadly to have the mud stymie us and have us here in the plain at the mercy of the rains."

With a mighty effort, they bent their backs with sloshing donkeys and camels under their already heavy loads laboring mightily.

As they moved, Lilith inspected each situation she encountered telling the Canaanites at one point to abandon some of their loads in order to speed the travel. She counseled the Lilim who, in seeking to save some of their meager treasures had stalled in the gathering mud. She told them to leave these mementos, which she told them, "You'll not need these in your new home."

Battered by the ever-increasing rains, they encountered trees athwart their path which they then had to circumvent. Their tents, poorly packed, began to be swept away by screeching winds; families had to pause to nurture children frightened by the ordeal that, it seemed, grew more dangerous by the interval. "We must not lose heart," Lilith told them, "we will reach our destination; it is destiny."

Suddenly Lucifer appeared, cloven hoofed in front of them on the path to the mountain. As they struggled along, Lucifer set the rushing waters upon them. Lilith could see a mighty wave cresting, move apace across the horizon toward the middle of her marching line. She moved to raise to it a mighty hand and stay its crash downward among the Lilim who would have all been lost or drowned. Lucifer appeared and was angry at this thwarting. He sent logs uprooted from far Lebanon of cedar wood to thrash the milling throngs. Again, Lilith diverted these to allow the passage of her people to proceed.

The mountain, now in sight, she took one of the mighty waves and had it form upon her own body a high road wherein many of the laggards were swept up along this watery sky road forward toward the mountain top. Lilith was able to stash her people in many of the lower mountain caves temporarily, to await the further climb to the main mountain top entrances above.

Lucifer said in a mighty roar "Lilith you have once again earned my enmity, your betrayal will bring to these people destruction and mayhem for generations."

Lilith, laboring with those still arriving at the mountain base, did not look at Lucifer, but kept to her task and said, "That may be Lucifer, but in all things we have our destinies, you have yours, and I have mine. These strings of fate we play out until the thread breaks."

Lilith continued to direct the influx of more thousands against the whipping rain guiding them up along the mountain trails, allowing some to rest in the lower caves and was gratified to see that many, of not most, had survived the deluge and the thunder of Lord's rage and Lucifer's attacks.

But to her horror, on the thrashing waters below, she saw a flotilla of small boats oared by what was clear to her over 100 fallen angels, she guessed. The fallen ones, who had survived thus far, sought the same refuge as she did for her Lilim. She could see their demon eyes and goat faces were mixed with Nephilim humans who stood side by side with their angel demon compatriots clearly bent on scaling the mountain and ejecting Lilith and secure it for their own redoubt.

Lilith called upon her tired warriors, the Canaanite arrow men and her flame throwers, and her own contingency of gas-givers who, upon a mountain ledge, massed for an assault from the approaching fallen angel fleet.

From the deck of the lead boat, a massive demon-angel rose above, his claws and hideous visage stroked the air menacingly and tilted directly toward Lilith and the warriors on the cliff.

"He is their leader, all arrows out the quiver," Lilith ordered. "We must down him sure, and that will blunt the eagerness of his minions and then we shall rout the rest with our flame givers."

But arrows flew and many stuck but the demon leader's fleet kept momentum and the demon leader rose twenty cubits above the fleet unsheathing his claws heading directly toward Lilith meaning to slash at Lilith's throat. Lilith took her short sword and slashed his killing claw. He gave a great shriek and retreated above her several cubits to gather himself for another plunge. Lilith cried, "You shall not have this place, you shall not despoil this ground again."

The demon-leader shrieked and focused again on Lilith's throat to make the deadly thrust with his other claw. As he drew it back for a second attempt, Lilith's long sword did its work while the demon foolishly focused on her short sword. This time her blow was just above his shoulder and his head spat green blood and his eyes bulged while head and torso separated, both falling down the mountain side in a maze of shrieking demon, rock and rubble.

With that dispatch, Lilith ordered her flame-givers to the heights and to hover above the first of the lead ships and make upon them a searing heat. She could see them attempt to launch their arrows against the flame-giver assault, but their attempt in this was of little consequence. Lilith ordered the boats set afire, and once lit, a flaming boat rammed the others setting those, in turn, aflame. Each boat, as it came to ignition, was forced by Lilith's hordes into close formation with the others until many hundreds of boats made one large burning pyre as the Nephilim and the demon-angels floundered in the rising waters--some on the boats seeking to quell the fires. Others drowned in the rising waves. Wave after wave rose over the demon warriors, crashing down until the many disappeared or died in the searing flames of the burning fleet.

Lord sat in his throne, observing this and said "By my word, she is a warrior-demon. But Earth can have only one Lord and I am he. Lilith, I shall have at your weakened force in due time."

"You may in this achieve a minor victory, but I shall reintroduce my earlier curse and by these desserts every child born of these Lilim, 100 shall die until the entire population of them dissipates."

"Lilith," he said, "enjoy this reprieve for in dancing a victory dance you have but ensured only ultimate defeat."

Lilith had no thought of this and sought as she gazed upon the burning fleet, to ensure the remainder of her people, Canaanites, Lilim, and exiled humans seeking refuge with her from Lord's wrath and Lucifer's revenge, would rise to their final secure place at the mountain top.

She urged them up man, woman, and child with encouragement. "Up with you to our haven here. We have in this place history. Here is where Adam and Eve took refuge when ejected from the garden. Here is the place where we shall begin a new nation for the children of peace, the lovers of the land, the mild ones who have the gift of tolerance and patience."

In that first night in the mountain, Lilith assessed the water supply. While the rains were all around and thunder clanged their ears, she sent a platoon of Canaanites deep within caves which lined the Petra amphitheater which was similar to the one they discovered at Mount Hermon.

These caves contained natural shelters and water distilled from steam from past eruptions. This had made in them natural wells from which precious water could be caravanned from deep within the caves to the thirsty population above.

Food was simple—unleavened bread, olives and some oils and this would have to last for the forty days Lord had stated the rains would last.

Chapter 37

But in the fifth day, the Canaanites returned and whisper-announced to Lilith, the news they had discovered. They told Lilith when she was alone of their discovery. "We were in the set of caves on the north face" the Canaanites said "and noticed whiffs of wood smoke and sought therewith its main source proceeding down the vast branch of a crystal cave we had come upon. Stealthily, we heard soft cries and came upon wooden cages lashed together with ropes of hemp and palm leaves, and inside, my Lord, were humans, Lilim, and others. One Lilim cried out to us and told us that all of the Azazel minions had not been killed on Mount Hermon and that they had taken possession of this cave. They raided villages and were using their Lilim and human captives for food, roasting them alive in the cave depths, especially savoring the young ones."

It was to Lilith, a sickness unto her soul. She said abruptly, "Again, the atrocity at Mount Hermon. Gather me my best flame-givers. We shall have at the beasts in the cave. How many you say are ensconced there?"

"About one-hundred I was told." said the man.

Lilith had before her a contingency of about two hundred and cried, "Let none escape alive this day and take care to harm only the evil ones. We shall, this time, leave no survivors." They scrambled to the cave mouth that their guide indicated lead down to the inner chambers.

Down in the early descent there was, as stated, the clear smell of stale of wood smoke and human flesh, sickening to the nostrils. Lilith lead the group and they made their way to an underground fork where the guide waved his arm left to indicate the direction where he had found the cages. Lilith moved quietly, her hand before her mouth, silencing the men and women in the cages who saw her approach. "We are friends, do not speak, least we are discovered."

The men and women covered the mouths of the children as a part of Lilith's advance group stayed with the Lilim and human prisoners to free them from their cages and to take them up to the surface, while Lilith paced on the downward path still deeper into the cave.

Their footfalls were so silent such that they could hear sounds ahead of them as well as above them. The inner cave had niches and smaller caves still which lined the walls of this inner sanctum where the demon-angels held their perches surrounding a great central pit of smoldering fires. From behind a hidden vantage point, Lilith stared out upon this scene, holding her breath against the stench rising from what must have been a central roasting room. There below, sitting on a throne of gold was a demon which Lilith took to be their king. Others sat and beheld him as he poured an incantation into a purple cup. Behind him were several cages of human Lilim clearly about to be sacrificed to the demon lust for blood and flesh.

"I'll have him first," Lilith said indicating the Demon-King. "You take a group to the left," she said to her first lieutenant. "And you take a group to the right and attack from that vantage point. I shall take the King and his throne and have his head as my own to rise up to show the rest that resistance is futile. Now, implement this plan quickly, as a diversion such, that I may have the element of surprise upon the Demon-King."

She pounced from her boulder vantage point, her eyes fixed upon every movement of the Demon-King. As she launched, she could hear her minions began their assault. She rose to a great height and dove straight away toward the startled king, who heard her shouting voice which said mid-flight "You are beasts of vileness and filth. May my sword be visit upon you the just death you deserve."

The startled King put his hand to his sword so as to meet Lilith in mid-air seeking to slash her torso and thereby bring her down. Lilith stopped in mid flight just beyond the swords reach and pounced forward just as the King's sword swung past his center forcing him to expose his chest to Lilith's incoming steel. Lilith thrust him full center and took a second to twist the blade so great her anger but that second was a second in excess because it gave the Demon-King time to backhand his blade and strike Lilith in her side even as she retrieved her blade from his bleeding chest.

Unfelt, the slash held no pain and Lilith was to her next move. She cut the demon's head asunder and watched it fall to his feet as his torso slumped back onto his throne. But the blow to his head from Lilith's sword began to bleed. She stabbed it with her sword and it rolled away into the pit of fires...

She turned from the dead beast to see that the other demons were being dispatched by her army of two hundred easily. But then she was overtaken by faint and dread fatigue as blood gushed from her wound. She thought to herself as she felt it; the Demon-King has laced his sword with poisoned oils.

Chapter 38

Lucifer, too, took measures in the flood to protect large contingencies of Nephilim and remnants of Samyaza's and Azazel's armies. The deluge threatened to wash them as well to oblivion in Lord's plan.

He had prepared a place for them inside a hollow mountain to the North of Canaanite territory, where food and water supplies were plentiful. It was a march of fifteen days with several hundred thousand of them under Lucifer's command. He had with him Canaanites who acted as guides, who provided them with the location of water holes along the way.

But Lord was upon them soon after the convoy had begun—bent on their destruction before they reached any safety point. Lord inflicted upon them grievous losses numbering in the tens-of-thousands and Lucifer had to sit with his councilmen to plan for their survival for the rest of the trip.

Speaking to them Lucifer said, "Lord has inflicted harm upon us, in this, there is no doubt. Nonetheless, we must persist. We are only five days out from our hollow mountain where we shall be safe against the floods. But hear my plan for the remaining time. Go to the human towns and take from them women and children and place them scattered among our ranks to lessen Lord's willingness to take their lives along with ours. He may not be affected a wit but this is something we must try."

It was done— and the humans were dispersed, but to no effect. Lord's wrath upon the marchers continued unabated. At night of the last day before they would reach the mountain top, Lucifer's minions were starved of food and water.

"Will there be at the mountain top food enough forty days of flood and rain as you Lucifer promised? Will we sit mountain perched and die slowly of starvation? We ask, Oh Lucifer, to take up with us these humans as hedges against lack of food and eat of them as we may need, as our ancestors did?"

Lucifer sighed a deep sigh and part of him was secretly repelled by this suggestion and part of him relished the thought, and humans were to become the food fodder his contingency would need to survive in their tenure on the mountain.

Chapter 39

Lord came to Noah in the waning days of the deluge and said to him, "Noah I have prepared for you a landing spot atop Mt. Arafat. You should prepare to found my new race upon the Earth there."

Noah emerged from the Ark and Lord made the animals to disseminate upon the Earth to make new life. He told Noah that he was to repopulate, to be fruitful, and multiply upon the Earth.

"But how," Noah asked, "is this to be achieved Lord? We are not many, in humans or animals."

"You shall," Lord said, "benefit from my decree now pronounced and from my new covenant with you.

"Here me Noah," Lord said, "I shall lift the curse upon the soil and you and your progeny can now sow grapes to make wine and grow olive trees and harvest figs such that you in these activities may produce ample harvests. My curse upon the ground ends with this, my pronouncement."

"You may say, as well, Noah that I, Lord, am repentant of having killed all living things and that I will not ever again destroy every living thing as I have done in this deluge. You may eat meat, too, from this day forward since its nourishments shall be important for you and yours."

"You may eat of the green plants," Lord said, "as once was done in the garden. But of this," Lord said, "you are forbidden to eat flesh with its life, that is, still with its blood and you are forbidden to eat the flesh of human kind."

"In all of this you may not kill, murder or cause life to cease in another human being. This is my covenant with you and as a sign I shall set into the sky rainbows so that all may see and be reminded of its existence."

Noah was the tenth generation from Adam and had position as the middle ancestor for the ten generations succeeding from the time of the flood to the birth of Abraham. These ten generations after Noah were the generations of Arphaxed, Salah, Eber, Peleg, Reu, Serug, Nahor, Terah, and finally that of Abraham.

With each, Lord sought to impress upon them piety. Some complied and Lord was pleased in them. These latter included Aprhaxed, son of Noah, Salah whose piety was such, his example became the example for of all Islam in matters of prayer.

Peleg's time period, was one when the sons of Noah divided among themselves the regions of the Earth for administration of Lord's word. But this resulted in wars among these sons and a reversion to behavior Lord frowned upon.

Eber found favor with Lord and he is credited with giving the Hebrews their name.

But Serug, Hahor and Terah did not find favor with Lord since Serug abandoned belief in Lord altogether, and taught the people to believe in idols. His son was taught by him, witchcraft, which caused Lord great grief.

It was in the time of Abraham that Lord looked again at the covenant with Noah to see what direction he would proceed with his minions on Earth.

Chapter 40

Lilith, in the generations from Noah to Abraham, lay ill from the poisoned sword of the demon king, a poison she learned had been given him by Lucifer.

The poison had intent not only to kill her but failing that to initiate a process whereby Lilith's immortality would be slowly drained from her ending in her death as an ordinary human. The poison was, also aimed at Lilith's beauty; to cause her to age in form and face, something previously, with Lilith, had not been the case.

Lucifer appeared above the mountain to pronounce further, "I have placed upon you all, followers of Lilith, further evidence of my powers. All of you would do well to consider joining us against Lord. All you who follow Lilith shall have for every child born, one hundred to die. In this way your spawn shall never grow and you shall be encased in this mountain top which will become your prison. Even if some among you survive, you shall have your years shortened from nine hundred to less than one-hundred and twenty. By these desserts my word is known, by my word this shall be done."

Aggrieved, Lilith lay for generations upon her bed whilst her lieutenants took to directing the defense of the mountain top retreat, because all this time assaults from Lucifer did not cease. Lucifer was intent upon her final demise and in separate assaults he struck her outer defenses causing her and her people much stress and fear.

"You have," Lilith said, "to keep your faith high in your hearts and this will nourish your souls. I know that we have been here these many Glicks and your courage is without bounds. Each child born causes one-hundred among us to die, meaning our population in this mountain continues to diminish. But you have remained strong. Fear not in this time of trial because one day we shall be free from here and return to the land and re-claim the farms and homes which others now occupy. That day will come sure as fire quenches the rain, as light follows night."

"Hosanna, Hosanna, Asherah, Asherah" they cried.

***

Lilith, by the time of Abraham, had recovered somewhat from her poisoning. She came before the assembled group, humans, Lilim and hybrids of same to make her words heard at the same time by all.

"First know, that the poison has failed in its intent, I remain alive and with you, and that I have just received word that a new remedy will be able to reverse this curse and return to me part of the robust immortality I once had."

"Hosanna, Hosanna," the group cried.

"Also, I am told that the remedy might restore to some of you your former fecundity without fear that you will suffer one hundred deaths among you for each child born."

"Hosanna, Hosanna" they all cried.

Lilith then said, "But to have these remedies become effective, in short time, rather than the process taking an eon, requires the semen of human males to take effect quickly on both you and I. That means we must steal among the human males in the dark of night and collect the seed quickly and, in amounts sufficient for both you and I. Collected; we shall bring it back and place in a reservoir for our use and experimentation. Now this I know has its bizarre tone and many among you will need to take council of it and think if this is something to do or to avoid or wait for the next remedy and eschew this one. Take your time of it and let us reconvene on morrow night, when we can take this and ponder deep our future."

With this, and the group dispersing, Lilith thinking about the thing with her solitary self. "I can," she thought, "pass this remedy by and evoke my patient strain for perhaps another eon and place my hopes there. But, am I to creep in the night as a semen gatherer and ignore my own disgust with that method of rejuvenation? Or shall I reject this concept and test an another at a future time. Is it better I should up again and be out of this cave and back into the world as an outcome even if the means is lower that I am comfortable with?"

She still struggled to make up her mind by the day following. She finally decided as she took her place before the assemblage. She said to them.

"I am up again, having spent the night measuring the distasteful means we contemplate to an end which we measure in terms of whether this tact of semen-gathering is worth the marble. I have concluded that it is. What say you council men and women, because it is you women who shall bear these hybrid young in thy womb and you men of the cave who will have to raise and provide for them?"

"Our numbers here under Lucifer's curse have dwindled down to a count from which our population may not recover. In our encasement here, we could all simply die and disappear. With the new remedy, we could take again to the sunshine and see our future reignite its possibilities."

The Lilim council-woman stepped forth, "We have counseled on this," she announced, "and the future is our main concern—to see that our children have one. We say to you, Lilith, we are strong with your plan. Let's discover quickly how it might unfurl into reality."

"I thank you, Adina," Lilith said. "Is it then that Adina speaks for all?

"Hosanna!" was the cry from all. Lilith discussed the detail of the plan with them where Lilim contingencies would be sent out disguised as owls. The birds would sit in the mid-trees and watch for the men to sleep and send to Lilith the notification of when best to alight and collect the booty.

"We can succeed," she said to them, "if we are swift, collect a clay pot full per night. Then swiftly, we are here back for its application to the female genitalia and thereby revive the hope for children who will survive this curse."

The first night was clear and cold. Lilith warmed her hands by rubbing them together and placing them on some of the Lilim and some of the Canaanites. The transmogrification was instantaneous and the owls and doves flew from the cave one hundred strong. The transformed beings, winged their way out of the mountain to separate into the countryside, to begin their vigil and to signal Lilith when to come for the male harvest.

Lilith perched atop a mountain abutment and listened for the first owl hoot and dove then from her great height toward the sound from whence it came. Sleek, she landed at the home where the owl blinked then turning his head to indicate the room where the man lay. Lilith crept silently, and inside the room, she was but a whispered

172

apparition to the sleeping one, who, she apprized, was in his night dreams ready to drop the seed. Lilith took his member and gentle-stroked it and there was her first harvest. There was another and another until before the dawn she had brimmed the clay pot over-flowing with what was required. Quick to the distribution, the women formed a long queue taking what they needed in silence.

Lilith sat and sighed, pondering what this enterprise would bring. There was little to do except to wait and see if this would produce the children the Lilim women needed to produce to ensure the future of their race.

It was in six weeks time when Adina approached Lilith to give the news that she was indeed pregnant from the filched seed and was now waiting to know as to how the pregnancy would proceed. Presently there were hundreds of similar announcements of women whose bellies began to grow. So many had the condition that Lilith decided that there should be a rejoicing and a feast.

In the dark of the caves, there had not been much dancing or faces lit without the prospect of children. Now this was no longer true and the tangible evidence was among so many that Lilith was able to count it as a great moment. She, herself, saw her recovery accelerate from her own applications of the seed. Hope grew among them all.

She stood before them that night and said, "I am in the midst of grasping again old powers long since taken from me, and it feels good. I see happy faces among us and that is good. People of the caves prepare then to multiple our numbers and return to the world below and now let us rejoice in and dance-dances that celebrate joy."

It was a happy lot on the mountain top that night and from far below you could see the candles lit and hear great shouts of "Hosanna, Hosanna."

"And I can say you in this tenth generation after the deluge that my recovery is now near complete Lilith said "and I can be again with you in the fields, on the hills and in the valleys of this Earth."

Chapter 41

Lucifer was as well occupied in the generations after Noah. He sat with Lukim and Nephilim councilmen to speak of it. "We have these last millennia much to count that we have achieved. We have laid low some of the sons of Noah such they have come to our side chaffing against Lord's arbitrary restrictions. See our great cities; see our great tower at Babylon. They are not evil creations but the arts of man seeking to expand and grow. Lord would have all the Earth obedient to his will and his will alone, whilst we all are stunted in our own growth and toil in the dirt of the fields forever in the name of specious independence. We have created, from our knowledge gains, the great civilizations of Atlantis; we have monuments to immortality in Egypt, in Tibet, in Babylon, in Assyria and beyond. Along the Tigress and Euphrates, we have tamed the wild rivers and made them fertile for our needs. We have created a hierarchy where the men of wisdom take slaves and use their own time to advance the future of the race with new knowledge and new tools rather than have the toil of our backs in the fields forestall all that for ritual obeisances to Lord."

"We have seen that our Patriarchs have been triumphant over the daughter's of Lilith. These women set a bad example when men, who hath made the Universe, were being murdered, and laid low by Lilith, her ilk of witches, harlots, and practitioners of the black arts. We have wiped her from our writings and instructed all our scribes to expunge this anomalous example of blaspheming from human remembrances and history. Lilith Asherah and writings of her shall never be found. We pause in this moment to savor our triumph."

Lucifer took himself to higher heights and said, "Let me now tell you the story of Job, so you might see the weaknesses of Lord's message and to make my point. Five generations ago, I determined to challenge Lord directly in the matter of a man named Job to seek to answer and display for one and all that the way of man's greatness is far superior to Lord's mean demands for empty obedience. I wagered Lord, that the man Job was pious only because he assumed Lord had blessed him with many riches. His piety, I said to Lord was, therefore, false. It would fall away, I said, in the face of adversity. Lord and I agreed Job would be the testing ground for our two philosophies. Where will Job's heart ultimately rest?" I asked Lord, "with his own future or will he choose you, Lord?"

"Job was a very pious man with seven sons, and three beautiful daughters and very prosperous with many herds of sheep and goats. He made sacrifices to Lord, many and often, but my view, which I pressed with Lord, was that Job was pious only because he was prosperous not because he loved Lord."

"I wagered Lord that Job would choose, "to keep his wealth, herds and family, rather than keep faith with him."

"Lord agreed to the contest and I began Job's ordeal with one proviso from Lord. Lord insisted that Job's life not be harmed or extinguished in this."

"I agreed and set upon Job hideous boils, which repulsed all around him and it distressed him so that he took pottery chards to scrape at them, to cut them away from his skin so that he would not be such a hideous sight. Job's friends come to him and for seven days they contemplated his calamity, some said, "You must have offended God for him to let this happen to you Job."

His wife joined in wonderment and said, "Surely, this is not the treatment of a just God."

"It was then, that I took all his children!" Lucifer exclaimed. "One by one, I destroyed them all. And then, I took from him his prosperity, his many animals and herds. He descended into poverty. But Job was a tough one. He made himself to pray to Lord and continuously said, "I am of the dust and to the dust, I shall return."

"I whispered to him in the dark of night that his piety was now going unrewarded, indeed, was being punished bizarrely. His friends agreed with me in a manner calling upon Job, to confess his sins for surely these misfortunes must be retribution for sins made or done. They did not believe Job was innocent in this. They believed he must have earned these retributions. They urged him to confess his offences against Lord."

"Job maintained his innocence," Lucifer continued, "and refused to blame Lord for his misfortunes, and said to all who would listen, 'I have no guilt, no act, which would qualify to bring this upon my family and I say, therefore, to all of you, this is not Lord's retribution. I have determined that another explanation must exist to explain this and have determined to ask Lord directly what the origins of my wretched circumstances are.'"

"Job went to the altar and called Lord and Lord made his presence known.

Job spoke and said, "I am here, Lord, to lay claim to my innocence and, do not assign to you in this, any blame for my calamities because you are a just God. My presence here is based on my surmise that you yet might have an explanation for how and why this has come to pass in my life and to my family."

Job was fearful, intent upon Lord's response, and hopeful that his directness would not cause offense with Lord and he, Job, would not have by this, created more grief for himself."

Lord responded, 'I have, Job, placed upon this Earth many creatures and all must be maintained and now I have with you, one who wishes to set upon me with interrogatories and answers to numerous questions. I say to you that this stance, you approach me with the attitude of the inquisitor; the moral superior who would, however innocently, set to place himself, his thoughts and his views above that of his creator. I am thy creator, Job, and inherent in this is my sovereignty over thee, and all the creatures that are my handiwork. Place thyself as one among many whose needs must be met; you and yours are not the only ones who matter. Man must not place himself above me, your Lord. Yours is obedience, even if what transpires on Earth is beyond your understanding. My word is your guide in your existence there, not a prompt to raise up questions to me, your Lord, your superior. In this you have, because by your behavior, never lost your faith and obedience will, by me this moment, be rewarded; even as I now say to you that questioning me, your Lord, also demonstrates that you, while pious are not perfect."

'In this I say, unto you, I will restore to you your children, your wealth and prosperity three-fold and place upon you the duty to tell all in the land of these, my decrees and understandings of the proper role of Lord and man."

"Job," Lucifer continued, "took Lord's words away with him and conveyed them among his friends such that a new understanding would be among them of these things."

Lucifer paused in his story telling, "Now some will say I lost the wager, and Lord won with Job, therefore, I was defeated. But I say to all, it was not the outcome of the battle that matters here, what matters here is what prompted the war. Here my meaning in this; Lord, failed to demonstrate an awareness that man was reaching to gain knowledge on his own, that man was listening and comparing what Lord offered to what I have already given them. Will blind obedience win out in the long run against wealth, power, and possessions? Will the simple life of peasantry and nomadic, hard-scrabble existences resist the temptations my cities offer? Shall man in Lord's own image, not in time, seek to be immortal even as Lord's example presents. Lo, I say unto you, in time most will be swayed by my temptations not the meager rewards Lord has offered."

"This chapter with Job," Lucifer said expansively, "is meaningful not because of the outcome of this first skirmish, but because it is an indicator of the onset of a new chapter in the war. And the war, my friends, I speak of, is the war for men souls."

Chapter 42

It was in the time of Abraham that Lord, Lucifer, and Lilith set out anew upon the Earthly stage to renew and play out their conflicting goals and intents. Here was the crux point where all of history was to fix its origins, the point where Hebrew, Christian, and Islamist, would take root in the lands of Jordan, Israel, and Jerusalem, where east and west converged before the split.

While it would take millennia for these outlines to congeal, it was clear here, in the time of Abraham, we saw their origins.

Lilith fresh, from her recovery, and now with a renewal of numbers among the Lilim, the Canaanites, and the hybrid humans, set out from Pela to reclaim their former possessions, homes, and places upon the Earth. It was at the Plains of Hatzor, the home of the Canaanites, that she and Lucifer first met after the eon of her poisoning. Never was there more determination in Lilith's eyes.

Lucifer set his army on the march to forestall her march to Hatzor.

Their two armies stood face to face on the plain below Hatzor. Lilith rode out on a satiny black stallion, which snorted steam from his flared nostrils, to meet Lucifer at the middle point. She was to see if he would relent or would seek to block her way.

Astride a steed of equal qualities, Lucifer said with a sneer, "I see you have come again." He maliciously admired her presence. "I see your poisoning did not succeed. You sit upon your horse, robust. Are you still the champion of the meek?" Lucifer laughed as his stallion reared above hers.

Lilith did not speak for long moments and leered at Lucifer's demonic presence. She finally spoke, "I am. I have had to endure this long hiatus because of treachery not at the hands of Lord but at your hand. I am fully aware, Lucifer, of your part in it. You, whom I once loved, have in this earned your rightful name. She turned to all the assembled hosts. Her horse tossed his head, pranced sideways until Lilith was able to lean forward and look straight into the depths of his malevolent eyes. "By all thy evil acts, Lucifer, I am this day renouncing the name of affection I had once given you. By your evil acts and deeds done in your name, henceforth, your name Lucifer shall be denoted as Satan, the deceiver."

Lucifer's eyes blazed at this public denouncement. "Do you call me evil; do you renounce then all we once were? Am I to take to heart these words, this sullying of our mutual histories?"

Lilith raised her sword and shouted, "By this oath and denouncement, you, Lucifer are no longer of my bed or ilk and I here this day renounce forever what you have become."

Lucifer sat a long moment and then wielded his horse around making a turn, and gave way to Lilith and her hosts who made way to Hatzor for their inhabiting.

"So," he said over his shoulder to her "the die is cast."

Lord, too, noticed the return of Lilith and in her first night in Hatzor he came to her in a dream and spoke to her. "I have repentance to do with you. I am guilty grievously in the objects I have pursued with you, robbed you of your beauty, and sought to encase you inside the mountain top. Understand Lilith, I do what I must do, as we all must, as we all have commitments which cannot be altered."

Lilith awoke with a start that night not sure of the visitation had taken place or not.

Meanwhile, on high, Lord sat with his ministers who complained, "Lord, are thou still in fancy for her? Do you believe that now she has renounced Lucifer, she is once again available to you? Why you would even in a dream, confess to her an error and seek her redemption? This will not end well for Lilith, who will as always, be in rebellion against you. She will not relent and become a friend."

Lord said, "It is true; I am repentant in some things with her. She is my creation; all my creations I love, it is within me to do so. Lilith is one whom I still yet love. Rebellious? True. She is. But I have a plan to see, that now she is alive, released again upon the Earth, how she can now be of use in our struggle against the Lucifer, the Devil incarnate. I will think on this and take my clarities as they come. No, I will not reject this reborn Lilith out of hand. We must see what can be made of this."

Chapter 43

Lord came to Abram in this same time. Abram's father, Terach, was a merchant and idol seller living near Ur in Babylonia—a merchant city where Lucifer held sway among the inhabitants who sought above all things, wealth, trade and, they, too, worshipped false idols. Lord determined that he would persuade one among them to abandon the Devil's ways and he chose Abram. Abram's father discovered that the boy had broken idols the father had for sale in his shop. Abram denied that it was he who broke the idols stating that the idols themselves had fought among themselves, the result being a broken arm for one of them. Terach, the father said "Idols are not alive!" This made clear to the young Abram that his father, the idol salesman, did really believe in the idols that were the source of his commerce and living. This was shocking to the young Abram who began an internal journey to find the true nature of God and idols.

Lord appeared to Abram and said. "Do not be afraid for I am before you the only true God in the Universe and I have placed within you the vision that all other Gods and Idols are false Gods and idols. You have seen this?"

Abram, after his fear had subsided said "Yes I have within me this belief. Was it you who gave me this wisdom?"

"Yes," Lord said. "Idol worship and the pursuit of the things of Mammon have made this city an evil one under the influence of Satan. I will give you a new vision. I will have you to renounce this life of the city and the idols of your father. For this I will make of you a founder of great nations. I am the true God and the only God. Abandon all other idols and Gods before me and I shall bequeath to you all this."

Abram was afraid of the apparition of Lord and did not know what to say.

Lord said with an ever increasing volume, "I have seen that you of your own volition have seen the fault in idolatry and understand there is only one God and that God is me."

"Yes I have seen," Abram said timidly.

"But before I bequeath to you this legacy you must pass tests of your fealty and sincerity."

"What are these?" Abram asked.

"First your name shall be Abraham not Abram; your new name is more befitting a founder of nations."

"Second," Lord said, "All peoples on earth will be blessed through you because I shall make you fruitful and your progeny shall spread across the Earth and from you shall spring all nations under my protection and they shall prosper under my name."

"Third, you must leave your city-life and be nomadic in the fashion of my true believers and travel to lands I have promised you, the lands of milk and honey."

"Fourth, you shall have two sons Ishmael who shall found the Islamic nations, and a son Isaac who shall be the Patriarch of the Jewish nation. To your descendents I shall give the lands from the river of Egypt, to the Euphrates and Tigris in the North and I shall give you dominion over the peoples therein, Kenites, Kenizzites, Kadomonites, Hittites, Perizzites, Rephaites, Amorites, Canaanites, Girgashites and Jebusites."

"Lord," Abraham said, "I am with wife and many roots here, leaving shall be difficult for me and I would speak of this with my wife Sarai."

Now it was that Abraham's wife, Sarai, was his half sister, being the daughter of Terach his father. There was between father and couple much tension over the marriage. More, Abraham was crowned by Sarai, whom Abraham understood to be his superior. Sarai was considered the most beautiful woman in the world and was favored by all who looked upon her. Abraham spoke to her of Lord's visitation.

"I have had a visitation from the one who is the only true God and, he said to me that he would have me found new nations, but, we must he said, leave from here and go to the lands he has bequeathed us. I am preparing to answer him and I told him I would speak with you on this."

Sarai was not only beautiful, but wise and superior to Abraham in intelligence, and between the two, this was acknowledged. She said, "I have, too, had the same dream similar to yours and I am convinced he is Lord; my predilection is to accept this covenant and proceed from this place and take the destiny the only God has assigned to us. We are here mired in conflict with our father who has made it difficult for us to live a peaceful life here."

"Lord has told me to adopt a pastoral life and abandon the sins of the city to return to the life of the desert and tending flocks. This seems a hard life."

Sarai said "This I would prefer to the life of strife as we have here."

Abraham agreed.

But unknown to Abraham, Sarai had visions and dreams which she did not dare share with Abraham, dreams of visitations not only from Lord but from Lucifer and Lilith as well.

Those stories are imbedded in history, written or no.

Lucifer was much agog with Lord's attempt to sabotage his successes in the cities and with the merchants. It was a direct attempt to push back the achievements of man. He visited Sarai and sought to convince here to reject Lord's plan for Abraham.

Lucifer said to Sarai, "You should have no fealty to this new single God, he is barely known to you, yet you offer all support, yours and Abraham's to him? What if he discovers you and Abraham are half-sister and half-brother? You will, I assure you, become victims of his wrath and will be spurned in the end. I assure you, Sarai, I would never be the one to reveal this, for surely it would cause your marriage to be seen in the eyes of this new God as sin. There would surely be there no lands of milk and honey since the faith here would have been broken from the beginning."

Sarai spoke unhesitatingly in this dream confronting the Devil. "I am confident, Lucifer, even in these visitation dreams you have paid me, of where my fealty lies. It is with my husband and the only God. I have come to understand this is so. I shall not waiver in this."

With this rebuke, Lucifer withdrew but cursed Sarai with a secret curse that rendered her barren. But this was unknown to her and Abraham, except all asked the question why there were no children? At an advanced age, Sarai agreed to have Hargar, her servant to become the concubine of Abraham, so as to produce children for the two of them. But Lucifer intervened once again and sought to block conception in Hargar as well.

Sarai was in grief and Lilith heard of her plight and visited her when she was in seclusion one night. Lilith said, "I am Lilith from on high."

Sarai was shocked to see Lilith's apparition and exclaimed, "I thought you had been poisoned and encased in the mountain forever. What a sight to see you are well or is this a dream for my eyes?"

Lilith said, "I am resurrected and am much recovered and come to offer my help in this. I am keen upon the two men Lord and Lucifer and their tendencies."

"What can I do?" Sarai exclaimed?

"Well," Lilith said, "I have for you a gentle brew which will lift from you the secret curse of Lucifer and you will be able to bear children even at your advanced age and I, too, can lift the curse on Hagar as well. But this must be a secret between you and me, because if those two get a hint of our liaison, their reactions will be unpredictable."

"Can you do something for me as well about my advancing age? I know I should not care, but I would like a small portion of my former beauty. It grieves me so to have it gone; that I scarcely can face people or show my face."

Lilith said, "Perhaps, but let us take the first step upon the road before we insist upon having already reached our destination. And one more thing, you must in this change your name from Sarai to Sarah. There is in names, "Lilith said, "the power to alter your destiny."

Sarah told Abraham told she has gotten a visitation from Lord and that she would have two sons, Isaac the second son was to be born to her, and Ishmael was to be born to another wife. Abraham was overjoyed.

Hagar gave birth to Ishmael and Sarah, as predicted, gave birth to Isaac.

***

But in Isaac's early years, Lord came to Abraham and commanded him to sacrifice the boy. Abraham was terrified and could not believe the request wondering why God had made it. But he did prepare the boy after discussing it with Sarah.

"I am dismayed beyond comprehension," Sarah lamented. "Why would Lord make this demand? What good can come of this?" Sarah sobbed. "I am not sure it is wise to take a young child and make of him a martyr. I stand opposed to this."

But Abraham prepared the boy in the dead of night and stole away as Sarah slept, taking Isaac to the altar preparing him for the sacrifice in the land of Moriah. It had taken him three days travel to reach his destination and the boy kept asking where they going and where the animal sacrifice would take place. Abraham had Isaac carry wood for the fire telling him the wood was for a sacrifice of a lamb for Lord.

"But where is the lamb?" Isaac asked again and again.

Abraham said finally, "Lord will provide one, once we are there."

Exhausted from the climb, the two took a small rest before the final preparations were to be made for the sacrifice. Isaac lay quietly sleeping as Abraham murmured to himself, "Lord this is the heart of my heart and Sarah's heart will be broken by this. I had not the heart to tell her my mission, and, rather, I stole away in the night. She will awaken and wonder what the scheme, but she will likely guess. I am in your hands in this Lord and all my faith is with you."

He took the sleeping Isaac in his arms and placed him on the altar, his sweet face arrayed in the sleep that children sleep. Abraham took his knife and cleaned the blade with a special cloth he had brought along for the occasion and decided that he would not hesitate; that he would raise the blade and plunge it sure to Isaac's heart and be done with the pain of it quicker that way. The blade rose and he plunged it down wanting to be sure that it was a clean cut, but, miraculously, there in Isaac's place was a ram. Isaac lay beside the altar still sleeping. An angel appeared to the shaking Abraham and said, "On the mountain, Lord provides."

Meanwhile, Sarah was at home asking all and anyone where Abraham and Isaac had gone. On the second night when it was clear that the two were not away on a day trip, Sarah lay weeping upon her bed. Neighbors had avoided her, Hagar, her servant, had disrespected her and convinced others in the camp that she Sarah was in league with witches, some saying that Isaac was not her son but a foundling of the devil.

As Sarah worried about the fate of Isaac, Lucifer appeared to her in a dream and said, "You placed your trust and obedience at all costs in this Lord and now I must tell you the fate of your son."

"Sarah sat up with a tearful cry. "You have news of this, what is the news? Tell me."

Lucifer gave her a comforting sound and said, "Lord commanded Abraham to take your son Isaac to a mountain in Moriah where he was sacrificed at the mountain altar."

"Oh," Sarah screamed as she fell to the floor, "my heart can tolerate no more grief than this. Too much weighs upon me. I am done. I cannot live with this."

"I am sad to say that little Isaac died this night as Lord requested," Lucifer repeated, "and Abraham plunged the blade deep so as to minimize the pain for the poor boy. He died peacefully and the blood was plentiful and Lord was pleased," Lucifer said.

Grief-stricken Sarah ran from the tent asking others to help her get to Hebron. But she did not make Hebron before she died of grief and was buried there and never did see Abraham or Isaac again. Her dying words were reported in Hebron by one who comforted her in her death-bed grief.

"How Lord, despite my undying love for you, can I hold love for you above all else; above family, above Abraham and Isaac, above my love of them when it is that you have also that placed inside me iron most a love of you? You have commanded me be fruitful and multiply and, placed inside me as well, a huge love of the offspring Isaac who sprang from my womb barren for all those years; and now my only son has now been sacrificed to your featly demand. I confess, I am unable to extract myself from this quandary on this my death bed; I now see Lord I would, choose to have my son Isaac with me at my side, even if it placed you second place in fealty. Yet, in this, I cannot be whole-hearted; hence, I am dead; split asunder--torn between my grief and your demands for loyalty."

***

Sarah's death was shocking to Lilith. She went under cover of night to visit Sarah's remains at the Cave of Machpelah where she sat next to Sarah's ossuary.

"We have been made the bearers of seed to be bought and sold among the men who now fight over the goods of this world; Lord and Satan are in a battle for souls but unmindful of the causalities the battle brings upon the women and the children. Surely this cannot be Earth's ultimate consequence. The cure here is worse than the disease. I promise you, Sarah that this is how the story on Earth begins but it is not how the story here on Earth shall end."

Chapter 44

After Sarah's death, Lilith returned to Hatzor to find delegations including Kenites, Kenizzites, Kadomonites, Hittites Perizzites, Rephaites, Amorites, Canaanites, Girgashites, and Jebusites—all angry that their lands had been claimed by Abraham and the sons of Isaac. More, they were the aggrieved, since a prophet had stated that the new Hebrew nation would succeed in taking their lands. They wanted Lilith to intercede.

"We are aggrieved in this," the Canaanites said, "since we are mother to the Hebrews and like a brother we have been to them. Yet Abraham's sons come from Ur into our lands to lay claim to what has been ours for centuries. What, Lilith, can be done about this? Is their God so powerful so as to make this demand succeed? Should we fight, should we grant obedience in this?"

The Hittites were supporters of war and urged preparations. The Kenites urged peace along with the Kadomonites. The Canaanites urged preparation for war and pointed out that wars demand for goods could be good for trade, especially at Sidon where there was much money to be made.

The Jebusites stepped forth and made a strong case. Their representative said, "Our prophets say that our lands in Jerusalem shall be the center of Abraham's new nation. We have occupied these lands for centuries and shall not budge."

The Rephaites lived in the area of Moab at Ar, the region east of the Jordan, and their representative was a giant man fully thirteen feet tall who stood and spoke. He was not well greeted and there were shouts of "Gargoyle! Nephilim! Demon-Angel!"

Lilith raised her hand and hushed the crowd and said, "I will hear his words."

At that the Rephaite warrior spoke. "Thank you, Highness, for allowing me to represent my people here. We, too, have seen this vision, a terrible vision, where the Israelite nation shall invade our lands and murder our people. The vision said that Og of Bashan shall be our last king, and that a David, in two hundred years hence, shall kill Goliath, one of our own, in a great contest."

"I hear cries here today of Nephilim where the sins of our ancestors, are revived and placed upon us as if we Rephaites were guilty of having committed them. We have lived in peace since those days and trouble no man's peace. All we ask in return is that we be left alone to enjoy our flocks in the fields and our tranquility. We are here today to ask that our arms be joined with yours to thwart this terrible vision and ensure that it does not become reality."

The Perizzites were located in the hill country of Judah and Ephraim and their king spoke for them. "The vision for us is most dreadful, one where a King Solo comes to power among the Hebrews and enslaves our people. We fight bravely and a peace is made but our culture is lost in this, our history, and our land."

The Hittites and the Amorites spoke jointly and said "We are peoples who have met this Abraham." There was a murmur among them all. "He traversed near our settlements and told of his mission from the one God. We only later obtained the details of the convent he claimed came from his God."

"We are small traders, on the one hand and hill people on the other, and have no great armies and weapons such as those we see in the visions. We have clung close to the land; we have tended our flocks and have seen our simple life sustain us for many generations. But," their representative said " in the visions, we see one nation seeking hegemony over all Canaan, crushing the many peoples who already live there, treating us as animals in the field, proclaiming our land as their promised land of milk and honey."

"The invading hoards do this," the vision said, "with the help of their powerful God, who gives them arms and miracles and witchcraft."

"They also, I have heard," the Amorite emissary said, "have learned the arts of war from a demon named Lucifer. Lilith, we have none of these supports. Our prospects, according to these lights, look dim. What combats can we offer against these powers? Tell us Lilith, how can be we proceed with any hope of success? Do you know this Lucifer?"

Lilith took to the high ground to address them all. "It is true; they have learned devil arts and demon-craft from the one known as Lucifer. I know him well. He was with me in their God's heaven before we both were cast down to this Earth as exiles."

There was a grasp among some of them because they had no knowledge of Lilith's relationship with the one they knew as Lucifer. There were immediate questions among them. "What then, are you- his partner in this? Are we being hoodwinked here? Why should we give you our trust? Are you then demon stock?"

Lilith waited for the questions to subside and stated, "I have no truck with this Lucifer, for he, once fallen to this Earth, has become, indeed, demon stock, delighting in sowing violence among you, teaching you the arts of war and witchcraft. I have severed all ties to him and he is my enemy. I have taken to the battlefield many times against him and I shall continue to do so. It was Lucifer, the Devil, who poisoned me. Make no mistake in this, Lilith is no friend of Satan, and by my sword I shall close upon him in some near encounter and have his throat at the mercy of my sword, immortal to immortal, for only such a one can kill such another one. This is my pledge in this place and time."

Her sincerity seemed to mollify some of them but one stood to say "What then, Lilith, of your relationship with the one God of which Abraham and his progeny speak? What power have you against this one?"

Again, there was a long wait for her reply.

"I knew this one God of which you speak, in another place on high. This is true. It was, she continued slowly, "at first a thing of love between Lord and me, because he created in me a being close to himself in power and beauty, for I was his first love, his wife. For such a gift it was, one which earned my gratitude to him forever. But, there was another. There was another born by similar means this one God also created, and his name was Lucifer, then the most beautiful of angels, who, too, held a high place, was highest among the high."

It was we, Lucifer and I, who fell in love and a child was conceived of this."

Again, a gasp goes up among them.

"A love," Lilith spoke up amid the din, "that was crushed by our God and the child was ripped from my womb brutally. We two were exiled from on high to this place to suffer in pain for eternity for love's sin which produced this child."

"So I stand before you today, an immortal, but I, too, cradle my regrets, among them that once upon this Earth, in these mortal bodies, we sometimes possess, we become susceptible to mortal frailties and can fall again, as Lucifer has done, to become as beasts in the field, eating the flesh of our fellows and bringing war and mayhem as our legacy not the peace I crave. Let me be clear, my mission here is to raise the meek, celebrate the mild, bless the peacemakers, and secure these blessings for the future and our children. From these goals, I shall not shrink or deviate. These are my solemn vows and commitments."

A hush came upon the crowd after Lilith's presentment. One among them stood after conferring among some of the chiefs and spoke.

"We have heard much here today, much to absorb and contemplate. Thanks be to you Lilith—a heartfelt presentation and clarification of your nature and your presence here. There is much to ponder, much to take in. We would rest on this and cogitate, and if it pleases you, come together again on the morrow."

Lilith nodded her assent and the group dispersed. She took to solitude to meditate upon her own predilections and priorities in this proposed venture.

Lord came to Lilith in a vision that night, and said to her, "Lilith, say you will not come against me in my prophecies for my people in the promised-land. Say you will not take up arms against me with those whom I have said must accede to my wishes that must, in this, be obedient. They are idolaters and pagans. In this they have taken up the ways of the Devil and surely in this you can see that we now have a common enemy and must mend the differences which now for many eons have separated us. Say that you will not intercede. Disperse these representatives. Surely you can see what will be will surely be."

"I cannot," Lilith said, "because I see that this covenant is but a harbinger of war and more war even as Lucifer, your enemy, teaches these humans how to make wars' implements. I cannot see in this much to choose Lord between you two. Make me understand my error in this. Surely you in your own laments chastise these descendents of Abrahams for their excess, their wars and bent toward conquering what is not theirs. I, too, have seen these visions that all this shall be so. Is this true? What is your plan in this—in allowing the Hebrews to conquer the lands of others?"

Lord spoke sincerely, "It is written and I have stated that all of this shall benefit all who live on Earth. These events, seen in the vision, are but the passageway to my vision for all Earth inhabitants."

"Benefits, Lord?" Lilith asked. "I am pressed hard to see how the dead, who will result from this, will benefit. And more, there are pacifists among them hindered by your own curse of original sin, and this combined with Lucifer's inducements, make for a combination in which the weak will certainly perish. I fear, Lord, this battle for men's soul is a bloody one."

Lilith bolted awake in bed that night from this vision and took water to her body, and her face, so disturbing it was to her.

***

At the moon's declension the Hatzor group reassembled and Lilith sat to hear their decision as to how to face their dilemma. They agreed on many issues within their councils, but not all.

Lilith did not speak to them of her vision because many of them had visions of their own to report.

One after another they reported their vision of the night before. One said, "Mine showed me seven hundred years of our history. I was shown men who are to be kings and prophets and the evil things they will do in our future. There was a man called Elisha who in coming from a town called Bethel, was mocked by children for having a bald head, he called upon the single God who made two bears come out of the wood and to maul forty-two of the children to death."

"There will be," another said, "a king called David who will conquer a city called Rabbah and approach the defeated king there and, in the vision, this King David will take the defeated King's crown from his head and put it upon his own head. He ordered all of the people of the city be tortured with saws, harrows of iron and with axes.

191

He made them pass through the brickkiln which caused hot fire to burn their feet."

"I saw the same King David invade the lands of the Geshurites, the Gezriites and the Amalekites. He will invade into Shur and even into Egypt. In Egypt, in the vision, it said he left neither man nor woman alive, took away the sheep, and the oxen, the asses, the camels, and the apparel and anything he could carry. He moved against the Jerahmeelites and the Kenites. He killed, every man, woman and child. This he did, too, in the vision; in the land he called the land of the Philistines."

"This David," a Hittite representative said, "was in my dream, as well. He sent Uriah, one of our mighty warriors, into battle at the forefront such that he would be surely killed for the reason that he coveted Uriah's wife. He took Uriah's wife as his wife and she bore him a son. Uriah's wife was called 'Bathsheba.'"

"Even the single God," the Hittite representative continued, "was displeased by this act and others where this David killed seven in the family of Saul in order to inherit his throne. And he took the wives of other men especially those of conquered Kings, many when he came out of Hebron."

"I have seen the one called Moses in the dream." said the Girgashite representative. He was truly capable of many evil things. While in Egypt in that land of Hebrew slaves, this Moses rose to high rank and he killed an Egyptian and hid him in the sand.

He ordered the population of a whole city killed but told his men to keep the virgins for themselves. He does this again and again."

There was, as well, the one in the vision called Solomon who is seen to order the murder by the hand of Benaiah, of the son of Jehoiada. This Solomon sought to kill Jeroboam who escaped to Egypt.

Another man offered, "This Solomon did freely consort with the evil one you call Lucifer, and made a pact with him to utilize demons to build the Hebrew Holy Temple. He went mad in the end but the Holy of Holies in the vision, the temple was made with a pact with this Devil."

"Lilith we say to you," Nabob said of the Kenites, "what manner of men are these? Are these visions true?"

"No more!" Lilith exclaimed. "We have seen enough visions for this round. We shall speak again tomorrow. Let us take our rest again tonight and have a quiet repast and ponder what we all have seen collectively and individually."

Lilith sat at the somber supper. As she reposed, some of the representatives came to her with questions as to her understanding of the visions. Many were interested if Lilith could save their peoples and their nations. They were fearful most since the visions were so vivid to them that few doubted their reality.

"Are they true?" they continually asked Lilith.

At length she answered each of them, and stated that her belief was that the visions were true; that they accurately reflected things that were to come to pass.

They all sat huddled at the gloomy repast contemplating how best to convey this news to their anxious, waiting nations. Lilith as well had to decide what her stance would be with Lord who must have given these visions to one and all.

On the next day, in assemblage, the various groups shared their plans as to what they would do.

"I, for one," said, Nebish, "will council my people to take their flocks and hide in the hills as we have always done in response to conquerors."

"I will," said another, "advise my people that we must stand and fight. Death will come, but if so, it should be in defense of our women, our children, our treasure and our goods. None can expect to live forever."

Others, opined that there could be negotiation and intermarriage with the conquers and, in a generation or two, there would be no distinction between the conquered and the vanquished.

Individuals within all groups, sat with despair on their faces, unable to take tactics seriously when strategy itself was doomed.

Lilith stood to tell them that she did not see how the disasters in the visions could be avoided; that Lord had the power to make the things in the vision come true.

"There is little, I see, can be done," she said. "I, too, have seen these terrible visions, as you have. Over these last nights, I have been equally horrified as to what I have seen. More, I am powerless to ascertain what can be done to avert this disaster where clearly many, if not most, of the victims will be the women and the children, where it will be the blood of the lamb spilt in the slaughters."

"I came to this exile," she continued, "hopeful that from Hell's prison, we might make here a paradise. This has not been so. My faith now is low-ebbed because of this, but not abandoned. I hear the rattle of the cages but we are not yet imprisoned. Take heart my people. We are at the edge, it's true, but we are not over the precipice, our road is lacking bricks and is mired in mud but our destination still looms ahead. Now we must take this time to hunker down and await our next attempt at righting these terrible wrongs--the ones to come as we have seen, and the ones being visited upon us now, even as I speak. Farewell to all; be with the higher spirits—heed not the demon call which will tempt."

She said her farewells to one and all and retired to Hatzor to make her plans to weather the coming eon of violence, hatred and war.

Chapter 45

There was to be no peace for Lilith at the Hatzor heights. Lucifer focused again upon routing her out of any refuge she claimed. He was bent upon having her dead beneath his sword. For seven hundred years, he made attempt after attempt to dislodge her from that place. He, the Hebrews, and many others came and went. But Lilith made her stand with her small band and kept the place secure despite the attempts to conquer it.

After seven hundred years had passed, Lord appeared to Lilith at evening dusk and spoke, "I am here, Lilith, in much distress," he said. "by my own hand I created Adam and Eve and the young Lilith. Man and woman I did create, from the depths of my love."

Lilith was startled to see Lord to appear in his original apparition. It had been eons since she had looked upon his face, now haggard and drawn.

Lord continued, "From the first attempt to grant them paradise, I gave only a few rules which I forbade them never to violate. They did so promptly, nonetheless. It gave me to eject them from the Garden into the Earth with your minions and those of Lucifer."

"That was to me," Lord said slowly, "another failure in a train of failures which began with you. I have been haunted as to where I failed you, how could a heart as dear as mine that gave its all to you, had in the end been rejected?"

Lilith did not speak.

"I have seen my creations scatter upon the earth and mix among you and Lucifer's kind; but, alas, I gave them again simple rules to live by, but, time after time, they succumbed to Lucifer's abominations. They allowed themselves to be draw up in pride, classes, and hierarchies. I saw them aspire to be immortal, to be Gods themselves, sample every manner of sin and degradation, until my eyes could not forebear the sight of them."

"I came down to Noah and told him I would bring a great flood and destroy them all so great was my frustration with them. So was my will, so it was done and

I had me then a fresh slate to start from, a new strain issued out from Noah's ark to spread out upon the land."

"My heart was full of joy at this, but as I looked down after the deluge at the many killed, the awful destruction, I asked what have I wrought?" he said. "I had great remorse. My heart was bleeding at my own deed. I needed redemption myself yet there was no one to minister to me in this. Who ministers to God's needs?"

"I told Noah I would never kill mankind again. I permitted him to eat of certain meats if necessary, releasing him from that constraint. I urged him to eat of the crops of the Earth. I recanted on many of my strictures so as to make my people's life on Earth easier. I gave Noah permission to till the soil and to make wine. I gave Noah permission to grow crops against the famine times. I gave them to keep my word and to be clean in all things and made in this clarity so as to alleviate confusion among them as to my wishes."

"But, again, my children made for me, a mixed gruel. They gave me black sand for my many gifts, offered me scorn in place of my love given. They fell to Lucifer's enticements; worshiped his false idols and made of other men slaves."

"Who has disappointed you so, Lord?" Lilith asked.

"Ah," Lord said slowly, "the very first sons of Noah straight away divided the world among themselves and proceeded to war among themselves over the divisions and made a catastrophe. Such grief for me, to see in the very first generations, many fell.

"Serug was first to deny me, to take up with false idols sacrificing unto them, and more, was accursed to the marrow of blasphemy. He followed on this to teach his son, Nabor, the same and added sorcery to his transgressions, no doubt a teaching learned from your lover Lucifer."

It was from this that Lilith drew in her breath to make a comment at the "lover" reference but chose not to at that juncture.

Lord understood her inhalation, and understood his comment was not well received.

"I am sorry for that. It is still sore with me, over that incident. But by my presence here, Lilith, I hope you understand I offer to you an apology."

She looked at him, shaking her head slowly, but she did not speak.

"Well," he continued, "Serug was father to Terah and he, in evil train, sold false idols for merchant gain placing up me great shame; great shame without even a hint of remorse. I grew then more resolved that the covenant with Noah was again a covenant failed, that I had to face yet another need to retrace and reexamine my purposes in creating man, and to admit to myself that Lucifer's forces were strong among many and many of those could not be retrieved to my side."

"I resolved after many Glicks of deliberation to make a new convent, to place upon the Earth a new understanding, to give man one more chance to come, of his own free-will, to come to my side and place the sword into the side of Satan. This was my plan. This was my covenant with Abraham, son of Terah."

Lilith nodded her knowledge of Abraham.

"Abraham, Abraham," Lord said, "the one in whom I cradled all my hopes of what could be on this Earth, this Earth now filled with exiles and sinners, followers of Satan, adherents to cannibalism, wars and mayhem. Abraham, my heart cried out, could father a chosen few among nations and thereby make new start of it in that place—a new covenant, not among the many but among the few."

I went to him, Lilith, and told him of his mission. Earth nations would start from a pure kernel planting new covenant seeds with the sons, Isaac and Ishmael, one would found, in my name, the Israelite nation, and the other who would father all of Islam. By these pure beginnings I would erase, and indeed, overpower the enclaves of sinners and retrogrades who had come to populate the Earth, and from this renewal, all nations of the Earth would see future benefits."

"This was my plan," Lord said grievously. "This was my plan. But the forward vision of this, the actuality is now clear."

"I gave the Israelites Isaac as their patriarch, but he disappointed me. I gave them Jacob, and he while still in the womb, quarreled with his older brother Esau and the two fought a deadly battle their entire lives through. Jacob tricked his brother Esau out of his birth right and lied in the attempt to exceed to his older brothers' rightful place as head of the family. I came to him, after his years in exile, and showed him the ladder of life which made the vision clear for human kind. 'In your life,' I said to him, 'you are ascending the ladder to heaven or you, in your life, are descending the ladder to the worst vestibules of hell.' That was my message to him."

"Only," Lord said quietly, "Sarah understood. She was the crown of Abraham and in asking Abraham to sacrifice Isaac; I lost her love through the chicanery of the Devil. She took her life thinking Isaac, her only son was dead."

Lord took a moment, apparently in contemplation and, folding his arms looked wistfully at the floor. Lilith watched at him in silence.

"But worse than all this, Lilith, is the story of the 900 years from the death of Abraham. I ensconced with the Israelites to keep my vows with them to make of them a great nation. I promised them to make them rulers over all nations in the promised-land, the Kenites, Kenizzites, Kadomonites, Hittites Perizzites, Rephaites, Amorites, Canaanites, Girgashites, and Jebusites. And I did. I gave them conquered kings, used my powers to aid them in these—bloody goings on. Their crimes were horrible. Many Israelites fell among themselves fighting for power, priesthoods, and money and the wives and goods of the conquered. They waged unjust wars and took for themselves, harlots, and unclean girls, of the vanquished for lust and lusts' sake alone. They made drunken orgies with idols, despite my warnings, and worse, Lilith, worse of all, I was bound by this promise, this covenant; I aided them in this. I gave them power to kill innocents bound as I was by my own promises. Bound as I was by my own promises." Lord's voice trailed off.

"And here we are at nine generations since Abraham, and once again I must make another fork in this road and decide what I must do, for I have a part in the calamity. I have made these creatures and I must form among them, a correction."

"I am here at a stopping point," he said, "I shall return in the short time and further puzzle this through."

He gazed at her, then and said, "Sarah most reminded me of you."

Lord left Lilith, after brushing her cheek, longingly.
Lilith was quietly stunned by what she had heard.
Exhausted, she allowed herself to sleep.

Chapter 46

Lord did return in the short time one night seemingly eager to continue his dialogue with Lilith. He sat across from her subdued at first and then he spoke.

"I remember most," he said, "your beautiful voice in worship, a voice heard above all the other voices raised; I could, amid them all, discern yours, lilting highs and sweet lows."

He sat on a protruding stone with Lilith opposite him lighting a lamp with a gesture of his finger and said "I must have at this new conundrum and I would ask you Lilith, to think with me on this to pursue with me a resolution."

"I have made, amongst the chosen ones," he said "a promise for a Messiah. Upon this promise I am bound to deliver, for a blessing once made cannot be revoked. But how to deliver upon this promise made is my dilemma. Lord then said, "My thought is this; to make it so and to have that Messiah be of my body, have my flesh come to Earth. I will walk among the humans."

Lilith was stunned, her face was pallid in the lamplight. She spoke succinctly, "Am I to understand, Lord, you propose to come to Earth, as I have, and make your presence known and lead in the affairs of nations? Is this so?"

Lord said, "My plan would be to take of the Holy trinity, the Father, the Son and the Holy Ghost and have the Son descend in bodily form and lead my people back to the fold. That is my thought. What think thee?"

Lilith sat back and said, "This is a plan for transmogrification. This is a plan not without great risk."

"I am aware, Lilith. For to come to Earth, to have part of the trinity assume human form is to acquire as well all of the frailties of humans, become susceptible to the temptations of Satan, to the exposures of disease and, while I will likely survive, my Son aspect will be likely transformed as was yours."

"You, Lilith, are the only being who has experienced this, other than Satan. His council I do not seek."

"Because you have taken human genes inside yourself, you are the model of what the costs may be and I am here to examine you and take your words and thoughts on this."

Here was Lilith's inner most secret and Lord was aware of it. She could tell by his tone and manner.

"I assume. Lord," she said "you have information on my current state, my transmogrification?" Lilith said. "I do," Lord said, "but I wanted to hear it from you."

Lilith looked at him deciding that this information should be imparted only to one she trusted and she was not sure she trusted Lord at this point.

"Why the sudden change of heart and attitude? He had been clear about his disappointment in his Earth creations, clearly his anger with them was present but why exactly was he here confessing at her table?"

Lord noticed her hesitation and said, "I guess that you wondering whether on not to trust...to trust me and my motives." Here is my second confession. In coming to Earth I shall be taking from mankind, all of mankind, my minions and yours as well, all curses and the original sin from the Garden. This is no small concession." he said pointedly. "Lilith, the people you have created here, would benefit, too, by this."

"It is my last effort in this enterprise. It is my last attempt to make of these populations God-fearing and amendable souls walking the ways of purity. Hear me, Lilith, these are my motives."

"And," he continued, "in this particular plan I will, in taking a bodily form, have need of you and your support."

"It is clear that Lucifer will, upon seeing me descend, will have all his minions to my side in a flice and I anticipate, thus vulnerable, he will attempt to kill me."

"I will either fail, be killed or forced to retreat. I am not sure in this of any victory if I attempt this alone. I am more sure of success, if you join me." He paused and gazed at her, hoping for an instant answer.

"Lilith, if I can be sure of your support, even though I know that, in asking this of you, a great risk exists in my plan for you as well."

"And what support is that Lord. Speak plain," Lilith urged.

"Transmogrification, as you know, means that with each resurrection, each extension into human-hood our immortality, yours and mine, is reduced. It can be altogether be squelched unto death, itself. The risk is undeniable. Of this, I am sure you are aware. Every battle you lead for these, Earth beings, you risk death. I assume a human form can cause the Son's death and yours—permanently or only short time...the result is unknown. We don't know because it has not been attempted, except for you and me. I see that you have been weakened due to this mixing blood with humans. And, I see that you are less eager to engage battle since some wound may weaken even more of your blessed state upon which your immortality depends."

"I see taking human seed into your own womb, that I caused to be barren," Lord said slowly. "has had it own costs for you. I would like to show good faith by the restoration of your femininity, complete with a fertile womb." Lilith did not respond.

Lord continued and said, "I am willing to take that risk with the Son but only with your help. I will need you to be with the Son and shield him from ultimate risk—even as we both shall, in this battle, have to fend off Lucifer's hordes-which shall be upon us sure. More, we both will have the humans as well to contend with. Can you do this task?"

Lilith sat pensively, trying to figure if any loophole existed in Lord's plan; anything that would drive her and her minions to their death.

"I can not! I will not," she finally said. "In this there is no history of trust between us, no reason to take your words as meaning what you say. In this I can lose much and gain little. Why would I not withdraw while you and Lucifer battle to the death? Leave me now," she said finally. "I need distance from you, and Lucifer, to contemplate all the words you have placed before me."

Lord disappeared, leaving trail of sparks where he sat and indication of his chagrin as to her answer.

Chapter 47

In the next 400 years Lord began to punish the Israelites for their transgressions allowing them to be conquered in retribution for their warring against others.

First the Assyrians conquered the Northern Kingdom and then Judea fell to Nebuchadnezzar II of Babylon. After a brief period of freedom the Jewish nation fell in 63 BCE when Pompey invaded Jerusalem, and Gabinius subjected the Jewish people to high tributes and oppression.

At this point Lord returned to Lilith and spoke with her.

"I have these years punished the Israelites and have caused among them the loss of all their territories because they displeased me and I have placed upon them a great Diaspora which afflicts them now and they are scattered in foreign places. The Romans hold sway there and I am preparing for my decent among them in Judea."

"Here, my Lilith, here is where the rent in heaven, itself, can be healed. Surely this is necessary to save the world of the humans you love, as I do. It is the opportunity to rid the world below of its sins and start anew with new voices, new believers."

"The events, of which I speak, shall commence in sixty Earth years--hence. Then I shall descend and be among them. I pray you will join me."

Again Lilith did not agree in this.

But before ten years had passed, Lucifer appeared to Lilith. She was in repose and he appeared at her back. Sensing his presence, she turned to see him at ease at the back of her rooms.

She gained her feet and drew her sword. "You would come to me this way and invade my privacy? Plant your feet, Lucifer. Expect no hospitality here only sure harm and death."

She leapt upon him toward planting her sword at his throat, backing him toward the wall of the cave where he made a face of fright but made no effort to resist.

"You dare come in my quarters, uninvited, and plan to make purring words to me. Is that your plan? I am sure you'll seek to advance another brand of soft deceit and I am sure you fully expect that your winnowing charm will first have my sentiment; and then my mind. Let me see, it shall end with your beseechment of me to be your ally in the war against Lord. Was your plan thus in this?"

"I have no plan Lilith," he grinned ominously, "I came tonight to heal not to war. I came not seeking help against anyone, but to offer it. Will you let me speak?" Lilith let loose her grip and ordered him to "Speak quickly, Devil, least your forked tongue end up at the tip of my sword."

Lucifer asked "May I sit?"

Lilith did not answer and he eyes fixed upon her measuring the distance from her temper and his throat.

"Sit," Lilith commanded, placing her sword at her side, within easy reach.

Seated, Lucifer said, "I am here with observations and an offer of support because, I am told Lord means to personally intervene on Earth and risk his own body and person in this endeavor which, by the rules that apply, he will surely weaken in this human form and become more vulnerable than ever."

"Now I have no plan in this but that of seeking justice," Lucifer revealed. "Lord in his descent can be made to know the sting of his own actions, toward you and toward me. We could, in this, extract our revenge. Tell me, do you do not feel this way as well? Would you like to see him humbled on this Earth?"

Lilith chose not to speak, but was aware of Satan's every nuance. His deceptions she could read like a book.

"He murdered our child Lilith," Lucifer said. "surely you cannot forgive this. I cannot."

Lilith bit her lower lip to remain silent.

Lucifer measured her face, her every expression looking for a clue as what path she might take in his plan against Lord.

"You may not know, but in his endeavors to make humans his worshippers he has sadly lost. They reject him and his endless quest for obedience. They favor themselves to rise rather than to scratch the ground to make a living in the dirt as Lord would have them do."

Lilith suddenly stood up and said, "Speak quickly, Lucifer, my hand is trembling, ready to strike. I would know your point in coming here." She leaned close to his face your sword drawn sideways aligning his throat. "I said speak," she commanded.

"My point," Lucifer said, "is this. If you, as I surmise, have no interest in justice here, at least remain neutral as I seek mine. That is all I ask."

"Neutral is it? This your point?"

Lilith outraged, struck at him with all her might. But Lucifer jumped up and away from the table utterly surprised. His hand had taken her sideswipe and he made a grimace. His hand had received a wound which promptly bled. He stared at it blankly for moment, and said, "I bleed Lilith. See I bleed! Our immortality bleeds away the longer we are here in this place the more human we become."

Lilith raised her sword again, but he had disappeared, leaving the distinct order of sulfur.

Chapter 48

By the end of the sixty years Lilith had made up her mind, as to what she would do if Lord came to the Earth. She called to him and he appeared.

"I have made up my mind in this and will do as you ask, but hear my conditions." Lilith said.

Lord looked at her thoughtfully and said," I am blessed in this that you have decided to join with me. I am grateful to you because I was not sure it could succeed without you. I thank you Lilith, sincerely so."

Lilith stirred and spoke. "I have these conditions before any final agreement is reached. I will undertake the education of the boy--you in human form--because as a child you are most vulnerable and need protection and as well as an education—one which will be needed to balance away the things he will hear in growing up. You, Lord, will indeed enter this world as a child and as a child will need to learn of your mission and receive protection from those who will sure look to do you harm."

"I will," Lilith continued, "take him at twelve and begin his education for that will be the way for him to perceive what his life is to be. Even you cannot simply place all this in his mind too quickly. It is something his human side has to assimilate gradually."

"Agreed." said Lord. "And what of the prophecies of the Messiah?"

"I shall cooperate in this and I assume you will as well." Lilith said. "And Lord," she continued, "you understand there is no assurance that you will survive this ordeal in your human form. This is understood I hope."

"Understood." said Lord.

With this agreement, Lilith came to Mary, Jesus' mother- to- be, to tell her of Lord's plan and to tell her of her having been chosen to give birth to the Jesus child. Lilith assumed the guise of Gabriel, an Arch-Angel, and she took the form of a female.

She told Mary that she was blessed and had found favor with Lord. "You," Lilith told her "will have the Jesus child placed in your womb by Lord and you shall call him Jesus."

Mary was very fearful of the vision and asked, "How shall I conceive when I have not lain with a man?"

Lilith said, "The Holy Ghost shall come to be with you and your son shall be the Son of God."

Lilith told Mary that she would be there to guide her in the child's education and this had been agreed to by Lord.

Mary asked Lilith if she was an angel of Lord, and Lilith told her she was and that her name was Lilith.

***

Lilith kept her word and looked over Jesus and protected him as he grew in early boyhood. She observed him growing quickly and it was evident that he was an extraordinary child having powers which ordinary humans did not.

Lilith brought him to her side when Mary told her that Jesus had brought some small animal back to life while playing with the other children. He did so to prove that his Father was the one God to these other children.

"He did this," Mary said "because the children were taunting him saying he was an illegitimate bastard and had no Father. They told him his house was a house of shame.

He performed the miracles to prove to them he was telling the truth. And there is more," Mary said, "he placed his hand up and caused a great fire to leap from his hand to the face of a boy who was taunting him. He allowed his anger to be released. If news of this spreads beyond the village to the wrong ears, his life could be endangered!"

Later, Lilith sat with Jesus and asked him what had occurred.

"They taunted me." Jesus said. "They said, 'how is it Jesus that you have a mother but no father?' Would you have us believe that you are Messiah come down to us from the house of David and are royalty? My mother says that you were born out of wedlock and all you say is false.'"

"They said I am not the son of God but of Joseph and Mary, born out of wedlock," Jesus said looking at Lilith. "What am I to believe in this?" My mother told me, everyone in our family says, that we are descended from the house of David, aren't we?"

Lilith spoke to him earnestly, "I know these things are painful to you, but you must remember that your Father would not want you to stray from his mission on Earth for you, or be distracted by the taunts of children. You must be strong and not return hatred for hatred, stone for stone. You must learn to give love for hatred and pray for those that taunt you, despise you. That is Lord's way."

"Your mother and I," Lilith continued, "want you to not use the powers your Father has given you. You must save this for another time when you are older."

Jesus said, "Tell more of my father and what it is he wishes of me on this Earth?"

Lilith told him of his Father in heaven and how he had created man in the hope of making man see the ways of piety. "But," Lilith said, "man was disobedient and made pacts against Lord's words with the Devil, and disrespected Lord in things; man had made upon the Earth violence and mayhem."

She told him that Lord was displeased but had vowed to send to the Jewish people a Messiah, one who would right wrongs and lead the pious to new paths. "That Messiah," she told Jesus, "is you as your family has told you. This is true."

Jesus had been told all of his early life that he was special, that his entire family was special and that he was on Earth to fulfill God's promise to send a Messiah. Jesus seldom questioned it.

Under the tutelage of Lilith, he went to temple and began to read the Holy Talmud, had begun to read of the Messiah that was to come; that the Messiah would be born in Bethlehem; that he would create a new ministry for the Jews and a new covenant; that some of the people would not recognize him as the Messiah; that he would be crucified, to save the souls of the sinners in the Earth; that the worshippers of idols and Mammon would be placed down and a new testament would be proclaimed in his name, in the name of Jesus the Christ. These things the young Jesus read about and what he read one day troubled him. He brought it to Lilith.

He came to Lilith one day and said, "Am I then to die as the Messiah? Is this my fate? Lilith hesitated but decided to tell the boy the truth.

"Yes," she said looking closely at young Jesus' face, "it is written and it is so."

"I am then to be crucified as the ones I have seen along the roads. Is this so?"

"Yes." Lilith said, realizing that the young boy was realizing the meanings of all the things he had been told since his birth, of his relation to the house of David, of his mission on Earth and now he was understanding that all of this was to end in his death as a mortal being and he would, in doing so, save the world and ascend to his father in heaven and undergo a resurrection.

He sat for a long moment and finally spoke. Lilith's heart went out to him, so sad his face was and it was clear that he was a boy, a mere boy realizing for the first time what it meant. Even Lord's presence within him did not come with any shielding against his, a boy's fears and emotions.

Finally, the young Jesus spoke. "Could you talk to my father?" he asked, "and plead for his intervention, if he will please take this burden from me? I am only a boy and too young to die. And Rabbi, I am afraid of this crucifixion. I like to bring the word of God, my Father to all-that pleases me, but to die in that way so young seems unfair. What are the reasons for this?"

Lilith spoke slowly in order that the boy would hear her clearly. "Oh no, you'll not die as a boy. No, that is not the vision seen. Only later child when you are adult and have learned all the things you need to learn will you then lead your ministry in Galilee, only then shall these things come to pass. All of that is years from now, not to worry, you are still but a boy."

"You must be brave in all of this," she continued, "and prepare yourself because upon your shoulders will rest all of the remainder of human history. Fret not. I know you will remember your Father's work when the time comes and he shall be by your side and make you strong. By your bravery others shall gain salvation, all these Earthly sins will be expunged and Earth people shall be free to come back to the fold and be free of the Devil's temptations."

The young Jesus was mollified but clearly it was much for the young boy to absorb. He looked very sad to her.

Chapter 49

Jesus at twelve started to attend Temple in Jerusalem with Lilith as his unseen his guide. It was a huge complex, very grand and very beautiful with thousands of Pilgrims coming each year to worship there.

Jesus would sit in its outer courtyard where hundreds of small groups met to discuss Holy Writ. He easily mixed in the many discussions taking place and the elders were much impressed with the young boy's knowledge of the Torah. Jesus asked a Rabbi if he could read and study the holy writ inside the building and he was taken inside. There he was given access to the holy writings. He was of particular interest to some of the priests because he asserted that his family was the direct ancestors of the House of David. Rabbi Shol agreed to be his sponsor and showed young Jesus the library there and often allowed him to sit in the religious discussions taking place there.

There was especial interest in him when he asserted one day in the discussions that he was the direct descendent from the House of David and that he was the Messiah.

He was approached by the Rebbe, Leader of Prayers, who sat next to Jesus and asked him, "Who are you and why do you say these things? You must come and join me in prayer and I will sit with you to learn more of this."

Jesus said unto him. "I am here on my Lord's work, which is to bring a new convent to the people and all here must make reform and amends because you have found disfavor in the eyes of Lord God, my Father."

The Rebbe asked him, "You say Lord God is your Father? Have you seen Lord God, your Father?"

"Well, no," Jesus said, "he is within me and will reveal himself his own way and time."

"Has Lord God your Father told you himself of your mission?"

"No, but I am sure of his desire for me is to complete it here on Earth."

"And you say that your Father has sent you here as the Messiah as written about in the holy writ?"

"Yes," said Jesus.

"Well," said the Rebbe doubtfully, yet with a ray of hope, "this makes you a very special person. You are welcome to join our services and join our prayers. Come, let us join the others."

Jesus took his place among them for the examination, with the Rebbe at his side; he began the traditional prayer of the Kaddish as others looked upon him.

"This is Jesus," said the Rebbe, "and he will be joining us in prayer today. He has questions for us and I have welcomed him to come pray with us today and receive answers to his questions. Jesus sit here," he said, "and ask of us what you will."

Jesus took a seat surveying the group and began his address with measure. "Why must we tarnish the holy temple with money-changers and charge the people for relics?" he asked. "Why must there be the Rabbinical classes separated from the people? How can we take the heel of Rome from about our necks and refuse the tribute they demand? This steals the crops from our fields." The young Jesus asked, "Where in the holy text, does it say Lord's word can be interpreted by anyone who says they are a Rabbi?"

The group greeted Jesus' questions only with silence, and the Rebbe cleared his throat and said sensitively, "Thank you, Jesus, for some very good questions. I am sure we all will take them for our discussion group and will pray upon them. Meanwhile you are welcome to read our text in the text room as you like. But remember, these are holy documents and you must use care with them, using only a stylus to read the scroll. It must not be touched by human hands."

Jesus nodded and moved toward the room the Rebbe indicated as the text room.

That evening Jesus said to Lilith, "It was frustrating. I am treated with respect but it is the respect of a precocious boy, there is no real understanding in them of my words; they smiled indulgently and ignored my words, praising me for my knowledge of the texts but my words did not enter their hearts truly. They speak of things I don't yet understand and they gave me questions from the Holy Texts I have not read," said Jesus as he expressed his frustration by pacing. "I need a Rabbi," he said, "with more texts to read, such that I may converse with them equally and not be waylaid by sophists and those who offer to me only mystical references and reports from the readers of entrails. What has my Father's work here come to?"

Lilith did not speak.

"I see there idolaters and the unclean, yet I am too young to make a remedy, I have no power I might use, these have been forestalled to me by my Father. I am forever, it seems, the Messiah who must wait."

"Yes," Lilith said "I know it must seem that waiting in your Earthly body is an eternity."

But Jesus was impatient despite Lilith's tutoring and assurances.

One day, Jesus' mother, Mary spoke to Lilith asking for her to help with Jesus who was missing. Mary said, "I ask you, Lilith, for your support. Jesus has been missing now for three days and we know not where he is. What can you do, in the name of his Father."

"I will see what may be done," Lilith said. Lilith took to the streets. She looked for him in the city but he was not to be found. She returned to Mary and together they awaited Jesus' return.

***

That night Jesus did return home late and lay restlessly on his bed in the late hour. Lilith came to him after all had gone to bed and asked, "What happened with you in Jerusalem these last days? I have heard many rumors."

Jesus barely twelve years old did not speak immediately and rolled over presenting his back to Lilith.

"I need you to speak freely with me, she urged, as she approached the woven mat bed on the floor. I would know what you have done there. Separate for me, the fact from the rumor because, as you know, I have with you a promise not to use your Father's powers. What is it that transpired there?"

Looking at her wearily, the young boy turned toward her, sat up with his knees to his chest. He spoke in a whisper. "I was there with my family and took leave from them to go to the temple to reread a text which was opened there for me to read at dusk."

"But in the courtyard Rabbi, there were livestock defiling my Father's purposes. There was dung and urination in that holy place. There were money-changers who took Greek and Roman money to exchange to Tyrian and Jewish money and the people were obliged to pay-- to buy entrance to the Temple, to hear my Father's word. In this the changers took their filthy profits while the poor who could not afford the price lingered outside; the blind, the sick and down-trodden were shut out. I could not in this remain silent."

"What happened then?" Lilith inquired.

"I took a cord and from it fashioned a whip which I used to drive them forth from the Temple yard out in the city to leave the place clean. I lashed out at them and removed all the animals which were unclean from my Father's house. I took their tables and spilled their filthy lucre and had them gone and released the doves to flight."

"Last to leave were the loan sharks who exacted exorbitant rates among the poor for borrowings to enter my Father's house for the dove sacrifices. For them a special lash came forth from my whip."

"The Temple leaders came out and asked me my business there and I told them my business was the business of my Father's house." He paused and looked at Lilith, a bit sheepishly.

She responded. "I will not chastise you in this, because your heart has heard God's word and now done I'll rest my tongue and say you have a path you must travel and this is but a step. But it was reckless, my son, and actions such as these should not be repeated. Your father would not approve you placing yourself in danger like this. Your family and I were worried. Jesus, leave the things of sinners for now; await your time to come and all wrongs will be righted in due time. This is your Father's wish."

Jesus agreed. Lilith placed a hand on his forehead to soothe it and to place within him a deeper understanding of her words.

"Now," she said, "your father's wish is that you leave this place with me. We shall go into the desert, go into the world. It is part of your education to see and hear the wisdom of all of Earth's peoples. In your travels you shall learn for ten years and upon your return Lord has prepared a place for you, and will call upon you to begin your ministry here in the Promised Land."

"Ten years? Jesus said numbly.

"It is his wish. He will be with you as will I. It is a necessary preparation for your mission to come. Upon your journey you shall learn many things of the world and become your Father's teacher in many lands."

Chapter 50

A month later Jesus and his family met together on the night before he was to leave upon his journey. There was Mary, his mother, and his brothers, James, sometimes called Jacob, Joseph, Simeon, and Judah. His two sisters were called Assia and Lydia.

James spoke for the sibling group and said, "We shall miss you mightily but it is clear you must be about your Father's work. We believe you will be safe in the hands of Lord in all of your endeavors."

"Our family," he continued, "is here to continue the work of the House of David and we shall bring to our oppressed people a savior from that line as the prophecy foretold; that the Messiah is Yeshua-you. You are here and shall fulfill the aspect of the coming of the Son of our Lord. In him all Earth shall be redeemed and Lord will establish among us a new covenant which shall bring down those who worship at the table of Mammon, who create great sinful cities, who shut out the poor and the blind, the sick and maimed. The simple people shall lead to a new Jerusalem."

Each stepped up to Jesus and to give him a present for his journey.

Mary gave him a pair of sandals, and said, "Take these. They will shield your feet from the burning sands, such that you might have more comfort along the way."

His brother Simeon gave him a parchment and said, "This is the holy word that you might share with the wise men you'll meet on your journey such that they might know the word of our Lord, the one God. God speed you my brother in this journey."

Joseph gave him a staff of cedar wood, "It is sturdy enough to smite those who would harm you," he said, "and strong enough to lift you over the most raging of waters." He gave Jesus a hug. "To you, my brother, all of God's glory" he said.

Judah stepped up. His eyes full of tears. He said, "You and I my brother, have shared secrets from on high and for that I am most grateful. My heart, and God willing, my strength goes with you to protect you from the beasts of those far lands and from the many travails you may encounter."

Assia and Lydia gave him vials of oil for trading along his way that he might eat and have water to drink.

Mary wept silently nearby and said to no one in particular, "He is so young."

James said, "My brother, you are a reader and I have for your travels the books you love. I give you the Talmud, the Avesta, the Vedas and these, the Psalms of David. I know they shall bring comfort to you in the night. These are mementoes of your debate with the Doctors at the Temple. Go with God."

Joseph, his earthly father, spoke last saying, "We shall keep our faith here until your return. Know and keep pure the beliefs of this family and Lord, thy God, on this holy mission." He asked everyone to bow their heads in prayer.

"We know there is but one God," Joseph said, "and that is thee Lord, as recognized by our brethren in Egypt, and as recognized by Pharaoh Akhenaton centuries ago who threw out all the priests and idols from the temples of Egypt. May your travels Jesus in Egypt land, be fruitful among our brethren there."

"Keep our faith and avoid the blood sacrifice because that is not the way of the Essenes. Do not eat the flesh of animals, thereby keeping your bodies clean. Spread God's new message that love not curses in the loving God's true way."

Spread God's new message," Joseph continued "one which is one of blessings, not curses and destruction; one where you are called upon to love those that hate you--not war upon them. Blessed are the scribes and meek for they shall inherit the Earth."

"Spread God's message," Joseph said, "that the meek shall be received in heaven by way of the purity of their souls, not by wealth or power. Keep you to the path of the Messiah. Remind all that the soul immortal is salvation from the physical bondage of the sufferings of this Earth."

"In India Jesus," Joseph said, looking at Jesus, "you shall learn the healing arts. In Tibet you shall read the writings of the Book of the Dead. Tell all you encounter that after we leave these earthly bodies our soul, as foretold in Egypt, shall be weighed by God and if found wanting shall receive its just reward."

Joseph finished by citing the final prayer. "None will be wealthy and none will be poor, and all shall work together in the gardens of the Brotherhood. Yet all shall follow his path, and all shall commune with his heart."

The next day Lord came to Jesus before he was to embark. Jesus said to him, "I am about to embark upon your work this day my Lord and my heart is both glad and fearful. Outside these, my homelands, I know little or nothing of these other places. I am certain out there, out there may lay many threats, beasts, barbarians, and giants, and the minions of the Devil himself. But my footfall shall be strong and unwavering in this. My faith in you, my Father, is unrelenting. I know it shall carry me away and as well as see to my safe return."

Lord said to Jesus, "Lilith will be your guide and she will protect you. I shall see you next at Qumran high atop the cliffs overlooking the Dead Sea. You shall study there with the brotherhood for three years. Thereafter, you shall be in India and Egypt for four years each and in Ur as well. Go with my blessings."

Chapter 51

Jesus set out for Qumran with Lilith by his side walking at night and early morning to avoid the heat. As they encountered fellow travelers and townspeople, Jesus said to them "I am Jesus of Nazareth and I am about my Father's work, may I count upon your hospitality?"

There were Essene communities and families along their route which Mary had told them would welcome the young boy and his Rabbi; so it was. Many of them had heard of the young boy Jesus and some had heard of his mission as Messiah and asked him about it. He reply was, "I am not designated yet--the prophesies have no fulfillment yet. I am on that journey now to seek the blessings of the wise men of the world. Only God can anoint me so." But he was greeted as the anointed one on the way to Qumran and Lilith sat with him as one family gave them dinner.

He preached to them of God's new covenant.

"Give the things of the world and its strivings away to support the poor of the brotherhood and perfect thy soul as the first order of business in this lowly body we have inherited. Press thy bread into the hands of those who have no bread at all; give alms to the poor, go among the sick and wounded for in ministering to them there is healing for thy own soul. Give thy love away as if it were a precious stone for surely it is valued higher than cold rocks."

In five days time, Lilith and Jesus arrived at the Qumran community where they were greeted and invited to attend the evening's meal. About 120 of the Essene brotherhood attended eager to see the young "Master," as some of them called him, and to speak with him and Lilith of news from Nazareth.

"I bring you greetings from Mt. Carmel," Jesus said, at the mid-point of the meal "and give you my thanks for harboring wayfarers such as we--allowing us to share your table. I am about the work of my Father, Lord."

"Hosanna, Hosanna," they cried as one.

"I shall not be among you long," Jesus said "because in a fortnight I am to meet a Raja from India who has promised guidance to the great teachers there. I would hear from them the wisdom they have to share."

"Tell us," the Essene leader said, "are you the chosen one, the vicar of God?"

Jesus said, "I am not chosen yet, my journey is one of discovery and at its end the Blessings of Lord will be revealed."

"In any event," Rana, the Essene leader said, "Our blessings go with you."

***

Jesus left that place and went down to India with Ravi, his Raja guide, providing direction to him and Lilith. Jesus, as they made their way, asked Ravi of Indian beliefs and customs.

"Tell me Ravi," Jesus said "I understand your path has many Gods, not one God. Is this true?"

"Yes", Ravi said, "this is the Hindu way. We have many Gods, Brahma, Vishnu, Shiva and his wives, and of course, Vishnu's many incarnations. We have many Gods and we worship them all."

"Is this not confusing?" Jesus said.

"Yes, but one cannot argue with the Gods and Goddesses of Hindu, it is not allowed." Ravi said.

"All things in our religion are Brahman; that is to say all things are holy, from the highest Maharaja to the smallest insect. All life is sacred to us because all things contain God. We are taught that God is not out there but within and one can achieve communion with God, our Brahman principle, from within. All things are therefore divine, don't you see. Once you became attuned to Brahman or God you attain enlightenment and, if one achieves a high state, one becomes released from the wheel of life and can attain the highest, Nirvana. The way to Nirvana we call Moksha. So you see Jesus, we, like you, seek salvation."

"Salvation, yes," Jesus said, "we too, seek salvation. What is the way to salvation among your people?"

"Well," Ravi said, "I can tell you but I would not get it right. Perhaps we should wait until we get home and I can take you to sit with our wise men. They know better than I. All I know is that there are three ways to salvation.

The first is karma yoga or good works. Each among us must do our duty by our families, our communities and our caste. We do this in this life to make up for bad karma, our karmic debt from past lives. You see, Master Jesus, we believe that each of us dies but become reincarnated if we have not learned the entire lesson in a given life we were intended to learn, or if we produced bad Karma in a past life. Bad Karma can make you an insect in the next life." Ravi said, "That is why you should not step upon the smallest among us; it might be a relative."

"I see." Jesus said.

"The second way," Ravi said, "is in *jnana* yoga, which is the way of coming to knowledge."

"Coming to knowledge?" Jesus said.

"Coming to knowledge is the realization that through raising our consciousness, though deep meditation that we are not individual selves in life but part of the great Brahman. Ah, once we have attained this level of consciousness, the ending of striving for individual outcomes, we are ready to be released from the wheel. But this is not so easy to do. Many Masters take many years of disciplined yoga to ready themselves for this step. This is *jnana*." Ravi said.

"Yes? And the third way?" Jesus asked.

"Well," Ravi said, "this is one most favored by the common people; it is the way of *bhakti* yoga and is the total divestment of one's individuality and the self-surrender to one of our Gods, to be come totally devoted to him or her, in acts of worship, in temple activities and pilgrimages. This is the *bhakti* way. But this is all so confusing, I should think, to one unfamiliar with our ways."

"Oh, no," Jesus said, "many of these ideas are similar to ones in my land. But tell me, Ravi, of the caste system in your country. I have heard of it. Is it a good thing or a bad thing?"

"Oh, it is a good thing, Master. If one has bad karma then one comes back and is assigned to one of four castes. We have four castes, or social classes each with its own rules and obligations for living. The high caste is the Brahman, or priestly caste. Second are the Kshatriyas, or warriors and rulers. Third are the Vaisyas, or merchants and farmers. Finally, the fourth caste is the Shudras, or laborers. Outside the caste system are the Untouchables. The Untouchables are the outcasts of Hindu society. If one has bad karma from a previous life then one, in reincarnation, returns to a lower caste. All is just in this."

Jesus did not speak for a while absorbing what Ravi had conveyed to him and finally said "I shall ask your wise man about this caste system. There is much to learn."

***

When the trio arrived in India, Jesus was taken to the Ashram where a high priest of the Brahman caste dwelled high in the mountains in the land of the Cheras. The Chera people were of the hills and the climb to the Ashram was an arduous one for the trio and, as they climbed, Jesus noticed that the air became thinner producing a light-headed effect.

"It is the way of enlightenment, since the high elevation heightens consciousness," said Ravi.

They entered the Ashram which was heavily decorated and had many incense pots and several worshippers. Jesus and Lilith sat pensively as Ravi went to seek the Chera priest. Presently, he arrived with a very thin man dressed in a simple white cloth garment draped over his body. He sat down before them in a yoga posture and spoke as his head moved slightly from side to side. "I welcome the young Master and his teacher to our Ashram and offer you every hospitality I may offer in this holy place. Many blessings to you."

Jesus said, "I thank you for your blessings, High One and ask that you indulge strangers who are here to learn of the world and to bring enlightenment and knowledge back to my people."

Ravi interrupted and said, "The stars have foretold that this young Master, Jesus, is the anointed one for all of the peoples of Canaan and I have agreed to show him our ways and to answer his questions, High One. We thank you for accepting him in this high place and for agreeing to speak with him."

"No matter; welcome young Master, many blessings upon you and to you Rabbi as well. Let us please proceed," the high priest said.

Jesus said, "I have noted many wonders in your country and seen many great sights. Ravi has been for us a great host and guide. He has spoken to Lilith and me of your religious beliefs, of your ways to salvation and they have been of great interest to me. I have much to ponder and many rich ideas to take back to my people far away. I see clearly, High One, you have as the highest goal to escape off the wheel of life; as you call it, to reach the highest state? I have read of this in my country, and there are many questions."

"Please," the high priest said," questions are a way to higher truth."

"Thank you," Jesus said. "My first question concerns the caste system you have here. It seems to me the untouchables in your system have a bitter life. They are like, in my eyes, the oppressed of my community, under the Roman heal. The sick are ostracized, the meek trampled upon, the peace-makers ignored. Tell me is that the case here as well?"

The High Priest did not reply. He stared at Jesus a long moment.

Jesus continued. "My ministry is to these, high one, and we have in our ministry renounced wealth and idols of all kinds. How are the needs of these unfortunates met here in your country? Do they have a path to salvation? Is their sole option devotion to your Gods, while not benefiting from the fruits of their own labor?"

The high priest looked first at Ravi and then back at Jesus, and finally said, "We believe that each in his life may accumulate what we call Karma. Karma may, depending upon the individual's behavior, be positive or negative. If positive, the individual in the next life may move up the Karma ladder. If an individual does not discharge his duties, or overcome, his or her own ignorances, then the Karma wheel swings backwards, and one is born into a lower caste at reincarnation. This has been proven to us over many centuries to be the case. There is no essential requirement of equality in this for all. Inequality is the Karmic return. Surely Master you can see that?"

"Actually," Jesus began, "I am at a loss to understand how God's plan could so easily be divined by the accident of one's birth. Surely no one among us is capable of reading God's mind; such a one would be as a God himself, or herself. I am heartened here, however, learned one, by the role of your women here. You have many female Gods in your pantheon. This amazes me. How can this to be?"

The priest's stone silence demonstrated that he was clearly stung by the bluntness of Jesus' words. He was not ready to move on. He spoke with an air of annoyance, "I would caution young Master that one should not engage in assumptions that one understands another's country after only such a short visit. That would seem, as well, to assume one had the powers of comprehension, only a God would have."

Jesus, taken aback, measured his words as he spoke, "I am humble, sir, in accepting your reprimand. I had no meaning to offend."

Ravi and Jesus walked down the mountain and Ravi said. "Humm, that was a nice apology but I fear much damage was done."

"Meaning?" Jesus asked.

"We should prepare to leave and not tarry here long," urged Ravi.

But Jesus did tarry. He went to the village square that very day and began to preach Lord's word beside a well where many came for water.

"Come gather with me," he said to a small group. "I am Jesus of Nazareth and I have come to this land to speak of the one God, one God in heaven. All other Gods are false Gods, there is but one God in his heaven and I am his messenger. My Lord promises you eternal life if you but believe in him. He rewards the suffering of this life and promises you that the meek shall inherit this Earth not the rich man, not the priests, not the powerful."

There was an immediate reaction to his speech among the crowd at the well and word got back to the high priest immediately.

The High One stood after getting this report said to his lieutenants, "This Jesus is here but one day, and already he demeans his hosts and our religion. I will have to devise a plan for us to be rid of him. He tramples upon the hospitality of his hosts. Invite him here for the solstice feast. I would hear what more he has to say and let me find out what this House of David is. Who is this man? To rally the untouchables against me is to play with fire—mine."

Before the feast day Lilith sat with Jesus to discuss the events and their thoughts concerning what they had seen and heard in the place. "I am much impressed with what I have learned here. What is new to me is the voyage of the soul to this Brahma, I would learn more. There is much to be learned here, much to contemplate. Your thought?" he asked Lilith.

"I am troubled for you, here," Lilith said clasping Jesus' hand. "In this body I am seeing you are not immune to the ways of this planet as long as you are in this human form. With the High One your impatience showed. These human traits are pulling at you, affecting you. I too, have been affected in my time here. The longer we here the more like them we become. The creator succumbs to the ways of the created. I see myself changing Lord, this transmogrification is progressing with me; my birthright powers, and my heart is now moved closer to the hybrid between what it was on high and what we have here below. It happens to all who descend from on high. It is a troublesome aspect."

"But tell me Lilith," Jesus said, "of the troublesome part related to me. What warning do you imply?"

"I am, Lord," Lilith said, "not sure it is wise to antagonize our hosts and stir the population against the rulers here. There will surely be retaliation. I am quite capable of defending us against whatever they might present to us but the conservation of my energies is also wise. An ill use of them now in the early part of our journey may harm us in the latter parts of this voyage."

"I see." Jesus said thoughtfully. "You are wise."

"More," Lilith said, "surely, Lord, has seen that the ideas we have heard here are at odds with much of what we see in the promised land, indeed at odds with those in our own family."

"Speak clearly to me. I would know your deeper meaning," Jesus said.

Lilith stood and began to pace, and said "Many, when we return, will hear from the Son of God who preaches blessings, love and an end of curses as speaking against Lord, the Father himself, and as you know Lord's ideas of a heaven, a migration of the soul, afterlife, love of one's enemies will all be new ideas for the people. Very new. We must think carefully. What we merely discuss here and what we embrace and promulgate upon our return will be very new in Palestine. Much of this will seem strange even to our friends back home."

"True." Jesus said

"And I need not remind you Lord that the mantle of the Messiah is heavy indeed since it must perforce end in your sacrifice, but more, the kernel of the issue is how to reconcile the Messianic message of leading the Jews up against the Romans in war and any new message which stresses the love of one's enemies. How will it ring in Jerusalem where the holy wrath of God is to come down upon the Devils of Rome and Lucifer himself if we return to preach the kingdom is not now of this Earth but a kingdom within? These are not compatible concepts and we run the risk of angering many and satisfying few."

"Weighty thoughts indeed Lilith. I have at this point only the intention to explore and learn but, in the end, my Father has whispered to me that my sojourn here concerns a new covenant and a new convent means new. Its content, as you rightly point out, is yet to be delineated. And true," he said looking intently at her, "there is need to thread lightly between change and what our friends will understand and accept. Indeed we need wisdom in these things to succeed."

"But," said Lilith, "we must now think of the immediate things which relate to the here and now. We should discuss the tact at the festival feast."

"I am weary," Jesus said, "and must sleep now. We should discuss this on the morrow."

But, on the holy feast day Jesus had not discussed his plans with Lilith and continued to speak in the streets of Chelsa. Lilith could see the high priests had his monks at the fringes of the crowds which grew larger and larger as news of this Jesus visitor spread to the countryside. More and more of the untouchables came to hear him speak and it was clear that they were beginning to grasp that the stranger was their champion, and frightened, they were not vocal in their agreement with his words but it was clear they had high regard for him. Some came to him after he spoke to kiss his hand and touch his cloak. These gestures were not lost on the minions of the high priest.

But Jesus drew substance from the recognition given him from the untouchables and their pleadings that he demonstrate his holiness by reaching out to heal the sick among them.

"Show us Jesus," they said, "show us the power of your God, can he heal as our priests do, can he make sickness flee from our bodies, tell us most high is your God greater than Shiva?"

Jesus was moved to compassion from their entreaties and began to reach out among them to heal. He laid hands on a blind man such that he in the instant was able to see again. He took a child into his arms and made it live again. He made from dirt in the ground loaves of bread for the hungry. After each of these demonstrations the crowds, next time, grew larger when he came to speak. More and more of them brought their sick and poor to healed and fed.

Lilith warned Jesus after ten of these preachings. "Lord, I have warned you of these temptations, none is greater to you than that of the worship of these Earth beings. It is a drug you would be well advised to avoid, for once drunk it quickly degrades to empty adulation and loses all spiritual content."

"Jesus shot back at her irritated, "I am, Lilith, about my Father's work and will not be stymied in this."

Meanwhile, Lilith could see that the high priests spies grew more and more agitated and more of more of them appeared at the preachings bringing along with them soldiers who stared at Jesus as if to warn him.

One spoke above the crowed, which grew hushed, shouting "What manner of witchcraft is this, who are you but a demon come among us to dazzle with magicians' cheap tricks. Once we taste of them we endanger our holy karma and come back to this Earth as a lowly insect. This will not allow a release from the Wheel of Life if we believe in this trickery. Begone with you stranger, Leave from among us least Shiva comes down in her terrible wrath and harm the entire lot of us."

Jesus looked at the solider and spoke. "I am here on my Father's work and I have only blessings for the people. I have only my hands to offer to heal the poor and the sick. Is this wrong in your land? Is it your custom to blaspheme the healer?"

The solider turned abruptly and left.

The next day was the festival feast day and Lilith and Jesus prepared to leave for the Ashram, Lilith walked in stillness, clearly troubled. She finally spoke. "I have prepared a plan for our taking leave of this place if we have to do so in haste; which I suspect will be the case. Be ready at my signal should this come to pass Lord, it is only prudent to prepare thus."

"I cannot disagree Jesus said wearily. "Life must be lived here, I see."

At the festival, Jesus and Lilith came to pay their respects to the high priest. It was clear that the meeting would be tense. A man approached them and said "Welcome. Sala welcomes you to this house of prayer." The high priest sat surrounded by a small group of his advisors who all starred intently at Jesus and Lilith, their displeasure scarcely disguised.

"I am so pleased that you have accepted our invitation to participate in the festival and offer again our hospitality for you visit here. How long I might ask do you plan to be among us and when would you be taking leave of us?" It was in Chelsa a rude comment.

"We are not sure, Highness, it is something unclear, your people have taken us to their hearts and we are much vivified in this."

"I am sure this is the case," the high priest said. "Let us join the festival now and may I suggest that rather than descend the mountain tonight you allow me to extend our hospitality further and stay with us. I have prepared guest quarters for the two of you, if this is something you will accept."

Jesus said, "We thank you again for yet another gracious offer." The two went to the festival and there were some among the crowd who approached Jesus and begged that he heal their wounds or lay hands upon them. Jesus stopped to minister to their needs but their number only grew and did disrupt the festival at several intervals. This did not go unobserved. Sala looked down from his window over the festival and growled lowly, "Tonight we will deal with him."

That evening in their rooms, Lilith sat by the door and said, "We are very vulnerable here. I have packed our things for surely the high priest will send here those to do harm to us. We have no choice, we must flee, be on our way to Tibet in the highest mountains. There I have word of one who will take us to the spiritual leaders there, Jesus," she said, with a piercing look toward him, "our time here is done."

With that the two quietly slid their door open and moved into the night.

At a distance the high priest watched them make their departure. He turned to a lieutenant who asked "Shall we apprehend them, Highness?"

"No," the high priest said, "Let them go in peace. We shall not be the ones to harm the Son of God."

But Jesus did not leave India immediately. Despite Lilith's protests he traveled from village in the general direction of Tibet but stopping in each village to preach his message of redemption of the poor and the sick. He continued to heal among them, despite the watchful eyes of the authorities who tracked all of his movements. Some of the soldiers brought their sick and wounded children for Jesus to heal and he did. Some became followers of his.

The High One, Sala, decided not to intervene. He said to his lieutenants "Harm him not as long as his path leads to the border."

It was on this trek to Tibet that Jesus learned that his earthly father, Joseph, had died. He was stricken with a great sadness as he paused with Lilith at the base of the high mountains. "I am here far away from him and can offer no comfort to Mary. Am I not" he said to Lilith, "the worst of sons? I shall write her and offer consolations to her, for surely her sadness must be great indeed. Do you think I should return?"

Lilith shook her head, no. "That would take many days travel and you would arrive very late in the process and could do little in that regard. A letter is best I think. We can have a traveler from here deliver it for you. James will be able to lead the family through this, he is capable."

229

Jesus sat for two days and composed a letter to Joseph which would be carried from community to community on his behalf.

He said "I have in my life known only my father in heaven and you my earthly father. In all these days you have stood with me, nurtured me and made many sacrifices for me and the work of my father in heaven. You believed in me and took upon yourself this great mission and I am sadden that you will not be here to see it to fruition. I am secure in the belief that now you are on high with my father who has seen fit to call you home now. He has his reasons which none can fathom. But tell him for me that I am about the work and his guidance is my only beacon. Tell him that Lilith is my earthly teacher and my protector in my time here. It will not be long before I am again with you. Jesus."

It felt good to have written the letter.

At the first monastery, Jesus was able to get a traveler destined for Canaan to deliver his message to Mother Mary. Lilith told the traveler, "Fear not, Lord will guide your way."

To Jesus she said "I will appear to Mary to tell of the traveler's journey to her, and of your care."

Chapter 52

Lilith made arrangements for Jesus to visit the sacred monastery of Lamaism and to visit with Meng-Tse, a Chinese sage, who was to introduce him to the writings known as the Tibetan Book of the Dead. The trek up the mountain trails was an exhausting one, but they arrived at the temple and were received by Meng-Tse.

Jesus was to spend three years learning the sacred texts there and comparing those writings with those of his family and those he had read in Temple. The Book of the Dead interested him most and Meng-Tse spent many hours discussing it with Jesus and Lilith. The Book spoke of Bardo's or the experience of consciousness from the moment of death to reincarnation.

Meng-Tse said in their first week there "We must see death as a passage of consciousness thorough several states. From the moment of expiration, the *chikhai* bardo brings a moment of brilliant light where the individual sees the blue ghost and this is followed by the *chonyid* bardo where visions of Buddha forms attuned to individuals capabilities and then there is the *sidpa* bardo which is the last step before re-birth."

"We can," Meng-Tse said, "experience other bardos in this life where we see in our ordinary waking consciousness, a bardo of *dhyana* or meditation and the bardo where we can enter a dream state while awake and gain clarity on many things if we train the mind to roll back its curtain of confusions. I believe this dream state, asleep or awake, can connect the individual to past lives and well as future ones and thereby utilize knowledges gained there from."

"One," he said, "is the collection of all of one's lives, past and future; the miracle is that we can meditate and bring unified knowledge of all of them together in one space for a short period of time."

Unlike our Indian friends, our Karma is not out of control or predestined, resulting in rigid castes and hierarchies, our Karma can be controlled by the individual. Our future is ours to make. By that I mean to say Karma can influence your actions, but you are the ruler of your intents, thoughts and action and, therefore, of the Karmic consequences. You are responsible for all this and no one else. One can overcome one's Karma in a rebirth. There is no devil making the individual behave badly. That is what the Buddha teaches."

It was in relation to this idea that the young Jesus had the most trouble comprehending. Does not the Buddha believe that there is evil in the world?"

"He does," Meng-Tse said, "but that evil intent and the actions which flow from that create evil is Karma; but this is man-made."

"As well, the Buddha said we must remember that the deed itself may be evil but can be mitigated by the whole of a person's life and in this way negative Karma can be obviated."

"In the Anguttara Nikava, Buddha said," Meng-Tse continued, "a man who has not cultivated his body, or his intents; his life will be a short life and even a small evil will send him to hell. But a man who has followed the ways of the Buddha will not fall so and may have long life. This small evil will not produce evil karma in the next."

These ideas greatly interested Jesus because some of them resonated with those of his family and the Essenes and even those of the Pharisees. He began to see how many ideas from many cultures had similarities and perhaps even common origins. He asked Meng-Tse where the great creation ideas in Tibet came from. Meng-Tse would only answer that "An answer to that would entail being the great Buddha himself."

At the end of his third year in Tibet, Lilith and Jesus prepared for the next leg of their journey which would take them to Egypt to review the sacred writings there and to meet with Essene leaders who had an established community in Egypt for hundreds of years.

Jesus said to Lilith, as he breathed in the shallow air from the heights of the steep mountain ranges, "I have learned much here but how these learnings are to be made a part of the gospel in Jerusalem and integrated into the preachings is a puzzle of great magnitude."

"Indeed," Lilith said, "the Buddha's way stresses individual responsibility but they do not have the heel of the Roman sandal on their necks as do our brethren at home. They do not have the urgency we do."

"And I am not sure," Jesus said, "that the expurgation of all evil in the world is a preaching I can do. I know evil exists in the form of Lucifer."

"I, as well," Lilith said.

***

On their trip into Egypt, the young Jesus and Lilith arrived in Ephesus where Jesus went before The Council of One-hundred in the Supreme Temple there. There was great excitement in the city at news of his eminent arrival. The Essene College there had over 200 students and Jesus' arrival had more that just passing interest, because there was to be a determination there, among the One-hundred as to whether or not he was to be anointed by them as the Messiah.

Jesus stood before them in the early morning and said "Greetings to all. I bring tidings from Mt. Carmel and the communities of the East. I have traveled many roads in coming before you today and I have learned many things."

The Council Leader greeted Jesus. "We have many years now followed closely your birth, your education and now your travels. Be sure that you are welcome among us. Join with us young Jesus in prayer. The Council men and the associate women stood and cited the Brotherhood prayer.

"Bless us, oh Lord, that we might be humble in all we do, each day;

May we not harm any creature, man, woman, child or animal;

May we seek Justice for all; may we seek not, nor participate in, the belittlement of any person or thing;

May we be given the strength to refrain from displaying superior prowess, mental or physical at the expense of no one;

May our very souls stay free of worldly gains and their pursuits.

May we never seek dominion over any man woman or child and we shall not seek or participate in any form of slavery, serfdom or the servitude of others.

May anger never cross our hearts and may we not indulge in unkind emotions.

May we seek moderation in all things and keep our silence among those outside the Brotherhood and speak softly.

We shall only participate in the peaceful trades, carpentry, planting, and merchants;

May we Lord relinquish all our worldly goods and gains to provide for the sick and the poor, the stranger and the downtrodden, for this is our mission in this world."

Finished Elias, their leader said, "We ask the Jesus to come forward."

Jesus came forward and Elias said, "I, Elias, place my hands upon you such that the Holy Ghost enters your earthly body and inhabit your spirit because only the spirit matters."

"I sit before you as a stranger and wash your feet."

With that Elias, kneeled before Jesus and took a cloth from a nearby bowl of water and began to wash Jesus' feet as was the custom among them. Elias, continued, "We hereby consecrate our belief that we must care for all, friends and stranger alike, we hereby by consecrate our belief that friends and foe alike may receive food from our hands, succor as relief from the travails of this world and kind words not rebukes." With that said he completed the washing of the feet of Jesus.

"Now stand, young Master," Elias said, "we would hear from you."

Jesus stood and began his address to the Council. "I am humbled and thankful to the Council for your welcome and I bring greetings to you from the community in Mt. Carmel. I am here today about the work of my Father who has bid me to carry the news of a new message to the peoples of the world, of the existence of one God, the only God."

"This God," Jesus said, "is the God of not a single people but all people of the Earth, this God is a God of blessings, and not a God of curses, and this God is a loving God and is the God of the poor, of the peacemakers. This is the true God and this is the true message of God."

Members of the Council began to murmur their assents to the words of Jesus.

"I come before you today seek your assent, an affirmation that I have been blessed by that God to be his representative on Earth at this time to carry this new message to all. I come today asking that, if it meets the wisdom and foresight you have among you to see that destiny in me, and are willing to grant me your support as the Messiah of David and the Messiah of the new covenant, then I will agree to take upon myself that mission if that is what is desired of me."

"I have been told from my birth that this is my destiny. I have since I can remember prepared myself and received so much love and support from so many who have helped me prepare. And now I come before you and the high council to look upon me, to look into my soul and apply your wisdom to my humble self and make your opinion known as to whether I am the anointed one or merely a prophet of another yet to come. I will abide by your decision."

Jesus withdrew.

***

That evening Lilith said, "They have welcomed you. That is good."

"Yes." Jesus said. "I have a spiritual home here which began before the days of Pharaoh Akhenaton who was inspired, I have read, to declare that all of the Egyptian Gods were to be replaced by the one true God. He did so at great risk to himself. He eliminated the priests in the temples and they revolved against him. After his death they obliterated his name from all the records, all of the temples and sought to deny him dignity in death. They reinstituted the old Gods and their power."

"But his name and his deeds were kept alive in this group. They are the scribes of history in Egypt. They are the preservers of some of the most important writings dating back to the great library at Alexandria."

"Indeed," Lilith said. "I wonder though are you not apprehensive of the decision of the Council?'

"I am," Jesus said, "but that is a matter in the hands of my father. He came to me last night and gave me news that I am to marry."

"Marry!" Lilith exclaimed, "That is wonderful news. Lord told you this? I am pleased, yet wonder how do you greet this development? Do you welcome it?"

"'I am very pleased. She is Mary Magdalene and I know her. My family has said that I should marry immediately upon my return. This is of great inspiration to me. I am, to take a wife in this body; this is something unknown to me."

"Lilith held her tongue remembering a marriage that she too had participated in long ago with the Father on high. It was with very mixed emotions she heard of this from the young boy.

***

The next day the Council convened and Elias stood to speak the decision of the Council.

He said "Jesus of Nazareth, we have conferred in this anointment and asked guidance from the Father, the one God. We sent our prayers to him and asked that he send us a sign to guide us. We have known of you and your birth in Bethlehem. We know, of course, of your family, may they be blessed. We know that many troubles beset your land and our communities there, who suffer greatly under Roman rule. We have laid side by side the principles of the Brotherhood with Davidic prophesies to see what will be resolution of the conflicts between the two. You shall have to achieve this with guidance from the Father."

"On our part," he continued, as he closely examined Jesus' presence, "we will pronounce from this day and inscribe in the parchments that you are indeed the Messiah spoken of in the Holy Writ, that you are the reincarnation of all of the great prophets of the past come now to relieve the suffering in this world and to bring a new message to the peoples of the Earth. So it is spoken here now, so will it be written in the parchments. Blessings be upon you."

With that Elias sat. His posture was humble and he trembled from being in the presence of such a Master.

Jesus rose from the ground which he sat and spoke, visibly overwhelmed with Elias' pronouncement, "I am humbled before you and very grateful for your recognition of my mission from the Father. There is in this Brother Elias much to ponder in your words concerning the reconciliation of the Davidic prophecy and that which has so long been given us in the Brotherhood. I shall heed those words carefully as I make my way back to

Jerusalem--my heart full of your love and praise for the one on high."

"There, as is Lord's will, I will marry and undertake the ministry of the word in his land."

Chapter 53

Jesus undertook the journey home, rejuvenated. He and Lilith decided to stop in Babylonia and Assyria to speak before communities there which had already heard the news of his anointment. There was great joy amongst the people, but Jesus told them that he had not begun his final ministry as yet and this would not begin until he reached home. The leaders there understood and simply stated "As you wish, Lord."

"But they did have questions; many questions for the young boy, questions which Lilith urged him not to answer. In Babylonia, leaders wanted to know if they should take up arms and await his signal to attack the Roman garrisons; if they would all be saved in the coming holocaust as the prophecy has predicted; if he was the Messiah. All these questions Jesus did not answer simply stating that answer to these questions were in the hands of his Father and they would have to wait, as he did, to learn of his Father's wishes.

A Babylonian leader named Arias came to Jesus the night before he was to leave for Nazareth and spoke to him of what had transpired over the nine years the young Jesus had been gone. "It has been a very eventful nine years Master," Arias, said, "much has occurred. First, James, in your absence, has lead the movement and has gone among the people spreading the word of your coming. He and your cousin, John, have told the people of the baptism rites and they have responded to their messages. Our ranks have grown greatly in Judea to the point where we are 5,000 strong there now and equal the numbers of the Pharisees the Sadducees and the priests. Judas, your brother, had done well also in taking up the case of the poor and spreading the message that they will inherit. Good work has been done Master. Many of the rebels are now in the hills and await your word to attack the Roman strongholds."

"Thank you Arias. Many blessings to you for your hospitality to Lilith and myself. I now must on the morrow be off and onto my Father's work," is all Jesus would say.

The next day, Lilith and Jesus were off to Nazareth. All along the way people greeted him with "Hosannas," while many simply nodded to him as he passed offering to keep his passing unnoticed and unreported least the Roman spies take note.

It was on a quiet evening when Jesus arrived at his home in Capernaum He was greeted by his mother Mary, his brothers, sisters, cousins having prepared a meal to mark his return. It was a joyous moment.

Jesus stood at the simple meal to acknowledge their good wishes and their many questions of his journey. "I am much humbled by the love you shown me tonight and the many years of support you, my family, have shown me and the community here in Capernaum has given me. I have been to many places and learned many things. I was in Ephesus where I met with the Council of One Hundred and they, with my Father's inspiration, proclaimed me the anointed one, and with that blessing, I am returned and prepared to begin my ministry here in my homeland."

"I have heard many wise words in India, in Tibet, in Egypt, in Babylonia and many other places and have met many who share our views and values, and those who do not. I have heard of the prophecies of many religions, in many countries; met with priests and wise men; and now I have come home. I am anxious to know of the news here. But first may we be with the Kaddish for Joseph, our earthly Father, who walked in the way of Lord and is now home with him; we thank him, Lord, for his many sacrifices upon our behalf; for his steadfast faith in us, and his support. He is home with you."

Jesus asked for a moment of silence in honor of Joseph.

***

There was then a lively discussion of what was to transpire with Jesus now that he had returned.

"We have many many expectations among the people." James said. "They are torn. Some say we should proclaim the end of days; that the Messiah has come and the Romans will now die in a blaze of righteous retribution just as the Davidic prophecy has foretold.

Some of the Brotherhood insists that we must not veer from the Essene way, that we should stick to our holy principles and not become rebels and kill. This would destroy who we have been for centuries and likely make an end to our communities. The Roman retribution would be severe and all our communities would be threatened."

"Still others say we should not remain the silent ones but come out with our message so that all might hear the message of the one who the Father has said is the Messiah, but do not choose war as the means to the kingdom. They urge a third way."

"What say you Jesus? What is best here?" asked James.

Jesus stood to address, brushing the desert dust from his clothing. He was mindful that much depended upon his words. He said, "I am aware of these ways of thinking. I have heard them from the Council, itself, and they, too, spoke of their concerns as to how these matters would be resolved."

"I am myself am awaiting guidance from the Father. But of these things I am sure. We must first begin the ministry and do as we have done, strengthen the movement and gain adherents by spreading the true word of God. That I am certain is the path we must take first. We say to the people the time is not right for rebellion. That Lord will act in his own time. This is our charge." Jesus said. "It is best to gather our strength."

"Besides," he said to them, "I have not yet seen my new bride and is it not improper to bring to her so soon upon my return, plans for war? We shall have time to speak of these things many times in the future. First, I marry now in my twenty-first year as is our custom. Let joy be our marker for this new beginning!"

"Mary Magdalene took my heart nine years ago," Jesus said "and I am betrothed to her."

Many in the room were surprised at this announcement because only James and Mother Mary knew Jesus had remained connected with her. But in fact Jesus had never forgotten her.

Jesus would only say, "She is the one chosen by my Father. So it is, so it will be done."

With that said they all agreed and the plans for the wedding of Jesus and Mary Magdalene began. It was a joyous plan they made. From all over Nazareth to Jerusalem, to Mt. Carmel and countries beyond the news that the marriage was to take place excited members of the community and many saw it as high honor to be invited even as the wedding had to be kept in secret least suspicions arise among the Romans. Additionally, as many pointed out, the news of Jesus' return had spread to the Pharisees and the Sanhedrin. This was an ominous event in the minds of many from these groups.

At the day of the wedding, Jesus sat receiving the best regards of more than twenty-five of his friends and relatives gathered to honor him. Many had simple gifts, all home made without destroying any thing, person or animal of the Earth. Many offered to wash his feet and place upon them oils and creams. All offered prayers for him, because most understood that underneath the celebrations Jesus, the young boy they knew, now a man, had agreed to most awful of deaths at the end of this; his passion.

Jesus saw Mary of Magdalene surrounded by her family, veiled from head to foot and was most pleased at the sight of her. She was in white linen, as was their custom, and his mother Mary told him she was very quick and bright and already an associate in the Brotherhood. Jesus was well pleased in her aspect. Her sister and brother, Martha and Lazarus, were there to vouch for her and Jesus was well pleased to be her bride-groom.

***

The wedding was in Cana at Joseph's brother's house. Jesus and his party arrived there in the early evening. As the ceremony began Jesus walked to the khuppah, the wedding canopy, which was covered with a prayer shawl.

He stood there as his betrothed, Mary, came in with her wedding party walking toward him and then circling him seven times as he stood under the khuppah. With each passing he found her more and more beautiful and she offered him blessing after blessing until she had counted all seven. Jesus was in this very happy.

"Blessed is he who comes!" cried the guests; "Blessed is he who comes!" they cried again.

241

He placed his ring upon her hand saying, "Behold, thou art consecrated unto me this right according to the Law of Moses and of Israel." He gave her a gold coin saying "This represents my commitment to you and to say unto you that my heart sings and my spirit rejoices, for you are my eternal companion."

Mary said "I will never leave you, my Lord, your light will always guide my path, and with you, I will create."

He could see in her eyes tears of joy.

Now it was that under the laws Jesus and Mary could not complete the marriage ceremony until a home had been prepared for them as their permanent residence. He spoke to her that night before she returned to her home in Bethany.

"I am the most blessed of men and I well pleased in you." Jesus said to her.

She said "I am most blessed in being wed to you and I believe that many will be blessed as well through your work for your father."

"We are, "Jesus said "most blessed, indeed, Mary love;" he said, "understand that in all my days here, you will be my best confident and Lilith as well. I am wed to thee and many nations who count me as their bridegroom. My Father has spoken to me of this and I now understand that my ministry must now begin in this land and come to its prophesized end."

Mary paused and gazed at him. She said "Let us not look so far into the future, let us take only tonight in our regard and accept this gift; this night as ours."

***

Jesus accompanied Mary to her home in Bethany. When they arrived there was an immediate clamor that he should speak to the people there who welcomed his return and were eager to hear from him the words of Lord. Lazarus urged him to come and speak by the fountain in Bethany. Jesus said "Lazarus; I do not wish to make a host of enemies before my timing. This will come soon enough. If I inflame the pious, this will only anger the unrighteous. Then we will have persecutions before I am prepared. There are many things I must do in quiet and peace."

But Lazarus was persistent in his request and at length Jesus agreed to make an address to the crowd by the fountain. It was a powerful speech in which Jesus told the assembled that; it was sin to raise your voice in unrighteous anger, to hide the truth for fear of retribution, that the system of all property and wealth going to the first male in each family was unjust in the eyes of Lord; that all should come forth and confess their sins in hope of forgiveness from Lord, that all children born are children of God and that the oldest child should not be favored over female children or younger siblings, that a man may live all the commandments upon Sinai, but if these commandments are not present in his thoughts and secret intents, it is as though they did not exist; that obeying these commandments grudgingly will be weighed on the Day of Judgment--not the pretense of action meant mainly to impress those in the temple.

"Whatsoever you sow you shall reap," Jesus said, "whether priest, first born, rich man or poor, all may have need to repent."

There was an outcry from some in the crowd who said "We have no need of repentance, who are you to say this to us? Another said "The day of the prophets is over, we are descendents of Abraham and Isaac and have no need of forgiveness."

Yagur, the Pharisee spoke and he said unto Yeshua, "By what authority do you say these things? Which prophets are you quoting that we may know that your words are of true merit? Jesus responded saying "I speak by the authority of God my father and it is from the words of Lord that I speak. Hear my words, oh men of the world, for by them you will be justified, and by them you will be condemned."

Another said "You speak in ways that are contrary to the law, for you have spoken that even those who are not a part of us, not one of the chosen, can still find equal favor with God simply because they live a good life."

Yagur continued saying "The time of the great Prophets is passed and you are blasphemous to speak as you do; you do not speak to uphold the laws that have been given, but think to make new laws unto yourself."

These few were stunned by Jesus' words but most began to whisper to one another and said, "Surely this man must be a great Prophet, for he speaks with the calmness of still waters, the confidence of a lion, and the power of thunder. He does not quote the Prophets that came before, but speaks as if he has been given the words from the very mouth of Elohim."

Jesus continued, "Any man who loves God with the depth of his heart also loves all that lives because Elohim has made it, and this man will live the Commandments of Sinai, even if he is from a far land and has never heard of them."

"Elohim, the only and true God, loves him and favors him, not because of who his father was, nor whether he was the first born or the last, nor whether he is a Hebrew or a Gentile, but because of who he has chosen to become inside himself; because of how he has chosen to live both seen and unseen by men; because of the light he gives unto the world."

"To each I say unto you," Jesus said that fateful day, "you are the Master. The light of your soul contends with the temptations of your body. Choose to be the Master of your body instead of its slave and you will find a joy and peace in this world such as you never have imagined, and a great reward in heaven, beyond the descriptions of men, built with every good you have ever sown."

"Who then," Jesus said, "is the adversary? Where is the root of evil? It is you. Man is his own enemy. To conquer yourself in a far greater measure than you are conquered by yourself, is the supreme challenge of life, and only those who succeed will pass the portal of judgment into eternal glory."

He came down from the fountain and walked among them. Many were the men and women who touched him and asked blessings from him; and many were those whom he touched and blessed with a portion of his light.

***

That night Lilith, Jesus and Mary Magdalene discussed the day's events. Lilith said "Surely, Lord, the die is now cast. Word of the sermon today will reach Jerusalem in two days and I am sure that the Pharisees

244

will have a meeting and decide what to do. We will then have to take up this ministry sooner than we had planned."

"Yes," Jesus agreed, "it would appear so."

Mary said, "There is much to consider here. I must say that much of what you have said Lord today was indeed shocking to many who would oppose your message and this is not something which can be ignored. Let me speak for a moment and give my sense of the impact this day has had and my remedy.

"Mary declared, "We should not take the lead in these spiritual matters least we divide opinion among the many and fragment opinion needlessly. Why not, as planned, not take the lead and allow John to gather adherents as he has done these many years. Your arrival need not entail his stepping aside. Secondly, while John has stirred many he, nonetheless, has identified you as the blessed one. This is good. Meanwhile, in the south your brother, James, has taken the leadership of the movement there. It is wise, I think, to make appearances and demonstrate what John has said but not necessarily take the leadership position at this time."

"I agree." said Lilith. "There is in this the Father's plan which does not implement for nine years as written in the Holy Writ. Let us not now hurry fate let we change the state of matters."

Jesus nodded his agreement.

Chapter 54

James and members of the family came to Jesus as well after the sermon at the fountain in Bethany.

James spoke for the group. "Lord," he said, "you have spoken of the end of days and that is a message most welcome in the south where the Roman control is greatest. Here in the north there is less a sense of their presence. Perhaps that is a factor. You have spoken to the people of the sins of anger, divorce, oath-taking and revenge. You warned against gluttony and wealth-getting. It was good, I thought, your statement that you did not come to destroy the Law of Moses but to fulfill the Laws was inspired. You have said to them they must learn new laws, laws which require them to turn the other cheek to anger and to love one's enemies. It was good to have said to them, I think, that the kingdom is within and the Son's of Man will have a kingdom not of this Earth, but above, on high."

"This latter," James said, "has allowed the Sanhedrin to ignore you for the time being. I am hearing their focus is more and more on John and me. I have spoken to many and they ask me of the Messiah in the Holy Writ, the Messiah who will come and lead the people in rebellion against the Romans. I have said that you are the Messiah of the writ but you have come also as the Son of God, come to supersede the writ and bring a new testament and a new word to the people."

"This part is the part which is most troublesome and most dangerous to us Lord," James continued, "we have two ideas of what you as Messiah ought to be and ought to do here on Earth. Where is the kingdom of God that the Son of God is to bring, they ask, on Earth or in heaven? Or within? These are troublesome questions we have to address."

His brothers and disciples all agreed in that Passover meeting that it was so.

Jesus rose and responded and said, "I am aware that these are questions among the people and as yet my Father has not chosen to reveal to me the answer he wants me to bring. But I say to you that there is no contradiction among the three. The kingdom is within, the Kingdom is above and I am the Son of God come to fulfill the prophesy of the Messiah and yet to extend to all peoples of the Earth a new testament for their learning. These are the words my Master has spoken to me and these are the tasks he has told me lie ahead for me. As to war, I am not come to bring war."

"Now brethren," he said, "I understand that these are new thoughts and it will take time for their meanings to come clear to the people. But we must be patient in this and not try to hurry the work. Lord acts through us. We do not tell him the timetable."

"I will," he said after pausing, "move among the people and show all the power of Lord, I will do his work not just speak his word. One has to do both. James, you and John should continue as you have because it is good that many ask questions. That many question now not only us, but the Pharisees as well is movement. This is part of God's plan. I need not remind you of that plan."

"We shall move in our haste but move at Lord's pace. Now let's eat."

James said finally, "So be it Lord, but understand the Zealots have promised the end of days and soon. To them this means expelling the Romans from our lands."

Jesus looked at James with a steadfast gaze. "I understand James. All things in the timing of Lord."

***

Lord from on high came to Lilith that night startling her. She said "Is that you Lord?"

"It is, me, Lord."

"I have no clear vision of you Lilith said, "Are you Lord from on High.

"Yes, it is me, Lilith. I have come to be with you and to speak my mind to you. I will speak my heart."

"Yes, Lord," Lilith said "please do."

"I have been with you and Jesus all these years," Lord said "and did not intervene because I was pleased in your shepharding, very pleased. Know, too, Lilith I am aware of the heart that beats within you and know that much of this is difficult for you, that you, too, suffer in this and that you, in your human body manifestation, risk your own immortality in taking on this assignment as I have asked you to."

Lord paused; "I am seeing as well there is risk and pain in the Son's body which I am feeling more and more. This is all new to me. I have never known physical pain, or hunger."

"There is physical pain and hunger in these bodies," Lilith said.

"I mean to say, as well, Lilith that my heart too longs for you, my wife, and I look forward to the day that you might ascend with the Son on high. I hope, that is, this will be your choice rather than stay in your humanly body on Earth."

Lilith turned her face away.

Lord continued appearing on her other side and peered into her face, "All my heart wishes for this Lilith. My forgiveness in this is complete. I am wishing that this is so for you as well."

"It is good to hear Lord," Lilith said tentatively, "that you have a new testament you are offering. There is much wisdom in what you are preaching in this body on earth; this is a Lord which I find more to my heart spiritually, this is a Lord which has seen fit to forgive mankind all sin, at great sacrifice to himself, the Son. Never has there been a greater deed done, and one which has unknown effects upon you, even in heaven. How will this earthly trip affect thy being on high? Surely there will be such effects. We know to visit Earth is to affect the spirit upon its re-assent on high. I trust that there will be no ill effects. We must talk of this more, such that I can understand and well advise the Son what may be in store for him upon his return."

"And yours, what of your return Lilith, Lord said.
"There is
nothing greater my heart desires than this."

Lilith did not respond.

"There is nothing greater in this heaven's history that would compare to your and the Son's return, arm in arm."

Lilith said, "Let me think upon this, Lord. Know, however, that I am many eons here on this Earth and none can say in what a return might eventuate. I shall think on this," she said wistfully.

Not long after Lord left, Lilith thought about the transpired conversation; sad, as she lay down. Perhaps she had already remained on Earth too long to expect to re-ascend safely.

The day following, Lilith told Jesus of her visitation with Lord. "Are you aware of these things in your earthly form?" She asked.

Jesus looked at her and said, "I feel these things and Lord makes me aware of them if he sees fit. But I am not aware of any of the details of your visit. Apparently it is my Father's wish that this be so."

"And what are you aware of this time" Lilith asked.

Jesus looked at her and said reverently, "I am aware how much he loves you and wants your forgiveness; he is aware of how much you have meant to me these years and I am aware how much I am grateful to you for the many blessings and love you have given me."

Jesus continued, "Thank you, Lilith, for as my Father has said through me, man and woman are equal in all things and he is showing all Earth people this as well through you and Mary Magdalene, my wife and closest apostle."

"There is another thing I am sensing as well in this."

"What is that?" Lilith questioned.

"I sense whenever I use his powers on Earth something changes within me. I feel his power pass through me, but this human body cannot sustain forever these surges. They make me feel weak after and I must rest. Is it the same for you as well, Lilith?"

"It is." Lilith said.

Chapter 55

At thirty, Jesus decided it was time to begin his ministry in earnest. John was becoming more and more a target and the Pharisees and the Romans alike began to focus on the two as major threats to their power. Jesus too, was attracting increasing numbers in individuals who came to hear him speak especially in and around Jerusalem.

He first determined, as was the new custom, to see his cousin John the Baptist, who would perform his baptism in the river Jordan. He decided to go alone.

"Greetings, my Brother, "John said, "I am so pleased to see you and offer to you my best wishes."

"Greetings, Brother John," Jesus said, "may you everyday walk in the light. I have heard many good things of your work."

"All of this," John said, "was in preparation for your return. In you, Master, I have delivered all my faith and all my love for the future. This evening, in the quiet of the evening stars, let us perform the Baptismal immersion. I have invited many to come to witness the event in your honor, Jesus."

Under a rising evening moon, over four hundred came to see John perform the full immersion of Jesus under the waters of the Jordan River. They crowded the river bank eager to see the ceremony, eager to talk to Jesus; some wanting him to heal them of ailments or to offer food to them.

John said, "In the name of the Father, the Son and the Holy Ghost, I commend your soul to these holy waters, which by the power of your Father reaffirms that you are the one, the one the Father has sent to us. I commend to all that can hear me. This man is the Son of God, the one."

There was a hush among the multitude, for John had many adherents, who considered him the major prophet, the Messiah himself. Many regarded John as the promised one.

"I urge all of you to follow this man, for he speaks the word of God. Give him your love as you would me, and more."

Jesus was cradled by John. Jesus was immersed and came up and spoke, "In my Father's name, I have come. In my Father's name I will fulfill his word."

It was the first time the adherents of John and those of Jesus broke bread together. This combing of groups did not go unnoticed.

***

The baptism was the beginning of Jesus' ministry in earnest. To purify himself at this inception of his ministry, he went into the desert to cleanse his soul, to fast, preparing himself for what he knew would be his martyrdom.

Lilith offered to accompany him but he said this was something he had to do on his own, that it was his mettle which needed to be tested. With a morning prayer he left to spend forty days in the desert, living alone, sleeping in the caves at night and performing meditations in the heat of the sun.

***

Lucifer saw Jesus undertake the journey and understood what it meant. Jesus was preparing himself. He came to Jesus after many days. Jesus was thirsty, hungry and very weak.

Lucifer spoke to him. "I see you are hungry Jesus. Why would you not make bread from the stones and eat to relieve your aching belly? Why would you not call upon Lord to aid you in this? No one here would see or care. Will not your ministry be about the feeding of the sick and poor yet you would deny substance to yourself? Is this to be the message you convey?"

Jesus looked at Lucifer and said, "You forget, Lucifer, I am the Son and the Father is within as well. We know you and your history and you intend no good here. The weakness of the stomach and the need to eat is not the focus of this ministry."

"I see," Lucifer said. "Then tell me, Lord, what is to be the focus for you? These earthlings will come to you time and time again, since you have made for them wine and bread, from water and stones to heal or feed them.

251

Surely you see they are hungry, many of them, and want to be fed as a part of your ministry. Surely this cannot be wrong."

"Man does not live by bread alone, Lucifer, that is my message here," said Jesus.

"I see." said Lucifer. "But, tell me, what exactly is to be your ministry?" Are you here to be the King of all Nations, is that the mission? Are you the Messiah of David; or are you to be the Son of God, who will not stay, but be raised again to heaven and then where will the poor, be once you have gone? Surely you can see these are essential questions for the multitudes."

"Here, let me show you the high places from the Temple Pinnacle," Lucifer said. "from there you can survey what could be your kingdom as far as the eye can see if you but join with me."

Lucifer showed the weakened Jesus the view from the highest point of the Temple in Jerusalem. Satan said, "Now, it would not be a bad thing, would it, to remain here on Earth and have rule and dominion over all nations--to do good and carry out the mission of Lord. Surely a thousand years of peace is not a bad thing? I had a wager with Lord over a man named Job, which said these humans are not followers of Lord, they are mine to rule. I wagered that earthlings favor comfort over obedience. I pose the same wager to you, Son of God, stay on Earth, exert your powers and we shall then see who these humans really love."

"Why not take the staff of rule and impose upon all nations the gift of peace? What say you Jesus, is your rule the rule of peace? Why retreat to heaven and thereby prevent that pain of crucifixion to come and allow peace to come earlier rather than later? Are these not good ideas, Jesus? Tell me your thoughts."

"I am not here for rule or power," Jesus said. "The way is the way from within--not rule over others, mine, or yours, Lucifer."

"Then free your self from the Pinnacle," Lucifer said. "I now place you at the very top. Will you call upon the angels for your rescue? Will you jump and count upon faith for your salvation before you land on the stones below? Tell me Jesus can Jesus save himself? If so why don't you?"

Jesus said, "I am immune to these taunts and did not come to Earth to prove I can save myself. That would be a vanity Lucifer, a mistake you, yourself, should understand. It is one you, yourself, have made."

Angered by this statement from Jesus, Lucifer, took a deep breath and said mildly, holding his venomous thoughts at bay, "If you could but see wisdom in my words, Jesus, you and I could easily rule these humans; simply make a truce with me, is all I ask. Is that not reasonable? Why war between us when I offer peace?"

"Upon what terms is the Devil's peace? Jesus said. "Clear, it is the peace of the slave and of avarice, of pride, of rank power; things I am here to strip away and replace with a spiritual mission. You have no such goal, this is clear."

"I see," said Lucifer, "but I fear, Jesus, you will have to choose among my proffered options because these are the ones these earthlings desire and, I say how to be a savior, if you don't give them want they want?"

"You are of a smooth tongue Lucifer, I know it was a gift from my Father, but here this final word; I am here not to give what is desired but to raise the candle higher."

Stunned by Jesus and reminded that Lord had created him, Lucifer said, "Then who am I, Lord, in the final analysis, am I the demon Lucifer or merely the Tester for you in mankind's affairs?"

***

Jesus arrived back home from Mount Quarantania exhausted from his spiritual journey but his mind was refreshed. His plans were clearly set before him.

"I am resolved now," he said to Lilith and Mary, let us begin our ministry."

"Yes, Mary said "I will call together the disciples you have chosen and have them ready themselves."

"Let us go first to Cana," Mary Magdalene said "I have relatives there and we have been invited to a wedding there," Mary Magdalene said.

There were about sixty people in the Holy Party as they began their journey to Cana. They went out from town to town making their way to Cana. Mary, Lilith and Jesus' mother, walked with him and many people stopped them and asked who they were and where were they going.

Lilith told them, "This is Jesus of Nazareth, who this day was beginning his ministry for the poor and the weak telling them of God's new covenant."

Some of the townspeople joined the party asking questions of Jesus, the two Mary's and Jesus disciples. "Who is he?" they asked, "and is he the Messiah? Will he bring food to us? Will he lead us to rise against the Romans? Will he show his power against our enemies?"

Food was provided food for Jesus' group that first night. Jesus spoke to them beside a house that was opened to them. The meal was prepared in his honor. He spoke to the group. Many had questions about his forty days in the desert and whether or not he had received messages from Lord.

"I was in the desert," he said, "fasting and an apparition came to me and tempted me, taunted me as will be the case with many of you. You will be assailed in our journeys by those that hate you on my account, those that will revile you and seek to test your faith in the one God, in the new covenant. I say unto you, any faith untested is," he paused, "a faith that is not yet born; any faith not placed in the furnace of the desert that does not return stronger, is a faith untested. So fear not, my friends, as we begin because if your faith is strong we will in the end, do his will."

One there asked him if he was not afraid of the Romans and if he was not afraid that they would know him and crucify him.

Jesus replied. "My faith in the Father is strong."

***

The following day Jesus' group arrived at the wedding in Cana. A man came out to him and said that the Pharisees had many spies who watched and reported everything they saw and asked Jesus if it was wise for him to come into the town.

Jesus said, "We will not move in fear." He continued, "All are to keep to our path to the wedding house."

Arriving at the wedding house, Mary Magdalene told the wedding group of Jesus and they all welcomed him.

Mary, his mother, thanked the host for welcoming them. But at some point his wife, Mary, told Jesus that the host had said that there was not enough wine for everyone, since Jesus and his party had exceeded the number they had expected would come.

Jesus told Mother Mary to wait by six barrels of water and after a short time there would be wine enough for all. He touched the barrels as Mary left to tell the host what he had told her and the wedding party was amazed when the barrels were tapped and found to be full of wine.

His disciples and family were amazed as well for this was the first time many of them had seen Jesus perform a miracle. They spirits were high as they prepared in the next two days to leave the wedding for Jerusalem their next stop on the journey.

As they walked, Lilith and the two Mary's spoke with Jesus as to what his mission in Jerusalem was to be. He would only smile and said "I will come to them to announce that I have arrived and my aim to be about my Fathers work. It is only fitting. We shall not hide from the authorities."

"The authorities?" Mary questioned, "but the people, Master, will also have heard of your miracles and they will be present, many will look to you to perform more miracles and to feed them. They will, as well, want to hear you speak."

"What you say, Mary is wise. I was last there in the temple with the money changers and my intent is to go again on tomorrow and to clean out the temple again as I did as a young boy."

News of Jesus' impending arrival preceded the party and Jesus was met with many on the road who came with their sick and dying, their ills and many were hungry hailing him as the Messiah, and wanted him to heal them. The party was stopped on the road and Jesus decided to address them to tell them of his mission.

As the two thousand people gathered before him, he spoke, "I am he who is sent here from the one God down to Israel to command Israel to repent in its ways. I am sent to warn of God, my Father's wrath which is sure to come."

"I call to the Pharisees to mend their ways, to end their hypocrisy, to end their perjuries against the people. I have seen them usurp places of honor at banquets, take silver coins from the poor to enter the temple; I have seen them wear fine and expensive clothing while many go hungry; I have heard them tell others to call them Rabbi in the face of these violations."

"These actions," Jesus told them shut out the poor from the kingdom of heaven by insisting upon silver and gold and sacrifices they could not afford. He said, "The Sadducees, as well, stress the minutia of faith while neglecting the substance of faith. "They stress the outer shell while neglecting to teach that the kingdom of heaven is within where my Father's kingdom lies, not in the blessings of a purchased faith. They neglect justice and mercy in favor of the tithe. There is greed and self-indulgence among them and wickedness wearing the guise of holiness. My Fathers kingdom," he told them, "is among you, the people, not in the sterile confines of the temple."

This was a great shock to many of them and there were cries of blasphemy among some of them. "How can you speak of such things, by what authority can you make these accusations?"

"I am Jesus," from the house of David and the Son of Man and I speak from the authority of my Father who is the one God." Jesus said.

Again there was shock among some who said, "Are you, Jesus, saying to us that you are the Messiah as prophesized in the holy writ?"

"Yes."

"Tell us, Jesus, are you the Messiah?"

"I am the Son of God, about my Father's work." Jesus replied.

This initial statement was electrifying to most of the multitude. Although some called him blasphemer, most called upon him to heal or ask that he feed them. Jesus walked among them and offered them succor and kind words. He told them his Father was the Father of all Jews and Gentiles. When he finally left them he said, "One should love God with one's entire heart, soul, mind and strength and one should love one's neighbor as one would love one's self."

It was later that same night, at the edge of Jerusalem, Lilith, and Jesus' disciples got word that the Pharisees and

Sadducees had heard of Jesus' words and were very upset. Mother Mary said to all "I do not think it is wise to continue on to Jerusalem and suggest we go back to Nazareth where we will at least have the greater protection of friends. Hear me on this. Danger lies in the streets of Jerusalem where any roof-top may harbor a rock thrower or the paid assassin."

Lilith said, "I agree, Jesus. Your words were very strong this day and did incite many there and I presume that the repeating in Jerusalem of your words has gained exaggeration. We are best to leave now tonight and return home."

"What say you Mary Magdalene?" Jesus asked. "Your council is wise."

Mary was thoughtful at first but spoke assuredly, "I say we go to Nazareth or Bethany. I was in the crowd today and some were very excited and in others faces I could see anger."

It was decided that James would go on the Jerusalem and there he could relate to the many what had transpired in Jesus' talk and to quell rumors among them.

The party, with Jesus, departed for Nazareth that very night and arrived in Nazareth days later.

Chapter 56

In Nazareth, a month later, Jesus began to speak in the local synagogues after deciding that it was best not to go to Jerusalem until late in the year, for his safety.

He went to a synagogue in Nazareth where he had decided to make an announcement of his mission in clear terms to temple members. He rose and spoke, "I have come today to speak clearly to all of my faith of my mission in the name of my Father. I have brought with me the scroll of Isaiah from which I will read. He produced the scroll, unraveled its handles and read, "The Spirit of the Sovereign Lord is on me, because Lord has anointed me to preach good news to the poor. He has sent me to bind up the brokenhearted, to proclaim freedom for the captives and a release from darkness for the prisoners; to proclaim the year of Lord's favor; and the day of vengeance of our God, to comfort all who mourn."

Then, Jesus announced that he was the Messiah of which Isaiah spoke. Then he rolled up the scroll, gave it back to the attendant and sat down. The eyes of everyone in the synagogue were fastened on him, and he ended by saying to them, "Today this scripture is fulfilled in your hearing."

There was astonishment among them. Many were furious with him and defamed him and calling him "blasphemer." Their anger was so great they seized him and shouted, "He clams to be the Messiah!" They grabbed him and took him out of town to a cliff where they meant to throw him down the cliff to his death.

But Lilith intervened, and the crowd grew fearful as she presented herself to the angry hoard as a Specter. It paralyzed them, some fell to the ground, covering their faces wailing. When Jesus turned to the synagogue members, at the cliff's edge, he did not fear them or the Specter. The people, frozen with fear, did not speak or move. Jesus faced them as he moved slowly past the ones near him; those that had meant to push him down the cliff. They crowd parted, and created a way for him to pass. Jesus went on his way back to Nazareth, unharmed.

Mother Mary spoke at the evening meal. "We were so terrified. It was our miraculous, Lord who sent Lilith to save you. Otherwise the ruffians would have tossed you over. Praise be to God, the Almighty. It is shame that here, in the bosom of our homeland, there are those that deny you despite all they have heard and witnessed."

Mary Magdalene said, "I have heard you say Master that there are many Gentiles here and they hear our message, but we should be in Bethany for a few weeks as we consider how best to continue the word."

There was among them that evening the cloud of fear, fear for the safety of Jesus and fear for the entire family since many of his disciples, too, had been threatened that day. But Jesus was steadfast. "You have little to fear. Have you no faith in my Father? He is here and he will protect his children."

But, it was an uneasy group which left for Bethany the next day.

***

After two months in Bethany, Jesus called his disciples together to make an announcement. At the evening meal he said "We have been here now two months and my Father came to me and asked why I am not about his business? He asked of me why was I not in Jerusalem where his message needs to be heard."

"This is something that is clear," Jesus said. "We must carry his message to the very gates of the city. I have many messages from leaders there who want us to come and speak to the people. I have sent word that we would come. Once there I have seen in a vision that I would go again, as I did in my youth to the temple because I have been told it is unclean there, that it is a barnyard and that the money-changers have again taken up residence there. It is my will that this be done."

There was a hush in the room because all there understood what this meant. To go to the gates of Jerusalem was to put one's head in the mouth of the lion, to invite all of the forces of that city that hated Jesus, to unite and rally and look to do him harm.

Over their objections, he said to them, "For this work I am placed on this Earth and I have no fear of harm. I am in my Lord's hands."

They persisted in their concerns but in two days as they were all preparing to leave, Lilith came to them at the evening meal assuming the form of a young man, hiding her flowing red hair and donned men's clothing.

Jesus introduced the disguised, transformed Lilith as Nilith and said, "This is Nilith, and Lord has told me that he is pure of heart. Nilith should accompany me into Jerusalem. Nilith has found favor with Lord and in him I place my trust."

Mary Magdalene, and Mother Mary had been told by Jesus of Lilith's agreement to accompany him in the form of the young man and this allayed their anxieties about the trip.

The day following Jesus set out with Mary Magdalene and Nilith. They planed to join James who was already there. He had prepared a place for them in the City.

***

Nicodemus, a member of the ruling council of the Temple, the Sanhedrin, heard Jesus' party had approached the city and spoke to the council. "I understand this Jesus," Nicodemus said, "has approached the City. I think we should understand from him directly, what his views are, what his intentions may be, in coming here at this time."

"Council members," he said, "I need not remind you, he has many adherents here in Jerusalem. We have no interest in an incident that will only serve to draw attention to him. Jesus may very well bring the Roman governor down upon us who will ask us if we can keep the peace."

Caiaphas, Chair of the Council, spoke and said, "I presume you are aware Nicodemus that this man has spoken blasphemy against the temple, has openly called for the wrath of God to come down upon us, the Council, indeed, the entire holy order here? He is dangerous, it seems to me. Jesus and his entire family. John, John the Baptist, his cousin, and the older brother James, both draw large crowds. We will, I believe, have to deal with him at some point. The question is how to do that without creating more problems for ourselves in doing so. What is your proposal in this?"

Nicodemus said "Let me, Council representative, go out and meet with Jesus and examine him, hear him, such that we may know him as a person. Let me hear his views such that we have first hand information before we act against him. We have no need of haste here, besides, we need to be able to identify him. No one here knows what he looks like."

The Council agreed this should be done and the day that followed, Nicodemus went out and sought to speak with Jesus on behalf of the Council. Jesus agreed to see Nicodemus and the two men sat alone before a simple meal of olive oil, bread and wine at the place James had secured for them.

Nicodemus had, before the meal addressed many others in the crowds, who had heard Jesus speak. He was much impressed with their reports of miracles he performed with wine and that Jesus had saved the royal governors son in the North. He heard, as well, that Jesus had made bread from stone.

As they sat Nicodemus leaned forward and examined Jesus' presence as if he might be an apparition. Decidedly not. He asked Jesus, "Tell me Rabbi, I have heard of the many miraculous signs you have made. I ask you, are you the Messiah, and are you from God?"

Jesus replied to Nicodemus and said, "I tell you the truth, no one can see the kingdom of God unless he is born again."

Nicodemus was skeptical of this response and asked Jesus, "How can a man be born when he is old? Surely he cannot enter a second time into his mother's womb to be born!"

Jesus replied that the Kingdom of Heaven requires the individual be re-born of water and the Spirit. "Flesh gives birth to flesh, but the Spirit gives birth to spirit."

Jesus said, "Belief in me as the holy spirit, as the Son of God, is the path to heaven, none other." Jesus told Nicodemus, more signs of this would be coming through him from the Father in heaven and ending by telling him "For God so loved the world that he gave his one and only Son, that whoever believes in him shall not perish but have eternal life."

In the presence of Jesus, Nicodemus was much disturbed and agitated as he searched himself for his own beliefs in these matters.

Nicodemus returned to the Council disturbed. He arrived and he told the Council, "I have sat with this man and examined him. I have heard the stories of his miracles. We have taken in the prophecies as the signs of the coming of the Messiah. I believe him to be the Messiah as he claims."

But the Council was incredulous at Nicodemus's words. "Messiah?" they said, aghast. "The Messiah, it is written, will come from Bethlehem not Galilee! Is this fellow not from Galilee? If so he cannot be the Messiah. But Nicodemus remained steadfast in his belief that Jesus was, as he claimed, the Son of God.

***

On the next day, Jesus came to Jerusalem and proceeded to the temple. H saw that nothing had changed at the Temple from his youth. He saw that animals were being sold in the temple, that their dung fouled the air and floor within the temple; he saw that the money changers were still there charging exorbitant rates to the poor to buy birds for sacrifice. He saw the poor were being shut out of temple because they did not have the price of entry. He fashioned a whip once again and overturned their tables and drove them all from the temple.

There was a great tumult over this action by Jesus and no one saw him for the rest of the day after the Temple incident. He returned later that evening. Lilith sat with him when they were alone and asked what had been his emotions in ejecting the money-changers. Jesus looked very repentant and did not speak.

"What I mean is," Lilith said, "this looked like a display of anger and even rage and, as you know, Master, this looks and was exactly contrary to what our message is to others. Anger and rage is war and we are opposed to such things."

"I don't know," said Jesus. "It was something which over came me and I had acted before I thought about it."

"It is more, Lord," Lilith said. "The longer the Son is in this body, the more he will be overwhelmed by the emotions of earthly humans. We must remember this because not to follow the message from the Father can hurt the work which must be done here. We must be away from here," Lilith said "to examine this. I see the Son transmogrifying."

Jesus, James, and Lilith left Jerusalem following day for Capernaum.

Chapter 57

Two months later in the second year of Jesus' ministry, his popularity grew to perhaps ten thousand followers; nearly double that of the Pharisees and Sadducees. He performed many miracles in that year and word of his ability to heal and to feed the hungry accounted for much of this popularity-- as well, the decision by Jesus to give some of his disciples the ability to perform miracles. They were sent out to many different parts of the Galilee, to Bethany, to Jerusalem and beyond. This made it more difficult for the authorities to identify one person as responsible for the miracles. It also meant that the number of multitudes who had heard of him more than doubled in the second year compared to the first year.

He sent out Peter, also known as Simon Peter, Andrew, brother of Peter, James, son of Zebedee, John, brother of James, Philip, Bartholomew, Thomas ,Matthew, the former tax collector, James, son of Alphaeus, Thaddaeus, Judas the son of James, Simon the Zealot, and Judas Iscariot, who was brother to Jesus.

His message became more and more focused upon himself in that his disciples told the crowds that whosoever believed in Jesus would have eternal life and that the end of times were near.

Jesus went through towns and villages, teaching and performing more and more miracles and exorcising demons from the afflicted, the poor and the rich as well. He was challenged in some cases by those who said he was gaining power over demons from the devil and, therefore, was in league with the devil. Jesus countered saying "Evil comes from evil, good comes from good."

His message became more insistent and he said to a group, the one "unpardonable" sin was blasphemy against the Spirit, "This," he said "will not be forgiven. Anyone who speaks a word against the Son of Man will be forgiven, but anyone who speaks against the Spirit will not be forgiven; he who is not with me is against me, and he who does not gather with me, scatters. Anyone who speaks a word against the Son of man, will be forgiven, but anyone who speaks against the Holy Spirit, will not be forgiven, either in this age or in the age to come."

This was a powerful statement. This Holy communication carried the message that only through he, Jesus, could the people be saved. This was becoming a Jesus-centered message and caused dissension among some disciples who wanted him to stress the Father in Heaven. Others, the Zealots, wanted him to stress rebellion. Still, others, wanted him to grow his popularity by feeding more people and healing the sick.

In this second year of his ministry, Jesus concentrated more on performing miracles.

He healed the servant of a Roman centurion.

In Nain, he resurrected the son of a widow by touching the coffin of the young man. Those there were filled with awe.

He quelled a great storm on the Sea of Galliee.

He brought back to life Jairus' daughter a nobleman when he came upon the mourning party.

He cured the blindness of two men whom he encountered on the road who proclaimed him as the Son of David.

But the most important event of the year was the Sermon on the Mount delivered by Jesus in Galilee.

On that day, Jesus discussed with Lilith, a new direction he planned to take in the preaching. "I am more and more convinced we must move away from judicial law and lay out for the people a new source of authority in matters of faith. Law should focus, as we have seen in Tibet and in Egypt, on perfecting the soul and moving toward the light, not following external ritual which has no meaning."

"Today," he said to Lilith, who appeared in the guise of Nathan, a young man, "I will speak of the soul, of adultery, anger, covetousness, retaliation and resisting evil. I will give them a prayer to the Father that they might be comforted in their times of need; I will teach, today, of love, not curses, and hatred; love for all peoples, even to those who hate you. I shall tell them to turn the other check and to pray for those who persecute you. I will tell them if they forgive men when they sin against them, their heavenly Father will also forgive them. But, if they do not forgive men their sins, the Father will not forgive them their sins."

"My Father" Jesus said pensively, "has given me these words to say."

And it was then Jesus did go down into Galliee and preach these teachings to those present. It made a great impression upon those there; such that many committed his words to memory such that it could be repeated to others, family and friends.

Chapter 58

The third year of Jesus' ministry began with the shocking news that John the Baptist had been beheaded. It was so distressing to Jesus; he withdrew on a boat to grieve the loss of his cousin, the man who baptized him. Crowds of people saw him do this from the shore.

Two days later, he returned for the evening meal during which the family ate in silence. James shattered the silence and said "John had many disciples. This day I have received many requests from his disciples to become part of our ministry. I replied that I would speak of it with you. What is your pleasure, Master, in this?"

Jesus looked very sad, lifting his head, and said only, "I am aggrieved in this and my heart bleeds over this unholy act. We are in our final hours and must prepare for what will come."

They all looked at him and understood his meaning.

Lilith spoke with him alone and said, "Many have challenged you in debates; yet still the number of your adherents continues to grow. But in this growth, there is also growing danger. They will come for you in this year. This is my prophesy. You have to prepare, Master, now you are the leader of these."

On the day that followed, Jesus spoke to a large crowd by the sea, and told them to take heart. John the Baptist was a good man he told them and would have everlasting life in heaven with his father. He told them the good soul would be weighted after death and those having weight from a proper and piteous use would move on to be with the Father in heaven. Those souls light in weight would be turned back and away from the face of Lord. The group by the sea grew in numbers, many coming to hear Jesus speak of John's death. By the afternoon over five thousand were there but there was no food, only five loaves of bread and two fish.

Jesus told his disciples sit on the grass. He took the five loaves of bread and the two fish and looking up toward the heaven, he gave thanks and broke the loaves. Then he gave them to the disciples, and the disciples gave them to the people. They all ate and were satisfied, and the disciples picked up twelve basketfuls of broken pieces that were left over. The number of those who ate was about five thousand men, besides women and children.

In later months, Jesus brought sight to the blind, and walked upon the waters in Galliee to the astonishment of his disciples. In that year, he took with him Peter, James and John the brother of James, and led them up a high mountain. There he was transfigured before them. His face shone like the sun, and his clothes became as white as the light and he told them he was the Son of God and the light which shone upon him was the light of God. While he was still speaking, a bright cloud enveloped them, and a voice from the cloud said, "This is my Son, whom I love; with him I am well pleased. Listen to him!"

When the disciples heard this, they fell facedown to the ground, terrified. But Jesus came and touched them. "Get up," he said. "Don't be afraid." When they looked up, they saw no one except Jesus.

This was the year Jesus raised Lazarus from the dead after having been told that he had died. Four days had passed; Jesus went to Lazarus' tomb and called out to him to rise. Lazarus then rose from death to life and came out from the tomb.

This was the year, as well, that Jesus brought his disciples together to tell them of his persecution, death, and resurrection soon to come.

***

All thirteen, including Mary Magdalene, seated to the right of Jesus, were there that woeful night. Supper lay before them untouched. Jesus said to them, "I have come to the end of my time here and must now look to complete my work. There are those who persecute me, hate me for the words I speak. There are those who would kill me, but I shall rise from the death of this body on the third day and ascend to my Lord, to the Father.

Jesus examined each disciple at the table, blessing them with all his heart and said, "And I will not be among you again."

There was great sadness among them because they all knew the prophesy; Jesus would go to Jerusalem, arriving on a donkey, praised as the Messiah, that he would be put on trial, betrayed by one among them; that they, his disciples, would deny him. Yet they protested that this would not be so and he said, "These are the wishes of my Father and it must be so. I am martyred here at his command such that all of mankind's sin may be expunged. I am to be crucified here such that all nations may have access to heaven. These are the words, these are the prophesies. As you all know, this is written in the Holy Writ and thus what our entire brethren and family has been given as its cross to bear."

"Five hundred years ago," Jesus said "Zechariah prophesied the Messiah would present himself to Jerusalem and shall enter the city while riding on a humble donkey and the next day," the prophet said "the king will be crucified. This is to be our fate, in my Lord's wish."

***

The Pharisees and the Sadducees were aware of the prophesy as well. They discussed it considering Jesus to be a potential threat who would come to the city where over 150,000 pilgrims were present for Passover. It was a volatile situation from their point of view.

In Council meetings, they said, "We know he means to enter the city, as the prophet has said, and declare himself the King of the Jews." one said.

Another exclaimed, "We shall have to see his end without angering the population and have his followers turn against us. There are many of them maybe ten thousand, now that John the Baptist's followers have joined him."

"He grows bolder each day as he has feed the poor and urged them to rebel against the laws of Moses and against the Temple," another said. "We should be done with monitoring him and place him to an end before he grows too powerful to be contended with."

"We should have the Romans commit the offense against him; they should be the ones to crucify him. We do not want his blood on our hands."

"We should send," one Councilman said, "one of us to examine him on questions, on taxes.

Another said. "We should ask him if he is the Son of God in open court, that is, what we should do. We should ask him to prove that he is the ancestor of David. All these things should be done."

***

Jesus agreed to see the representatives of the Pharisees and the Sanhedrin outside Jerusalem. They sat to examine him as he stood before them in a tent. The asked him his views on issues important to the Jews. Jesus turned to each one in the circle as he answered their questions.

One asked him, "Do you think that we Jews should pay tribute to the Romans, tribute which is bankrupting our nation."

Jesus spoke slowly saying "Let me see a coin. They presented to him a Roman coin called a denarius. "Whose face is on this coin?" Jesus asked? Whose portrait is this? And whose inscription?"

"Caesar's." they replied in unison.

"Then," Jesus said to them, "give to Caesar what is Caesar's, and to God what is God's."

One by one, they left—leaving him standing inside tent feeling stymied by Jesus' answer. Jesus followed the last one out and came into the City after them. Jesus went straight to the Temple Courts. They found him there teaching to small groups and hatched another trap for him asking him, "By what authority are you doing these things? And who gave you this authority?"

Jesus replied, "I will also ask you one question. If you answer me, I will tell you by what authority I am doing these things."

Jesus said "John's baptism—where did it come from? Was it from heaven, or from men?"

They discussed it among themselves and said, "If we say, from heaven, he will ask, then why don't we believe him?' But if we say, from men—we are afraid of the people, for they all hold that John was a prophet." So, they answered Jesus, "We don't know."

The members remained in the Temple after Jesus left. They were most frustrated and infuriated with Jesus in these things. They vowed to kill Jesus.

270

Chapter 59

A few days before Passover, Jesus met with his disciples and he again told them of his plan to ride into the city on a donkey and they all told him that if this was his wish then it would be done. He told them that his wish was to have a last supper with them before the Passover meal.

They agreed.

The night before the Passover meal, Lilith in the guise of Nathan, sat with Jesus to take the measure of this, the event for which he had spent his entire Earthly life preparing for.

"I am in this, Lilith--prepared because you, my Father, and my family have made me so. I have spoken with my Father and he is prepared to welcome me back on high at the ascension."

"Yet, Lilith I am only a mortal here," said Jesus, "and I have never been crucified. I asked Lord if there was a way to lighten my burden in this or to take it from me."

"What did he say?"

"He said he had told the Jews and Gentiles of his new covenant and had made to them a solemn promise which had to be kept. He told me that my sacrifice in this body would remove all the sins of all the peoples of the world and this would give all of Earthly people a new opportunity to walk in faith, cleansed."

"These were his words to me," Jesus said. "Yet, I still have this deep sadness within me. I have a family here which I love, I have a child with Mary; Sarah, is yet only nine. I have my dear-dear Mother here and all those who have placed their faith in me. Yet, I shall not remain here. I shall ascend and leave them with only their faith to sustain them. I shall ascend with Roman rule still in place. I asked my Father what is to be the fate of all here, the Jews, the Gentiles the poor, the Lilim, the Lukim, all those which inhabit this place? I asked Lord to tell me of these things. He said to me that I must have faith in his plan. And it was he was gone."

"What is your thought? Shall I go forward with Judas and the thirty pieces of silver? I have a Sanhedrin, who says he loves me, and is willing to participate. I have

271

made arrangement for Mary and Sarah to leave Jerusalem soon after, soon after it is over. All of you my disciples say they are strong of heart. So why do I grieve so in this body?"

"And what of you Lilith, will you ascend as well to reunite with your husband, my Father?"

**

On the night that followed, on the day before Passover, Jesus broke bread with his disciples and gave thanks to them and to his heavenly Father. Mary Magdalene, seated to the right of Jesus, wept silently and Peter reached over Judas and placed a comforting hand on her shoulder. As they ate, Jesus said, "Take and eat, this is my body." He took the cup, gave thanks and offered it to them saying, "Drink from it, all of you. This is my blood of the covenant, which is poured out for many, for the forgiveness of sins."

Jesus did go into Jerusalem the next day riding on a donkey given him by followers, as the prophecy had stipulated. Crowds greeted him with great joy as the authorities looked on determining to see an end to him. Later that evening Jesus sat with his disciples again.

Mother Mary, Sarah, Martha and all of his brothers were there and wept as they prepared themselves for the ordeal.

Jesus took Judas aside and told him to do what he had to do. Judas wept and did not want to go, but Jesus told him that this was what he had to do. Judas slipped silently from the group.

They all left after and went the Garden of Gethsemane on the Mount of Olives. This was the place Jesus felt was closest to his Father's heaven. He asked his disciples to stay alert but they all slept after Mother Mary, Martha and Sarah left.

Jesus went with Lilith to a nearby stone altar to pray. He prayed and asked Lord, again, if it be his will to make the sacrifice and if there was a way that the burden could be lifted from him, in this ordeal.

Lord told him "This is the way, This was written and can not be changed."

Jesus returned to the others and Lord spoke to Lilith alone.

"I am grieved for my Son, and clear to me is that, I too, have no understanding of earthly pain. I am, Lilith, in this to be suffering with him in this body?"

"Yes, you will Lord. It will be true suffering. They will scourge his body with whip nails and make him to carry his cross to the crucifixion site. Nails will be pounded into his flesh; into his feet, wrist and hands. Jesus shall hang by his flesh until he suffocates, or his blood runs dry. You shall suffer, as well, with him as one, Lord."

"So be it," Lord said.

Judas returned with the Temple Guards. Some of the disciples rose against the Guards. Peter used a sword to cut off a man's ear. Jesus said "No, those who draw the sword will die by the sword." He healed the man's ear and allowed himself to be arrested and led away.

His disciples followed the group trying to see what would happen to Jesus. Peter followed them into courtyard of the high priest. He was asked if he was a disciple of Jesus and Peter said, "No." Peter left and outside he again denied Jesus when asked if he was a disciple. Before dawn Peter thrice denied knowing Jesus.

***

The high priest Caiaphas looked down upon Jesus intently. He spoke slowly to the captain of the Temple Guards and said, "Why is this man before me and what is the charge against him?"

The captain began to read from his scroll. "The Nazarene, Jesus, has been accused of blasphemy, of sedition, of impiety and of desecrating the temple, of claming to be the Messiah, the Son of God, and a leader of Zealots."

"Who is witness against this man?" Caiaphas questioned.

The captain said, "Many have witnessed his preachings, High One, and heard him speak where he freely admits these things."

Caiaphas, of course, had heard of Jesus, knew of his teachings, but understood very well that the situation with

Jesus was a delicate one. The city was full of pilgrims for the Passover holiday, the Romans were ever watchful of any incident which could spark a rebellion against their rule and thereby interrupt grain supplies to Rome. Pilate was ever cruel in his political ambitions and ruthless. He would make the Jews pay mightily if they failed to maintain order. That responsibility, small as it was, was given over to him and the Sanhedrin and none of his compatriots would likely want to risk Roman cruelty. The man, Jesus, had then the largest following of all of the prophets in Jerusalem. That to Caiaphas, was an additional iron in already blazing fire; he was a threat to the temple and the traditional ways; he was a threat to the very livelihood of the temple Rabbi's.

"What say you Jesus of Nazareth to these charges? What is your plea?"

Jesus did not speak.

"What say you Jesus of Nazareth to these charges? Are you guilty of these or are you not guilty of these?"

The captain stepped forth and slashed Jesus across the back caused Jesus to cringe with the pain. "Answer the High One, Nazarene!" he shouted. Jesus turned toward the man and looked at him intently and the captain backed away.

"No." Caiaphus said to the Temple guard. "I will interrogate him more. You understand," he said urging Jesus to speak, "if you do not speak you are subject to my ruling here without your being able to tell your side of all this. What is your plea?"

"I do not recognize the authority of you or this hearing. I answer only to my Father above in all matters," Jesus said.

"Well," Caiaphus said, "your Father? Who is your Father?"

"My Father is above and I am the Son of Man and descendent of the House of David," Jesus said.

"So you say that you are then you are the Messiah of the Holy Writ?" Caiaphas asked.

"I am," Jesus said simply.

Caiaphus looked at Jesus intently, "You understand, Jesus of Nazareth that such a claim is not blasphemy and therefore this is something which is out of the hands of the Sanhedrin; we here only rule on questions of the Torah and the holy writ. I find no blasphemy in your claim but I do see that you were accompanied by many zealots who seek to overthrow Roman rule here in Jerusalem. Are some of your disciple Zealots, do they seek the overthrow of Roman rule here?"

Jesus said, "I cannot speak for them."

"Are you a Zealot?" Caiaphus asked Jesus slowly.

Jesus replied, "I am on a mission here from my Father to fulfill the prophesy and I am his Son."

"So you are then the Messiah," Caiaphus declared. "So be it."

He then turned to the Captain and said, "This man has no religious heresy I may rule upon. His crime by his admission here is sedition. Take him to Pilate."

***

Pilate, too, had heard of Jesus and he was impatient with the situation that Caiaphus had placed in his lap.

"Who is this man?" he asked the Temple Guards, "and why do you bring him before me. What business is this?"

"This man, Jesus of Nazareth, is accused of blasphemy, of sedition, of impiety and of desecrating the temple, of claming to be the Messiah, the Son of God and an admitted leader of Zealots," a Priest said.

Pilate looked at Jesus a long searching moment and a man standing near him, whispered, "He is cousin to John the Baptist."

"Oh." Pilate remarked. "I ask you," he said to Jesus, "are you the King of the Jews?"

Jesus replied, "So sayest thou."

The Priests who had accompanied the Temple Guards began to speak. Some said "He is a blasphemer, High Governor, and sought to disband the Temple and rouses the people against paying their taxes. He is a Zealot, leader Highest. We brought him to you, Governor, because we are only responsible for religious matters. We brought him to you as the law requires."

Pilate said to them, "I am aware of the game here and I make no finding as to whether he is King of the Jews or no. I see here that he is from Galliee. This man is not, in any event, in my jurisdiction. Take him to Herod; he is

275

from Herod's district. Herod is in Jerusalem this day. Take him to Herod. I find no fault in this man."

When Herod saw Jesus, he was much curious because of the miracles attributed to him. He asked Jesus to perform a miracle for him. But Jesus did not speak before Herod. Herod asked him if he was Zealot. But Jesus did not speak. Herod asked him if he was the King of the Jews and their Messiah. But Jesus did not speak.

Herod realized that the man, Jesus, was related to John the Baptist and to condemn him in Jerusalem during Passover would likely spark unrest. He said "I find nothing in what this man says. He does not speak. Take him back to Pilate."

Lilith spoke to Jesus on the return to Pilate, so that none could hear. "Why did you not speak?"

Jesus spoke to her, whom none could see. "Herod is Jewish and could not fulfill the prophesy. It must be Pilate."

Pilate entered the Judgment Hall and saw it was Jesus, again. "So he sent you back to me? Herod is ever the dodger." Looking at Jesus he said "I ask you again, "Art thou the King of the Jews?"

Jesus replied, "Sayest thou this thing of thyself, or did others tell it thee of me?"

Pilate answered, "Am I a Jew? Thine own nation and the Chief Priests have delivered thee unto me, what hast thou done?"

Jesus answered, "My kingdom is not of this world, if my kingdom were of this world, then would my servants' fight that I should not be delivered to the Jews, but now is my kingdom not from hence."

Pilate, therefore, said unto him, peering at Jesus intently; "Art thou a King then?"

Jesus answered, "Thou sayest that I am a king. To this end was I born, and for this cause, came I into the world, that I should bear witness unto the truth. Every one that is of the truth heareth my voice."

Pilate's eyes narrowed. Jesus had stated that he was indeed a King seeking his rightful place on the Throne of Israel. This admission could not be ignored. He did not know what Jesus had said to Herod but he feared that if he did not act against Jesus, a dispatch would be on it way to Rome from Herod, claiming that, he Pilate, had refused to act against one who had admitted sedition. He ordered that Jesus be scourged and delivered for crucifixion.

**

Lilith watched from afar. She could not intervene. She felt a presence and Lord was there beside her. He looked stricken. He did not hide his face from her. He was truly devastated by the event, the event that he, himself, had sought, had decreed. But now, now it was upon him, upon him in his earthly body, Lilith could see Lord as Jesus was afraid of earthly pain.

Jesus was being taken from Judgment Hall by the Roman soldiers who mocked him, struck him, and prepared him for the scourge. They tied him to a wall and began to lash him.

They used a whip with pieces of metal at its ends and began the flogging. The first of forty blows landed with a great ferocity, as the soldiers looked on, A second followed quickly. Lord jerked and cried out, "Lilith I feel these. I feel these blows in my body."

Lilith took Lord's hand. It was true. Lord's entire body wracked with each blow upon Jesus. He was feeling the searing pain as Jesus felt it. He had not expected that the connection would be this close, that he would feel the pain as Jesus did. Lilith could see tears well up in his eyes. The third blow. "I feel the very skin in his body, in my body, tear away from the flesh! This is what pain is Lilith? I have never experienced such as thing. How do Earth people endure this?"

"In the human body such pain is normal." Lilith said.

The fifth blow started and Lord braced himself. "I shall not turn away from this scourge. I shall endure even as my Son endures because this is the covenant I have made. The Sixth Blow, the Seventh, Eighth, Ninth and Ten. "He is suffering so!" Lord lamented. "How can this much pain be endured? How much pain is there in this Earth, Lilith?"

The Eleventh blow.

"Have I done this, have I caused such pain as this among the humans? Have they caused this among themselves? Lord began to weep. "I have much to repent here as the agent of this torment. How vulnerable their bodies are, how much pain they endure."

The Twelfth blow.

"Yes, Lord, in the early exile there was much pain since the Earth was a molten inferno and death itself offered no release from the burning; since immortality itself barred the door, death itself offered no release." Lilith said.

The Thirteen, and on to the Thirty-Fifth blow.

Jesus was unconscious now and unmoving. They threw water on his face to revive him, but to no avail.

The Thirty Eight blow and Lord cried. "How much pain I see has been caused by my own actions. I have been justified in doing so but I now see what it meant to them."

The Thirtieth Ninth blow, "I have not felt pain in this way from inside a human body before.

The Forty blow and the scourge was at an end.

Lord said "I shall not again inflict pain upon them Lilith. By this I, myself, and the son have been cleansed and repent even as we have cleansed the people of earth of all their prior sins. We have started here a New Testament, one born in my own pain."

As the lashes flayed the back and skin of Jesus, Lucifer taunted Jesus. "Son of God, you may now see how pain feels. There was no pain in heaven, Son of God, but there is here."

The Thirty Fifth blow.

"These human bodies know great pain and that is what you have offered them. I promise them great pleasure and you wonder why so many have chosen to walk with me rather than endure the scourge of these human bodies. I say to you Jesus, pleasure is their weal and pain they avoid. So elementary. I have learned this myself here," Satan gloated.

The Fortieth blow.

I say to you now-- you and Lord-- understand pain as it exists outside Heaven's Gates, such that you might learn from this pain that you, yourselves, have inflicted upon others. These humans are vast reservoirs of pain, even as they are also vast reservoirs of pleasure and guilt. I understand them," Lucifer said with mock consolation. "You don't."

"And this," Lucifer whispered to Lord finally, "is but a prelude to the crucifixion."

They took Jesus from the flogging area and prepared him for the crucifixion. They gave him a cross to bear and put a crown of thorns on his head and mocked him as the King of Jews. On lookers spat upon him as he hefted the cross unsteadily, weak from the beating.

Many gathered to watch him, some praying for him, some mocking him. "Why Lord some said, "will you not save your own son?"

Others, said, "Where is your Father now Jesus, why doesn't he save you from the Roman lash? Soon you will be dead."

"My Father," Jesus said "is in heaven and I will be with him soon."

Lilith and Lord watched as Jesus struggled along encountering Mary his mother, Simeon and others. There was enormous fear because even to be seen in the crowd might draw suspicion from the Romans. The Sanhedrin had Temple Guards there since there was the possibility of a major disturbance from Jesus followers or from Zealots who might use the occasion to spark a rebellion among Jesus' followers, many of whom stood by silently, heeding Jesus' admonition to them: "It is written so shall it be." He had said to them to "be of good faith because through my suffering all sins will be forgiven and I shall rise in three days and walk among you once again."

He again called out to Lord to draw from him the burden and Lord said to Jesus "I am with you in this sorrow; I feel every pain in you. I, the Father, you the Son, and the Holy Spirit must persevere."

Lilith said to Lord "All this seems to bow to the prophesy, to follow you Lord in your will. This must be for you an indication that the humans indeed have faith, that they love you."

"I am pleased" Lord said."

They took Jesus to the Crucifixion site. They strapped his hands to the cross and they nailed his feet but he did not cry out in pain. Lord cried out in pain. His side was pierced. He then cried out in pain and Lord cried out in pain. They gave him something to drink and he drank from the cup and cried to Lord, saying "Forgive them Father, for they know not what they do."

Mary, and Mary Magdalene, knelt below the cross and Jesus told them not to fear because "Before this day I will be in heaven with the Father."

For six hours he was on the cross, his breathing becoming slower and slower, the blood from his side wound bled and he was weakening.

"I am with him in his body," Lord said to Lilith. "I have tremors in my earthly body, I feel what he is feeling, my blood, my heart beats only slowly; I cannot move my hands, they are numb; the pain is great. I have never imagined such pain, my thirst is great, so great; I cannot breath; I am beginning to feel what death is like for the Earthlings. It feels like fading away, the spirit rises, the soul begins to prepare itself; my lungs are collapsing and I am drowning."

Then Lord looked at Lilith and said "He is dead in the Earth body. He is dead. I must bring him home. I must bring him home, Lord said weeping softly. I must bring him home. He stood and opened his arms saying. I must receive his spirit. It is done. It is done."

A spirit appeared beside Lord. It was Jesus. Lord held him and said, "I am proud of you. I love you, my Son. This pain is over and we can now go home."

Jesus wept at the sight of Lord and Lilith. "I am home he said softly."

"You are home" Lord said weeping.

Lilith cried.

Lord took the still-weak Jesus in his arms and said to Lilith "I must remove him from this place and take him on high. This earth has harmed him. He needs to be home. We must ascend."

"He looked at Lilith and reached out to her and she touched his finger tip briefly. My heart goes with you." Lilith said.

With that Lord and Jesus were gone.

***

It was a desolate place on Calvary that day. A great suffering had occurred there, a great loss of one man, a man who died for all. A man who, in dying, had sacrificed that others might live.

In heaven there was a great rejoicing for two months. Heavenly choirs sang heavenly songs as Lord and Jesus stood on high before all the hosts, the Angels and the Cheribums who assembled to sing praises of Jesus who had returned. Jesus looked very weak still.

Heaven itself had changed because Lord and Jesus had come to know earthly pain. Lord said, "I am today Cherubim blessed to have the Son back among us. These last months have been for me the beginning of a new covenant-one born of my new understanding of compassion. It is so easy if you are high to forget the low. It is so easy to look down rather than reach down. Praise be to Jesus, the son. All blessings."

Jesus stood beside Lord and the hosts and said, "I am risen from that Earth to be again with you. I was about my Father's work and his work was done there. All Earth has now a new beginning, all sins there have been expunged and there in new hope among the Earth people of good will."

Lord said, "And we have here too, among us another newly risen one."

With that Lilith, came forth and joined the two standing between Lord and Jesus.

"Lilith, my wife is home, too," Lord said. "Without her the work on Earth as Asherah, our word and mission could not have been done. Without her there would have been no Jesus coming home."

"And today," Lord said, "she tells me she will bless me with a son."

***

Lucifer looked on. "So, they are all in heaven again." He seethed, "So there will be a second son. I will be here."

THE END